I0593328

Book 2:

Between City and Sea

2nd Edition

ISBN: 978-0-6451986-3-8

Cover Design by Brand Artisans Australia
www.brandartisans.com.au

– Acknowledgments –

A big, huge thanks to everyone who contributed to making this whole project happen.

Anita and Jeremy Walker, Amanda Bentley, Karyn Tulloch, Ben and Tracey Kreplins, Kate and Tim Brand, and Karen Weaver for donating to the editing process.

Amanda Bentley for once again being my test subject and creative sounding board. Thank you for your endless support and your feedback on all the manuscripts, it's appreciated beyond words.

Tavis Shearer for being my safe zone for an entire decade, even when I didn't entirely understand nor fully appreciate it.

To the rest of my family and friends who have helped and supported me in immeasurable ways, this book wouldn't have been possible without any of you.

And to the people who came into my life to teach me some challenging lessons, thank you for making me stronger.

– Dedications –

As always, my first message is to my not-so-little dude. Tyler my love, you've gone through a lot in your ten years on this planet and even though we've had some super-tough times, you've never failed to put a smile on my face. Your sense of humour and your resilience will serve you well in life and I have no doubt that you will do something amazing. You are a beautiful human and there will never be enough words in the dictionary to articulate how proud I am to be your parent.

Mum… what else can I say?
You have been the steady, stable light in our lives through all the dark and uncertain times. Even when your own sparkle was fading, you still continued shining brightly to help us find our way back home. This world is a better place for having you in it.

To my little sis Anita (younger in years but much more mature than I), thank you for your enthusiastic support of this project from the very beginning. You have encouraged me all the way through and have always made me feel like I'm actually a talented writer! Love you so much.

Contact N.J. Ewing

Website: www.brandartisans.com.au/njewing
Facebook: www.facebook.com/njewingauthor
Instagram: www.instagram.com/njewingauthor/

Sales and Distribution enquiries to Brand Artisans Australia
Email: info@brandartisans.com.au

Between CITY & Sea

N.J. EWING

brandartisans.com.au

- Prologue -

Fresh Blood

Hello again. So you made it back to Stonerland huh?

I'm impressed that you've returned. I thought maybe the first book might have scared you off, but obviously you've got a strong stomach.

Not many romances include death, rape and murder, yet here we are.

I'm glad you've made it this far down the rabbit hole, because there's still a lot more of the story to tell. I know you're probably on the edge of your seat, wondering what happened to Granger, but before we get back to the matter at hand, let me give you the 'Cliff Notes' (or 'Carlton Notes' as the case may be), of the situation thus far...

RITCHIE

- RITCHIE CARLTON -

Much like humans have defined time in accordance with the appearance and death of Jesus Christ, life at Artemis Advertising could be broken down into two distinct time periods: B.G. and A.D. The only difference with our timeline being that we had a third phase in between those two, which we could refer to as C.G. or Cyclone Granger.

It might've been by sheer coincidence that Ashley Granger's arrival at our company marked a dead-set turning point for our small group of misfits but, co-inky-dink or not, life was definitely not the same from the moment she stepped foot in the Artemis building. It wasn't that Ash directly caused all of the drama, but her presence undoubtedly created stratospheric chaos in our little world. I mean, don't get me wrong, I always thought she was a ripper chick, but there was no doubt trouble had a way of following her around. She was Cyclone Granger. Spectacular and awe inspiring to witness, but if you got too close you risked getting sucked into the vortex.

Maybe that was part of her allure? Perhaps it was an adrenaline rush, like storm chasing. We could put my best mate, Nathan Stone, into the 'storm chaser' category. Stoner was a man who had run from relationships his entire life. Before Granger (B.G), he had made a conscious effort to avoid any sort of emotional connection with women, but when Ashley arrived, he was instantly smitten by the tall, blonde, force of nature. Everything I'd known to be true in relation to Stoner and relationships, was no longer applicable.

To be fair to Ashley, Nathan Stone was a force of nature himself. The obvious metaphor here would be something to do with 'blowing', but I'd hate to be predictable, so I'll just say that Nathan was a whirlwind of female destruction. He had the uncanny ability to whip women into a frenzy and, prior to Ashley, wherever Stoner went, he would leave a trail of broken hearts shattered behind him. Not only that, but Nathan had never failed to disappoint in the inappropriate entertainment arena.

Case in point... the week before Granger's arrival, he had been held captive as a sex slave by our French client and her stripper friend in Paris. Needless to say, controversy was hardly a new concept to Nathan Stone. Falling in love however, that was seriously out of character. Something changed in Stoner from the first moment he saw Ashley sitting in our office cafeteria. It was as if her mere presence had caused some sort of transformation in his DNA.

The first weekend after Ashley arrived at Artemis, it was prolifically clear that Whirlwind Nathan was on a direct collision course with Cyclone Granger. We could see the typhonic winds on the horizon, but there really was no stopping them.

I'd never seen Stoner love-sick over a woman before, so it was an interesting experience to see him with that goofy look on his face, as he and his new love interest, joined my non-girlfriend Amy and I, on a non-date. If Nathan's doe-eyes weren't enough proof that he was totally smitten, then the fact that he was denying the nature of their date was his final undoing. Usually, Stoner was less than subtle when parading around his latest conquests, but with Ashley, he continued to deny his attraction to her.

"You can't seriously think that any of us are buying your non-date bullshit?" I teased him when Amy and Ashley had disappeared off to the bar together.

"Like I said Ritch, we're just hanging out," he answered coolly, sipping on his whiskey as if his wholesome date with Granger was nothing out of the ordinary.

"Nathan, she's got the hots for you," I told him bluntly.

"Do you think so?" he asked with a pretense of cluelessness which was betrayed by the look of arrogant content on his face. He had the demeanor of a croc who'd got the chook.

"You can't go from your Sandrine sexcapade to this girl-next-door date and not expect me to ask questions," I said with a casual grin, determined to get a rise out of him. "Unless Granger's got a dark side?" I mused, knowing that I was pushing the limits of Nath's self-control. His jaw clenched slightly but he didn't flinch, so I went in for the kill. If he took the bait, the only possible conclusion was that he was in love with her. "I mean… she'd have to be some sort of deviant to fuck a low-life like Dom Doyle right?"

Stoner plonked his glass on the table and stared at me incredulously.

"Are you fucking serious?" he snarled. "What the fuck is wrong with you dude?"

"What the fuck's wrong with you?" I asked, already suspecting I knew the answer. Nathan was not normally inclined to defend the virtue of his various women. "Why are you so touchy about this one?"

"I'm not touchy about her," he snapped defensively.

"Yeah, not touchy at all," I teased with a chuckle. I felt a bit sorry for the guy. He had no idea how to be in love… but that's also what made it so much fun. "So, what's the go then?" I pressed, unwilling to let it go.

"There's no-go," he replied with a stern face, "and don't bring up the Sandrine thing again," he huffed. I nodded in agreement. The scowl on his face told me that I'd pushed him far enough for now.

"Sorry mate, it's none of my business," I said, raising my hands in surrender. Upon my capitulation, Nathan's scowl downgraded to a mild glare.

"So you'll drop it?"

I bowed my head, conceding to his request. The only person Nathan was fooling was himself, and honestly… I don't think he was even successfully doing that.

"I'll butt-out now," I assured him.

"Thank you," he said, as he caught sight of our women returning with another round of drinks. The moment his eyes locked on his non-date, his mild glare flipped upside down and turned into what could only be described, as a dopey look of total adoration. "So Ashley… where do you stand on music?" Stoner asked once he'd helped her back to her seat. The poor girl was looking green at the gills.

"In what context?" Granger asked with an awkward chuckle.

"What sort of beats are you into?" I clarified for her, knowing where his line of questioning was about to lead, having been subjected to the bloke's musical obsession for nearly a decade.

"I've spent a lot of time and effort, teaching these guys about music," Nath explained to Ashley flirtatiously, "so if you're going to hang-out with us you'll need to be up to par."

"And if I'm not up to par?" she replied with a wicked smile. The woman could certainly hold her own, even when she was drunk as a skunk. In fact, I'd never seen anyone handle Nathan quite as well as she did. Aims flashed me a grin, clearly thinking the same thing I was.

"Then I guess I'd have to give you a proper musical education," Stoner answered without missing a beat. Ashley chuckled and nodded with approval, biting her lip as she contemplated her next response. I felt like I was watching some sort of painful girly rom-com movie, but I couldn't look away. Instead of waiting for Granger to answer, Nathan pointed at her as if he was a game show host. "Your favourite album right now. Go."

"Phase by Jack Garratt," Ashley responded coolly, "it's an oldy but I love it."

"Solid choice," he said, legitimately impressed by her answer.

"One point to me," Granger joked, squirming in the limelight.

"Okay, question two," Nath continued. "Name an artist you own every album of."

"Ed Sheeran."

"Oooh I love Ed Sheeran," Aims agreed emphatically. "Nothing hotter than a Ginger," she said, flashing me a wink. Being the only person to see my pubes on a regular basis, Amy was one of the few people who knew for a fact that I was a natural ginge. Back when I'd had hair, my nickname had been Ranga – Australian Slang for Orangutan – but thankfully without my bright orange dreadlocks, no-one in London was any the wiser… until they saw me naked that is.

"Okay, since you're a girl I'll give you Ed," Stoner adjudicated fairly. "What about your all-time favourite band."

"Ugh that's too hard," Granger replied with a cringe. "Pass."

"You can't pass." Nath said.

"Why not?"

"Because that's the rules," I interjected. "We all had to sit through it, so you can too."

"Fine," Ashley conceded, "then maybe Temple of the Dog… or Rolling Stones. No. Panic at the Disco? Or Journey? No, Led Zeppelin."

"I need your final answer Granger," Stoner said as if they were on Millionaire Hotseat.

"Okay, I'll go with Led Zep," She decided confidently. "I can't resist the power of D'Yer Mak'er."

"Wow," Nath said with surprise, "I wouldn't have expected that." He then spontaneously broke into song at the exact same time as Ashley and they both sang loudly, "Oh, oh, oh, oh-o-ooh, you don't have to go-o-o-ooh," before giggling like schoolgirls. It was sickeningly adorable and so unlike Stoner, like invasion of the bodysnatchers in reverse.

"I can't believe you know D'Yer Mak'er," Ash said after they'd finished their little sing-along. "No-one ever knows what I'm talking about when I say that. The only Led Zeppelin song people usually know is Stairway to Heaven."

"Well then you've clearly been hanging-out with the wrong sort of people," Nath said with a wink. Aims peered over at me again we couldn't help but share a chuckle. For a non-couple they were very in sync with each other.

"Okay final question," Nathan announced with a smile, "your favourite song of all time."

"Wicked Game," Granger said without thinking.

"Original Chris Isaac version or one of the covers?" Stoner asked as if it mattered.

"Depends what sort of mood I'm in," she answered with a shrug as Aims rolled her eyes.

"Okay nerds, enough of the music talk," she said, interrupting Ashlan's cozy conversation. "Let me tell you a story about the time Nathan got caught wearing nothing but a beanie..."

After that night, things continued to get weirder with every passing day. It was as if Nathan had descended into Wonderland and we'd all jumped through the looking glass alongside him. Ryan, Kat, myself and Amy. It was as if our little crew had veered off into a parallel universe, where our lives were playing out as an alternate reality. The phrase, 'Curiouser and curiouser' was certainly an apt way to summarise our collective journey.

In the series of events that followed, let's title it: 'Adventures in Stonerland', we all joined in the crazy voyage of love, heartbreak, romance, infidelity, violence, sex, stalking, drugs, murder plots, birth and then... death.

Which is where we resume our story...

Stories from the City: Part 3

Stone Cold

- Chapter 1 -

Ashes to Ashes

- NATHAN STONE -

I stood in my girlfriends' blood splattered apartment staring at my own vomit all over the floor. Losing Ash was too much to bear.

"What's he doing in here?" One of the Coroners asked gruffly as he carried my dead girlfriend towards me in a giant black plastic bag.

"This is his apartment," the cop said, squeezing my shoulder in solidarity as he nodded towards a photo of Ash and I on the sideboard.

"I don't care," the Coroner growled, "no one should be in here until we've removed the body." The 'body'? The fucking 'body'? Rage and sorrow coursed through my veins. How dare he. I stood up straight and wiped my mouth with the back of my hand.

"That 'body' is my girlfriend arsehole," I said, not bothering to contain my rage as I stepped up to him.

"Your girlfriend?!" he asked with a shocked laugh.

"I'm not sure why that's funny," I snapped, as fury rose in my chest.

"Because this is a bloke," he said, nodding at the body-bag. "A very heavy bloke in fact, so if you could move out the way and let us get him down the stairs, that would be great."

"A bloke?" I asked in confusion. "What do you mean?"

"I mean this is a man," he said with amusement. "There was a woman here earlier, but they loaded her into the ambulance."

"Was she…" I trailed off, not wanting to say the word 'dead'. He dropped the tough guy act and gave me an understanding smile.

"The police officers were taking her statement when we arrived, so she can't have been critical," he answered with a nod.

"Oh, thank fuck," I blurted, as the breath that I'd been holding, finally released in one long sigh. My tears of grief were replaced with tears of relief, and I wept like a baby as I stood in the center of a room full of strangers.

"I found this on the floor in there," the Coroner said calmly, as he handed me Ashley's phone. "I think it's your girlfriends."

"Thanks," I said, taking the phone with a shaky hand.

"No worries," he nodded. "Now seriously mate, this guy is heavy so if you could move out the way…"

"Oh, sorry," I said in a daze, stepping aside so they could get out. I shoved Ashley's phone in my pocket and watched them lug their heavy load out the door. What the hell had happened?

As I surveyed the trashed room, I spotted the shattered case of the CD I'd made for Ash lying on the floor in pieces. I picked up what was left of it and pulled my note out of the broken plastic feeling another round of tears trying to escape from my eyeballs. I pinched the bridge of my nose to try and stop them, but it was no use.

"Let's get you out of here," said my new best friend, the cop.

"Yeah," I nodded, following him out the door and down the stairs to where the coroners had loaded the body-bag onto a trolley bed. I studied the bag and realised that whoever was in there was obviously way too big to have been Ash. My stomach lurched as the pieces finally fitted together. I already knew the answer, but I asked anyway. "Who's body is that?"

"Umm…" the second Coroner glanced at the paperwork in his hand. "Doyle," he said with a grunt as he tried to push the stretcher through the front door of the building.

"Dominic Doyle?"

"Yeah. You knew him?" he asked distractedly, having trouble getting the stretcher through the narrow door-frame.

"Unfortunately," I said with a stiff nod, as the metal frame got wedged in the door, "nasty piece of work."

"Well from the looks of him, your girlfriend put up a good fight."

"Couldn't have happened to a nicer guy," I muttered under my breath.

"Speaking of your girlfriend…" piped up the first Coroner as he peered over his shoulder out to the street, "…the ambulance is still out there if you want to see her."

My heart pounded excitedly. Ash was still there?

"Thanks!" I said, springing into action and jumping gracelessly over the stretcher. Pain shot through my hips as I used Dominic's dead body as a springboard, and landed on the other side of the blocked door-frame with a thud, wincing as a sharp pain shot through my freshly healed knee.

"Oi!" the guy shouted in disgust.

"Sorry!" I yelled back insincerely, hobbling at Olympic speed towards the parked ambulance. "Ash!" I shouted, frantically banging on the closed doors, "Ashley!" I panted and stepped back as one of the doors swung open.

"Nathan?" came Ashley's groggy voice from behind a female paramedic. I peered past the woman, desperate to see Ash. I needed to see her face and touch her skin to make sure that she was really alive.

"Ash," I said, seeing her wide eyes staring out at me. She was bruised and bloodied, but she was alive. The paramedic stood back as I ignored the sharp pain in my knee, and jumped into the back of the van.

"Hey," I breathed quietly, with more tears in my eyes.

"Nath," Ash whispered as I took her face in my shaking hands. Her cheek was purple and swollen, her eyebrow was tacked together with little white plasters, and her right arm was in a sling with a massive bandage covering the back of her shoulder. I kissed her forehead, trying not to inflict any further damage on her battered face.

"Thank god you're alive," I sighed, as I inspected her for any further injuries. She reached out to stop me fussing and, as her hand landed on mine, I noticed that her wrist was red raw. I traced my hand lightly over the nasty bruising and then looked up at her face. "This is my fault. I was supposed to keep you safe."

"This isn't your fault Nathan," she whispered quietly as she grasped my hand. "I'm alive and that's more than we can say for him," she added dryly, inclining her head stiffly towards her apartment building, where the Coroners were navigating Dom's stretcher out onto the street. I glanced out at the body that, only ten minutes ago, I'd thought had been Ashley's.

"I thought that was you," I whispered, swallowing back another wave of tears. "I thought you were dead."

"Well, I'm not," she said with a pained smile. "I'm okay."

"We've really got to stop meeting like this babe," I said, pushing a wayward strand of hair off her face. Ash chuckled tiredly.

"Yeah I'm a bit over Ambulances," she replied with tears welling in her own eyes. The siren gave a short wail.

"We've got to get going now," said the paramedic, heaving the doors closed. "We've already called it in, so the hospital is expecting us."

"Okay," I nodded and sat down on the bench next to Ash, still grasping her hand. "What happened back there? Why was Dom in your flat? How did he get in? How did he know you were going to be here?" I hadn't intended to interrogate her, but the questions came spilling out of my mouth before I could stop them.

"He broke in. He was waiting for me," she said exhaustedly. I took a breath and studied her face. There was something else going on inside her head. I leaned over and placed my hand gently on her cheek.

"I should have been with you."

"Sorry to interrupt," the paramedic said awkwardly, clutching a clipboard and pen. She cast me a furtive glance and then turned back to Ashley, holding out the clipboard. "The incident report said aggravated sexual assault, so I've requested a rape kit, but they'll need your consent."

I exhaled loudly as if I'd been punched in the gut. Dom had raped her? The thought of that cunt putting his hands on my girlfriend caused another vomitus feeling in my throat. Ash peered over at me nervously and my stomach lurched as I saw the answer in her eyes. Ash shook her head at the paramedic.

"No thanks," she said as she pushed the clipboard away.

"I think it would be wise to have someone look you over," the paramedic said, sharing a doubtful glance with me.

"Honestly, I'm fine," Ash re-iterated pointedly to both myself and the paramedic, fighting the obvious fact that something terrible had happened to her.

"I know it's awkward," said the paramedic kindly.

"It's not awkward," Ashley replied tersely, "the guy's dead, so it doesn't really matter what he did."

"Okay," the paramedic conceded gently, "I'll leave you to discuss it with the doctors at the hospital."

"There's nothing to discuss," Ash snapped. "Besides… it was nothing that he hasn't done to me before."

"Holy shit," I whispered under my breath, swallowing back more acidic upchuck as it threatened to escape my mouth. I planted my face in my hands to collect myself. The last thing Ash needed was for me to freak the fuck out. I took a deep breath and rubbed my face. Anger, fear and grief welled inside my chest so violently that I felt like I was going to explode.

"It's okay Nath," Ash reassured me, peeling my hands away from my face, "I'm okay."

"But he…" I choked on the uncomfortable words, "…raped you?"

Ash's eyes dropped to her lap and she nodded. "I'm so sorry," she whispered.

"No," I said, taking her face in my hands as she tried to avoid eye contact, "you have nothing to be sorry for, do you hear me?" I leaned down to look her in the eyes, but to no avail. "Never apologize for what happened back there. It's that cunt who should be sorry, not you."

"He can't be sorry Nathan, I killed him," she said flatly, finally looking me in the eyes. "Dom's dead."

"Yeah, he is," I replied with a macabre chuckle. It was an inappropriate response, but death couldn't have happened to a more deserving bloke.

"I killed him," Ash re-iterated as her eyes glazed over. "Nathan… I killed someone."

"Not just someone Ash. It was Dom. Please don't feel guilty over that psychotic prick."

"I don't feel guilty," she said quietly, "that's what worries me. I don't feel bad at all. I thought I would, but I don't. And I don't even feel the slightest bit of regret for what I did. I just feel…" she sighed, "…numb. And relieved. I feel relieved that it's over. Dom's gone and we can finally get on with our lives," she took a deep breath. "It's finally over."

- ASHLEY GRANGER -

As we sat silently in the back of the speeding ambulance. I felt like I'd been run over by a truck, emotionally as well as physically. So much had happened in such a short space of time, yet my life had been irrevocably altered for both better and worse. The memories would haunt me always, but at least I knew they would never be anything more than memories, because Dom was gone now. The hell was over. I could finally get on with my life. A decade of living in fear had come to an end in one climactically violent show-down. If I was honest with myself, there had probably never been a chance of any other conclusion to our story. It was always going to be either Dom or me, and I was glad it hadn't been me. I grasped Nathan's hand and he looked down at me, stroking my hair with this spare hand.

"You're safe now," he said gently. I nodded and relaxed my head against the pillow. My adrenalin-rush had begun to wear off and the exhaustion (and the pain meds) had started to kick-in. My eyelids fluttered closed and I let myself drift off into a void somewhere between waking and sleeping. I could hear what was going on around me, but it was distant, almost like I was at the other end of a long tunnel.

Slowly the noise faded away and I welcomed the peacefulness. Dark blue patterns swirled around the back of my eyes until, from stage right, entered Dominic. I wanted to open my eyes, but I was too far from awake to pull myself out of the nightmare, so I was forced to re-watch the awful scene play-out again as if someone had rewound the movie in my head...

I was back in my flat and Dominic was coming at me. Spurred on by my instinct to survive I madly flailed the kitchen knife with my hands still bound tightly by Dom's belt. I saw his knife slice my skin a few times, yet I felt no pain. His big hands bore down on my wrists and the knife slipped from my grasp and clattered to the floor.

We both looked down and watched it slide across the tiles. There wasn't time for me to recover it, so I grabbed the heavy frying pan off the rack. Aiming for Dom's head, I swung hard but not quickly enough. Dom saw it coming and grabbed my arms as the pan collided with his head. He cushioned my attack but, in the process, lost his balance and we both tumbled to our knees. I scrambled quickly across the floor commando style, with wrists still tied, to get my knife before Dom could get to his.

I reached out for the knife, clutching it just in time to see Dominic climbing to his feet. He swore and rubbed his head, then locked his stone-cold stare on me.

"Fucking cunt," he seethed, spitting blood in my direction. He didn't seem to have noticed that I was in possession of the knife and, with an almighty grunt, he dove straight at me. Without thinking about it, I held the knife tightly in both hands and aimed it at right his chest. He was hurtling towards me so fast, that by the time Dom had realised what was happening, it was too late. With his full weight bearing down on me, neither of us could stop it.

The stab through his chest was so swift and deep that I felt the force of the puncture reverberate through my own body. My stomach churned. It was sickening. The feel of the impact; the tear of his flesh; the spurt of blood; Dominic's pained cry and the shock in his eyes; it was all like something straight out of a horror movie.

Dom clutched his chest and collapsed lifelessly on top of me. Blood began to dribble out of his mouth as he stared at me with shocked eyes. I scrambled out from underneath him, scooting backwards as far away from him as I could. He gasped for breath and attempted to speak, but seemingly unable to voice any words. After a moment, his body grew still and his eyes became vacant.

I held my breath, waiting for the nightmare to end, yet half expecting him to make another miraculous recovery. Finally, with one last strained gasp, Dom's eyes rolled to the back of his head.

"Oh my god," I sighed in disbelief, as tears rolled from my eyes. I sank against the oven door in relief and pain. My whole body began to hurt, especially my shoulder. I unwound the belt from my wrists and yanked open the collar of my shirt to take stock of my injury. I couldn't see it very well, but I could see enough to know that it was a deep gash. I pulled the tea-towel off the oven and shoved it inside the back of my shirt, wincing in pain as I pressed it hard against my injured shoulder.

I clutched my make-shift bandage with one hand and sank back exhaustedly against the oven. My head was struggling to process the situation. None of it felt real. I let my eyes flutter closed. I was tired, aching and so cold that I was shivering convulsively. I must have dozed off for longer than I'd realised because the next thing I remembered was the ambulance arriving.

"Hello?" one of the paramedics called from the front door.

"In here," I said, struggling to sit up as they made their way through to the kitchen.

"Don't get up love, just stay where you are so we can check you over," the lady told me. I nodded and sank back down to my previous position. The pair surveyed the gory scene, and the expressions on their faces said it all. "You look like you've lost a lot of blood," she added as she knelt beside me.

"Most of it is his," I told her, nodding towards Dominic as the man checked for a pulse.

"He's gone," the guy confirmed, "I'll call it in." My eyes wandered over Dom's body lying lifelessly on the floor. I'd killed him. I'd killed Dom.

"What's your name love?" The woman asked, snapping me out of my daze.

"Ashley," I answered quietly, as I watched the man put a plastic sheet over Dom's body. That was it. That was the end of it. Dom was dead. It was all over.

"Ashley," called a disembodied voice. "Ash?" My body jerked awake and my eyes flew open as I returned to the present. "You okay?" Nathan asked, stroking my hair to bring me back to reality.

"Uh-huh," I said in a daze.

"It looked like you were having a bad dream."

"Just a bad memory," I muttered, looking up to see that the ambulance doors were open. "We're at the hospital?"

"Yeah, they're about to take you in," he said with concern. I nodded through a foggy haze. Whatever painkillers they had me on were good ones.

"Hi Ashley, we'll be taking care of you from here," said a Doctor.

"I can't go in with you," Nathan told me, letting go of my hand, "but I'll be in the waiting area, okay?"

"Okay," I breathed, not wanting him to leave. "Can you call my parents and let them know?"

"Sure," he agreed with a solemn nod.

"Please don't tell them everything. I don't want them to know about the…" I trailed off, unable to say the words. Nath nodded with understanding and ran his hand over my hair.

"I'll take care of it."

"And I don't want anyone to come down here," I said, grasping his hand. "I can't face anyone right now."

"Okay," he agreed as they began to wheel me away from him. "I'll be in the waiting room when you get out," he called as they pushed me towards the ER.

"Thank you," I mouthed, keeping my eyes locked on his until the heavy double door swung closed between us.

- NATHAN STONE -

I stood outside the ER, not mentally prepared to go inside yet. The last time I'd been at that hospital I was half dead on a stretcher. Just being outside the building was enough to bring back the memories of those dark days. Why did shit like this keep happening to us? This was CSI, NCIS, Law and Order level drama… not something that happened to normal people. But then again, Ash and I definitely weren't normal people.

"Are you the husband?" a little blonde nurse broke the silence, causing me to nearly jump out of my skin.

"Yes," I lied, figuring I'd be able to get more information if they thought we were married.

"Then I need you to come with me to fill out some paperwork," she told me gently. I rubbed my face in worry as I began to process the events of the last few hours. "When can I see her?" I asked pushing back the tears that were threatening to overflow.

"Once the surgery is complete," she told me with a reassuring nod. "Why don't you come in and grab a cup of tea while I get the admission forms?"

"I think I'd rather stay out here for a bit," I said awkwardly.

"Okay," the nurse said, nodding. "I'll bring them out."

"Thanks."

She left me alone and I took a deep, calming breath. It was a struggle to process everything that had occurred over the past few hours.

I pulled out my phone and scrolled down my contacts list to the one person I wanted to talk to most. Ryan McPherson. Up until a few months ago, Ryza had been my sanity checker. He'd always been the person I'd called when I'd done something stupid or was stuck in a situation that I couldn't charm my way out of, but now he was locked up in rehab and uncontactable. I sighed and tapped on his name anyway. I knew he wasn't going to answer, or even get my message for that matter, but I was hoping that talking to his voicemail might provide me with some semblance of clarity.

"Hi, this is Ryan, leave a message after the beep."

"Hey Ryza, I know you probably won't get this message, but I really needed to hear your voice," I paused, sighed and rubbed my eyes to fend off the tears. "I don't know what to do man. Shit just got really real. Ashley was attacked by Dom tonight. She's hurt but she'll be okay. She killed him if you can believe it. Our feisty blonde," I laughed sadly and paced the empty car park. "I wish you were here man. I'm so lost right now. I'm standing outside the hospital, but I can't go in. I feel like I'm reliving my accident all over again, only it's worse this time because it's Ashley inside."

I stared up at the inky sky, which had turned a dark shade of purple. The crescent moon sliced through the darkness, shining brightly like it was offering a slither of hope amidst the turmoil.

"I've got to call Geoff and Mary and tell them, but I have no idea what to say," I continued confiding in Ryza's voicemail. "I guess we should all be glad that it was him and not her. It could have so easily been Ash lying in the morgue right now, but it isn't. It's Doyle, which means the nightmare's finally over." I closed my eyes and sent out a silent prayer of thanks to any god that cared to listen. For the first time in my life, I actually felt like there was someone or something watching over us. Ryan's voicemail beeped to tell me that my message was finished whether I liked it or not.

I sighed and opened my eyes, looking down at Ashley's phone in my hand. It was time to call Geoff and Mary. Shoving my own phone into my back pocket, I took a deep breath and dialled Geoff on Ashley's phone. I began pacing the pavement again as I put the phone to my ear.

"Hey cupcake," Geoff said at the other end of the line. "Ready for Paris?"

"Geoff. Hi. It's Nathan," I said nervously, rubbing my sore hips as I hobbled down the footpath. I was aching in places I didn't even know I had.

"Nathan?" he asked with surprise. "Why are you calling on Ashley's phone? What's going on?"

"Ummm…" I mumbled, not knowing where to start. Would he be relieved or disappointed that he didn't get the chance to kill Dom himself?

"Nathan, what's happened? Is Ashley okay?"

"She's fine," I said quickly, "there was a bit of an incident, but she's safe."

"Oh, thank god," he breathed with relief. "Does this have anything to do with Doyle?"

"Yeah," I said with a sigh. "Dom's dead Geoff, but he attacked Ash tonight."

"How? When? Where was she? How did he get to her?" He asked in quick succession, making my head reel even more than it already was.

"She went back to her flat alone and he was waiting for her there.

"How did he know she was going to be there? Why did she go on her own?"

I sighed again, feeling overwhelmed. I had all the same questions as Geoff and very few answers to give him.

"She went to get her passport while I was in a meeting. I don't know how he knew where she was. I didn't even know she was going there," I said hopelessly. "All I know is that he attacked her and she defended herself."

"She killed him?" he asked, in shock.

"Yeah," I confirmed grimly. Geoff fell silent, processing the many layers of meaning that piece of news brought with it.

"I wish I'd gotten to him first," he said grimly, breaking the tense silence

"Me too," I agreed.

"Is she okay?"

"She's pretty shaken up and a bit battered, but she'll be fine."

"That's good," he said, "which hospital is she in? We'll come up and get her."

"I wouldn't worry, it's just a few stitches and they'll be discharging her as soon as they're done. We'll be home before you even get here."

"Okay, we'll pick her up from your place then."

"It's fine Geoff, I've got this," I told him with a certainty that I didn't feel.

"But what about Paris? Don't you need to leave first thing in the morning?"

"I'm not going to Paris anymore." Work was insignificant given the circumstances.

"Okay," he said quietly. I could imagine him rubbing his chin at the other end of the line.

"Look Geoff… I hope I'm not over-stepping here," I said, feeling weirdly awkward about the idea I was going to propose, "but I've got a beach house in Cornwall, so I was thinking I'd take her down there for a few weeks while she recovers."

The line was silent for a moment, and I held my breath, awaiting his response. Ashley was a grown woman, so I didn't need her father's permission… but I really wanted it. I'd always had Gaz as a father-figure, but there was something about Geoff that made me desperately want his approval. Perhaps it was because I was in love with his daughter, or maybe just because he reminded me of my own Dad. Strong, but caring; Wise, yet mischievous; Proud, yet humble; Noble, but willing to do whatever was required to keep his family safe. Geoff was the sort of man that I'd always wanted to become.

"That sounds like a good idea," he said eventually.

"Thanks," I replied with a sigh of relief. "I've got a guest room, so you and Mary are welcome to come and join us."

"That's a nice offer Hotshot, but I think it's probably best if we let you have your space," Geoff answered with his innate parental wisdom.

"Okay," I said, nodding my head. "I'll get her to call you in the morning."

"That would be great," Geoff said appreciatively. "Enjoy your break. God knows you two need it."

"Thanks Geoff. And the offer is still there if you change your mind about coming down."

"Cheers," he paused for a moment before speaking again. "I'm glad she has you Nathan, you're a good man."

I teared-up with pride. "I'm glad I have Ash. It was her who turned me into a good man."

"That's not something someone else can give you Nathan," Geoff chuckled. "Anyway… we'll see you in a few weeks' lad. Take care of our girl."

"I will. Bye Geoff."

"Bye Nathan."

- RITCHIE CARLTON -

I stretched out my well-worn body and rolled over to see Aims pulling on her jeans.

"Are you off already?" I asked disappointedly. I don't know why I thought she might have actually hung around this time. After two years of being her fuck-buddy, the novelty was wearing a little thin and I hated that I seemed to have taken the role of the woman in our non-relationship. Our situation had done serious damage to my ego over the past few years, and I was wondering whether I'd ever reclaim my balls, or if my loss of man-hood was terminal.

"Yeah," she replied with a casual shrug.

"But I'm going to Paris in the morning. We're not going to see each other for a week."

She zipped her jeans and turned to face me.

"Ritchie, it's only a few days," she said with a disdainful snort.

"You always have an excuse Aims," I said, leaning back against the bedhead. "Why are you so adverse to staying the whole night?"

"I'm not adverse to it Ritch," she replied with a smile, "it's just that I don't see the point." It felt like a knife in my heart. She couldn't see the point?

"Wow, thanks," I answered with a grunt, holding back a whole host of other words that were much less polite.

"You know what I mean," she said flippantly.

"No, I don't think I do."

"We spend every day together Ritch, I don't see what the big deal is with sleeping in the same bed when we spend most of our waking hours together."

"We work together Aims," I said dryly.

"Exactly," she agreed lightly, as she bunched her beautiful mahogany hair on top of her head. "Look Ritch, you know I care about you right?" she asked, sitting on the end of the bed to put her shoes on.

"You do?" I questioned doubtfully.

"Of course I do."

"Well, that's news to me."

Amy sighed. "Come on, don't be like that. We both agreed right at the beginning to keep this open and casual," she said condescendingly as she finished putting her shoes on. "What we have is perfect Ritch, let's not ruin it."

"Right," I agreed obediently.

"It's the best of both worlds, right? Sex on tap with no commitment."

"I don't know how to respond to that," I answered honestly.

"Then don't," she replied chirpily, kissing me on the cheek. "I'm off. I'll see you when you get back."

"Fine," I sighed, watching hopelessly as she bounced out of my bedroom.

What had just happened there? How did she always manage to shut down that conversation? I definitely must have handed over my balls when I agreed to the fuck-buddy deal. I peered under the sheet to double check.

"Hey boys," I greeted my useless balls, "looks like I don't need you anymore, so you might as well take a break," I sighed hopelessly, before flopping back on the bed.

This was not how I'd envisioned life in my late thirties. The universe certainly had a cruel sense of humour. Here I was, desperate to settle down and have kids with a woman who had a severe aversion to committing; while Nathan Stone, the king of the man-whores, was falling in love with the girl-next-door. What sort of twisted irony was that?

I laughed with self-pity. Would Aims ever want to be a proper couple? It didn't seem like it. She was so adamant that things were perfect as they were, and any time I broached the subject she got defensive about it. She was the one in control for now, but I couldn't wait forever. I wasn't getting any younger. The longer I let it go on, the harder it would be to lock her down. I'd have to make a decision soon, before it was too late.

I didn't want to be an old dad. I didn't want to be the guy huffing and puffing his way around the footy field with his kids. My brother would be getting married at the end of the year so maybe that was a good deadline. If Amy wasn't ready to commit to me by December when I left for Sean's wedding, then I'd call it quits.

Until then…I'd be her committed sex slave.

- KAT McPHERSON -

It felt strange being in my own bedroom again. The last time I'd slept in that bed was the night I'd broken Ryan's heart. I glanced over at his empty pillow and my mind replayed the awful moment when I'd told him I'd slept with Beau. A million emotions had crossed his face in that one horrible second. What had started as a look of drunken happiness, had quickly turned to shock, then disbelief, then pain, then hate, then rage, and sadness, and grief, and the worst of all... betrayal.

Seeing that betrayal in his big brown eyes had been unbearable. That had been the moment I'd realised that I'd broken my own heart at the same time. I still hated myself for being responsible for that shattered expression on his face and I was never going to let that happen again.

I rubbed my tired eyes to clear the painful memory. Ryan and I were good now and that awful chapter was behind us. All we needed to do was get him out of rehab. Once he was home, life could go back to the way it was before any of the drama happened. Well... except that we now had a baby of course.

I rolled over quietly and peered into the Port-a-cot beside my bed, breathing a silent sigh of relief when I saw that Mia was sound asleep. It was only 9pm and she'd already woken to feed three times so I was absolutely exhausted. Looking after a newborn was hard work.

I'd learned quickly that I could no longer divide my life into days; I had to break it down hour-by-hour, so I didn't have any expectations on when I 'should' be sleeping or waking. It was purely a matter of survival. Sleep, feed, eat, repeat.

Things would get easier once Ryan was home, but in the meantime, I just had to push through and do the best I could. It had taken us so long to get pregnant with her, that I didn't feel like I had the right to complain about it. I just needed to appreciate being a mum and enjoy the process. Ha. That was much easier said than done.

I refrained from running my hand down her plump, caramel cheek and laid back down, snuggling into my soft, fluffy pillow. I needed to grab some sleep while I had the chance.

I closed my eyes and let myself drift off, as memories of blissful times spent in this bed swirled through my head. The first night Ryan and I ever slept in this apartment; the day we got engaged; the night of our wedding; the moment we found out that I was finally pregnant with Mia, and then the day that we passed the 'safe' point of the pregnancy; and the morning of Nathan's birthday… before Ashley had reappeared. That morning had been the last truly joyful moment that Ryan and I had shared in our bed.

Not that our broken marriage had anything to do with Ashley. It wasn't her fault we'd fallen apart; it was mine. Ash had merely been the torch that had shone a light on all the cracks in our relationship. I was the one who'd destroyed us. I'd been too caught up in my own insecurities to see the reality of the situation and because of my compulsive need to feel desirable, I'd made a fucking stupid decision.

But that was in the past and I couldn't change it no matter how much I wanted to, so I'd have to let it go and move forward. The past was history, and all that mattered now was the present and our future.

Mia's cries cut through my sleepy thoughts and I sat bolt upright before rolling over to get her out of the port-a-cot. I could hear the muted noise of the television coming from the lounge room, so I knew Rosie was still awake.

Cradling Mia in my arms, I leaned back against headboard to feed her. I was finally getting the hang of breast feeding and although it still hurt a little, I was finding it easier and easier. It was nice mother/daughter bonding time, although it was a little harder to appreciate that bonding opportunity when I was sleep deprived. I peered over at the clock. It was only 10pm but it felt like midnight. Time no longer held any meaning. Rosie popped her head in the door.

"Do you need anything?" she asked quietly.

"I'd love a cuppa."

"One Shirley cuppa coming right up," Rosie said with a wink. Our mother believed anything could be solved with a good cuppa. It was part of the Shirley Tailor philosophy of life: 'drink tea and ignore your problems'.

"Thank you," I stroked Mia's head and closed my tired eyes. Parenting wasn't an easy gig.

- RYAN McPHERSON -

Another fucking night in rehab. No matter how many weeks passed, being held captive in a clinic didn't get any easier, and now that Mia had entered the world, every second away from her and Kat felt like torture. It almost made things worse knowing they were back home in our flat. They were so close yet so far away and on top of that, I was worried about Kat having to care for a newborn on her own. It certainly wasn't what we'd envisaged parenthood to be at the beginning of her pregnancy. But then again, nothing had gone to plan lately.

Our world had been turned upside down several times over so, by all rights, we should have been experts at rolling with the punches. Sometimes literally. I was deep into my brooding when there was a knock at my bedroom door.

"Come in," I called, and the door opened to reveal the night orderly. "Hey, what's up?" I asked curiously. I didn't usually get room checks this late in the evening.

"Ryan, your lawyer is on the phone."

"What? Geoff? Why?"

"I don't know, but he says its important."

"Okay," I said, my stomach churning with concern. What could possibly be classed as important legal business at 10pm on a Monday night? Was it about my application to defer? Or perhaps I'd inadvertently broken the terms of my sentence when Mia was born? Maybe Peterson had contested the verdict and was fighting my deferral. I took a deep breath and followed the orderly to the office, where I hesitantly picked up the phone.

"Geoff?" I asked down the line, "is everything okay? I'm not going to prison, am I?"

"Ryan, calm down, it's got nothing to do with your case," he said calmly. "As far as I've heard you're doing really well, and I haven't heard back about the deferral yet."

"Oh, thank god," I breathed a loud and long sigh of relief.

"I just played the lawyer card, so they'd let me talk to you." He was calm and controlled but his tone was solemn.

"Very cunning," I said as my panic waned, "so what's going on?"

"I wanted to let you know... since you've always been a good friend to Ash... that there was an incident tonight."

"An incident?" I asked, with renewed anxiety, "Is she okay?"

"She's okay," he confirmed grimly, "but Dominic Doyle is dead."

"Dead?" I asked, stunned.

"Yes."

"Well, that's the best news I've heard for a while," I joked in disbelief. "What happened? I bet Ash's relieved."

"I suspect so," said Geoff sounding far less excited than I would have expected him to be. "It was Ashley who killed him. He tried to attack her and she defended herself."

"Holy shit," I whispered as the air evacuated my lungs. "That's extreme. Is she coping alright?"

"I haven't seen her, but Nathan tells me she's fine," he said evenly, "he's taking her down to Cornwall while she recovers." He paused, waiting for some sort of response from me but I didn't have one. "Sorry if I've distressed you Ryan," Geoff said compassionately, "maybe I shouldn't have rung. I just thought you'd like to know."

"No, I'm glad you did," I said appreciatively, "I hate being in the dark about everything. I feel like no one wants to tell me anything because they're all worried I'm going to go on another bender or something."

"They're just looking out for you," he said sagely. "I can't speak for your other friends, but I know Ash and Nathan miss you Ryan. They're keen to get you back into normal life as quickly as possible."

"Huh," I balked at his use of the word 'normal', "I don't know that things will ever be normal again."

"Mmmm…" Geoff agreed quietly, "Ash certainly has a talent for landing herself amidst drama." I chuckled in agreement.

"At least now her and Nathan can get on with their lives."

"My thoughts exactly."

"Can you pass on my best wishes if you speak to them?"

"Will do lad."

"Thanks for thinking about me Geoff," I said quietly.

"Not a problem," he said kindly. "Hang in there. Not much longer and you'll be out of there and starting afresh with your own family."

"Yeah," I agreed sadly, "although right now a few months feels like forever."

"Just take one day at a time Ryan. That's all you can do."

"I know you're right, it's just hard."

"I bet it is," Geoff empathised. "Have your parents been back since the baby was born?"

"No, thank god. I think they got the message."

Geoff sighed sympathetically. "I'm sorry you had to go through that lad. It must be heartbreaking to be betrayed by your own parents like that."

"Honestly Geoff, bribing my wife to leave me is sadly not one of the worst things they've ever done."

"Well, I'm still sorry," he said kindly, "just know that I'm here if you ever need to talk."

"Thanks Geoff."

"And Ryan… I know you might not believe this right now, but I'm really proud of you."

"Proud of me? Why?" I asked with confusion.

"For owning up to your mistakes and facing the consequences head on. It takes a big man to do that."

"Well… thanks," I replied, bashfully, "but it probably would've been better if I'd just not gone off the rails in the first place."

"Maybe, but maybe you needed go through this. The world works in mysterious ways Ryan and I think in a few years you'll look back on this as a positive experience."

"I hope you're right."

"I'm rarely wrong," he joked. "Well, I should let you go or they'll start getting suspicious."

"I think they already are."

He chuckled again and his deep rumbly laugh was somehow comforting.

"Goodnight Ryan, we'll talk soon."

"Night Geoff. Thanks again."

- NATHAN STONE -

By the time the nurse returned with the paperwork, I was still loitering out the front of the hospital.

"How about you come into the waiting area and have a seat love?" she suggested kindly. "It will be more comfortable than waiting out here."

"Okay." I nodded like a zombie, and she led me through the double glass doors, into the waiting area. With a deep breath, I limped inside and flopped down on one of the blue vinyl chairs, groaning from the excruciating pain in my knee and hips.

My healing bones were all aching badly, and I could only imagine what my physiotherapist, Wayne, would have said if he'd seen the state of me. My body hadn't healed enough for me to parkour my way up to Ashley's flat the way I had, but my injuries had been the last thing on my mind when I'd thought her life was hanging in the balance. I rubbed my aching knee and dialled Gareth.

"Nath?" Gaz asked worriedly down the line. "Is everything okay?"

"Something happened Gaz," I said calmly. "I'm fine, but Ash got hurt."

"What do you mean?"

"She got attacked Gaz," I said bluntly, "by the same guy who ran me down."

"What? I don't understand," he said with confusion. "I thought they couldn't find the guy."

"They couldn't… but he found us. It was Ashley's ex and he tried to kill her tonight."

"Holy shit, is she okay? Are you okay?"

"We're both fine, but she's in shock. She killed him Gaz. He came at her with a knife, and she defended herself."

"Fuck."

"Yeah… so… we're not going to Paris tomorrow."

"Nath."

"I'm sorry Gaz," I continued quickly. "I know it's shitty timing but that's just how it is."

"Sandrine will be pissed if you disappear again Nath," he said in disbelief. "Can't you drop Ashley off at her parents' place and go without her?"

"Yeah, I could, but I'm not going to," I told him honestly. "I'm taking her down to the beach house for a few weeks."

"You can't be serious Nathan," he said in shock. "Our biggest account is on the line and you're just going to fuck off to Cornwall for a few weeks?"

"Yep."

"I need you here mate… or more specifically, I need you in Paris."

"Fuck Paris," I said angrily. "I know you need me Gaz, but Ash needs me more."

"Nathan, if you do this, I'll have to hand the account to someone else."

"Do whatever you have to do," I said with a defiant nod. "This is more important than work."

Gaz sighed, "but you've worked so hard."

"Yeah," I agreed unemotionally, "but I guess I just realised that there's more to life than work," I paused. "Just promise me that Ash will still have a job when we get back. She'd be devastated if she got fired because of this."

"Of course! I wouldn't fire her for getting attacked, I'm not a heartless cunt," he said defensively. "Ash can take as much time as she needs to recover. It's you that I can't wait for, I need someone leading this account immediately."

I breathed a sigh of relief. "Okay."

"Okay? Does that mean you'll get your arse to Paris in the morning?"

"No," I said apologetically.

"Don't do this Nath," he pleaded, sensing what was about to come, "you're in shock right now".

"I'm sorry Gaz," I paused, "but I quit."

"Nathan."

"You'll have my letter of resignation in your inbox in the next few days."

"I won't let you ruin your career."

"See you in a few weeks Gaz," I said decisively.

"No Natha-"

I hung up and rubbed my tired eyes. I was a little shocked that I'd walked away from my career, but more shocked that I didn't care. Work didn't matter anymore. Ashley was my priority now. If there was one thing the whole evening had taught me, it was that I didn't want a future without Ashley Granger in it.

- ASHLEY GRANGER -

"Okay Ashley, you're all done," said the Doctor as she finished stitching up my shoulder, "but I really wish you'd let me look you over properly."

I stiffened, tired of having the same conversation with the medical staff. All I wanted was to get home and have a shower. I felt disgusting and dirty; I needed to get home and get clean.

"I won't consent to a rape kit," I said coldly, sliding off the stretcher. The doctor sighed patiently.

"I know this is a sensitive issue but as a care of duty I have to encourage you to talk about the sexual assault."

I cringed at the term. Why did people have to keep saying it?

"I'm fine," I replied curtly, too shamed to discuss it with anyone.

"I know it might feel embarrassing or shameful, but it's better if you can talk about it."

"Honestly, I'm fine," I re-iterated, "like I said to the other lady, it was nothing that he hadn't done before."

"So this wasn't the first time he'd assaulted you?" she asked with concern. I huffed with amusement.

"No," I answered politely. Not exactly the first time, or the second, or even the tenth. I'd lost count of the times that Dominic had forced me to have sex with him over the years, to the point where I couldn't even make a rough estimate. "Ten years of repeated sexual assaults in fact, except back then he was my boyfriend."

"Oh," she replied speechless, "could I at least talk you into seeing our resident psychologist?"

"No," I told her adamantly. "There's someone I've seen before, so I'd rather go back to her."

"Sure," agreed the Doctor as I edged towards the door, anxious to get home.

"I'm sorry. I know you have to ask, but honestly, I just want to find my boyfriend and go home."

"Please promise me you'll speak to someone. You've been through a traumatic experience Ashley, and with sexual assault it's quite often the psychological effects that have the greatest impact."

"Thanks," I said with a rigid nod. "I'll do that."

"Okay," she replied with a concerned smile as she led me out into the hallway. I nodded absently and peered out into the waiting room where Nathan was resting, looking adorably disheveled. His head was flopped against the wall and his feet propped up on the chair opposite him. His face was tinted with a shadow of ginger whiskers, and his shirt was stained and crumpled, with one side of his collar up and the other side down. He would have hated anyone seeing him in such a state of disarray, but for me, it was my favourite version of Nathan Stone. "Take care Ashley, and just remember that you don't have to go through this alone."

"I'm not alone," I told the doctor, without taking my eyes off my gorgeous man.

"That's good," the doctor replied, patting my non-injured shoulder. "Good luck Ashley."

"Thanks," I said peering back at her before I made my way across the waiting area to Nathan. I leaned over him and ran my hand lightly down his stubbly face. "Fancy meeting you here," I joked quietly. Nathan's eyes flew open.

"Ash," he said scrambling to his feet. "How are you? Are you okay?" he asked, as he rubbed his bloodshot eyes.

"I'm fine," I reassured him, "but I'm ready to go home."

"Yeah, me too. I'm pretty over this place," he said with a smile, offering me his hand. "Let's go." I took his hand and we walked silently outside into the cool night air. "Shit," Nath muttered, stopping in the middle of the footpath. "We don't have the car."

"Oh yeah," I answered, cringing at the thought of ever having to go back to the flat again. That place certainly wasn't my home anymore.

Nathan looked around. "There's a cab rank over there," he said, pointing towards the solitary black cab sitting in the taxi rank. "That will be quicker than calling a car."

"Yeah," I agreed, following along behind him, hyper aware of the fact that I was still covered in blood.

"I'll pick up the car in the morning," Nath said, squeezing my hand. He opened the door of the waiting taxi and helped me in.

"Holland Park thanks mate," he told the driver, who nodded and chuckled when our eyes met in the rear vision mirror.

"I wondered whether you two ever found each other," said the old man with a grin.

"Oh my gosh," I exclaimed with shock, as I realised it was the same lovely man who had taken me to my job interview at Artemis.

Nathan's jaw dropped. "You took me to the station that day," he said as the penny dropped.

"I sure did," the driver replied with a wink. "I take it you got her pen back to her then?"

"I sure did," Nathan repeated, looking over at me with an intense expression that made my heart flutter. It was a mixture of love, concern, and exhaustion, but it left me with absolutely no doubt as to how he felt about me.

"And did you get the job love?" The driver asked me as we pulled out onto the quiet street. I tore my eyes away from Nathan.

"I sure did," I echoed, not wanting to break the pattern.

"That's great."

"I can't believe that you remember us," Nath said with amazement, "you must have driven hundreds of people since that day."

"Yeah, but you two were a love story waiting to happen."

"Tonight's been more of a horror story," I mumbled exhaustedly.

"I'm sorry to hear that," said my favourite cabbie with a look of fatherly compassion, "but it looks like this guy is taking good care of you," he added, pointing over his shoulder at Nathan.

I peered up at Nathan, "he is."

"Then it's still a love story," the driver said, giving me a wink in the rear-vision mirror. I smiled and dropped my head onto Nath's shoulder. He wrapped his arm around me so gently that anyone would have thought I was made of glass. I let my eyes close and the images of Dominic's lifeless body on top of me sprung straight back into my mind. I opened my eyes again and snuggled further into Nathan. He kissed the top of my head and let his chin rest there for a moment. Maybe our relationship wasn't a typical Disney romance, but it was a love story of epic proportions.

"Hey," Nath whispered into my hair, "I was thinking I'd take you down to my beach shack in Cornwall for a few weeks."

"You have a beach shack?" I asked, looking up at him with surprise. He'd never mentioned a place in Cornwall before.

"Yeah," he said with a shrug. "What do you think? Do you want to get away for a while?"

"But what about Paris?"

"Fuck Paris," he said nonchalantly, "you're more important."

"No Nathan, I can't let you ditch Paris. You'd be throwing away all of your hard work." Nathan snorted with disdain at my choice of words.

"Pardon the pun?" he teased with self-deprecation.

"You know what I mean," I replied with a warning look. He huffed like a child and shook his head obstinately.

"I don't care about work."

"Yes, you do," I said, taking his hand, "and if you cancel this trip, you'll regret it."

"No, I won't."

"Yes, you will." I smiled with a bravery that I didn't feel. "Nathan, we're going to Paris."

"But-"

"No buts. It's not up for discussion. I won't let you throw this opportunity away because of me."

- NATHAN STONE -

Ash was like a dog with a bone. She didn't stop nagging me until I agreed to rescind my resignation.

"If you don't call Gaz and un-quit then I'll do it for you," she insisted sternly. It was an idle threat given that I was in possession of both of our phones, but it was enough to make her point clear.

"Okay, I'll rescind my resignation," I acquiesced, "but only via text. I'm not calling him again."

"Fine," she agreed with relief. I studied her tired face. She wasn't in any shape for traveling let alone attempting to maintain a professional façade. "Are you sure you're up to a work trip?"

Ash stared intently out the window and, for a moment, I thought she was going to pretend that she hadn't heard me.

"It will be a good distraction," she answered eventually, without taking her eyes off the quiet street beyond. I watched her silently, feeling completely helpless. She was pushing down her pain for some misguided belief that my job was important. I wanted to hold her and kiss her and make her see that she was my priority, but I knew that wasn't what she needed, so I took her hand in mine and sat silently for the rest of the ride home.

Fred was sitting on the doormat to greet us when we finally walked through the door, weary and worn. The place was still lit up and my satchel was sitting in the middle of the bench, exactly as it had been when I'd rushed out the door to go search for Ashley.

"Hey Freddie," Ash said groaning as she bent down to pat our chubby cat.

"Are you hungry?" I asked Ash, popping my keys down on the table. "I'll cook you something."

"No thanks, I just really want a shower," she said with a waver in her voice. I nodded and choked back a lump in my own throat. Now that we were back home, the nights events were beginning to feel very real.

"Okay, well you go do that and I'll put on a pizza or something in case you change your mind."

"Honestly babe, I couldn't stomach it, but you should eat something."

"I don't think I could stomach it either," I said, running my hands through my already disheveled hair. The memory of her blood-splattered apartment was still playing on my mind, as was the thought of Dominic forcing himself on her. Ash slipped away to shower and I looked down at my vomit-stained shirt.

"Gross," I muttered, unbuttoning the shirt as quickly as I could. I balled it up and threw it at the washing machine. An incinerator would have been a better place for it but lying on the kitchen floor in front of the washing machine was where it would stay for now. I stood shirtless in the lounge room feeling adrift.

"What do you think Fred?" I asked the cat as she wrapped herself around my legs, "should we still go to Paris or do I call Red and tell her not to worry about feeding you?"

I patted the cat gently and sighed, groaning in pain as I stood up again. Wayne was going to have a few choice words to say about my Action-Man shenanigans when he found out that I'd scaled a flight of stairs and parkoured over a dead body.

- ASHLEY GRANGER -

I flicked on the hot tap and let steam fill the bathroom as I stripped off my dirty clothes. I held the bloodied pile in both hands and stared at them in disgust. I could still smell Dom on them. Instead of putting them into the laundry basket, I threw the whole pile in the bin. I didn't want to keep anything that would remind me of tonight.

I wiped a couple of tears off my cheeks and jumped into the steaming shower. It was scorching and made my skin turn pink on contact, but I needed it hot enough to kill the germs. I grabbed my loofah and lathered it with soap. I scrubbed and soaped repeatedly until my skin was red raw but no matter how much soap I used or how hard I scrubbed, I still felt dirty.

I dropped the loofah on the floor and collapsed against the tiled wall with despair. I breathed deeply, careful not to make any sound as I wept with an anguish that penetrated my body and soul. Even though Dom's attack had been cut short this time, it had been so much worse. Last time I'd already resigned myself to a lifetime as Dom's prisoner, but this time... this time, all I'd been able to think about was Nathan. This time I'd had something to fight for; a reason to live and someone who'd shown me what real love was.

In that one horrible but brief moment, Dominic had destroyed it all. He'd contaminated me and left a stain on my beautiful new relationship that could never be removed. Nashley was now forever tarnished and there was nothing I could do to unsully us.

Tears poured down my cheeks as I sobbed silently against the cold tiles. I would have to pull myself together convincingly enough to make the trip to Paris in the morning. If I didn't get on that train, then neither would Nathan. He wouldn't leave me behind if he thought that I wasn't coping, so his career depended upon my ability to push aside my misery.

- NATHAN STONE -

I kicked off my shoes and headed into the bedroom, unbuckling my belt as I walked through the door. I was shirtless, shoe-less and mid belt-removal when Ash emerged from the bathroom. I froze on the spot, feeling like a wildlife photographer who'd stumbled across a white unicorn in Epping Forest. I finished removing my belt and Ash shuddered as it slid out of the final belt loop.

"You okay?" I asked, as she cautiously edged past me.

"Yep," she said in a whisper, before quickly retreating into the walk-in-robe. The bandage on the back of her shoulder was soggy and stained with blood.

"Can I change the dressing you?" I asked, still standing at the bedroom door.

"No, it's fine," she said from inside the wardrobe. It wasn't fine, but I didn't want to push her.

"Alright," I agreed, feeling disheartened at the growing distance between us, "I'm just gonna jump in the shower okay?"

"Sure," she said from her wardrobe hidey-hole. I stood and stared in the direction of her muffled voice. I was at a complete loss. I assumed she would probably need some space, but she was completely withdrawing from me. How was I supposed to help her through such a massive thing? Especially if my mere presence made her shudder. I drooped my head in defeat and went for my shower.

Ash was already in bed when I emerged, and by the time I climbed in next to her, it was well past midnight. I crawled under the covers stifling a groan as I felt a wide variety of aches and pains twinging all over my body. Everything was hurting, but I tried not to make a sound as I flopped against the pillow. I looked over at Ash and she was peering up at me with an expression that I couldn't decipher.

"Are you okay?" I asked again, wondering what was going through her mind. She nodded silently, closing her eyes as a tear dripped down her cheek and soaked into the pillow.

"It's finally over," she whispered, opening her eyes again.

"Yeah," I said quietly, stroking her cheek with my thumb. "It's all over."

- ASHLEY GRANGER -

Despite being exhausted, it took me a long time to doze off that night. My body was weary, but my brain was fighting against sleep because every time I closed my eyes I saw Dom's face. He was haunting my dreams. My worst nightmares were being replayed in full colour and surround sound. Most of the memories were short flashes, but there was one moment that played over and over again. Dom grunting on top of me. The dream was so vivid that I felt like I was re-living it.

"Get off!" I screamed, sitting bolt upright. My heart was pounding and the room was so dark, it took me a moment to realise that I was safe in Nathan's bed.

"You're okay," Nath said, reaching out for me in the dark. His fingers wrapped reassuringly around mine and I breathed a sigh of relief, gripping his hand like it was my lifeline back to reality. "You're at home," he said soothingly, "you're safe now."

I slowed my breathing and snuggled into Nathan's chest, needing to feel the safety of his arms around me. He froze for a moment, and then wrapped me up in a tight hug, stroking my hair as I buried my head into his chest. How would he feel if he knew exactly what Dom had done to me? And even worse, that my body seemed to enjoy it. Would he still want to be with me or had I ruined everything?

"I'm sorry," I whispered hiding another wave of tears, "I'm so sorry."

"You have nothing to be sorry for," he said quietly into my hair. The guilt weighed heavily on my chest and I couldn't bear it, so I rolled onto my other side and curled up into a ball with my back to Nathan.

He sighed almost inaudibly, but in the quiet night the faint sound reverberated through my ears like thunder. I hugged my knees into my chest and let my tears fall silently down my face. How were we going to get through this? Would we survive?

- KAT McPHERSON -

With my eyes still closed, I hung over the port-a-cot, patting Mia gently. It was the fifth time she'd been up during the night, and I felt like a zombie. Was this normal for a newborn or was there something wrong with her?

"Come on babe," I whispered soothingly, "I'm here. You're safe. Go back to sleep honey." Mia responded by crying louder. "What's going on kiddo?" I asked, continuing the back-patting as per the instructions in one of the millions of parenting books I'd read. On the most part, they were useless. They all contradicted each other, so it was hard to know which advice to listen to. Let them cry it out, or cuddle them? Have a strict sleep schedule, or go with a child-led sleep routine? Dummy's are good vs dummy's are bad. Co-sleeping vs cot only. It was way too much for a sleep-deprived brain to handle.

When Mia still didn't settle, I tried a different tactic. I wasn't a great singer, but I was desperate so I was willing to try. "When you try your best, but you don't succeed," I sang quietly, going with the first song that sprung into my mind. "When you get what you want but not what you need…" Coldplay was possibly not the most appropriate choice, but I was rolling with it.

"When you feel so tired, but you can't sleep," I chuckled tiredly at that line, "stuck in rever-er-erse." Mia finally began to settle, so I rested my head against the rail of the port-a-cot and continued singing with my eyes closed until she was quiet and breathing a steady rhythm.

- NATHAN STONE -

In the early hours of the morning, I left Ashley in bed and set-off to pick up the car and her passport. When I arrived at her flat blurry-eyed, aching and exhausted, there was still police tape everywhere and cops loitering all about the place. I climbed out of the town car and took in the scene before me. The street was a hub of activity, but in a much more serene way than it had been the previous evening. The mood was eerily calm as all the police officers and investigators tended to their business like it was a normal day at the office.

"Nathan." I heard a deep Scottish accent call from behind me. I turned around to see Jock striding towards me, wearing dark sunglasses, jeans and a leather jacket, with what looked suspiciously like a gun holster hiding beneath it.

"Jock?" I asked with confusion.

"Is Ash okay?" he asked, reaching out his hand.

"Yeah," I muttered in shock, shaking his massive, outstretched paw. "What are you doing here man?"

"I heard about Dom," he said, glancing over my shoulder to survey the scene unfolding behind me. I took a step back from the ginger giant and studied him suspiciously.

"How could you have heard about it? It only happened last night." Jock slid his shades up onto his fiery red hair, then pulled out his wallet from the back pocket of his jeans.

"I'm a cop Nathan," he said, showing me his badge as if I wouldn't believe him.

"I know, but how did your Scottish contacts hear about this so fast?"

Jock opened his mouth to respond as one of the Policemen called out from the other side of the barrier.

"Detective Campbell," the guy said, as he motioned at Jock, "they need you inside."

"Aye, I'll be a minute," Jock said, dismissing the uniformed officer with an authoritative nod. I stared at Jock, then at the cop, and then back at Jock again as a heavy feeling began weighing in the pit of my belly. My brain was fuzzy from sleep deprivation, but the information was slowly sinking in.

"Detective? What the fuck Jock?"

Jock peered around, tucked his badge back into his jeans pocket and then sighed. "I'm still a cop Nathan. I've been undercover."

"Undercover for what? What could possibly have been going down at an Apple store?"

"Nothing," he said, rubbing the back of his thick, rugby player neck. "I never worked there. We just took the opportunity that day to try and get a lead. It was a last-minute operation to get an in with Ash," he shrugged guiltily. "The Kesha angle wasn't working so it was a last-ditch effort."

"The Kesha angle? What do you mean? How does Kesha fit into this? Why did you need to get close to Ash? How did you even know she'd be at the Apple store?" I asked without stopping for a breath. I had so many questions.

"Nathan, I know you've got a lot of questions, and I'm happy to answer them but right now I've got work to do. How about we go grab a coffee after this?"

"What? No. I've just come to get Ashley's passport. We're going to France this morning."

"Aye," he said with a nod as he waved over the same cop. "Could you please locate Ms Grangers passport?"

"Sure."

"It's in the top drawer of her bedside table," I told him in a daze, unable to process the situation unfolding in front of me. The cop trotted off to do as asked, and I turned back to the not-so-jolly red giant. "Jock…" I prompted. He sighed again and despite his cool and calm exterior, he squirmed awkwardly, as if telling the truth was going to cause him physical discomfort.

"I was part of a task force trying to locate Doyle. We found out that he wasn't in prison and I was assigned to investigate Ash, so I befriended Kesha to try and build some trust."

"Oo-kay…" I said, not sure whether to punch him or ask him more questions. I opted for more questions… for the time being. "But how did you know Ash would be at the store?" I asked suspiciously, "she only decided to do that the night before."

"We tapped her phone," he said, looking down at his heavy leather boots.

"Are you fucking serious?" I asked, as rage flared through me. "So, there was never any spyware on her phone?"

"There was… but we jacked the app so that we had access to all the same info Doyle did."

"You did what?" I roared, ready to forgo the questions and punch him instead. "Did you even delete it that day when she went to the store?"

"Yeah, I did, and when I saw the look on her face I realised that she had no idea about his escape."

"You thought she helped him escape?"

"That was one theory."

"What was the other theory?"

"That he'd go after her. Either way, we knew he'd make contact with her."

"Holy fuck," I muttered, rubbing my hands over my face. "This is fucked up Jock," I said, stunned. Adrenalin coursed through my body again, this time with renewed vigor. "Is that even your name?"

"Aye it is," he shoved his hands in his pockets. "I'm sorry Nathan, I know this is a shock, but Ash was our only option."

I stepped so close to him that we were nose-to-nose.

"So, you used her?"

"No," he said quickly. "I mean… initially maybe, but then I got to know her and-"

"No way, you don't get to use that excuse," I snapped, clenching my fist tightly. "You've been lying to her all this time and every day that you didn't come clean, you put her in more danger."

"I couldn't say anything while Dom was alive, I could have blown the case or put her in worse danger. If Dom had found out that I was a cop he would have-" Jock's words were cut short as I punched him hard in the face.

"You selfish prick," I growled angrily, before several police officers descended upon me. One of them grabbed my shoulders but Jock put his hand up to wave the guy away.

"It's fine," he said calmly, wiping a trickle of blood from his nose as if it was no big deal. "I've got this." The cop looked between the two of us, and then released his vice-like grip on my shoulders. "Honestly, it's fine lads," Jock reiterated to the officers, until they finally nodded and backed away, keeping their eyes trained on me. Jock sniffed back the remaining blood and glanced down at me with complete composure.

"I deserved that," he said with a nod.

"Yeah, you did," I agreed coldly. "Do you have any idea what she's been through? You could have saved her from that attack."

"Nathan, I was just doing my job."

"If you'd done your job properly, you would have put him away months ago."

Jock shook his head, "it's not that simple."

"Yeah, it is," I snarled. "You should have told her what was going on the second that you realized she wasn't involved, but instead you kept stringing her along so you could use her as bait."

"That's not what I was doing."

I snorted angrily. "Are you trying to convince me, or yourself?" I paused and sized him up for a moment. "You say you love her, but you handed her over to a psychopath on a silver platter," I closed my eyes and took a breath to calm myself down, then looked up at Jock with disgust. "Did they tell you he raped her last night?"

Jock's jaw fell. He looked pained, more so than he had when I'd punched him. It was clear that my words had hurt him more than my fist had.

"He rap…?" Jock let the word trail off. I cocked my head and enjoyed seeing the weight of his guilt bear down on him like a ton of bricks. It didn't make my pain any less, and it certainly didn't help Ashley, but it did feel like a very minor win in what had been a horrendous 12 hours.

"You can lie to yourself all you like Detective, but we both know you could have stopped that from happening. If you really loved her, you would have put an end to this months ago."

Jock sighed and ran his hand across his ginger beard. "I do love her Nathan, and I never meant for any of this to happen."

"Well, it did," I snapped nastily, "and that's on you." Again… hurting him didn't fix the situation but it felt really good.

"I just wanted to protect her from Doyle," he said with obvious regret. "I even tried to get her away from London."

"They're all waiting for you Detective," interrupted the officer who'd brought back Ashley's passport. The guy handed me the little maroon book and I turned back to Jock.

"You'd better go Detective," I said frostily. Jock nodded curtly and stepped around me, stopping by my side with his bulky chest pressed against my shoulder. I kept my eyes trained on him in case he decided to return the favour and punch me in the face. Instead, he glanced down at me with beseeching eyes.

"Please don't tell Ash until I've had a chance to talk to her."

"You won't ever be talking to her again," I huffed in revulsion. The Detective sighed.

"I still have to question her Nathan."

A flash of red flared inside my head and I grabbed the front of his shirt, pointing my finger in his face.

"Stay away from her Jock. You've done enough damage."

"You know I'd never do anything to hurt her."

"You already did," I said, slowly letting go of his shirt. "And if you go anywhere near her again, I swear to god I'll kill you myself. Just leave her alone," I added, before pushing past him to get to my car.

"Nathan," Jock called after me as I stormed away. "At least tell her I'm sorry."

"Bye Detective," I said over my shoulder. I pulled out my keys and jumped straight into the drivers' seat of my Tesla. It was the first time I'd sat on that side of the car since I'd bought it. I flopped back against the cream leather and rubbed my face.

"Fucking prick," I muttered, glancing over at him, then down at Ashley's passport in my hand. "Damn it," I swore as I hit the steering wheel with aggravation. How was I supposed to tell Ashley that she'd been used as bait?

I glanced around the busy street, remembering all the shitty things that had happened at that place. The worst things had all happened right there on that street. We needed to break our ties to that fucking apartment. Ash needed a fresh start and she wouldn't get that if she still had that flat.

It was time to close this chapter of our lives, and I wasn't going to turn the page, I was going to burn the fucking book, page by page, until it felt like none of it had ever happened.

– Chapter 2 –

Revelations

- KAT McPHERSON -

Not long after I'd finally fallen into a decent sleep, Mia woke and cried for her breakfast. I peeled my eyes open just as Rosie came running into my room, silent as a ninja, with a bottle in-hand, ready to go.

"Shh…", she quietly cooed to Mia.

"Morning," I mumbled, rolling over and rubbing my burning, tired eyes.

"Oh damn," Rosie swore, with a startled jump. "Morning babe. Sorry, I was trying to get the bottle done before she woke up." She put the bottle down on my dresser and carefully lifted Mia out of the port-a-cot. "It sounded like you had a relentless night and I wanted you to get some sleep."

"Aww Rosie, that's so sweet," I said, touched that she was helping out so much. "Sorry if we kept you awake."

"Don't be silly, I love being here to help. I just wish I could stay longer. Now, you relax, I've got this," she said, sniffing Mia's nappy with wrinkled nose. "Phew kid, let's get you out of that stinky nappy." Rosie gently cradled Mia in her arms and grabbed the warm milk bottle. "Go back to sleep, I'll look after miss stinky pants."

"Are you sure?"

"Of course! You hardly slept all night," Rosie said jiggling Mia in a very maternal fashion, "and you need to get your beauty sleep if you're going to see your husband today."

"Thank you," I said gratefully as I flopped back against the pillow.

"I'm only here for a few more hours, so make the most of me," she said with a wink as she carried Mia towards the door. "Consider me your own personal Mary Poppins."

I chuckled and watched them leave the room before letting my eyes drift closed again. This time I quickly fell into a deep sleep and dreamed of my future with Ryan.

It began with blissful days spent in our flat watching Mia crawl and play on the floor. We were happy and laughing, cuddled up together. Life felt good. We were not only back to normal, but better than before. I caught his eye and as lost myself in his warm chocolate coloured gaze. We moved into a big country house with a second caramel baby tucked gently in Ryan's arms. My heart glowed at the sight and a joyful giggle drew my attention to the garden behind him. Mia tottered happily around in the garden wearing a frilly pink dress that I'd never have bought her in a million years. It looked like something straight from the Shirley Tailor Kids collection.

Then, as if my thoughts had conjured her, my Mum appeared out of nowhere, accompanied by my father. They were dressed up in colourful early 1900's outfits straight from the chalk-drawn fairground scene of Mary Poppins. Mia squealed excitedly when she saw them, and my parents bundled her up in warm hugs as the baby become a little boy who ran into their arms alongside a now school aged Mia. The happy foursome skipped over to the bright pink ice-cream truck that had popped up out of thin air and proceeded to order one of everything.

I turned back to Ryan, who was glowing with joy, and we were both transported into a luxurious white bedroom with huge French windows overlooking the ocean. He was now naked, and his dark chocolate skin looked almost magical against the crisp white of the room furnishings. Ryan held my gaze with a sexy, confident smile that I hadn't seen before, and desire flared in the pit of my belly. He reached out his hand for me and as I moved to take it, he slowly morphed into Xavier.

I tried to back away but his grasp on my hand was too tight and I felt panic beginning to rise in my chest, escalated further when Xavier turned into Beau.

"Where's Ryan?" I ask anxiously as I stood staring at my ex best friend with my heart in my throat.

"He's gone," Beau said unemotionally. His sad eyes bored into me as he gripped my outstretched hand. The look of betrayal on his face pierced my heart and I felt tears spring to my eyes.

"I'm sorry," I whispered, wracked with guilt.

"An apology won't change the fact that you're a whore Kat," he taunted.

"What?"

"You're a whore Kat," he repeated, as grey smoke started filling the room. The smoke grew so thick that I could no longer see Beau, but I felt him release his grip on my hand. I was free, but I was all by myself in the growing smoke cloud.

"Beau?" I called, as the smoke grew thicker and darker. "Xavi? Ryan?" I called desperately, struggling to breathe in the thick smoke.

I could hear fire crackling somewhere behind the smoke and the room suddenly felt hot. How was I going to escape when I didn't know where I was? The smoke stung my eyes and the sound of the flames roared in my ears, even though I couldn't see them. I dropped to the floor, coughing as I heard an almighty explosion and the world turned black and silent.

When I opened my eyes, I was on a deserted beach, lying with my face against the cold, white sand. Scrambling to my bare feet, I searched for signs of life on the isolated coastline.

"Ryan?" I called into the empty void, as I ran ungracefully through the soft sand. "Mia?" As I scrambled along the seemingly endless beach, I knew I'd find nothing. I was alone.

"Kat?" a voice echoed from behind me. I turned to see Rosie, standing in a bright pink dress, with baby Mia in her arms.

"Rosie!" I ran towards her with tears streaming in my eyes, but as I got closer, she and Mia drifted further away. I ran harder and faster, but no matter how fast I ran, I could never get to them.

"Kat," Rose called with her hand outstretched.

"Rosie," I bellowed again as they both began to vanish into a blur.

"Kat wake up," Rosie's voice cut through my dreams and I zoomed back to reality.

"Huh?" I asked groggily as I realised I was at home in my bed.

"It's nine o'clock," she said, stroking my hair gently, "it's time to get up and go see your man."

- RYAN McPHERSON -

After breakfast, the Medical Director, Tony, summoned me into his office to discuss my application for a sentence deferral. Geoff had seemed confident that we'd get the request granted, so I strutted through Tony's door with a spring in my step, expecting to hear good news. I knocked on the open door.

"Hey Tony."

"Ryan, have a seat," he said, motioning towards the chair opposite him.

"Thanks." I made myself comfortable as he shuffled a stack of papers. I smiled and watched patiently as he read through my case notes. Nothing would ruin my good mood, because soon I'd be home with Kat and Mia, getting our new life started. Tony flipped through a couple more of the papers then placed them down on the desk and looked at me with an ominous expression.

"I've had a chance to look over your application," he said solemnly, "and I've talked to all of your therapists."

"Great, when can I go home?" I asked, certain that the ruling would go in my favour. He shook his head and clasped his hands together like a judge delivering a guilty verdict.

"I'm sorry Ryan, but I can't approve it," he said unapologetically.

"What? Why?" I asked desperately, almost falling off my chair with shock. He leaned forward with a calm confidence, which made me even angrier.

"From what I've been told," he said coolly, "you've been making great progress, and I feel that having a break now would set you back." I stared at him open-mouthed.

"But I'm all good, I don't need to be here anymore. I'm fine now."

"No Ryan, you still have a way to go," Tony said sternly.

"But I have a wife and a newborn to look after."

"I understand that, but arguing isn't going to change my mind," he said definitively. "I've made my decision."
I flopped back in my chair with hopelessness.

"So, there's nothing I can do to convince you that I'm better?"

"I'm afraid not."

"Please Tony…" I begged.

"That's my final answer Ryan," he said with a shrug. "It might sound harsh, but I honestly believe it's the best thing for you, and your family, in the long-term."

"I don't see how," I sulked like a sullen teenager.

"Look, I understand that you're upset, but if it's any consolation, I don't think you'll need the full three months here. I'm happy to talk about an early discharge, but that's as far as I'm willing to go."

"That doesn't help me right now though."

"It's better than the alternative," he replied, with a tinge of warning in his tone.

"Yeah," I agreed humbly, bowing my head like a subordinate pack wolf. He didn't need to remind me twice.

"That's the best I can offer Ryan, so I suggest you work hard for the next month and get yourself home to your wife and baby."

"Thanks," I said amenably, knowing that he was the only thing standing between me and prison. I rose from my chair and turned to leave.

"Keep up the good work Ryan," Tony said condescendingly.

"I will," I replied through gritted teeth, before letting myself out. I sped hastily out of Tony's office and Sloan was waiting around the corner to hear my news.

"What did Tony say?" she asked excitedly before seeing the grim look on my face. "Eek. Let's go grab a coffee in the lounge," she suggested, patting my shoulder like I was a lost puppy dog. We wandered out to the lounge room and I slumped onto one of the cushy sofa's while she grabbed us each a mug of gross instant coffee. "Here, coffee makes everything better," Sloane said, handing me a cup of blackish liquid that didn't look like what I'd classify as coffee.

"Not sure we could call this coffee," I sulked.

"It's the best we've got," she said with a shrug as she flopped on the couch next to me. Sloane wriggled around and hooked her leg over the arm of the couch as if she was settling in to watch an episode of Bridgerton.

"I take it from your cheery disposition that you didn't get the deferral," she said, sipping her so-called coffee.

"Got it in one," I said, pointing at her like she was a contestant in a game show. "He thinks it will hinder my progress."

"Well, that's a load of bollocks," she said defensively.

"Yeah, that's what I said, but he's the only thing standing between me and prison so I didn't feel like I could argue the matter."

Sloane patted my shoulder again. "That sucks Ryan, I'm so sorry."

"It's not your fault," I replied with shrug.

"Do you think they'd let Kat and Mia come and stay here?"
I laughed at the thought of anyone choosing to stay in that place.

"It's not really a baby-friendly environment," I said, seeing that she was being serious.

"No, but wouldn't be worth asking the question anyway?"

"I don't know, I doubt Kat would want to stay here."

"She just wants to be with you Ryan, I don't think she'd care where you were," Sloane said with the wisdom of someone twice her age.

"Maybe I'll ask," I replied with a shrug, when one of the orderly's waved me down.

"Ryan, you've got a visitor," she called from the doorway, "it's your wife." I grinned like a school kid at the prospect of seeing my wife, and Sloane nudged me playfully in the ribs.

"Ryan and Ka-at sitting in a tree-" she teased.

"Thanks," I said to the orderly with a wave, then put my hand over Sloane's face and gently pushed her away. She laughed and almost toppled off the sofa.

"K.I.S.S.I.N.G," she sang amidst her giggles. It was like having a little sister around and although Sloane could be annoying at times, I enjoyed her company. "Can I come and meet Mia?" she asked with an excited smile.

"Sure, why not?" I said, offering her a hand up.

- RITCHIE CARLTON -

Nath and Ash were already waiting outside the boarding area when I walked into the Eurostar terminal. They looked decidedly like a married couple as they faffed around, getting themselves organised. Ash was rummaging through her bag and Nathan was doting over her like a little old man.

"Morning Stones!" I teased from afar. Ash looked up and I nearly recoiled when I saw the state of her face. She was sporting a nasty black eye, a split lip and a row of stitches across her eyebrow. "Holy shit Granger, are you okay?"

She nodded silently and Nath rested one hand on her shoulder, as he shook my hand with the other.

"Hey Ritch," he said, shooting me a meaningful look.

"Everything okay?" I asked with concern. He nodded stiffly and patted me on my arm. I gathered that it was bad, but I couldn't fathom why they were both here while Ash was in that state. I opened my mouth to ask as much when Cody arrived.

"Hey dudes," he greeted us, breaking the tension.

"Hey mate," I answered cheerfully, shaking his hand as he joined the group. With Ash hidden behind Nathan, Cody hadn't seen her face yet. "This is a bit of a change for you hey?" I asked, trying to keep the mood light.

"Yeah, they usually keep me chained to my computer," he joked, shrugging off his backpack and popping it down on the floor.

"Where all good computer geeks should be," I teased with a wink as he moved towards Ash to say hello. Ash emerged from behind Stoner and Cody promptly stepped backwards.

"Whoa, Ash, what happened to your face?" he asked aghast.

"Long story," Nathan answered on her behalf. "Is everyone ready to go?"

Cody shot me a quick look of concern then picked his bag up again and threaded his arms back through the straps as if he'd never removed it.

"Yeah sure," he said, visibly perturbed by the bizarre situation.

"Righto then," I said loudly. "Paris here we come." Being an Aussie, I'd never been one to splurge on transportation. We traveling antipodeans had a habit of scrimping on the methods of travel in order to spend the saved money on visiting extra destinations. As such, I'd never traveled in business class on any vehicle, so when I discovered that Stoner had booked us business seats, I was pretty chuffed. It was certainly a lot fancier than cattle class. "Wow, not half bad Stoner," I said with admiration, as we boarded the business class carriage.

"Yep, I'm definitely a fan of traveling in style," Cody agreed with a laugh.

"Only the best for my team," joked Stoner, as we located our seats. We stowed our bags and unloaded our devices, pleased to find all the essential amenities, like USB ports and power outlets. "I might run down to the bar and grab us all some coffees," Nath suggested, shooting me that same meaningful look that he'd given me at the station.

"Need a hand?" I asked, taking the hint and getting to my feet.

"Yeah cheers," he said with a nod, then turned to Ash and squeezed her shoulder. "You okay here with Cody for five minutes?"

Ash nodded but didn't say a word. Although she was trying to keep a smile on her face, she was like a shell of her former self. I'd never seen Ash so subdued before, not even the day her crazy ex had showed up. I glanced back at my troubled friend and then lead Nathan along the isle and out of the sliding door.

"Talk to me," I said, once we were safely inside the other carriage.

"Dom attacked Ash last night," he said in one long breath. I stopped walking and turned to face him.

"Dude…" I said, as I gripped his arms and stared at him in stunned silence. Now that we were alone, he looked like he was only barely holding his shit together. "Fuck man," I said, not knowing what else I could say. "Are you both okay?"

Nath shook his head and then sank to the nearest seat with his head in his hands. His shoulders began to shake with hidden sobs, so I patted his back and took the seat opposite him. In all the years we'd been friends, I'd never seen Nathan break down. I leaned forward and held his shoulder as he wept silently, but didn't speak until his sobs began to subside.

"What happened?" I asked. He straightened himself up, wiped his face with the back of his hand and then continued as if nothing unusual had occurred.

"She went back to her flat to get her passport and he jumped her at the door."

"Holy shit," I said, annoyed that Nathan hadn't gotten to the fucker first like he'd planned. "I take it the cops got him then?"

"Nope," said Nath shaking his head, "she killed him."

"She what?" I asked, thinking that I must have misheard him.

"She killed him," he repeated. He took a deep breath and looked me in the eye. "He raped her Ritch, then when she got away, he came at her with a knife. Thankfully she got him better."

"Fuck," was my highly intelligent response. I couldn't believe what I was hearing. It was a huge amount of information to process in one short second and I was momentarily lost for words. I rubbed my bald head like it would grant me a wish. "I don't know whether to be pleased or concerned."

"Me either," Nath said, raking his hands through his hair. He sighed heavily, looking like he'd aged ten years in ten seconds. "We're not coping so well," he admitted quietly.

"Yeah, I noticed." We both stared at the ground for a bit. "I can't believe you still came on this trip."

"Ash insisted," he said, leaning back in his chair. "I wanted to take her down to the beach house, but she refused."

"That sounds like Ash," I said with a nod.

"I don't know what to do for her man. How do I help her through this? She's pretending that she's okay but she's clearly not. I'm scared to touch her in case it triggers her and I want her to know that she can talk to me about it but I don't want to question her." He paused and shook his head. "I don't think I'm equipped for this Ritch."

"From what I can see Stoner, you're doing everything right. I don't think there's much you can do besides be there for her and that's what you're doing. She'll talk when she's ready, in the meantime, just… hold space."

Nath nodded. "Thanks Ritch."

"No worries mate," I said, slapping him on the shoulder, "shall we get those coffees then?"

- KAT McPHERSON -

I stood out in the reception area waiting anxiously to see Ryan. I wheeled the pram around the room, looking at the large garden-view window and brightly coloured paintings hanging on the wall. The place looked more like a hotel than a rehab centre. Not that I knew what a rehab centre was supposed to look like.

"Oh my god is that little Mia?" squealed a high-pitched voice from behind me.

"Holy shit," I mumbled under my breath as I turned around to see Pop-Star Sloane Sutton, running towards me.

"It sure is," said Ryan proudly, as he trailed along behind her.

"Aww she's so adorable," Sloane cooed as she fawned over Mia. I stood silently staring at her, star struck. Sloane looked up from the pram and grinned at me. "And you must be Kat. I'm-"

"Sloane Sutton," I answered in shock.

"It's so nice to finally meet you," Sloane said grasping my shoulders affectionately. "Ryan's told us so much about you."

"He has?" I asked, looking at Ryan, as he carefully extracted Mia from the pram.

"I feel like I already know you," added Sloane, "and let me tell you… this man worships the ground you walk on," she teased with a wink.

"He does?"

"How is it being at home on your own? I think it's so romantic that you moved back down to be close to your man."

"I-"

"You probably haven't had any time to be on your own I suppose? I'm sure you've had all your friends around," she said without giving me time to respond. "Who was the one that delivered Mia? Ashley? I bet her and Nathan have been fussing over you."

"Oh," said Ryan, as if he'd just accidentally farted.

"Actually, no, they're in Paris at the moment," I said giving Ryan a quizzical look. He shrugged, indicating we'd circle back to that later.

"Ooh, I love Paris," she said wistfully, "it's so magical."

"Yeah, they're on a work trip," I replied, charmed by her child-like enthusiasm, "so I'm not sure they'll get to do much sight-seeing."

"Anyway Sloane," Ryan interrupted with a kind smile, as he bounced Mia in his arms, "I think we might get this little lady out into the garden." The look on his face told me there was something on his mind. In fact, it looked as though there were probably several things on his mind.

"Of course," Sloane said with a grin. "I'm so sorry, I get a little over-excited sometimes. My life is so boring compared to yours that I think I've been living vicariously through Ryan."

"I'm sure your life is probably way more exciting than ours." I that said with a laugh, stunned that an international pop-star would find my life exciting. I couldn't believe that Sloane Sutton knew so much about my mundane little life.

"Not really, just work," she said with a sad smile. "Anyway, I should leave you guys to have some family time."

"Thanks Sloane," Ryan said with a grateful smile.

"It was so lovely to meet you Kat, and if you guys ever need some private time, I'd be more than happy to look after this little cutie," she added, gently stroking Mia's cheek.

"Thanks, that's really kind," I said, blown away by how lovely and down-to-earth she was.

"I mean it. Any time," Sloane smiled and patted Ryan's arm, then bounced away out of sight, leaving me to wonder whether I'd imagined the whole thing. I looked at Ryan in amazement.

"Did that really just happen?"

He grinned and kissed Mia's head gently. "It did."

"You didn't tell me that you were in here with Sloane Sutton."

"We aren't allowed to tell anyone," he said with a shrug. "They have really strict confidentiality agreements because so many famous people 'visit' this place," Ryan said with air quotes.

"I can't believe Sloane Sutton knows who I am," I laughed with shock.

"That's just how I roll baby," he joked with a grin, strutting around to my side of the pram. He kissed me firmly on the lips. "It's good to see you Mrs McPherson."

"It's good to see you too," I said threading my arm around his waist. "We miss you."

"Oh god and I miss you," he said with smile, before staring down at Mia lovingly. "Yes, I do. I miss my girls." He sighed and ran his finger down the side of her face.

"What's on your mind babe?" I asked, seeing the concern in his eyes.

"Let's go outside," he suggested, motioning towards the glass double doors at the other end of the room. I nodded and followed him outside as he cradled Mia in his arms. Ryan and Mia got settled at a little bench and once I'd finished fussing with the pram I took a seat next to them and put my hand on Ryan's leg.

"So what was the fart face all about?" I teased.

"What fart face?" he asked with a shocked laugh.

"When Sloan was talking about Paris," I explained with a teasing smile, "you looked like you'd accidentally parped."

He laughed loudly and my soul felt lighter at the sound.

"God I love you," he said, giving me a kiss. "It wasn't about Paris, well... not exactly anyway. I'm guessing you haven't heard?"

"Haven't heard what?"

"Maybe Ritchie doesn't know," he muttered to himself.

"Know what?" I asked, wondering why he'd suddenly started talking like Abed from the show, Community.

"Sorry babe," he said, snapping back to reality, "Geoff rang here last night to tell me that Ash and Nath aren't going to Paris now."

"Why? What's happened?"

"Ash was attacked by her ex-boyfriend last night."

"Oh my god! But isn't he in prison?"

"Not anymore."

"Whoa. Is she okay?"

"Apparently so. Geoff said that she only had minor injuries, but she killed Dom in the process of defending herself. Nathan's taking her down to the beach house while she recovers."

"Holy hell," I said, at a loss for words.

"Yeah, pretty much." We sat in reflective silence for a moment, thinking about all the drama we'd witnessed over the past three months. Ryan bounced Mia on his lap and I let my mind wander back to us.

"Have you heard anything about the deferral yet?" I asked, changing the subject.

"Yep."

"No, please don't say-"

"They're not granting me the deferral babe."

"Fuck. Why?" My heart shattered into a million pieces.

"Because they feel that it would be counter-productive to my progress."

"I don't understand."

"There's nothing to understand," he said sadly. "I fucked up and now I have to deal with the consequences," he sighed heavily. "I'm so sorry babe."

"Hey, it's okay," I assured him, "we'll figure something out."

"This isn't how it's supposed to be," he said shaking his head. "I should be there helping you, not stuck in this fucking place."

"To be fair, it is a pretty nice place to be stuck," I joked, looking around at the lush gardens.

"Except for the psychotic soap star who has it in for me."

I peered up at him with interest. "That Rodney guy is a soap star?"

"Oh shit, I wasn't supposed to say that," he said with a fake cringe.

"It's not Rodney Baker is it?" I asked with curiosity, excited that my husband was hanging out with famous people.

"I can't say," Ryan said nodding his head playfully, "but if I could, I would say yes."

"Oh my god," I said with a laugh. "Rodney Baker is now your mortal enemy?"

"It would appear so."

"And you thought rehab was going to be boring."

"I guess not everyone gets to piss off a soap star," Ryan agreed with a grin.

"Or make friends with a pop star," I said, nudging him, "I still can't believe you know Sloane Sutton. Do you think she'd come and perform at Mia's first birthday?"

Ryan laughed loudly. "I know you're joking, but she probably would," he joked, "if I ever get out of this fucking place."

"It's only another month or so, right? We've totally got this."

My husband peered down at me with his big, brown puppy dog eyes. "I love you," he said kissing my forehead. "Maybe you should go back up to Rosie's for a while."

"No," I said adamantly, "I don't want to be that far away from you. I'll be fine, I promise."

"Okay," he nodded, "we'll work it out." Ryan rearranged Mia so he could drape his arm over my shoulder. I leaned my head on his shoulder as we both sighed. Just when we'd thought life was getting back to normal we'd been thrown another couple of curve balls.

- NATHAN STONE -

We'd been on the train for two hours and Ash had spent the entire trip staring vacantly out the window. She'd barely said a word all day, as if the effort of speaking would suck the remaining life out of her. Ritchie sat alongside Cody in the seats opposite us. He was uncharacteristically quiet, with his head buried in a book. I could only assume he'd been stunned into silence after my meltdown. In all the years we'd known each other, I'd never cried in front of him. In fact, I'd never cried in front of anyone before now.

Cody seemed to have picked up on the solemn vibe and had spent the entire train ride intently scrutinizing his laptop screen with a pair of massive white headphones clamped firmly over his ears.

I glanced over at Ash again and a few strands of her wavy blonde hair were hanging loosely around her beautiful, but damaged face. She was completely despondent. I had no idea what to do for her. She was present in body, but not in spirit and it was hard to tell if, or when, she would ever return. She pressed on her eyebrow, just below the neat little row of stitches and noticed me staring at her.

"Thanks for taking care of everything this morning," she whispered tiredly, "I really appreciate it. I'm not ready to go back to the flat yet."

"I'm your boyfriend, that's my job," I said with a grin, trying to disguise my discomfort. I felt a brief wave of guilt for not telling her about Jock but pushed it down with a gulp of bitter coffee. It wasn't the right time to tell her. There was already too much drama going on to add that piece of betrayal into the mix. "I was thinking maybe we could move you out of there permanently when we get back."

"Yeah, okay." Ash nodded and turned back to her window just as the darkness of the tunnel was replaced by the vivid colours of the French landscape. Her eyes widened in the bright light and the sunshine reflected off her damp cheeks. She quickly swatted at the tears and peered over her shoulder to check if I'd noticed.

"You don't have to do this you know?" I told her quietly. "You can stay in the hotel and I can tell everyone you're sick."

"I need to do this Nath."

"I'd argue that point if I thought I was going to win," I teased with a cheeky smile. "But you've clearly got your stubborn mind made up." One corner of her mouth turned up in what looked like a semi-smile.

"I don't deserve you," she said, turning away from me again.

"Come on Granger, we both know it's the other way around," I said, squeezing her leg gently. Ash recoiled against the window the instant I touched her so I quickly retracted my hand as she stared at me wild-eyed for a moment. "Sorry. I didn't mean to scare you," I apologized, with my hands in the air.

"No, I'm sorry," she said, with a stiff smile as her face softened and she straightened herself up. "It's not you. I guess I'm still a little jumpy."

"You don't have to apologize ba-" I nearly called her babe, but then thought better of it. "Please don't feel like you have to apologize."

Ash nodded silently and resumed staring out the window. She was hurting and it was killing me that I couldn't fix her. I was used to being a problem-solver, but this was one problem that I wouldn't be able to solve no matter how hard I tried. The damage had been done and there was nothing that I could do to reverse it. She had been violated and, even though Dom was gone, the memory of his attack would remain with her forever.

I felt another round of tears stinging at the back of my tired eyes but I couldn't let them fall in front of her, so I shook my head to clear them away. I had to keep it together. I rubbed my eyes subtly so that no one would notice, then flicked through my phone, pretending to be enthralled by my Facebook feed.

Once we arrived in Paris, I hustled along my weary tribe.

"We'll head straight over to Delfontaine Headquarters for our kick-off meeting, then check-in to the hotel afterwards." I informed the group, as I hailed us a taxi. "Unless you want to go straight the hotel?" I offered Ash quietly.

"No. Let's go," she said walking straight past me.

"Ladies first," Ritchie said, shooting me a concerned look as he gallantly waved her into the car. I shrugged and began loading up our luggage while Ash slid into the back seat. Ritchie waited until Cody was in the car before joining me at the boot. "Mate, is Ash really up to this?"

"Probably not, but she wouldn't take no for an answer."

"And what about Sandrine?" Ritchie asked in hushed tones. "Does Ash know?"

"Yeah, but not the full gory details."

"Solid," Ritchie agreed with a hint of condescension. "So how do you want to handle Sandrine then?" He asked curiously. "What if she wants another round?"

"I have no idea," I confessed, peeking around the upturned boot to make sure the other two weren't listening.

"Well, I've got your back man."

"Thanks," I replied with a nervous sigh.

My stomach was churning by the time we walked through the big, heavy doors of Delfontaine Cosmetics. Ashley had successfully plastered a fake smile onto her face and Ritchie was doing his best to keep the mood light, but I couldn't shake my nerves. I was pretty ticked off at past Nathan. He'd left me a rather long string of messes to clean up and I was starting to think that a time machine would be a pretty decent investment right about now. Hopefully future Nathan could sort that out and then come back and tidy all of this up for me.

"Ah bonjour Nathan!" Sandrine greeted me animatedly, with the customary double cheek kiss. Ashley stared at the sophisticated French woman with the fake smile frozen onto her face.

"Bonjour Sandrine," I answered nervously, super conscious of the fact that Ash was watching the woman like a hawk.

"So good to see you again." Sandrine purred.

"Sandrine, I'd like you to meet my team." I blurted abruptly, trying to divert her attention away from me. Sandrine's gaze shifted to my crew of merry men…and not-so-merry woman. Sandrine cast her eyes briefly over Ashley's damaged face with an indeterminate expression then hungrily assessed each of the boys, darting her eyes over them as if taking a mental inventory of their attributes. I had obviously been flattering myself in thinking that I was the only Artemis man she was interested in.

"Ritchie is our Program Manager…" I stuttered slightly, as Ritchie stepped forward to introduce himself.

"G'day," he greeted Sandrine in his rugged Aussie accent, shooting her an uncontrollable grin before shaking her hand so vigorously that she was almost thrown off balance.

"Bonjour Ritchie. Vous êtes Australien?" Sandrine asked with a husky laugh, eyeing his muscled forearms. Ritchie stared blankly at her.

"Yes, he's Australian." I clarified in what I hoped was a cheerful tone. "Il ne parle pas français." I added teasingly, before gesturing towards Cody. "And this is Cody, our Tech expert."

"Hi," Cody said simply, as he shook Sandrine's hand timidly.

"Bonjour Cody," Sandrine greeted him with a sleek smile. Her overt sexual energy was way too much for poor Cody and he shrunk back quickly towards Ash.

"This is Ashley, our Creative Lead," Cody said, pushing Ash forwards in an attempt to escape Sandrine's hungry stare.

"Bonjour Sandrine," Ashley greeted her politely, with an outstretched hand as if nothing were awry, "it's lovely to finally put a face to the name."

"Bonjour Ashley." Sandrine smiled and shook Ashley's hand. It seemed like a reasonable introduction.

"Nathan's told me a lot about you," Ashley informed Sandrine meaningfully, her tight smile still holding solid. I groaned inwardly as a flash of comprehension fluttered across Sandrine's face. Her eyes flicked between Ashley and myself but, thankfully, Didier appeared out of thin air and broke the tension.

"Nathan!" he greeted me loudly. He couldn't have timed it better if he'd tried, which made me wonder if he had indeed planned his timing.

"Didier!" I exclaimed in relief, as he rushed over and double kissed my cheeks with genuine fondness.

"Nice to see you my friend!" Didier said in perfect English.

"And you Didier," I chuckled, slapping him affectionately on the back. "You're looking better than when I last saw you."

"Oh dear. Oui, I don't know why I thought I could keep up with you youngsters," Didier replied with an embarrassed chuckle.

"You did well old fella," I nudged him with a smile and introduced him to my team, starting with the boys. After the obligatory handshakes, Didier turned his attention to Ash.

"And that must make you Ashely," Didier said charmingly, as he kissed Ashley's hand, pausing briefly as he caught sight of the dark bruise on her wrist. A look of fatherly concern fluttered across his face, but he recovered so quickly that if I'd blinked I would have missed it. "The English rose between the thorns," he joked with the sort of sophisticated charisma that only older men could pull off. Ashley laughed half-heartedly, but seemed to be very comfortable with Didier.

"I'm not feeling very rosy right now I'm afraid Didier."

"Don't you fret mon cherie," Didier said, gently tapping her chin in a fatherly fashion, "this beautiful face will be shining again in no time." Sandrine cleared her throat and put an end to the sweet moment.

"Didier, could you please show the team through to the boardroom while Nathan and I discuss a few matters?"

"Oui," Didier agreed, casting a knowing glance in my direction while Ashley tried to hide her discomfort at the situation.

"Merci," Sandrine replied curtly, taking my arm and leading me in the opposite direction. I peered back at Ashley helplessly, before Sandrine herded me into an empty office and closed the door firmly behind her. The click of the handle felt like a gun cocking before the death shot. "Vous regardez bien Nathan," Sandrine purred, as she turned back to me.

"Thanks Sandrine," I answered awkwardly, "you look good too."

"Aurélie has been asking after you," she said with a sly smile.

"Haha," I chuckled pathetically, trying to buy some time while I came up with an appropriate response. I backed away from her subtly as she stalked closer. "Sandrine…" I began.

"You don't want to have any more fun with me," she interrupted disappointedly, gleaning my intentions from the single word that I'd articulated.

I breathed a sigh of relief. "I'm really sorry."

"Eh c'est la vie," she answered with a casual shrug.

"So… does that mean we're okay?" I asked, hoping it wasn't a trick.

"Nathan, you should know by now that I'm not a sentimental woman," she smiled saucily. "Besides, you've brought me some friends to play with." French women were most definitely not backwards in coming forward.

"Well, I aim to please," I joked awkwardly.

"Cody will be a fun challenge," she said with great enthusiasm.

"Well, he'd definitely be a challenge Sandrine," I spluttered nervously, "he bats for the other team."

"Pardon?"

"Cody's gay Sandrine."

"Oui, that makes sense. Ah well, the Australian will do," she replied with a dismissive wave of her hand. I cleared my throat awkwardly, keen to get back to Ashley.

"Was there anything else you wanted to discuss?" I asked, shuffling my feet.

"Ashley."

"What do you mean?" I asked, with a sneaking suspicion that Sandrine had already figured out the situation.

"She's very pretty."

"Yes, she is," I agreed nervously.

"What happened to her?" I floundered for a moment, caught off-guard by her question. Sandrine waved her hands in apology. "Eh ça ne fait rien, it's none of my business."

"She got attacked," I told her with a crackle in my voice, "last night."

"And she still came to France to meet me?"

I smiled and nodded. "She's a determined woman."
Sandrine appraised me with knowing eyes.

"You're in love with her."

"No, I'm not in – it's not – I…" I sighed with resignation. "Oui. Is it that obvious?"

"Oui Nathan."

"Oh."

"Ah, Ne sois pas bête Nathan! Just embrace it."

"I'm trying," I admitted openly, "but honestly, everything has been so crazy lately, I'm expecting I'll fuck it up." It was a mystery even to myself as to why I was sharing that particular information with a client. Even if it was a client with whom I shared intimate knowledge.

"Nathan, we're the same you and I…" Sandrine informed me, "we are a breed unlike others. Little people live little lives, and have little goals," she said waving her hand disdainfully towards the door. "They're programmed to work and breed and that's all they know. They fall in love at the drop of a hat because they're too scared to be alone. But for people like us… love is not something we just give away. Sex is easy, but falling in love is much harder, so when we do, we put our whole heart into it. When people like us find love Nathan, we do everything in our power to keep it." She paused and studied me in an eerily maternal way.

"You won't fuck it up mon amour, because you know how special it is. Ashley is yours now, and that need only change if you choose it to."

I stared at Sandrine, speechless. Her idea of love was slightly disturbing, but the sentiment resonated. She was right about one thing… I would do everything in my power to make my relationship work.

- RYAN McPHERSON -

I sat silently through group therapy, with my mind a million miles away.

"Ryan, let's swing back to you," said Byron. I had to physically restrain myself from groaning out loud. He always seemed to 'swing back' to me.

"What for?" I asked as amicably as possible.

"Your deferral," he said simply. I rolled my eyes in agony.

"What's a deferral?" Asked Rodney, "and why does he get one?"

"I don't get one," I seethed quietly through a clenched jaw. Byron stepped in before the situation got heated.

"A deferral is something you don't need to worry about Rodney. You're here by choice, Ryan is here in place of a prison sentence. A deferral is an option to serve a sentence at a later date due to extenuating circumstances."

"Oh," said Rodney, turning to me, "so they wouldn't let you out hey?" He asked with a wry grin. I scowled and crossed my arms over my chest as if it would offer me protection from the grilling that was about to come.

"Ryan?" Prompted Byron, "how do you feel about Tony's decision not to grant your deferral?"

"Ugh," I groaned as my head flopped backwards with exasperation. This session was like Déjà vu. The room fell silent as everyone waited for me to lose my shit. I took a deep breath to calm myself and then looked around the room of expectant faces. All eyes were trained on me and I could feel my face burning with both rage and embarrassment. Byron broke the tense silence.

"Why is that question so frustrating for you Ryan?"

"I just…" I said with a huff before checking myself. "I just feel like it's Groundhog Day in here."

Byron nodded, "okay, so you feel like you're having to repeat yourself?"

"Well, aren't I?"

"Perhaps," Byron said with infuriating composure, "or perhaps it's just the same responses appearing in different situations. I find it interesting that, frustration and anger are your default settings."

As much as I hated to admit it, Byron was right. No matter what the situation was, I always defaulted back to anger or frustration, or both in some cases. Even back in my Mareechi's days with Ashley. Even when I was at uni with Nathan. Even when I was a teenager at high school… even when I was a kid. Now that I was thinking about it, I'd been frustrated and angry my whole life. Ever since…

My stomach lurched as a nasty demon stepped out from the darkest depths of my soul. I'd spent my entire life pushing that demon further and further down into the darkness but here it was, larger than life, clear as day and as vivid as if it was standing right before my very eyes. I swallowed back the vomit that began to force its way up my throat.

"Ryan are you okay?"

"Uh-huh," I mumbled, unable to articulate words as my repressed trauma surfaced into present time.

"So, what do you think is the underlying feeling behind those emotional responses?" Byron asked, after giving me a moment to ponder his words.

"Shame," I answered instantaneously. I didn't even need to think about that one, I could feel it coursing through my veins at that moment, infiltrating every cell in my body. "And betrayal," I added, thinking of the role my parents had played in creating the shadow monster.

"Good," he nodded his approval, "and where does that come from? What do you think might be the root cause?"

I sat in silence as I tried to find the words. I searched through long-forgotten, horrific memories as they began rising to the surface in quick succession. There was only one answer. I snapped out of my ruminations and looked up to see the whole group watching me with interest. Even Rodney.

"My parents," I said breathlessly as my stoic façade crumbled down around me.

"Bingo," said Byron proudly. I felt tears stabbing at my eyeballs and Byron's tone shifted so that his next words were spoken like a concerned parent. "Ryan… what did they do that caused you to feel ashamed?"

I stared around the room through blurry eyes as I re-lived a sickening period in my childhood that I'd long since buried somewhere deep in my subconscious. Memories that I had pushed down so far that I'd fooled my conscious mind into believing they'd been nothing more than nightmares. But they had been real, and for some reason, they'd chosen this moment to step out into the spotlight.
I swallowed hard and fought hard not to cry.

"They fed me to the wolves," I almost whispered.

"What do you mean by that?" asked Byron gently.

"They loaned me out to their depraved friends. Or maybe they sold me for money, I'm not sure." My eyes darted over the shocked faces staring at me. The room was so quiet that even the silence felt loud.

I could taste bile in my mouth, as the recollections made me feel sick to my stomach. In my 35 years on earth, I'd never articulated those memories out loud, but as I heard my words echo through the deathly silent room it was hard to believe that I'd managed to avoid them for so long. The visions were so vivid they were hard to deny.

"I was about three or four, or probably younger because I couldn't talk properly yet. They used to have these creepy parties…" my words trailed off as silent tears began streaming down my cheeks. I hated that I was sharing my deepest shame this with these people, but I wasn't able to stop it now. The words, and the tears, were flowing beyond my control. I wiped my cheek and attempted to regain my composure.

"Go on Ryan, this is a safe space to share,"Byron encouraged me when I failed to continue.

"They willingly handed me over. They just gave me to those men without a second thought. They stood and watched, while these disgusting monsters dragged me kicking and screaming into a dark room…" I sniffed loudly and rubbed my hands over my face, trying to force the memories back into the shadows where they'd been safely hidden for three decades.

I heard a sob from across the room and looked up to see Sloane breaking down in tears. Rodney was uncharacteristically quiet, listening intently with his arms tightly crossed. Angelica had tears running down her own cheeks and Byron looked both proud and disturbed simultaneously. He smiled kindly and nodded his head with encouragement.

"Now that, Ryan… is what we call an epic breakthrough." Everyone in the room nodded in agreement but seemed to be stunned into silence. "Right, well I think that's a good place to leave it for today," declared Byron. "I think we could probably all do with some reflection time after that. Ryan could you stay back please?"

"Yeah," I nodded as the rest of the group filed out. Sloane came over and gave me a huge hug. I returned her embrace as she wrapped her arms around my waist, and we stood for a moment in silence. Without a word, she stepped back, squeezed my shoulders and then followed the others out of the door.

Byron waited for the rest of them to vacate the room. "Let's have a quick chat."

"Sure." I nodded and veered away from the exit to where he was standing.

"I just want to make sure you're okay before you leave."

"Yeah."

"That was a pretty heavy session for you. I'd like you to go see Victoria for a one-on-one."

"What? Now?"

"Yeah, I think it's really important that you keep going with this. Leaving it there could send you into Post Traumatic Stress."

"Okay," I agreed, seeing his point. We'd discussed my relationship with my parents many times, but this revelation took it to a whole new level. Byron patted my shoulder.

"You did well today mate. This will be a turning point for you."

"I've never talked to anyone about that before. I hadn't even thought about it to be honest, so it's a shock for it all to come back up after so many years," I told him honestly. "I'd completely blocked it out of my memory. I guess I must have figured that ignoring it would stop it from being real, but ignoring it just made me bitter and angry. I have no idea why it's suddenly come back up."

"That happens more often than you'd think, but whatever the reason, I'm glad it did. At least while you're here you've got all the support you need to work through it."

"True," I agreed. That group session was the first time I'd ever really pinpointed the heart of my issues. I finally understood why I'd always felt betrayed, and rejected, and unwanted. My entire life had been tainted with an invisible veil of unworthiness and distrust.

"And once you've worked through this, I'll be happy to recommend you for an early discharge."

"Really?" I asked stunned.

"Really," he confirmed, "but don't get too excited, you've got some tough work ahead of you first."

"I know."

"But this is good progress," he assured me. "Now the healing can really begin."

- KAT McPHERSON -

Despite the fact that I had Mia, I'd never felt so alone. Rosie had gone home; Ryan was stuck in rehab; my parents were two hours away in Framlingham; Nath and Ash were in Cornwall; and Amy still wasn't talking to me, which meant that neither was Ritchie. Seeing Ryan at the rehab centre every day wasn't going to be enough. I wanted him home but there was only one way I could see the Medical Director agreeing to release Ryan. Unfortunately, it wasn't a palatable option, but it was the only option I had left. I glanced over my shoulder at Mia in the back seat.

"Let's see if we can get your daddy back," I told her, feeling sick in my stomach at what I was about to do. I wiped a tear from my eye and unbuckled my seatbelt. My only hope was 'Plan Beau'. Taking a deep breath, I climbed out of the car and lifted Mia out of her capsule. I gripped her tight and looked up with trepidation at Beaus terrace house. What if he slammed the door in my face? What if he screamed at me? What if I ended up making things worse? But I knew I had no other choice.

Cradling Mia carefully against my chest, I made the torturous walk up the footpath to Beau's porch. I pressed the button and, after a moment, he opened the door, his eyes nearly popping out of his head when he saw me standing on his front steps.

"Kat? What are you doing here?"

I swallowed nervously, "I need to talk to you."

He huffed and rolled his eyes, "and where were you when I needed to talk to you?"

"I-" I stopped talking. I had no answer. It was like my dream had come to life. Mia grumbled so I patted her gently. "Sorry she's due for another feed," I apologised nervously.

"Wow," Beau said, looking at Mia like she was an alien, "you really are a mum huh?"

"Yeah," I said with a nod, "most of the time, that's what happens after being pregnant."

"I know, I just... like, haven't seen you since..." he took a deep breath and then fell silent. I looked up from Mia and flashed back to my dream. Even if he did end up calling me a whore... I still owed Beau an apology.

"I'm really sorry for what happened," I said sincerely. Beau leaned against the door-frame and crossed his arms over his chest, while I patted Mia's back gently.

"What did happen Kat?" he asked through gritted teeth, "because I still don't understand."

I bounced Mia on my shoulder and looked up at Beau, feeling like an ant under a magnifying glass.

"I made a huge mistake," I said, deciding not to beat around the bush, "I know I hurt you and I shouldn't have done what I did and I'm really sorry for that."

"Sorry that you ditched me or sorry that we had sex?"

"Umm... both," I looked at my feet, unable to hold eye contact with him. "If I could take it all back, I would."

"Which part?" he asked, "the part where we hooked-up or the part when you ghosted me?" he waited for a response, but I had no answer for him. Beau shook his head. "Do you even care that you left me hanging out to dry?"

"I didn't leave you hanging out to dry," I jumped in defensively. He scowled and stepped out of the door onto the top step with the same look on his face as he'd had in my dream.

"You ran away and left me to deal with your mess Kat."

"But it wasn't like that," I argued, desperately wanting him to understand.

"That's exactly what was it was like," Beau said firmly. "You told your husband what we did, then let him come at me while you hid up in Sussex. I took a beating for you. Twice."

"It sounds pretty awful when you say it like that."

"It was pretty awful. And it's not how you treat your friends."

I looked back down at Mia, feeling the weight of my guilt beginning to suffocate me.

"I know," I agreed with a sheepish nod, "I've been a shitty friend."

"But we're not anymore, are we?" he said, clenching his jaw.

"Not what?"

"Friends," he said through clenched teeth, "you've made that abundantly clear."

"I'm sorry Beau," I apologised sadly, "I didn't realise I'd hurt you so much. I thought you'd just move on," I said, clasping Mia to my chest. Beau snorted angrily and shook his head in disbelief.

"How little you know me Kat," he said with disappointment. "What was I to you? I would have got it if you'd told me that it was just a one-off, or even if you'd wanted no strings attached sex. Like... I would have respected your space and I wouldn't have said anything to Ryan," he shook his head and sighed, "but you told me you loved me, then you completely betrayed me. You dumped our whole friendship down the toilet and threw me under the bus and you didn't even have the decency to explain or apologise." Beau chuckled with disgruntled amusement while I stood, stunned into silence. "You didn't even bother to call to see if I was okay after your husband beat me unconscious. Did you even care that I was in hospital for two weeks?"

"Of course I cared."

"Well you've got a funny way of showing it."

"I've been dealing with my own shit Beau."

"Yeah, that makes two of us dealing with your shit then." He shoved his hands in his pockets and looked me up and down. "Why are you even here Kat?"

"I... I needed to ask you something," I stuttered, thrown off-course by his truth bombs.

"And what's that?"

I took a deep breath and looked Beau in the eyes, trying to appear confident.

"Ryan couldn't get a sentence deferral so I was hoping that you could drop the charges."

Beau stared at me incredulously. "You want me to get Ryan out of rehab?"

"Yes."

"Are you fucking kidding me?" he grunted. "You fall off the planet for months, and now you suddenly return to ask a favour. That's rich."

"Beau... I need him. I can't do this on my own. If you care about me as much as you say you do then, please do this for me."

He rolled his eyes and shook his head. "You've got some nerve."

"Please, I'm begging you," I said with tears in my eyes. "I need my husband home. I need him Beau. I'm falling apart without him. This is so hard, and you're the only one who can help. I'm sorry for everything that happened, but if there's any part of you that still cares... please help me get him home."

He chewed on the inside of his cheek. "Would you even be apologising if you didn't need my help?" he asked disdainfully. I stared blankly at him, unable to tell him the truth. Beau sneered down at me with disgust. "You need to leave Kat."

"Please," I begged, swallowing back tears.

"Get out of here Mrs McPherson," he said solemnly as he stepped back inside. "If you ever come back here again, I'll get a restraining order on you too," he said, before slamming the door shut. I stood staring at the closed door and wiped the tears off my cheeks. I'd blown it. How the hell was I going to get my husband back?

- ASHLEY GRANGER -

The work distraction had been helping. Our day was so busy I'd barely had time to think. The Delfontaine account was shaping up to be a really exciting project, and with such a big budget we would be able to pull-off some ground-breaking campaigns. It wasn't until we checked into our hotel room that reality began to catch up on me. Nathan swiped us in and stood awkwardly at the door as I wandered into the plush, yet tiny room.

"Do you want your own room?" He asked, hovering inside the doorway.

"No," I said quickly as a wave of panic flashed through my body. "That's really sweet Nath, but I don't want to be on my own." He nodded and closed the door, studying my face as if searching for a sign of the old me. I smiled and squeezed his arm gently. "I'm still in here, I promise. I just need a little time to come back properly."
Nathan nodded sadly and shoved his hands into his pockets.

"Take all the time you need."

"Thanks."
He shrugged and edged a little closer.

"Did you want to go for a wander?"

"Actually, I'm feeling pretty tired, do you mind if I take a nap?"
Putting on a happy face had used up the last of my energy and I had nothing left in me. Even being awake felt like too much effort. Last night I'd fought for my body; my life; and in the end, I'd fought for my freedom, but I couldn't fight anymore. For fifteen years I'd been at war and now I was done. All I wanted to do was close my eyes and forget

the world existed.

"You do whatever you need to do," Nath said with a weary nod. "In fact, I'm pretty exhausted myself, I might join you."

I crawled into the bed fully clothed and rested my aching head against the soft pillow. Nathan was still standing at the end of the bed. I couldn't tell whether he was giving me space or if he was feeling weird about the fact that his girlfriend was now tarnished goods.

"You getting in?" I asked with a wobble in my voice. What would I do if he didn't want me anymore? He nodded, kicked his shoes off and laid down on top of the covers, glancing at me with a forced smile. "Let's get some rest huh? It's been a long 24 hours."

"Yeah." I snuggled into the blanket and Nath rolled onto his side, leaving me to stare hopelessly at his back as he pretended to be asleep. I swallowed back tears and let my eyes close as I drifted into a restless sleep. When I floated into the darkness of slumber, Dominic was already waiting for me. I tried to turn back, but my body wouldn't let me. I was trapped in sleep as my demon drew ever closer. I couldn't tell which of us was moving forwards, but there was no avoiding him. Dom grinned, malice and joy flickering in his black eyes.

"Why are you here?" I croaked, forcing my throat to push out the sound. He shrugged, with the evil smile still playing on his lips.

"This is your dream Princess, you tell me."

"I didn't ask you to come here."

"Yet here we are." Dominic glanced around the endless black void and when his eyes returned to mine, we were standing in the lounge room of my flat, watching the scene from the previous evening begin to play out. My stomach churned as I watched him throw me over the sofa. I squeezed my eyes shut tightly and covered my ears with my hands.

"I don't want to see it," I sobbed, trying to block out the sights and sounds of my real-life nightmare. With a flash of hot light, I was suddenly tied up in a chair, forced to watch the horrific event unfolding. Dominic hovered over my right shoulder, delighting in my panic.

"Looks like you've got some demons to face sweetheart."

"You're my only demon," I snarled, trying to wriggle my wrists free.

"Are you sure about that?" He whispered tauntingly into my ear, "because from where I'm standing, it looks like you've got a few quarrels with yourself."

"Fuck you," I growled, fighting so hard against the ropes that a few trickles of blood dropped onto the arm of the chair. Without even moving, Dom appeared in front of me, squatting at my feet so that his face was aligned with mine.

"You might hate me, but we both know it's yourself that you really despise," Dom said with his dead eyes boring into my soul. "Do you really think Stone will still love you when he finds out the truth?"

"What truth?" I asked the demon.

"That you wanted it Ashley."

"But I didn't."

"You know you did," he said leaning right up to my face so that his lips were nearly against mine, "and we both know you enjoyed it."

"That's not true," I argued as he reveled in the pleasure of torturing me. Dom grabbed my chin and forced me to watch myself getting violated. Tears streamed down my cheeks as I re-lived the trauma all over again.

"You're nothing but a dirty little slut Ashley," he teased, his creepy laugh reverberating through my head. "And it won't take long for your boyfriend to figure that out."

"Stop!" I yelled, waking myself up with a full body jerk. I sat bolt upright in the unfamiliar bed and Nathan reached out his hand.

"Hey, you're okay," he said sleepily, "it was just a dream."

I took a deep, calming breath, comforted by the sound of his voice, and then flopped back down onto the pillow.

"More like a nightmare," I mumbled, pulling the duvet up to my chin.

"Well, you're safe now," he said reassuringly, "and I won't let anything bad happen to you again."

I grasped Nathans's hand and let myself fall back to sleep but the nightmare never returned. My sleep was dreamless after that, and what felt like only minutes later, my eyes flew open when someone thumped on the door. Adrenaline flooded my body again.

"You guys ready yet?" Ritchie called loudly from the hallway. Nathan let go of my hand and rolled off the bed in a daze, fumbling for his phone in the darkened room.

"What time is it?" he asked groggily, squinting at the bright light of the phone screen. "Shit, it's seven o'clock."

"Nath, Ash, come on. It's time to go," Ritchie bellowed.

"On our way," Nathan called through the door. "You go ahead, and we'll meet you there."

"Righto," Ritchie said from the other side of the door. Nath glanced at me and ran his hands through his ruffled hair. "I guess the world keeps on turning."

"I guess so," I agreed, standing up from the bed too quickly and causing myself to blackout momentarily. I swayed on my feet and

Nathan grasped my shoulders to steady me.

"You okay?" He asked with concern.

"Yeah, just gave myself a head-spin." I answered, re-focusing my eyes as the blackness cleared.

"Maybe you should stay and rest?" Nathan suggested. "You're looking a bit pale."

"Honestly I'm fine," I assured him, "and I don't want to be alone." Nathan looked like he was about to kiss me, but he must have changed his mind because he squeezed my shoulder instead.

"Then you won't be."

- RITCHIE CARLTON –

I returned to the lobby where Cody was waiting impatiently.

"We'll meet 'em there," I explained vaguely as I ushered him outside and down the wonky footpath. The restaurant Nathan had booked wasn't too far from the hotel, so I figured we'd just walk.

"Aren't we getting a cab?" Asked Cody, traipsing along behind me.

"Nah, it's not very far," I said with a shrug, "only a twenty-minute walk."

"Twenty minutes?" Cody whined exasperatedly, "but we've just spent the last three hours walking around Paris."

"Mate, you're only twenty-eight, this should be a walk in the park for you," I joked, guffawing at my own hilarity, "or a walk in Paris as the case may be."

"You're a comedian," he replied dryly.

"Stop sulking," I said hooking my elbow around his neck, "it's a beautiful evening in gay Par-ee," I announced loudly in my best French accent. "This is your city mate," I teased giving him a noogie before I released him from the headlock.

"You're a dick," he said huffily, as he stood upright and fixed his usually well-coiffed hair.

"That is my name," I agreed good-naturedly and glanced sideways at him, "that's probably why you love me so much," I added with a grin.

"You wish," he said, punching me hard in the bicep. Well… as hard as a computer nerd could punch anyway. "You're not my type Carlton," he said with a cheeky wink.

"Just as well," I said with a smile, "you wouldn't be able to handle me anyway," I teased with a laugh. "Come on whinger, let's pick up the pace or we'll never get there."

Cody was panting a little by the time we reached the restaurant. I couldn't believe how unfit the kid was. He was ten years my junior and I could have easily run rings around him.

"Bonne soiree," a lanky, square-jawed waiter greeted us at the door, and Cody practically climbed over me to talk to the guy.

"Bonne soiree," he replied, with a goofy grin on his face, "nous avons une table reserve Artemis Advertising.

"Oui," nodded the waiter with a smile, "tu es le premier a arrive," he said. I looked at Cody for a translation, but he was too busy gawking at the waiter, who was still saying stuff in French.

"Merci," Cody said, once the waiter had finished talking. I shrugged at Cody for an explanation and he rolled his eyes. "We're the first ones here," he explained.

Apparently, being on-time wasn't fashionable in France. We followed the waiter through the main dining area, out to a private section of the Bistro, hidden from the rest of the diners. The room looked like a very fancy greenhouse, with wall-to-wall glass windows and completely filled with plants. It reminded me of the greenhouse at Kew Gardens. Candlelight flickered from the long row of tea-light candles, lined up along the middle of the giant table. The reflection of the dainty flames on the glass windows made it look like the entire room was filled with stars

"Wow, the Atrium," breathed Cody in awe of the candle-lit, glass-walled room.

"It's like being at Hogwarts," I said, as I pulled out a chair in the middle of the white-clothed table. "Una Cerveza por favor," I asked the waiter and Cody slapped me over the head as I sat down.

"Ritchie, that's Spanish," he scolded me in a hiss, before turning back to the attractive waiter. "Duex biere s'il vous plait," he told the waiter apologetically. The waiter nodded and smiled then, once he was out of earshot, Cody turned on me. "Are you trying to embarrass me?"

"What?" I asked with bewilderment. I did love to embarrass people but I hadn't done anything of the sort. "Why would I be trying to embarrass you?"

"Could you please stop saying stupid shit in front of Guillaume."

"Who's Gi-om?" I asked, completely confused.

Cody threw his arms up in exasperation. "The waiter," he said dramatically, "and it's Guillaume," he said melodramatically emphasizing the pronunciation with his hands.

"Well, I didn't know he had a name," I mocked, "besides, who cares what the waiter thinks?

"I do," Cody said meaningfully.

"Oh," I said as the penny suddenly dropped, "shit mate, you like the waiter."

Cody sighed and rolled his eyes as he took a seat next to me.

"Yes Ritchie, I like the waiter," he confirmed.

"I guess he's pretty good-looking," I said, attempting to make up for my total obliviousness

"He's absolutely gorgeous," sighed Codes.

"So, are you going to do something about it?"

"I guess," he said uncertainly, "but not until after dinner."

"Richard," called a sultry voice from behind me. Cody froze like a deer in headlights and cowered behind me. I twisted in my seat to see Sandrine Delfontaine posing in the Atrium doorway, wearing a skin-tight, red dress that left very little to the imagination. I stood up to greet her.

"Actually, it's just plain Ritchie," I said reaching out my hand to offer her an escort to the table, "like Ritchie Rich."

"Merci," she purred, holding me captive in an intense stare.

"Hi Sandrine," squeaked Cody.

"Cody, so lovely to see you," cooed the woman, not missing a beat. "What do you think of the Atrium?" she asked him smoothly as I pulled out the seat next to mine.

"It's amazing," he said before getting distracted by the waiter, who had returned with our beers. He blushed as the attractive man handed him the bottle. "Merci Guillaume."

Sandrine began speaking to Guillaume in French, so fast that I think even Cody struggled to understand the conversation. I shot him a wink as I noticed that Guillaume's gaze kept creeping back to Cody. Obviously, the attraction went both ways. I sat down and leaned in close to Cody to give him a nudge.

"He likes you too mate. You should ask him to come out with us afterwards."

"Maybe," Cody mumbled as he watched his crush trot off to do Sandrine's bidding.

"Why don't you go ask him for a wine menu or something?" I suggested. Cody nodded, took a deep breath and rose from his seat.

"Excusez moi," he said to Sandrine, before ducking out of the room behind Guillaume. Sandrine swiveled around on her chair and focused her laser-beam stare on me again.

"So, Richard," she said, crossing her legs elegantly.

"It's Ritchie," I corrected her again.

"I like Richard," she said authoritatively, as if that closed the matter.

"Okay." I laughed with astonishment at her self-assurance.

"Why don't you tell me about yourself," she prompted as my phone buzzed on the table. Amy's name flashed on my screen as my phone rang emphatically. I took a long, slow gulp of my fancy beer, delighting in making both women wait for my answer. Sandrine watched me with curiosity as I glanced between her and my phone. I let the phone ring out and then placed the beer bottle back down on the table and studied her with my ginger brow raised.

"What do you want to know?"

"Was that your girlfriend?"

"Not exactly."

- RYAN McPHERSON -

My session with Victoria was even more intense than Group Therapy had been. Now that I'd opened the floodgates, more and more memories had begun to surface. Each one was more detailed than the last, and they battered me relentlessly in wave after wave until I was sure I'd die from the pain of it all. I didn't want to remember. I wanted to keep it all hidden, but I'd gone too far for that to be a possibility.

After thirty odd years of successfully locking away all the horrifying memories, it felt brutally unfair that I had to relive them now. I didn't want to remember the hunger-filled expression on the pointed face of the depraved man who'd viciously stripped me of my virginity. I didn't want to see his beady black eyes lecherously assessing my small naked body. I didn't want to feel the fear, the confusion, the helplessness, the desperation or the pain. It was too much.

"How could I have buried something like that for so long?" I asked Victoria, "and how do I go back to a normal life now that I've remembered?"

"It's actually very common to suppress traumatic experiences Ryan, particularly in early childhood. It's a survival mechanism. The human brain is fascinating and complex."

"Okay… so why can't I keep it buried?"

Victoria smiled warmly, "because suppressing it isn't healthy." She waited for me to say something, but I remained silent. "How about you tell me about that first night?"

"Do I have to?"

"You don't have to, but it might help you process your feelings."

I closed my eyes and let my mind float back to the night my innocence was stolen. It was the most horrific moment of my life, and

I still didn't understand how I could have forgotten it.

"My parents had hosted those parties before, but usually my nanny had me upstairs in bed before anyone arrived," I explained, as I watched the scene play out in my head. "For some reason, Lindy had taken the night off-"

"Lindy was your Nanny?" she asked.

"Yeah," I nodded with my eyes still closed. "I had trouble getting to sleep without her special song or our bedtime story."

"Then what happened?"

"I'd tried to get to sleep for ages, but I could hear music, so eventually I gave up and snuck downstairs to see what was happening." I felt bile rise in my throat at the memory of what I'd seen. At the time I hadn't understood what I was seeing and, in fact, even as an adult it was hard to believe what my own memory was showing me.

"Go on," Victoria encouraged me, when I failed to articulate the sordid vision.

"It was a sick, twisted party," I blurted, swallowing back the lump of vomit that was threatening to force its way out of my throat. "There were naked adults everywhere, doing pretty much everything you could imagine… and a lot of things you probably wouldn't want to imagine." I cleared my throat to dislodge the lump, then continued. "I hid behind the sofa to look for my parents but most of the adults were wearing masks, so I couldn't tell if they were there or not," I paused again, and opened my eyes. "I don't think I can do this."

"Yes, you can. You're in a safe space Ryan," she reassured me, with a gentle smile. I sighed and stared down at the floor.

"I noticed another kid sitting in the far corner of the room, at first I thought he might want to play, but then I saw that he had a dog collar around his neck. I obviously had no fucking idea what was going on, but I knew it wasn't good. There was an old guy standing next to him – well, I thought he was old at the time anyway. He was holding the leash that attached to the boy's collar. I was so scared, but I couldn't stop watching. I wanted to know who the kid was and what he'd done wrong to be put on a leash. I tried to get his attention a couple of times, but he didn't seem to notice me, even when he looked straight at me." My voice cracked, and I felt tears overflow as the memory of his vacant eyes, pierced my soul. "That was when they dragged him away by the lead and a whole group of them started doing awful things to him," I blubbered through snot and tears. I wiped my nose with the back of my hand, and Victoria handed me a box of tissues. "I should have helped him."

"That's a big burden to carry, Ryan," she said, leaving the tissues on my lap. "How do you possibly think you could have helped him? You were a child in a room full of unsafe adults."

"I still should have tried," I said, blowing my nose loudly, "but I freaked out and tried to run back up to my room."

"Tried?" she asked curiously, "so you didn't make it back to your room?"

"No," I answered solemnly, "that's when he found me."

"He, who?"

"The guy who stole my virginity," I said breathlessly.

"Tell about him."

"What is there to tell? He was a sleazy old perve, who liked fucking little boys."

"Okay, so tell me about how he found you."

"He saw me dash out from behind the sofa. I didn't realise he was standing there until he grabbed me by the shoulder. I tried to get away, but he was grasping me so tight that his creepy long nails were digging right into my skin." My heart was pounding, and my throat was tight. I felt as scared in real time as I had been that night. Even after all those years, it was too painful to re-live. I couldn't talk anymore. The emotion was too big, and the pain was too much to bear. I broke down into an uncontrollable fit of tears. "I can't do this," I told Victoria, wiping at the tears that were streaming down my face.

"It's okay Ryan," Victoria said, gently patting my knee, "we can park that for now. Tell me about your nanny."

I didn't want to tell her about my Nanny. I didn't want to talk anymore. All I wanted to do was curl up in my bed and sleep forever, but Victoria wouldn't let me. We worked through my less torturous recollections for over two hours, and by the time I left her office I barely had the strength to walk. Even though we hadn't gone into the worst of it, I still felt like I'd been hit by a truck. Regardless, I forbade myself from retreating into my room. Instead of hiding, I forced myself to go the dining room and eat dinner with everyone else. If I could do that, then I could get through this thing, one small victory at a time.

I was the first one at the table and, as I sat silently pondering over my revelations, I heard someone pull out the seat next to me. Expecting to see Sloane, I turned to greet her with a smile and flinched when I saw Rodney standing there.

"Mind if I sit here?" he asked calmly.

"Errr… sure," I said, motioning for him to sit with a disconcerted shrug. I eyed him suspiciously as he sat down, and wondered what he had in store for me. Rodney said nothing. He just tucked into his own meal in silence. I glanced over at him a couple of times, trying not to make it obvious that I was doing so. Other people joined us but we didn't exchange one single word for the entire duration of dinner. It wasn't until the end of our meal that Rodney finally spoke.

His knife and fork clinked onto the centre of his plate, followed by his crumpled napkin. Silently, he took hold of his empty dish and cleared his throat. I looked up as he leaned ever so slightly closer to me.

"I guess we aren't so different you and me," he said quietly, then pushed his chair back and excused himself from the dining room. I stared after him in shock. The man who had recently vowed to make my life a living hell, had just offered me a very large olive branch and I had no idea what to do with it.

- KAT McPHERSON -

When we got home from Beaus, I walked in the door and dumped Mia's nappy bag on the kitchen bench. There was no way I could get through this without Ryan. I'd only had one night alone with Mia and I was already cracking like a prisoner subjected to Chinese Water Torture. I popped on my 'cheery music' playlist and put Mia into the bouncer. It was nearly 8pm but, in our newborn hour-by-hour survival schedule, time was irrelevant. Not having the enthusiasm to cook a meal, I ordered home delivery for myself and started dancing around the room to the music, determined to remain positive in the face of adversity. Mia watched as I spun around and sang to her. Somehow, we would find a way to get Ryan home.

I was feeling ravenous by the time I heard a knock at the door and jumped with a start, wondering how the delivery driver had got through the communal front door. I left Mia strapped in her bassinet and went out to the entry hall, cautiously opening the door. I peered into the hall and my jaw dropped. Amy was standing in the hallway, holding Ryan's keys.

"Amy? What are you doing here?" I asked, stepping back to let her in.

"I've been collecting the mail for Ryan," she said pointing towards the mailboxes in the hallway, "but then I heard the music..."

"Thanks for doing that for him."

"That's what friends are for," she said with a shrug, handing me the mail. "So does that mean you've moved back in then?"

"Yeah. Do you want to come in?"

"No," she replied bluntly.

"Oh."

"Here," she said, holding out the keys, "I guess I don't need to collect the mail anymore."

"Thanks," I said sadly, taking the keys from her hand. "Did you hear about Ash?" I asked, assuming Ritchie would have told her by now.

"No," she said blankly, "what about Ash?"

"I thought Ritchie would have told you?"

"I haven't spoken to him since he left," she said with a look of concern, "what's going on with Ash?"

"She got attacked last night."

"What? How? Was it her psycho ex? Is she okay?" she asked in one long barely comprehensible sentence.

"Yeah, apparently it was her ex, but according to Ryan, her dad said, that Nathan said, she was fine and he was taking her down to Cornwall."

"Thank god," she sighed with relief, "how did he find her?"

"I don't know," I said with a shrug, "that was all Ryan told me."

"Shit."

"Yeah."

We both fell silent and then Amy backed away from the door.

"Anyway… later," she said, turning away. My heart felt like it was breaking.

"Do you want to meet Mia?" I asked desperately, not wanting her to leave.

"Not today," she said, looking back over her shoulder as she made her escape towards the main door.

"Aims, are we ever going to be okay?" I called after her. Amy froze and shook her head but didn't turn around.

"I don't know."

"Aren't you even going to hear my side of it?" I asked with frustration. "You haven't even talked to me about it, you've just shut me out."

She turned around angrily, "you shut yourself out the moment you fucked Beau."

I recoiled, feeling as if I'd been slapped in the face.

"I know what I did was shitty," I said, stepping out into the hall, "but Ryan and I have made peace with it, so if he can forgive me, why can't you?"

"Because Ryan's a better person than both of us."

"Aims-"

"No Kat," she said, shaking her head, "I don't want to hear it," she sighed and fell silent, staring at me with a look of complete betrayal.

It was the exact same look that I'd seen on Ryan's face. Anyone would have thought that she was the person I'd cheated on. "After everything with Ash, and all the angst and drama of thinking that she was stealing your man. After all that… you cheated on him. I just can't understand it."

"I was upset and insecure and I made a mistake."

"That's not an excuse," she replied unemotionally.

"I know," I agreed humbly, "there are no excuses for what I did… but that was the reason. I'm a flawed human and I've regretted that stupid decision every single day since."

"Ryan was nothing but faithful to you."

"I know."

"He's a good guy and he didn't deserve the way you treated him."

"I agree."

"You completely ruined him," she said, pushing forth like a dog gnawing at a bone, "he destroyed his life because of you, and now he's stuck in rehab with a criminal conviction on his record."

"Is this really about me and Ryan or are you still angry at yourself for what happened with Alex?"

"Alex has nothing to do with this."

"Are you sure about that?" I asked kindly. "Look Aims, I know a thing or two about guilt, and ignoring it doesn't make it go away. But if it makes you feel any better, I don't think you could possibly hate me more than I hate myself for cheating on Ryan."

Amy snorted and shook her head with disgust, "was he worth it?"

"Who? Beau?"

"Unless you fucked some other guy?"

I cringed and chewed on the inside of my cheek, trying not to take her hostility personally.

"No," I said calmly, "he wasn't worth it." Amy was silent. I sighed, at a loss as to what to do. "Is there any way I can make you stop hating me so much?" I asked desperately, feeling a surge of tears bubbling to the surface.

"I don't know," she answered quietly.

"I miss my best friend," I spluttered as the tears broke and began to roll down my cheeks. Amy's eyes were glistening too, but she turned away and gripped the door handle.

"She misses you too," she whispered over her shoulder, before letting herself out the building while I stood in the hallway crying. It was hard to tell whether they were tears of grief or gratitude, but at least we'd made some headway. Maybe there was hope of getting at least one of my best friends back.

- ASHLEY GRANGER -

Our team-bonding dinner proved to be very interesting indeed. Ritchie and Sandrine had begun bonding much more than was strictly necessary in a work context, as did a few others. The expensive French wine flowed freely, and the pseudo-subtle innuendos and harmless flirtatious glances, very rapidly escalated into provocative sexual propositions and blatant under-table groping, largely instigated by Sandrine. It appeared Nathan was off Sandrine's menu.

"What did you say to Sandrine today?" I whispered to him curiously, "she didn't flirt with you at all after your 'private chat.'" I said, emphasizing the inverted commas with my fingers.

"I told her that I was madly in love with you."

"No, you didn't." I replied dryly.

"No, I didn't," he agreed with an embarrassed chuckle, "all I said was: 'Sandrine…' and she figured out the rest."

"That sounds more realistic." I replied, hiding a yawn. Even after our extended nap, I still felt shattered.

"Fancy calling it a night?" Nath asked quietly, as the room echoed with clinking glasses and merry chatting. It was nearing midnight and we were only waiting on a few people to finish their coffees, so it seemed like a reasonable time to make an exit. I nodded silently, feeling too drained to utter words. "Right, we're off," Nath declared loudly. "Ash still isn't feeling too good so I'm going to get her into bed."

"Yeah, I bet you are Stoner!" Cody laughed, winking at me, as the rest of the table erupted into drunken hysterics.

"Err… I wasn't meaning it like that," Nathan stuttered awkwardly, casting me a furtive glance. He was probably worried I was going to freak-out.

"You're not coming out with us?" Sandrine asked disappointedly, as everyone else resumed their cheerful chatter. Her arm was slung over the back of Ritchie's chair, as she leaned right over him to speak with Nathan. Ritchie's eyes skimmed quickly over Sandrine's ample cleavage as it peeped unashamedly out of her tightly fitted, crimson dress. If Sandrine noticed his subtle perve, she didn't let on. "It won't be the same without you," she teased Nathan with an over-exaggerated pout.

"I get the feeling you'll be well entertained," Nathan told her with a wink as he helped me up from my seat.

"True," Sandrine agreed with a chuckle, her eyes wandering over Ritchie's solid torso.

"Have fun kiddies," Nathan called to the table as we excused ourselves, "but not too much fun. Don't forget that we have a project meeting at 10am."

"Aye-Aye Captain," Ritchie answered with a cheeky salute.

"Night everyone," I mumbled as cheerfully as possible, before we escaped into the lobby. Nathan guided me over to the Taxi stand.

"Come on, there's something I want to show you and before we go back to the hotel," he said with excitement.

"Well that sounds mysterious," I said with a tired smile as he opened the taxi door for me.

"Not really," Nathan smiled, showing me into the cab. He gave the driver directions in fluent French, and then smiled proudly as he sat back in the seat, looking as though he wanted to wrap his arm around my shoulder, but instead wedging both his hands between his knees.

"What are you up to?" I asked, only having picked up a small amount of his instructions to the cab driver.

"You'll see." He replied with a nervous smile. "Unless you'd rather go hang out at Le Crazy Horse with the others?"

"Ah so is that how you and Sandrine ended up…?" I let my sentence trail off as I was hit with a graphic visual of Nathan and Sandrine doing the dirty.

"Do you really want to know the details?"

"No, I don't think I do," I admitted, swallowing back a little bit of vomit.

"Okay." He nodded approvingly, as if I'd made the right choice. I leaned back in the seat and covered another yawn. The taxi slowed to a halt in front of a dimly lit park and I peered out the window at the dark tree lined footpath, before glancing back at Nathan in weary confusion. Did he honestly expect me to wander around a park at midnight?

"Please trust me," he answered my unasked question with a smile and advised the cab driver to keep the meter running. Nathan climbed out of the taxi enthusiastically, but I didn't move. "You'll be safe, I promise."

I stepped dubiously out of the cab and was met with the most glorious sight. Behind the manicured row of trees, stood the Eiffel Tower, majestically lit up like a giant Christmas tree.

"Wow," I breathed in awe. It was much more impressive in real life than it was on the telly.

"Wait for it…" Nathan replied, looking at his watch. "Three, two, one…" Right on cue, the lights on the tower began twinkling magically. "Welcome to Paris Ash."

"It's gorgeous Nathan." I whispered with tears in my eyes, spell-bound by the sparkling lights.

"I couldn't let you come to Paris without seeing the Eiffel Tower." I tore my eyes away from the magnificence of the tower light show and studied Nathan intently. I smiled involuntarily, as my heart almost over-flowed with affection for the beautiful man.

"Thank you," I said, squeezing his hand tightly.

"My pleasure," he said, letting his eyes wander over my face with a look of great concern. "Now, let's get you back to the hotel."

- RITCHIE CARLTON -

Shit was getting crazy at the aptly named, Le Crazy Horse. The club certainly lived up to its reputation. Our evening had grown increasingly debaucherous, and I suspected it was primarily due to the free flow of cocaine, cognac and cigars at our table. The three C's had dissolved everyone's inhibitions and indeed perhaps had also relaxed our morals somewhat. People were hooking up left, right and center. Cody had dragged the waiter out with us and they'd been snogging unashamedly all night, but I couldn't judge since I'd already pashed Sandrine in a moment of drunken desire. I was pretty confident that it wasn't going to be a one-off.

After consuming at least my body weight in fine French cognac, I had to excuse myself for another piss. I stumbled into the men's toilets and started my slash when I heard moaning coming from one of the stalls. I froze mid-piss, wondering whether to continue as planned given the somewhat private, yet very loud, nature of whatever was occurring on the other side of the stall door. It wasn't often that I heard other men getting their rocks off, so it was an unusual experience to be privy to that personal moment.

The moaning got louder, but my bladder was un-perturbed by the situation and demanded to be emptied. I finished my wee as quickly as humanly possible while the dunny-stall sexy-time seemed to be coming to a climax. I quickly washed my hands and sprinted out of the bathroom so that I didn't have to meet the moaner in a very awkward post-cum interaction.

As I turned the corner into the hallway that led back out to the main room, I was accosted by a slim figure in a bright red dress, who pushed me up against the wall.

"I've been looking for you," Sandrine purred into my ear, "one of my girls is very taken with you Richard, shall we bring her home with us?"

"Sandrine, it's just Ritchie…" I said, buying time as I figured out how to respectfully decline the offer to be abducted and tortured in the name of sex.

"Or are you more of a one-woman man?" Sandrine asked, running her finger up the front of my trousers. My cock jumped to attention and spurred me into action. If Sandrine wanted to play power games, I'd show her how it was done. Alpha Aussie dude came out to play and I grabbed her by the arse, pulling her tight against my body to show her exactly what my intentions were.

"You won't even be able to think about your friend once I get started on you," I said gruffly into her ear, as I pinned her petite body effortlessly against mine. She looked up at me with lust raging in her eyes.

"Inouï," she whispered breathlessly. I didn't speak French, but I got the general gist of what she was saying. It was clear from the look on her face and the rise and fall of her ample chest that she was turned on by the tough guy act. Spurred on by her obvious approval, I spun us both around, pushed her up against the wall and snogged her hard. A little whimper escaped her mouth as my tongue ravaged hers, and it was hard to believe that this was the same woman I'd met at the Delfontaine Headquarters. It wasn't unusual for high-ranking women like Sandrine to be turned on by the warrior man play. One small taste of Alpha Male and they melted like putty in my hands.

"Still think we need a third person?" I asked, as I plucked her up off the floor and leaned my body against hers so that she was wedged between me and the wall with my hard-on pressing firmly between her thighs. The breath caught in her throat momentarily and she acquiesced, obediently wrapping her legs around my waist.

"It would seem not," she said huskily, as I firmly squeezed her bum cheeks.

"Shall I fuck you now or later?" I asked arrogantly, fully embracing my role of tough guy. Before Sandrine had time to answer, Cody and the waiter guy emerged from the men's toilets, holding hands and giggling like teenagers. A surge of nausea swept over me as I realised that there was a 50/50 chance I'd just heard Cody cumming.

"Ritch!" said Cody with a guilty smile on his face. I stared at him in horror.

"Codes," I replied with an awkward nod. There were so many levels of discomfort about the situation that it was hard to tell which was the most excruciating. Thankfully, Sandrine was shielded from his view at that angle and I had silently resolved to keep it that way, until she unwrapped her legs from around my waist and popped her head out to see what was going on. Cody's smile exploded into a grin. He now had as much dirt on me as I had on him.

"Sandrine," he said cheerily, "having a good night?"

"Oui," she said calmly, "et toi?"

"Oui," he replied with a satisfied smile.

"Well, this has been fun, but we all have better places to hang out than the toilet hallway," I said, taking control of the situation. "Goodnight Codes, I'll see you back at our room..." I looked between him and the good-looking waiter who appeared to have no idea what was going on, "...alone," I told Cody sternly, "there's no fucking in our room."

"Fine, but same goes for you."

"Fine," I agreed, reaching out to shake his hand, before I realised where it had probably been. I quickly retracted my hand and smiled at Guillaume. "Au revoir," I said pleasantly, using one of the three French words I actually knew. Guillaume and Cody nodded their farewell and I turned back to my date. "Sandrine," I called authoritatively, holding out my hand as if summoning a dog, "we're going to your place."

Sandrine's connections turned out to be very useful, and the manager slipped us out the back door of the club without anyone noticing. The two of them were ensconced in a very lengthy conversation in French when a big black limousine came gliding up the dark lane way. They both looked up at the bright headlights and hugged each other farewell.

"Merci Claude," said Sandrine, as the limo came to a halt in front of the door.

"Bonne soiree," Claude said, waving as we climbed into the luxurious limo. Sandrine gave instructions to the driver and then wound up the window between his section and ours. The car moved off and Sandrine poured us both a glass of champaign.

"So what was that all about?" I asked her curiously as she handed me an icy cold glass of bubbly.

"With Claude?"

"Oui," I said, testing out my French accent.

"He was asking why I wasn't taking one of the girls," she said honestly. I nearly spat my drink out.

"So... you do that often do you?'

"Only once a week."

"Once a week? Shit, then you're not hooking up with the right men Sandrine," I told her, putting my glass down on the little table next to me.

"No?" she asked, looking a little shocked as I plucked the glass out of her hand and put it down next to mine.

"No," I confirmed, kneeling on the floor in front of her. "I know you like being in control," I said, as she watched me with intrigue, "but tonight I'm in charge." I grabbed her bottom and pulled her to the edge of the seat. She gasped with surprise, but her eyes flashed with hunger. "I'm going to show you how a real man does it," I told her as I gently pushed her knees apart. Her mouth fell open as I ran my hands purposefully up her thighs and then planted my face in between them. Sandrine let out a little whimper as I got to work, and within minutes she was writhing beneath my tongue. I rubbed my thumb against her clit and she moaned loudly, before quickly scrambling to regain some form of control. With my faced wedged firmly in her crotch, she attempted unsuccessfully, to undo my jeans but, like a sex ninja, I swiftly secured both her wrists in my right hand and with my left, I plunged my fingers deep inside her.

Sandrine cried out in pleasure and I felt her body pulsate from the inside. With my fingers firmly planted, I sat up and whispered into her ear

"I'm the one calling the shots here Sandrine. You'll get off whenever I want you to."

"Oui," she panted, still in the throes of her orgasm.

"And I'm going to make you go again… and again… and again, until you can't go anymore."

– Chapter 3 –

The changing of the guard

- NATHAN STONE -

After a night of restless sleep with Ash having continuous nightmares, I awoke in the morning bleary eyed to the sound of my alarm. I groaned and rolled over to snooze my phone. We were supposed to go downstairs for breakfast with the boys, but my body wasn't happy about it. I yawned and glanced over at Ashley. She was still sleeping… or at least pretending to be. I rubbed my eyes to get them working properly, but all it did was make them blurrier.

"We've got breakfast," I muttered.

"Mmhmm…" she mumbled with her eyes still closed. "You go. I'll be down soon."

"Okay," I agreed reluctantly, rolling out of bed. "Are you going to be okay here by yourself?"

"Yeah. I just need a shower and then I'll be down."

"Alright," I said, pulling on my trousers, "I'll see you down there."
I shrugged into my shirt, slipped on my shoes and headed downstairs to meet the boys. I spotted the two of them sitting at a table next to the buffet, which was hardly surprising given Ritchie's appetite. They both looked shattered but in good spirits.

"Morning Stoner," chirped Ritchie cheerfully.

"You're looking very relaxed today," I teased, punching him in the arm. "No bruises then?"

"Well, I didn't get tied to a table and paddled if that's what you're asking," he mocked with a grin.

Cody looked shocked at Ritchie's comment so I acted as if I didn't have the slightest clue as to what he was inferring.

"But you definitely have some gossip to share," I said, shooting him a warning glare as I took the seat next to him.

"What can I say… the woman certainly knows her way around a cock," Ritchie joked, heeding my unspoken warning. Cody spat his juice back into his glass to avoid snorting it out his nose.

"Holy shit Ritchie, give a guy some warning before you say things like that," said Cody, wiping his face with a napkin as he pushed his soiled glass to the edge of the table.

"Oh right, so the guy who got a blowjob in the bathroom of Le Crazy Horse is suddenly a prude," Ritchie goaded him. Cody grinned, partly bashful, but mostly proud.

"Fair play," he conceded.

"Wow, sounds like a good night was had all round," I teased. I looked over at the food and decided that I didn't have the energy to eat.

"You look like you need a coffee Stoner," Cody said, passing me the coffee plunger.

"Yeah, you look like shit," agreed Ritchie, "anyone would think it was you who pulled an all-nighter."

"I did. Ash was having nightmares all night," I said, darting a glance towards Cody. He knew the top-line story, but I still didn't want him knowing too much.

"Don't worry Nathan, no one will hear it from me," Cody said, sympathetically.

"Yeah, he's too preoccupied with his hot little French fella to care," Ritchie joked, laughing mischievously.

"Sure am," Cody agreed, waggling his eyebrows, "he too, knows his way around a cock."

Ritchie exploded into his usual raucous laughter.

"Oh my god, they're multiplying," I muttered, pouring myself a cup of black coffee. "So, are we telling Red about your romp with Sandrine or is this a 'what happens in Paris', kind of situation?"

"I'm going to tell her," he said with a shrug, "it's not like she'll care."

"Are you sure about that?" asked Cody dubiously. Ritchie nodded and shoved a croissant into his gob. "She's made it abundantly clear that we're not a couple," he said with his mouth full of pastry.

"Ritchie's sick of being Red's sex toy," I translated on his behalf, in case Cody didn't speak Aussie Bush-pig.

"I never said that," Ritchie rebutted, swallowing the massive chunk of croissant.

"No, but you're not happy with the current arrangement," I reminded him.

"That is true," he agreed with a sigh.

"Well, on the plus side, I guess you'll find out how she really feels when you tell her about Sandrine," said Cody with a cringe. He clearly didn't think things were going to pan out the way Ritchie expected.

"Do you know something that I don't Codes?" Ritchie asked, eyeing

Cody suspiciously.

"Not at all," Cody answered, raising his hands in surrender, "I just think you may be underestimating the wrath of a woman scorned."

"How is she scorned when she's the one who keeps reminding me that we're not together?"

"I didn't say it's logical Ritchie," said Cody, sounding more camp than I'd ever heard him, "but no matter how much they deny it, women are innately monogamous."

"And you know this because you've been with so many women?" Ritchie teased sarcastically

"The irony about being gay, Ritch, is that you suddenly become a beacon for women, and because you're a safe zone they tell you everything – whether you want to hear it or not. The main thing I've learned is that ladies do not like sharing their man."

"He's got a point," I said, coming to Cody's rescue. Or Ritchie's. I'd completely lost track of who needed my help by that point.

"Speaking of ladies," said Ritchie, changing the subject, "is Ash coming down?"

"Yeah, she's on her way."

"Do you think she's going to be okay?" Asked Ritchie. "Nightmares aren't a good sign."

"Honestly... I don't know. She's completely shut down."

"Just give her some time," suggested Cody, breathing in the scent of his steaming hot coffee. "It would have been pretty scary getting attacked in her own flat. She just needs some time to work through that trauma."

"Apparently this guy is now the woman oracle," Ritchie scoffed disdainfully pointing his thumb at Cody.

"I'm just offering some insight," Cody said with a haughty shrug.

"I think you're probably right Codes," I agreed reluctantly. "Maybe I'll take her up some breakfast."

"Good idea, but at least east something first," said Ritchie as he threw me a flaky golden croissant from the pile on his plate. "You're no help to anyone when you're hangry."

"Aww, you're the best wife a man could ask for," I teased, taking a bite of the perfectly baked pastry.

The boys bantered as we ate and drank, but I couldn't concentrate on the conversation when I knew Ash was upstairs by herself. I grabbed a couple more croissants and a pot of coffee and excused myself from the table.

When I opened the door to our small room, I could hear the shower running, so I set the coffee and croissants down on the table and knocked quietly on the bathroom door.

"Ash, are you okay?" There was no answer, so I put my ear against the door. I could hear her crying and my heart wrenched in my chest. Was it better for me to go in and comfort her or to leave her alone? "Ash?" I asked again, "can I come in?"

"Yeah," she squeaked quietly. I opened the door slowly and stuck my head into the steamy bathroom. Ash was slumped on her knees on the floor of the shower, with her arms wrapped around herself. The bandage on the back of her shoulder was bright pink and starting to peel off. She looked up at me red-eyed. "I was trying to get ready," she mumbled before one huge sob escaped her lips, opening the floodgates for her sorrow.

"Oh shit," I said, jumping into the shower fully clothed, as she wept uncontrollably. I sat next to her on the wet tiles and wrapped her up in my arms as the water pelted down on us. She dropped her head against my chest and gripped the wet fabric on my shoulders as she cried. "I've got you," I whispered, pulling her in tight. I leaned against the wall, cuddling Ashley into my chest, and let my own silent tears fall, knowing that they would be disguised by the steady stream of water rolling down my face. Her pain was mine, and although I had no idea what she was going through, I could feel how much she was hurting. "I've got you," I repeated. It seemed to be the only thing I could ever think to say when she needed comforting.

We sat on the shower floor for a long time - an hour at best guess - until Ash began shivering. My body was stiff and wracked with pain. I helped her out of the shower and wrapped her in a towel, before peeling off my wet clothes. I let them fall to the floor with a plop, and we dried ourselves in silence, both too drained to talk. I wrapped the towel around my waist, in case my nudity was too confronting for Ash, but she hadn't seemed to notice.

"Come on, let's get you back into bed," I said, moving to put my arm over her shoulder before thinking better of it.

"Okay," Ash agreed without argument. I'd genuinely expected her to put up a fight and try to talk me into going to work, but she just nodded and shuffled out to the bedroom. She sat on the edge of the bed, wrapped in her towel, staring blankly at the floor with her wet hair dripping droplets of water down her shoulders as I did my best to replace the soaked bandage. She looked almost catatonic. Coming to Paris had been a dumb idea.

I checked my phone. It was 9am and I had several missed calls from Ritchie, probably wondering where we were. I shot him a quick text to tell him to go ahead to the Delfontaine offices without us and then sat down on the bed next to Ash. I'd never seen her so distraught before. She was jumpy and skittish, almost as if she had become a different person. Dom had changed her. This was not who she was, this was the damage he'd caused. He'd not only violated her body, he'd broken her soul.

"Ash…" I said quietly. She broke out of her trance and looked up at me with bloodshot eyes. We stared at each other silently, and she nodded in agreement to my unspoken question.

"Yeah," she said quietly. "It's time to go home."

- RYAN McPHERSON -

At 9am on the dot, one of the ladies came to tell me that a visitor had arrived so I made my way out to the foyer, expecting to see Kat and Mia. I stopped dead in my tracks when I realised that the woman standing in the reception area was not the one I had anticipated. Kellie was staring out the window to the Water Garden.

"Kellie?" I asked with surprise. She turned around and smiled stiffly.

"Hey," she said quietly. It was the most subdued I'd ever seen her, but then again, it was also the first time I'd really seen her sober. She almost seemed like a different person.

"It's nice to see you," I said, ushering her over to the seats, "what are you doing here?"
She remained standing, gripping her purse tightly.

"I needed to see you," she said, looking cautiously around the room. I bit my lip and cringed inwardly, knowing that I had to have the dreaded conversation.

"Kell… I should tell you… Kat and I are back together."

"Yeah I heard," she said, "and that's great, but there's something I need to talk to you about."
My stomach dropped.

"Oh, that sounds ominous," I said, my heart pounding in my chest. Was she going to tell me that she had HIV or Hep C or warts or something? She glanced around again.

"Is there somewhere private we can go?"

"Yeah," I nodded, taking her arm, "let's go out to the garden."

"Okay." She followed me outside and we got settled on one of the benches in the Japanese Water Garden. No one ever came out to this area so we were unlikely to be interrupted. We watched the huge koi swimming around the pond for a few minutes, but I couldn't take it any longer.

"So, what's up?" I asked lightly, "are you okay?"

"Not really," she paused and sighed, "I'm pregnant Ryan."

"Oh shit," I said, feeling oddly relieved that it was a pregnancy rather than a bout of Chlamydia.

She turned to me apologetically, "I know you and Kat just got back together... I wasn't even going to bother you with it, but I thought you should at least know."

"I appreciate that," I said resting my hand on her shoulder.

"I'm not asking anything of you Ryan, I'm not keeping it. I've got an appointment booked at the clinic next week, but I didn't feel right doing that without telling you first."

I looked down at my hands with mixed feelings. I couldn't believe that I'd made such a big mess for everyone, but at the same time, the thought of having another child wasn't entirely undesirable.

"Oh," I said, unsure what to say, "are you okay?"

"Yeah, I guess so," she said with a shrug. Kellie peered up at me with a shy smile. She looked so young and innocent that it was hard to consolidate her with the amorous party girl that I'd known. I rubbed her shoulder.

"I'm sorry you've been going through this on your own."

"Thanks, but it's my own fault," Kellie answered, glancing down at her hands, "I accidentally missed a couple of my pills and I thought it would be fine."

We sat in silence for a moment, watching the koi again. It was quite calming really. I looked down at Kell.

"Do you want me to come to the appointment with you?"

She shook her head, "that's really sweet, but aren't you kind of stuck in here?"

"Yeah, but I can put in an application for day release."

Kellie laughed nervously, "sounds like a prison."

"It basically is," I joked, "actually, it's more like a daycare for adults."

"Fun," she joked with a worried smile.

"So... you definitely don't want to keep the baby? Because if you did, I'd be there for both of you."

She squirmed awkwardly. "Ryan I'm twenty-five, I work in a nightclub, and my lifestyle isn't exactly conducive to parenthood. Plus, I'm about to do this apprenticeship..."

"It's okay, I get it," I said, patting her arm, "and I respect your decision. You're the one who it effects the most. It's just that I don't want you to regret it. Things change once you have that little human in your arms."

"I appreciate that, but the truth is, I'm not really a kid person anyway. I never saw myself being a mum and I just... I don't think I've got it in me," she said with a sad smile, "and honestly... I kind of like my life the way it is."

"Okay," I nodded, feeling a mixture of emotions, "I'll support you either way."

"Thanks," she said with a grateful smile. "Anyway, I'd better get going. I just thought it was important that you knew."

"I'm glad you told me," I said, "and I'll pay for the appointment, but I'll just need a few days to figure out how to make that happen without technology."

"You're not allowed technology?"

"Nope, besides TV and DVD's we're on a total ban," I said rolling my eyes, "I guess they think we're going to contact our dealers or something."

We both chuckled and I showed Kellie out to the reception area.

"Good luck," I said, squeezing her arm, "and if you change your mind about wanting me at the appointment, you know where to find me," I joked.

"I'm sure I'll be fine, but thanks," she said with a tight smile, "and thanks for being so cool about this."

I smiled and gave her a hug, "hey, it took two of us make this happen so we're both responsible for it."

"Yeah, but not all guys would step-up," she said, smiling sadly at me, "you're a good guy Ryan, Kat's really lucky to have you."

"I'm not sure if she'll agree with you when I tell her about this."

Kellie stepped back from me.

"Don't tell her Ryan," she said with concern written all over her face, "you only just got back on track, this could ruin everything."

"I have to," I said with a shrug, "we agreed to be honest with each other."

"Yeah but..."

"Like I said Kell... you and I both made this mess together, so we both have to deal with the fallout. Just because we're not keeping the baby doesn't mean it never happened."

Kellie nodded, "that's true."

"I know you can't call me while I'm in here, but if you need to talk, I'll be here. Literally."

"Thanks," Kellie said, before heading for the door. She looked back over her shoulder and smiled, then walked out into the real world.

"Who was that?" asked Sloane, sneaking up behind me.

"Geez Sloane," I said, jumping with surprise at her sudden presence, "you scared the shit out of me."

"Spill it McPherson, who was that girl?"

I sighed and rubbed my face. "That was Kellie."

"Your druggie fuck buddy?"

"She's not a druggie," I said, bristling at Sloane's description of the mother of my soon-not-to-be child.

"Please don't tell me you're seeing her again," Sloane said judgmentally, "because Kat's really lovely and I'd hate to see her get hurt."

I sighed and glanced sideways at Sloane, "can you keep a secret?"

"Nope, secrets aren't allowed here remember?"

"In that case, I'm going back to my room."

"Okay, okay," she said grabbing my arm as I walked away, "I promise, I'll keep your secret."

"Kellie's pregnant... and it's mine."

Sloane's jaw dropped, "holy shit Ryan."

"Yeah."

"Is she keeping it?"

I shook my head, "no, she's not in a good place to be a mum and I think she's made the right decision."

"But?"

"I guess I just feel bad," I said with a sigh, "Kat and I tried so hard to get pregnant. It took us two years and three miscarriages before we got Mia. But just one crazy week with Kell and..." I gestured towards the door.

"Yeah."

"And I feel bad for Kellie," I admitted, rubbing my face again, "she's going through this by herself and that can't be easy."

"It's not," Sloane said knowingly. "Been there, done that."

I sighed, as the guilt weighed heavily on my shoulders.

"I'm paying for the appointment but it's not the same is it?"

"Not really, but there's not much you can do right now."

"True."

"Are you going to tell Kat?"

"Yeah, I have to," I said solemnly, "I can't pretend it didn't happen."

"Are you sure that's a good idea? What if she freaks?"

"Then I'll just have to deal with it."

She patted me on the back, "Byron would be very proud of you," she joked. We both laughed and she threw her arm over my shoulder. "Come on Daddy, let's go raid the snack cupboard before your wife arrives."

- RITCHIE CARLTON -

I'd given Sandrine the rundown on Nathan's situation with as much confidence and tact as I could muster. Stoner seemed convinced that I was capable of leading the big-arse account, but I had never been responsible for any projects of that magnitude, so I had to wonder whether his trust was born out of necessity rather than genuine belief in my abilities. What if I fucked it up and let everyone down? Or worse yet, what if I lost us the client?

"That won't happen," whispered Cody, whilst we were waiting for our team meeting to begin. "Nathan would have lined up a replacement if he thought you wouldn't be able to handle it, Ritchie."

"I suppose so," I said with a shrug, still unconvinced.

"Besides, Sandrine didn't seem too phased," he said logically, as if her amicability was evidence of my competency in running a multi-million pound account. We watched Sandrine as she moved about the room, and when she caught us staring at her, she shot me a subtle wink before resuming her conversation.

"I don't think it counts since we've shagged," I whispered to Codes, my eyes still on Sandrine.

"It counts more," he said, as the Delfontaine team took some time to gasbag about the absence of Ashley and our fearless leader.

After another ten minutes of gossip, Sandrine got down to business. Awkward would have been a nice way of describing the meeting. It seemed as if most of the French team believed Nathan's abdication had more to do with my relationship with Sandrine than his own personal circumstances.

I did my best to keep up a professional façade, but it was one of the most excruciating situations I'd ever been subjected to. Every time Sandrine looked at me, at least one person would grin like an idiot, or shoot me a knowing wink. I wasn't a stranger to colleagues having insight into my sex life. I'd been shagging Amy for two years so I should have been used to it, but somehow having a fuck buddy within the company felt like a totally different kettle of fish to fucking a client. I finally understood why Nathan had been so tight-lipped about his foray with Sandrine. By the time the meeting was over, my nerves were totally shot.

"We've got desks set up on the third floor, so we'll use the afternoon for admin and emails, then we'll all meet for dinner," suggested

Sandrine. "We've got a table booked at L'Astrance for 9pm."

"Crikey, 9pm?" I asked no one in particular, "it better be good if I have to wait that long to eat," I mumbled as I headed towards the door.

"Richard, would you mind staying for a moment?" Asked Sandrine as the rest of the attendees began to filter out of the room.

"Sure," I nodded. Cody shot me a knowing wink before making a swift exit from the room.

Sandrine waited patiently for everyone to leave and then closed the door behind the last of the stragglers, who smiled and nodded their amusement. My office affair felt much sluttier in the cold and sober light of day.

"I've been waiting all morning to get you alone Richard," Sandrine purred as she turned to me with a lusty look in her eyes, "I haven't been able to get you out of my head."

"Really?" I asked with an arrogant swagger, as I called on the power of Alpha Male again. Sandrine strutted over to me and backed me into the boardroom table, pressing her body hard against mine.

"Really," she whispered into my ear. "I'd like to fuck you again," she said, grabbing my crotch firmly.

"As I recall, I was the one doing all the fucking," I teased, hardly able to believe what was happening. I'd always kept work and sex quite separate, but there I was, getting groped by my insatiable client on her boardroom table.

"Will you fuck me again Richard?" Sandrine asked, rubbing my cock through the thick fabric of my jeans.

"I think we could arrange that," I said, grabbing her off the floor by the arse and spinning us around so that she was sitting on the table. Sandrine gasped and let out a throaty chuckle to signal her approval of my vigor. I ran my hands up her smooth thighs to extricate her knickers, except I couldn't find them. I lifted her dress right up to her waist and looked at her with pleasant astonishment.

"Oh, you are naughty," I said as I discovered that she wasn't wearing any underwear. "Have you been like that all morning?"
Sandrine's eyebrow flickered teasingly.

"Oui," She nodded with a wicked smile.

"No wonder you're so antsy," I teased, taking another glance at her nakedness. "Fuck you're sexy," I said smashing my lips against hers. I was so turned on that I was literally about to jizz in my pants. I didn't have time to get naked, so I just undid my zipper and plunged straight into her. Sandrine laid back on the table with her legs wrapped tightly around my waist as I gripped her hips and banged her frantically. We were both so horny that it couldn't have been more than a few minutes before we were moaning and grasping each other. "Well fuck me," I declared in contented exhaustion as I rested my palms on the table either side of Sandrine's head.

"I just did," she quipped with a saucy grin.

"I think technically I fucked you again," I joked, as I extracted myself from between her thighs and helped her down off the table. "Seems like I'm the one doing all the work in this relationship," I joked as I straightened myself up. I zipped my jeans and peered over at Sandrine as she primly smoothed down her dress. She caught my eye and shot me sexy smile.

"Maybe that's the way I planned it," she purred with a wink, as I had the fleeting realisation that what I was doing with Sandrine wasn't much different from what I was doing with Amy. The only distinction between the two was that I wasn't in love with Sandrine.

- KAT McPHERSON -

The morning had been a disaster. Mia had fed so many times over night that she'd spent the entire morning pooping like a super-trooper. I'd already changed her nappy three times since we'd woken up and just as we were about to walk out the door to go visit Ryan, she did the poop to end all other poops. I plonked the bags down on the counter and pulled Mia out of her pram, with bright yellow poo leaking through the leg holes of her onesie and all over the blankets.

"How can all of that come out of one tiny human?" I asked her, feeling simultaneously disgusted and impressed. I sighed and took her into the bathroom to clean her up for the fourth time that morning. Eventually, we made it out of the door and down to The Lodge.

"Hey sweetheart," said the lady at the desk when I finally rolled the pram through the foyer, "you're later than expected."

"Yeah, we had a rough morning topped off by a nappy explosion just as we were about to walk out the door."

"I don't miss those days, that's for sure," she joked, "I'll go get Ryan for you love."

"Thanks." I wheeled Mia's pram over to the big window so we could watch the birds flitting around the garden.

"Hey gorgeous," Ryan called chirpily, although I could tell that something was wrong. Oh god, what was it this time? He smiled brightly and gave me a kiss. "Late start this morning?"

"Nappy explosion," I explained, rolling my eyes playfully.

"Eek."

I stepped back and studied him.

"What's wrong?" I asked, seeing through his happy act. Ryan rubbed his face and sighed.

"Let's go set up in the sitting room," he suggested, taking the drivers' seat behind the pram handles. I stood for a moment as he began to wheel the pram off towards the visitors sitting room. Whatever was on his mind wasn't a small matter. He turned and looked over his shoulder. "You coming?" he asked with an amused smile.

"Yeah," I said, catching him up. We laid out Mia's blanket and set her up on the carpet so she could have some tummy time. Ryan laid down next to her and propped his head in his hand as he stared at her lovingly. I watched him watching her, and I was about to ask what was going on in his head when he beat me to it.

"Kellie came to see me this morning," he blurted awkwardly. I froze with dread. Holy shit. Why would Ryan's ex-fuck buddy reappear out of nowhere?

"Oh," I said, trying to stay cool, "and why was that?"

"She had something to tell me," he said solemnly. My stomach churned with a feeling of impending doom.

"Please don't tell me she wants you back?" I asked breathlessly.

"No, it's not that. But..." he paused.

"But what Ryan?"

He took a deep breath, "Kellie's pregnant… and it's mine."

"What?" I breathed in shock.

"She's not keeping the baby, she's got an appointment booked next week, but I wanted to tell you because we promised to be honest with each other."

I stared at him blankly as my mind raced at a million miles an hour. Even though she wasn't keeping it, this was still a massive piece of news, and I didn't quite know how to process it. I felt jealous at the fact that she'd gotten pregnant so easily... and to my husband no less. I was furious at Ryan for being so stupid, but then I'd been just as irresponsible as he had. Beau and I hadn't been careful either. I ran my hand over my face and tried to gather my thoughts.

"Ryan, this is huge."

"Yeah, I know and I'm really sorry," he said, sitting up to hold my hands. "I fucked up big-time and it just keeps coming back to bite both of us in the arse." I looked down at his hands around mine.

"I don't know what to say."

Ryan sighed, "are you okay?"

"Yeah," I said with a nod, "but there's a lot of things going through my head to be honest."

"I understand."

"I think I need a walk. Can you sit with Mia for a bit? I need to get outside."

"Yeah, sure."

"Thanks," I said, climbing to my feet.

"Kat, are we okay?" Ryan asked, grasping my hand.

"We're okay Ryan, I just need a moment to clear my head." I wandered out to the gardens and breathed in the fresh air. In a matter of months, our little world had gone from boring, to completely mental. I dreaded to think what could possibly come next.

- NATHAN STONE -

My decision to take Ashley home was a contentious one, but I hadn't intended to piss anyone off. Gaz had had a few choice words about me abandoning my post. It was purely a matter of priorities, and, in my mind, there was no question as to where mine laid.

"Surely she can get herself back to London," Gaz had said incredulously. I peered into the carriage where Ash was napping peacefully. Peaceful sleep had been hard to come by for her lately, so I was glad that she'd drifted off so easily.

"No Gaz, I'm not leaving her alone again," I told him sternly down the phone line as the Eurostar glided smoothly through the French landscape. "Besides, it's already under control. Ritchie's got everything covered and Sandrine's been informed of the change."

"Oh really?" he asked pompously, "and no one thought to run it past me first?"

"No," I said honestly, "it's my responsibility so I got it sorted. I've also booked Francesco on the 3pm train to stand in for Ashley."

"Francesco?" he asked incredulously. "Why the hell would you put Francesco on such an important account like Delfontaine?"

"Because we don't have anyone else Gaz. Amy doesn't have enough experience to head up an account of this size and neither do any of the other AD's. Francesco is the only Creative Director we've got."

"Francesco is a fantastic Creative Director Nathan, but he's a fucking liability when it comes to talking with clients. He's not equipped to fill-in for Ashley."

"I know, but we're out of options."

"What about Kat then?"

"Kat's still on Maternity leave," I replied with confusion, "you know that."

"Yes, I do know that, but given everything that's going on, I'm sure they could probably do with a bit of extra income right now."

"I think Kat's got enough on her plate without having to worry about work.

"Well, we won't know unless we ask her, will we?"

"Fine," I sighed, rubbing my face in a very Gaz-like manner. "I'll call Kat and ask but I'm not cancelling Francesco's ticket unless she agrees."

"Fine," Gaz conceded. "When's Beau's replacement starting?"

"Uh... the thing is... we haven't exactly found anyone yet."

"Why not?"

"None of the candidates have been right."

"Oh, for God's sake," he mumbled grumpily. "In that case, get Beau back on Delfontaine ASAP. I'd like him on that 3pm train."

"But-"

"But nothing Nathan. You're leaving me in the lurch, so you've forfeited your decision-making rights as far as I'm concerned. Get Beau on that train this afternoon."

"So, you want Kat and Beau working together on our biggest account of the decade?"

"It's not ideal, but it's the best solution we've got."

"You're the boss," I said with a resigned shrug. "I'll get it sorted."

"Thank you," he said, falling silent for a moment. "And, dare I ask when you intend to come back to the office?"

"I don't know," I told him, feeling nerves rise in my chest, "I've handed over to Ritchie indefinitely."

"What the fuck are you talking about?" Gaz barked down the line.

"I'm going back to the original plan and taking Ash down to the beach house."

"Are we really going to have this discussion again?"

"I hope not," I said snidely, "because that's what's happening whether you approve or not Gaz."

Gareth sighed and fell silent for a moment.

"Nathan," he said, sounding defeated, "as your godfather I understand where you're at and honestly, I'm proud of you. You're stepping up and taking care of your woman and that's no small thing.

"But?" I asked, knowing there was more.

"But as your boss, I can't let you dictate when you do and don't work."

"Okay, so what are you saying?"

"I'm saying that I need someone reliable on this account. If you go to Cornwall, you won't be coming back to lead the Delfontaine account."

"I understand," I said simply. "Ritchie's got this Gaz. I'll see you in a few weeks."

"You'd better."

I hung up the phone and ducked into the bar carriage to order a glass of whiskey. The hostess poured me a large glass and I headed back to our carriage, sipping the smooth liquid as I tried to keep my balance on the rapidly moving train.

I peeked in on Ash, who was still curled up in her seat, sleeping with her head propped against the window. I knocked back the remainder of my drink, plopped the empty glass onto one of the unoccupied tables, and ventured back out into the luggage area to call Kat.

- KAT McPHERSON -

As I sat on the wooden bench, staring out into the beautifully manicured gardens of The Lodge, I contemplated the ridiculousness of my current situation. My husband's ex-girlfriend was pregnant with his child; my friend had been attacked by her ex-boyfriend; and my ex-best friend still wasn't talking to me. Our boring little life had rapidly gone from mundane to insane.

My phone buzzed in my hand, and my heart leapt into my throat when I saw Nathan's name on the screen.

"Nathan," I said breathlessly as I answered, "are you guys okay?"

"Hey Tails," he said with forced cheer, "I take it you've heard then?"

"I have. Ashley's Dad rang Ryan."

"I see."

"How are you both holding up?"

"We're fine."

"Don't bullshit me Stone."

He laughed half-heartedly, sounding dejected and broken.

"You know me too well mate."

"So do I get the real answer or are we going to play pretend?"

"We're not okay," he admitted with a long breath. "Ashley had a meltdown in Paris so I'm taking her down to the beach shack."

"You went to Paris?! Ryan said that you guys were going straight down to Cornwall."

"Ashley insisted."

"That sounds about right."

"Hey, sorry to get down to business Tails, but I can't talk for long. I need to get back into Ash before she wakes up."

"Okay..." I said with confusion, "what business?"

"How would you feel about filling in for Ash on the Delfontaine account while she recovers?"

"What? Me? Why?"

"We need someone we can trust on the Account and you're our first preference. If it's too much with Mia and everything I totally understand."

"Wow... umm... can I think it over?"

"Sure, take a few hours, but we need an answer fairly quickly so we can book you on a train to Paris tomorrow."

"Paris?!"

"Yeah, we need to introduce you to Sandrine and her team, and it makes more sense to do that while the other guys are there."

"How long for?"

"A few days. They're due to come back on Friday."

"Two nights. Okay, let me chat with Ryan. Give us an hour to talk it over."

"Will do."

"Chat shortly."

"Chat soon."

All thoughts of the pregnancy situation vanished from my mind as the possibility of going back to work dangled in front of me like a carrot.

- RYAN McPHERSON -

I was lying on the sofa in the empty sitting room with Mia sleeping peacefully on my chest. I peered down at her cherubic little face and I couldn't imagine what I'd do if anything bad ever happened to her. I knew without a shadow of a doubt that I'd give my life for that child without a second thought. She was my heart, and her safety was the most important thing in the world to me. How could my parents have sat back and let their toddler get repeatedly raped under their own roof?

It was hard for me to fathom how they could have handed me over so willingly. Were their hearts so cold that they genuinely felt no twinge of reluctance when they'd offered me up for sport? If anyone ever hurt Mia, even a fraction of the way that those men had hurt me, I'd be murderous. The cops would literally have to use dental records to identify the bodies because I wouldn't leave any recognisable trace of the scumbags who did it. Yet my parents hadn't done that. They'd actively participated in making it happen. How could they? Kat returned from the garden looking somewhat shell-shocked.

"Hey," I said quietly, trying to sit up without disturbing Mia.

"Hey," she replied, carefully sitting down beside me on the couch.

"How are you feeling about everything?" I asked, hoping that 45 minutes in the garden was enough time for her to forgive me.

"Honestly, I don't know," she said, brushing off my question with a wave of her hand, "but you won't believe what just happened."

"Tell me."

"Nathan just rang."

"How's Ash?"

"Not good by the sounds of it. She insisted they went to Paris and then had a meltdown while they were there."

"Shit."

"He's taking her down to Cornwall."

"Okay."

"But that's not why he rang. He wants me to fill in for Ash on the Delfontaine account, while she recovers."

"Wow," I said with surprise, "and how do you feel about that?"

"Honestly, I'm quite excited by the prospect, but they want to send me to Paris for a few days and I have no idea how to make that work with Mia."

"Babe," I said, taking her hand, "if you want to do this, we'll find a way to make it work. Why don't we see if Rosie could come down for a few days?"

"She only just went home; I can't ask her to do that."

"Okay… what about Amy?"

She looked at me with raised brows. "Seriously?"

"Okay, maybe not Amy," I conceded. "Why don't we ask if you can leave her here with me?"

Kat perked up. "Do you think they'd let us do that?"

"It can't hurt to ask."

"And if they said yes, you'd be okay with that?"

"Babe, I'd be ecstatic about that. I'd love to spend some one-on-one time with Mia." I looked down at my gorgeous girl and stroked her tiny hand. "Assuming Sloane and Angelica don't steal her away from me."

We both laughed quietly.

"Okay," Kat said with a smile as she patted Mia's head, "let's ask."

"So… does that mean you're not pissed about Kellie?" I asked nervously. She gritted her teeth at the reminder of our little drama.

"Can we park that conversation for a bit? I don't have the brain space for that right now."

"Sure," I said as my stomach twisted in knots. What if the pregnancy was the final straw that broke my marriage beyond repair?

- NATHAN STONE -

Much to my annoyance, Beau was more than happy to return to his old position, despite my best efforts to deter him. Feeling frustrated, I ordered another whiskey and returned to my seat, where Ash was still sleeping. I was starting to wonder if she was just pretending to be asleep to avoid talking to me.

I took a sip of my drink and let my eyes run over her beautiful but damaged face. She would be fuming when she found out that I had, for all intents and purposes, quit my job. I wasn't regretful about my decision to let go of the Delfontaine account. I would have done it again without a second thought, in fact I'd give up everything for Ashley if it ever came to that, but what I was concerned about was the fact that she was going to blame herself for it.

I brushed a strand of hair off her face and Ash stirred. I quickly retracted my hand in case it freaked her out and, as she opened her bloodshot eyes, the view outside plunged into darkness. The train zoomed through the tunnel with the roar of the high-speed engine echoing off the walls. Ash focused her eyes and looked out the window at the pitch-black view.

"Hey sleepyhead. We're nearly back on English soil," I said as she rubbed her neck. "Did you want a night at home, or shall we head straight down to Cornwall?" My gut told me that I needed to keep Ash away from the city for a while. Nothing good would come from hanging around the town where so much drama had happened. At least at the beach she'd be away from everything that reminded her of Dom.

"I don't mind."

"How about we pick up Fred and head straight down?"

"Yeah." She nodded casting her bloodshot eyes over my face. "Are you okay?" she asked, sitting up in her chair.

"I'm fine," I said with as much sincerity as possible, "just tired and worried about you."

She smiled and laid her hand on my knee.

"You're a good salesman Nathan Stone, but I know when you're lying."

"Please don't worry about me," I said, taking her hand, "I need you to focus on yourself right now."

"I can't not worry about you."

"Well, you'll have to find a way to put it on hold for a little while."

"Okay," she agreed, resting her head on my shoulder. "I love you Nath," she whispered as I kissed the top of her head gently.

"I love you too," I said, just as my phone vibrated loudly on the table, making us both jump in surprise. I flipped over my phone and saw that it was Tails calling. "Sorry babe, I've got to take this."

"No worries," she said, removing her head from my shoulder.

"Tails," I said as I stood up to answer the call, "what's the verdict?"

"We're in."

"Really?"

"Yep. They've agreed to let Mia stay with Ryan for the rest of the week, so I'm going to Paris!"

"You're a legend Tails."

"I know."

"There's just one thing I've got to tell you before-" My words were cut off by Mia screaming in the background.

"Oh bollocks," she said as I heard Ryan's muffled voice in the background, "I've got to go Nath. Just let me know my ticket details and I'll be there."

"But Kat, there's something you need to know," I said through the deafening wails of her hungry baby.

"Sorry Nath, I can't hear you," she said as the clattering sound of her phone dropping, echoed through my head. "I'll call you later Nathan," Kat shouted down to the phone wherever it now laid. I hung up and returned to my seat.

"All okay?" Ash asked seeing the look of concern on my face.

"All good," I said, not even trying to disguise my angst. Ash frowned. I sighed and put my phone down on the table. "Kat's going to cover for you until you're ready to go back."

"That's good news, isn't it?"

"Sort of. The problem is that Gaz insisted on Beau resuming his old position and I didn't have time to tell Kat that he would be there."

"Oh dear."

"Yeah. Big Oh dear," I confirmed, chewing on my lip. "Well... I guess I'd better call Ritchie and let him know what's going on."

- RITCHIE CARLTON -

It had been difficult to convince the team to focus, given the events of the morning, so Sandrine and I gave everyone an extended lunch, and ducked over to her 'house' (it was more like a mansion), for a 'lunch meeting' (which consisted of neither lunch nor a meeting). After our particularly athletic session, we both flopped back on her king-sized bed, sweaty and breathless.

"You know Richard…" Sandrine said, rolling onto her side and trailing her finger up and down my bare chest, "you could stay here with me."

"Instead of my hotel you mean?" I asked, tucking my hands behind my head.

"No, I mean in Paris… permanently," she said, letting her suggestion hover in the air for a moment. I rolled onto my side so I was facing her.

"You want me to move to Paris?"

"Oui. You could work here on secondment until the end of the project and then join Delfontaine as my second in charge."

"Isn't Didier your 2IC?"

"He's retiring at the end of the year, and I need to replace him with someone I trust."

"Oh," I said, trying to stay cool as I waited for my head to stop reeling, "that's a tempting offer Sandrine."

"Then you'll consider it?" she asked with her hand poised against my chest.

"I'll have a think on it," I agreed, "but there would be a lot of things to consider. For instance… is this a purely a professional offer, or would it extend to our private activities too?"

"Only if you wanted it to," she said, propping herself up on one arm, "you could live here with me. It would be nice to have you around."

"Sandrine…" I let my sentence trail off. I had no idea what to say. Did I have the word 'Sex Toy' printed on my forehead somewhere? "I don't-"

"Bah," she waved her hand in the air, "it was just an idea," she said with a shy shrug of her shoulder. "It was silly."

I heaved my tired body into a seated position and rubbed her arms reassuringly.

"It's not silly, I'm just in a different space, that's all," I said, astounded to see such a fiercely independent woman allowing herself to be so vulnerable. "If you'd asked me two years ago, I wouldn't have thought twice about it, but I'm nearly forty and I'm ready to settle down and have kids."

"I understand," she said with a nod, "I can't help you with kids Richard, but I am affiliated with a lot of very powerful people and we could make all of your other dreams come true."

"What do you mean?" I asked, feeling like there was something else underlying her offer.

"Anything you want… we can make happen for you."

I rubbed my scalp feeling overwhelmed by the turn our conversation had taken. I ran my hands from the top of my bald head, down my face and over my eyes as I exhaled loudly.

"Why me?" I asked, unable to believe what she was offering. "You don't exactly seem like a one-man sort of woman."

Sandrine sighed and took my hand. "I'm not, but I like being with you Richard. You're the only man that's ever made me feel…" she paused and pondered over her words, "like a woman."

"Really?" I asked, astonished.

"It's not easy being a female at the top Richard. Business is still a man's game and we women must act like men to get anywhere. People have certain expectations…" she said with a sad look on her face. "With you, I don't have to pretend to be anyone… I can just be."

My jaw dropped at her words and I squeezed her hand.

"Sandrine, I think that's the nicest thing anyone has ever said to me."

"Does that mean you'll stay?" she asked hopefully.

"I don't think so," I said gently, "If I moved over here, I'd be giving up any hope of ever being a father."

"I understand," she said with a sad nod.

"But we still have a few days together-" I started to say as my phone rang loudly inside the pocket of my trousers, which were lying on the floor. "Excuse me for a second Sandrine, I'm waiting to hear back from Nath." I rolled off the bed and fumbled around for my phone. It was indeed Nathan. "Hey mate, how's Ash?"

"She's uhh… okay," he said with a quiet sigh.

"Okay," I said with a nod, even though he couldn't see it, "I'm here if you need to talk."

"Thanks man," he answered with the tone of a man who was trying his best to keep his shit together. "So, listen, the Delfontaine update is that Tails has agreed to fill in for Ash. I've got her booked for tomorrow morning."

"Awesome," I exclaimed with a fist pump, forgetting Sandrine was there to witness my undignified moment.

"But Beau is coming back as Lead Copywriter," Nath added quickly.

"What?"

"Gaz insisted and Peterson agreed," Nath said grimly. "He's due out there this afternoon."

"Fuck."

"Yeah," he agreed, "I haven't been able to warn Tails, so could you deal with that one?" He sounded like a broken man.

"Sure thing boss."

Nathan laughed exhaustedly. "You're the boss now Ritch. As of this moment, the Delfontaine reigns are officially yours." Little did he know exactly how accurate his words might be.

- KAT McPHERSON -

I dialled Nathan's number and paced the gardens again as I waited for him to pick up.

"Tails," Nathan said at the other end of the echoey line.

"Hey Nath, sorry about before, Mia was in need of a feed." I could hear background noise that sounded like he was driving. "Are you on the road?"

"Yeah, we're back on English soil and on our way to the beach house."

"Okay good. How's Ash?"

"She's fine, you're on speaker so you can chat to her if you like."

"Hey Kat," Ash said lifelessly.

"Oh my god Ash… I'm so sorry to hear what happened, are you alright?"

"I'll be fine, how are you going? How's Mia and Ryan?"

"We're all great, just concerned about you."

"That's sweet, but honestly I'm okay. Nathan's taking good care of me," she said quietly.

"You've got yourself a good man there."

"I sure do," she agreed. "Hey, thanks for covering for me in Paris."

"Of course, babe! It's not a problem. I'm actually quite excited to get my brain working again."

"How will you go being away from Mia for a few days?" Ash sounded so empty and hollow that I barely would have recognized her voice if I hadn't known it was her.

"I'll be perfectly fine," I said cheerfully, "besides it will be good for her and Ryan to have some time together."

"I'm sure it will."

"Umm… have you spoken to Ritch?" interjected Nath.

"No, why's that?" I asked curiously, as Sloane jogged into view.

"There's something that you need to know about Paris," he said solemnly.

"What's that?" I asked as Sloane grinned and waved at me.

"Kat, hey!" she called, making a B-line in my direction.

"Hey Sloane," I called, waving back as she ran towards me looking effortlessly beautiful. "Sorry Nath, I've got to go. I got your confirmation email with the train tickets, and I'm all set to head out at 11am tomorrow."

"But Tails…" Nathan argued as the popstar beamed at me like we were long lost friends.

"Just relax and take care of our girl Nath," I told him sternly, "Ritchie and I have Delfontaine covered."

"Cool but-"

"Ash, you rest up and make sure he does the same," I told her, ignoring Nathan's protests.

"Will do," agreed Ash with a half-hearted laugh.

"I love you guys."

"We love you too," Nath said.

"Give Mia a big kiss from me," Ash added.

"I will," I said with a nod, "see you when you get back." I hung up the phone just as Sloane threw herself at me for an enthusiastic hug. I laughed, feeling a little taken aback by her affection, but her smile was so infectious it was hard not to get swept up in her energy.

"Where's Mia?" she asked, draping her arm over my shoulder. For someone who'd just been for a run, she looked and smelled annoyingly fresh. I always looked like a sweaty beetroot after a workout.

"She's inside with Ryan," I said, nodding in the direction of the lounge room, "I had a few things to sort out, but I'm all done. Why don't you come and hang with us for a bit before Mia and I head off? We have some news and I'm pretty sure Ryan will want you to be the first to hear it."

"Sounds exciting, I'm in!"

- NATHAN STONE -

We drove to Cornwall predominantly in silence after Kat's phone call, so I flicked on the playlist that Ash had made for me back when I was in hospital.

"Is this my playlist?" she asked curiously.

"Yeah." I nodded my head with a smile, feeling a blush creep up my neck.

"Does that mean you liked it?"

"To be honest, I didn't get much further than 'Honey', because I had it on repeat for the entire time I was in the hospital."

"Really?"

"Of course. It's sexy as fuck," I said a little too honestly, given the circumstances. I cleared my throat and concentrated on the road, "that song kept me going Ash. It made me feel like you were spurring me on, and it gave me a reason to get better." Ash fell quiet and I hoped that I hadn't triggered her.

"I nearly didn't put that one on there," she said quietly.

"Why not?" I asked, peering at her quickly.

"It's pretty provocative," she answered with a blush, "I didn't want to be too... whatever."

"Are you forgetting that I was the man-whore of Artemis?"

"Well we'd only kissed once at that point, and you wanted to take it slow so... it felt like a gamble."

"Call my phone," I said, pointing to our phones that were sitting in the center console.

"What?"

"Call my phone," I repeated.

"Why?"

"Just call my phone Granger," I instructed her with a grin. She nodded and picked up her phone, giving me a curious sideways glance as she dialled my number. When she hit the green button, 'Honey' came blaring out of the car speakers.

"You made it my ringtone?" Ash asked with mild amusement. I was satisfied with 'mild amusement'. It was the closest she'd come to being her normal happy self since we'd left the hospital, so it was a step forward.

"I did indeed," I said unashamedly, "you'll forever be my honey." After that we descended back into silence. I quietly hummed along to the music and Ash dozed on and off with Fred's cage at her feet.

As the hours passed, I had to concentrate harder and harder on ignoring the excruciating pain that was wracking my entire body. My parkour efforts at Ashley's flat had wreaked all sorts of havoc in my healing bones, and sitting for so many hours had exacerbated it. My knee was crying out in agony and both hips were aching like I was an arthritic 80-year-old man.

There was a nice farm shop at the halfway mark, so I pulled off the motorway. Ash was still sleeping so I climbed quietly out of my stupidly small car, to stretch my damaged legs with a pained groan.

"Fuck," I whispered to myself, as pain flared through every inch of my battered body. After having a good stretch, I peered in the window to check on Ash. Deciding it was best not to wake her, I hobbled inside to take a slash and pick up some supplies.

Still groaning like an old man, I grabbed a basket and filled it to the brim with farm fresh produce. I was at the checkout about to pay, when I saw Ash dash through the door with panic-stricken eyes. She was trying to look calm, but I could see that she was anything but.

"Ash," I called, waving, worried that something bad had happened.

"Nath," she breathed with a huge sigh of relief. She plastered a fake smile on her face and joined me at the cash register.

"Is everything alright?" I asked, rubbing her arm gently. She flinched when I touched her, so I quickly pulled my hand away and focused on packing the shopping.

"Sorry," Ash said quietly when she realised what she'd done. Her stoic expression faltered slightly, and I could see unshed tears sparkling in her eyes.

"No need to apologise," I said, piling the last of the veges into a cardboard box. "I'm just worried about you. Are you okay?"

Ash swallowed hard and shook her head. "I'm as okay as I can be," she eventually replied. I paid the cashier and propped the over-flowing box under my arm.

"Sorry if I gave you a fright," I said quietly, as we left the shop. "I didn't want to wake you, but I needed a pee and we're going to need supplies once we get to the shack. I haven't been there for about six months so the cupboards are bare."

"It's fine. I'm fine," she said with an unconvincing smile.

"Did you need a coffee, or a pee or anything?"

"Yeah, I might run to the loo."

"Do you want me to wait?"

"No, probably best we don't leave Fred alone for too long."

"True," I agreed dubiously. "Will you be alright on your own?"

"I'll be fine," Ash said, squeezing my arm. "Thank you."

I watched her walk to the bathroom and, once I was satisfied that she was safe, I headed back out to the car. I shoved the box of food into my tiny boot and joined Freddie in the car.

"How you going chubs?" I asked Fred, peering down at my fat cat in her cage. She looked up at me and rubbed her head against the cage, so I stuck my fingers through the gate to give her a pat. "What do I do Freddie? I have no idea how to help your mum."

- RITCHIE CARLTON -

I was dubious, to say the least, about working alongside Beau Peterson after everything that had happened between him, Kat and Ryan; but he was our only option. I would have to play nice whether I liked it or not because the account was depending on him.

Nathan had booked the poor bloke on a cattle class ticket, and rather than pre-ordering him a town car, he had left Beau to fend for himself with the local public transport system. By the time the guy arrived at Delfontaine headquarters, he looked like he'd been hogtied and dragged through the bush backwards.

"Peterson," I said with a stiff nod, as he all-but stumbled into the reception foyer.

"Carlton," he replied in his smarmy Yankee accent.

"How was the trip?" I asked as if I didn't already know the answer. I was being a dipshit, but it was the last chance I'd have to make his life a misery, so I was making the most of it.

"Fabulous," he said sarcastically, "I was wedged between a window and a fat lady, so it was a most pleasurable journey," he added, massaging his neck. "The metro was also a five-star experience, but I suspect that was all part of the plan, wasn't it?"

"You can dispense with the hostility mate," I said calmly, taking control of the situation, yet also deliberately avoiding his question. "Regardless of what's happened in the past, we're working on the same team now, so we're gonna have to be on the same page."

Beau nodded slowly, cautious of my olive branch. "Fine," he agreed eventually.

"And Kat is going to be here tomorrow. She's filling in while Ash is away, so you'll have to build a bridge there too."

"Kat's going to be here? Nathan didn't mention that."

"I know," I said, unable to hide a grin, "he figured you wouldn't come if you knew."

"Fucking fantastic," he said with a grimace. "This should be super fun."

"It'll be great," I said jovially, slapping him on the back. "Look Peterson, I know it's been a tense few months, but the agency can't afford for us to fuck this up, so we're gonna have to put aside our personal shit."

"Sounds good to me," he agreed, eyeing me suspiciously, as if he was expecting me to smoosh a cream pie into his face or something.

"Truce?" I stuck my hand out towards him. He looked warily at my outstretched hand for a moment before grasping it.

"Truce," he agreed as we shook hands.

"Ripper," I said, squeezing his hand firmly, "and same goes with Tails."

"Yeah, fine," he said, attempting to extract his hand from my firm grasp.

"I need to make myself very clear," I said, as I gripped his hand and pulled him towards me, "if you hurt or upset her in any way at all… I'll make Ryan's attack seem like a walk in the park."

Beau's jaw dropped and he tried to pull away from me. "Are you threatening me Carlton?"

"I sure as hell am," I confirmed unashamedly. "Tails is like my little sister, so if anything happens to her, I take it very personally."

"Nothing is going to happen to her."

"Good," I said chirpily, releasing his hand so he almost toppled backwards, "it looks like we're on the same page then."

"Yeah," he muttered, rubbing his hand with a veiled wince.

"Sandrine is… tied up, this afternoon," I said, unable to hold back a subtle smirk. "You'll meet her tomorrow when Tails arrives. I've scheduled in some team briefing time while Cody catches you up on everything."

"Well, not everything," joked Cody as he joined us in the lobby. He patted Beau affectionately on the back. "There are a few things that I probably don't need to mention," he added with a wink.

"Yeah, I'd be pretty happy not to hear about your antics with the French men," agreed Beau, shaking Cody's hand, before the two of them went in for a hug.

"Hey man," said Cody, slapping Beau on the back affectionately.

"Hey Codes, it's good to see a friendly face here," said Peterson, shooting me a look of distrust over Cody's shoulder.

"I'll grab your suitcase," offered Cody gallantly, as he released Beau from his man-hug. He took the handle of the wheelie case and threw his other arm over Beau's shoulder. "Let me show you to our office," he said, gallantly ushering Beau out of the reception area.

I rubbed my bald head and chuckled to myself. "This is exactly why everyone thought you were gay," I mumbled under my breath as I followed along behind the two lovebirds.

- NATHAN STONE -

The Cornish countryside zoomed past us and, eventually, we rolled down the gravel driveway to my little beach shack. I'd never invited anyone to the beach house before. Not even Ryan. It was my escape from the real world; my own personal zen-den. A hundred percent me, with no frills and nothing for show. Just a private little chill-out zone where I could surf, read and escape the rat race. Ashley, who'd dozed off again, stirred as the car drew to a stop.

"Hey sleepy head," I teased quietly, as she looked around to get her bearings.

"Are we here?" she asked tiredly, rubbing her bloodshot eyes.

"Welcome to my humble abode," I joked nervously, as I switched off the ignition.

"It's beautiful Nath. When you said it was a shack, I was expecting something a lot more basic."

"Well, it's not exactly the height of sophistication," I answered with a shrug. I climbed agonizingly out of the sports car, trying not to wince in pain. Ash stood and closed her eyes, breathing in the fresh air.

"I've missed the salt air," she said wistfully, "I haven't seen the ocean since I got back from Bali."

I unlocked the house and she followed me in, carrying Fred in her cage. The shack certainly wasn't up to my usual luxury standard, but I liked it.

"Sorry, it's not very fancy," I apologised, feeling self-conscious about the level of comfort to which she might have been expecting.

"Don't apologize, it's gorgeous," she said, letting Fred out of her cage. Ash patted the fat cat on her head and then wandered through to the living room.

I seized the moment to rub my aching hips, and Fred wound herself lovingly around my legs, almost as if she could sense the pain I was feeling. If I'd been able to bend over without groaning, I would have picked her up for a cuddle. I watched Ash as she stopped and stared at the table in the corner of the room where my pink salt lamp was sitting.

"You have a Himalayan Salt lamp?" she asked with an expression that somewhat resembled a smile. I cringed with embarrassment that she'd noticed my girly choice of lighting.

"Yeah," I shrugged self-consciously, "it's supposed to keep away negative energy or something. I bought it at the local markets."

Her eyes held mine and I searched the dull green pools to see if there was still a sparkle hidden in them somewhere. For a moment I saw a glimmer of the real Ash, but then it faded. I shoved my hands into my pockets and forced a smile to my face.

"How are your legs after that drive?" she asked with concern.

"The drive was fine," I said casually. She narrowed her eyes skeptically.

"Like I said on the train Nathan, I can tell when you're fibbing."
I smiled and nodded my head.

"Yeah, I'm pretty sore," I confessed, "but I think it was my superhero antics at your flat that did the damage, not the drive."

"Nathan," she said disapprovingly.

"It was extenuating circumstances," I said defensively.

"Okay, I'll give you that one," she agreed sadly. "Would you like a massage?" Despite the fact that it was an innocent offer, my brain went straight to the gutter as I envisioned her rubbing oil into my bruised hips.

"No thanks, I'm fine. I should unload the car," I blurted, hurriedly turning for the door as I abandoned my indecent thoughts.

"Okay, I'll help," she said, following me outside. We offloaded the food first, then grabbed our bags before I showed Ash the rest of the house.

"The master bedroom is just through here," I told her, guiding her down the hallway to our room. It was my favourite room in the house, with large French doors that over-looked the ocean, showcasing the blue sky.

"It's so beautiful," Ash said, plonking her bag on the bed so she could look out the window. With her hands wrapped around herself, she gazed out at the sparkling sea below. "Nathan, this place is magical."

"Yeah, I love it," I said, shoving my hands into my pockets again. It was the only thing I could do to stop myself from accidentally touching her. "I always come down here when I need to think."

Ash turned to face me. "Thanks for this. I really appreciate you bringing me down here."

"It's my pleasure. We both needed to get away," I said with a shrug. Ash was going through this super heavy thing and there was nothing I could do to lighten the load for her. "There's no pressure, okay? You don't have to talk, or even acknowledge me if you don't feel like it. This your recovery zone so just do whatever you need to do, and I'll be here whenever you need me."

Ash smiled faintly, "I love you Nath."

My heart flipped and landed in my stomach.

"I love you too," I said as a wave of relief washed over me. She smiled and tried to hide a yawn.

"I know I slept most of the way here but I'm really tired."

"Okay, I'll let you rest," I said, turning to leave.

"Actually… would you mind staying?" she asked quietly.

"Of course not."

"Thanks," she said, taking another look out the window before kicking off her shoes. I followed suit and sat down on the bed cautiously, moving slowly as if she was a flighty deer. It was probably unnecessary, but I'd never dealt with someone recovering from a sexual assault before, and I didn't want to risk triggering her. I needed to get some professional advice. Was I supposed to encourage her to talk about it, or was it better not to mention it at all? What was the etiquette for that sort of thing?

I made myself comfortable on top of the covers while Ash crawled into the other side of the bed. She snuggled down into the feather duvet and pulled it right up to her chin. Had she been on full-form we undoubtedly would have had some sort of rhetoric on the ethical quandaries of Duck Down, but we didn't. She just cocooned herself in my morally questionable quilt and closed her eyes.

I crossed my ankles and leaned back against the sturdy beechwood headboard, unsure what to do with myself. I peered down at Ash and, as if sensing my gaze, she reached out from underneath the duvet and rested her fingers inside my palm. I closed my hand lightly, softly encasing hers inside it, and then breathed a quiet sigh. We were so close, yet so far away.

- ASHLEY GRANGER -

I felt like a zombie. Something inside me had broken and I couldn't put it back together again. I could barely talk, barely keep my eyes open, and barely even think. It was like I was floating above myself watching my body go through the motions, while my soul hovered in the clouds. I was detached from myself, from Nathan… from the world. The worst part was that I didn't know how to come back. My spirit had fled my body, so I was trapped in this shell of a human being, unable participate in life.

The light touch of Nathans hand around mine was the only thing tying me to reality. Nothing else felt real. Warm tears escaped from behind my closed lids and rolled sideways down my cheeks. How would I ever come back from this? How would Nathan ever love me again once he heard the details of Dom's attack?

I squeezed my eyes tight and tried to push away the memories, but I couldn't. Nothing would ever undo what had happened. It had been stupid for me to think that I could carry on as usual. I should have listened to Nathan and not gone to Paris, but I honestly thought I'd be okay.

In my defense, I had managed to hold it together incredibly well for a whole day. I'd kept the smile on my face, I'd talked shop and I'd even socialized. In fact, I'd been fine right up until the point I got that fucking text from Jock.

His message had come through just as I was about to get in the shower. All it had said was, "I've let you down. I'm so sorry."

I had no idea how he'd heard about the attack, but his message had been enough to push me over the edge. As I'd climbed into the shower, something inside me had snapped and I was gone. The sobs had erupted from me and I'd had no strength left to fight them.

From that point on, I knew that the woman formerly known as Ashley Granger, would never be the same again.

- RYAN McPHERSON -

The hospital administrator gave me keys for the storeroom so that I could grab some things to prepare for Mia's arrival. Apparently, it was common for them to have babies staying at The Lodge, so none of the staff seemed to find it unusual that Mia would be joining us for a few days.

"There's a bouncer down here," called Sloane from the other side of the stuffy, cluttered storeroom. "And a play-mat thingy."

"Awesome," I grunted, trying to dislodge the port-a-cot from underneath a pile of boxes.

"All good there?" she teased, appearing behind me with the mat and bouncer in her arms.

"This fucking thing doesn't want to come out," I grumbled, tugging on it again and nearly sending the whole pile tumbling down on top of us.

"Whoa," said Rodney, as he walked past with impeccable timing. He quickly ducked inside the door and held up the boxes to prevent the avalanche.

"Thanks Rod," breathed Sloane, who was face-to-chest with Rodney as he stood with his arms over her head, propping up the unstable pile of boxes that had been about to collapse on top of her. "That was perfect timing. I'd hate to die from being crushed by a mountain of dusty old crap."

Rodney looked down at her with a blush, as he finished steadying the tower. He stepped back and shrugged modestly, and modest wasn't a word that one wouldn't normally use to describe Rodney.

"It was nothing," he said, brushing some dust off the front of his shirt. "Do you need a hand McPherson?"

"Yeah, that'd be great," I said appreciatively, surprised that he'd actually called me by my surname rather than 'rich boy'. Sloane fell uncharacteristically quiet while Rodney helped me extract the trapped porta cot. "Cheers man, you're a lifesaver," I told him gratefully.

"Literally," said Sloane, smiling bashfully at Rodney. And bashful wasn't normally a word I'd use to describe our little popstar princess either. What was going on with those two today?

"No worries," said Rod, taking stock of our haul. "What are you guys doing with a bunch of baby stuff anyway?"

I opened my mouth to respond but Sloane beat me to it.

"Ryan's daughter is staying for a few days."

"Really? Why's that?"

"His wife has to go on a work trip," Sloane said, as the two continued to discuss me as if I wasn't standing within hearing distance.

"Oh cool. Glad I packed my earplugs," joked Rodney, causing Sloane to giggle like a five-year-old girl. I watched the scene unfold, unable to tear my eyes away. It was like watching a slow-motion car crash.

"I never realised you were funny Rod," Sloane said, hitting him playfully on the chest, "why have you been hiding that sense of humour?"

I cleared my throat loudly, needing to end the pain. "I think we've got everything," I said, trying to maneuver around the pair, who were blocking the only exit.

"Oh, yeah," said Sloane, with a blush. "You wanna come help us set up Mia's stuff?" she asked Rod.

My jaw dropped and I stared at her, open-mouthed, in shock. I couldn't believe that Sloane was voluntarily offering her company to the man she usually referred to as 'CockRod'.

- RITCHIE CARLTON -

Once Cody was pre-occupied with giving Peterson the full tour, I slipped down to the garage, for which Sandrine had given me a security access tag. I ducked through the underground passage and into the secret entrance to her residence. I did have to wonder why she would possibly need such an elaborate set up, but with Sandrine, it was best not to ask questions. I popped my head out the door to check that the coast was clear, and then snuck upstairs to the master bedroom.

I closed the door behind me and turned to see Sandrine still lying naked, spread-eagled on the bed, exactly as I'd left her. Her wrists and ankles were bound to the bed posts with red silk rope, and she looked exceptionally pleased to see me.

"I've been waiting very patiently," she said with a saucy smile.

"So I can see," I said like a school teacher. "You've been a very good girl, and good girls deserve rewards," I told her, kneeling on the side of the bed, with my pants still on. I eyed her naked flesh. She was such a perfect specimen of the female figure that it was hard to believe she was in her fifties.

"What will be my reward?" she asked breathlessly as I let my fingers trail over her body.

"I'm still deciding," I said wickedly, enjoying torturing her. "Maybe I'll start here," I pondered, running my fingertip over her already hard nipples. She moaned quietly and wriggled against her restraints. I grinned and took my hand away. "But maybe not."

"You're teasing me Richard," she said, almost approvingly.

"Am I?" I asked with feigned innocence. "Do you like it?"

"Oui," she nodded and bit her lip as I ran my hands up her thighs, stopping right at the point she wanted me to touch most. She arched her hips as best she could with her ankles tied, and moaned achingly when I left her waiting. "Please," she begged breathlessly. I smiled devilishly and stood up from the bed, watching her intently as I walked towards the door. "No," she said, with panic, thinking that I was about to leave.

"You want me to stay?" I teased.

"Yes," she said desperately.

"Then you'll need to convince me," I said arrogantly, beginning to feel very at home in my new Alpha Male role. "I want you to beg for me Sandrine."

"Please," she whimpered, "I need you, Richard."

"You need me to do what?" I asked mockingly.

"I need you to fuck me."

"Hmmm…" I said, drawing it out for as long as humanly possible. I was very much enjoying our little game, partly because it was fun to watch her squirm, but mostly because it was payback for kidnapping my best friend.

"I want you inside me now," she begged. I pretended to think on it for a moment as I watched her writhing in desperation.

"Okay," I agreed. I grabbed the back of my shirt and pulled it up over my head, not bothering to unbutton it, then very slowly stripped off my pants for maximum torture points, "but I'm not untying you."

"What?" she asked with slight concern. I ignored her question and climbed on top of her.

"This was your idea Sandrine," I reminded her firmly, as I wedged myself between her thighs. "You wanted to me to take control so that's what I'm doing," I said, then immediately began to fuck her as hard as humanly possible. After several days and nights together, I knew Sandrine liked it hard and fast, but this time I could feel a difference in myself. There was anger behind my ferocious pounding as if every push, purged more of my suppressed rage. It wasn't really Sandrine that

I was pissed at, but since she was an eager participant I felt no guilt. Sandrine moaned loudly and raised her hips to match my movements. I could tell that she wanted to touch me, but I wasn't having it. "No," I barked, as she attempted to wriggle one of her hands out of the rope.

"But-" she said, before I silenced her with a fierce kiss. I pinned both her wrists down and continued my angry thrusting. Sandrine dropped her head against the pillow and let out a breathless cry. I felt her body begin to tighten around me so I moved faster, dripping with sweat and puffing with exertion. I was determined to make us both come hard. It wasn't long before she was crying out in ecstasy so, with a growl, I let myself go. Once I was done, I rolled off her.

"Phew," I breathed, lying back against the bed with my head resting on her secured arm.

"See Richard," she panted breathlessly, "we would have so much fun here together."

I sat up and let my eyes wander over her body as she laid spread-eagled, sweaty and spent.

"Sandrine, I've got a woman waiting for me in London," I blurted, feeling a bit guilty that I'd let things get this far without mentioning my arrangement with Amy. "Actually, I'm not sure if she is waiting for me," I admitted, "but I'm in love with her."

"Oh, I see," she said in an eerily cheery tone. "She must be very special to capture your heart."

"Yeah, she's pretty amazing."

"And what's her name, this amazing woman?"

"Amy. Amy Vaughn." I said, climbing off the bed and pulling my pants back on. "She works at Artemis too. In fact she's actually the Art Director on your account."

"Hmmm…" Sandrine's face gave nothing away as she watched me get dressed. "And she's the woman you plan to settle down and have children with?"

"If she'll let me."

"Okay," she nodded, seemingly appeased by my answer, "I can't begrudge you your dream Richard, but please don't say no yet. Take some time to think it over."

"Fine," I agreed, sitting down on the armchair to put my shoes on.

"I'll hold Didier's position until November just in case you change your mind."

"If that pleases you," I said, with a resigned sigh.

"It does."

I nodded and rose from the chair, strutting over to the bed. I bent down with my face close to hers and took hold of the red silk rope on her right wrist.

"Then I'll think on it," I told her, with my lips only inches from hers. I smiled and pulled the rope so that it tightened around her wrist. Sandrine gasped and her eyes flashed with surprised desire. I repeated the action on her left wrist rope and finally let my lips brush hers. "But for now, you can lie here and think about how you would make it worth my while."

- NATHAN STONE -

I sat in my old cane rocking chair, with a large glass of whiskey in hand, listening to the sound of the waves crashing against the shore outside in the darkness. It was past midnight, but I was wide awake. I took a sip of the amber nectar and leaned my head back against the chair as I rocked slowly back and forth, reflecting on the events of the last few days. When had my life gotten so out of control? Up until the day my Dearest Ashley had literally stumbled her way into my life, my whole world had been well ordered and meticulously designed to ensure that I was always holding tight to the reigns. I'd had a plan and I'd always stuck to it; Build up and take over Artemis Advertising. Everything I'd done before that fateful moment in front of the taxi, had been strategically engineered to propel me forward towards professional triumph. Yet I felt no sense of loss for the life I'd left behind. I'd never needed anyone until I met Ash and now that I had a taste of love, I never wanted to let it go. I would have given up everything to take away Ashley's pain. In fact, I would have gladly given my own life if I thought that it would help her in any way.

My illusive girlfriend was, at that moment, sleeping soundly in my bed, where she'd been snuggled up since we'd first arrived at the shack. I'd taken her dinner, but she'd refused to eat it. She was probably exhausted from the trauma and needed to sleep it off. Ashley was going through some heavy emotions and there was no easy fix for that. Her healing wasn't a problem I could solve. Despite that fact, I had deep desire to do something to help her, but I had no clue what. How was I supposed to take care of Ash if she wouldn't even wake up long enough to eat a meal?

I sipped my drink and glanced down at our phones sitting side-by-side on the coffee table. They'd both been buzzing constantly since we'd left Paris, so it was a nice change to see them lifeless and silent.

I swapped my drink for my phone and scrolled through the long list of messages. Ritchie, Gaz, Geoff, Amy, Kat, Beau, Ritchie again, but the name I most wanted to see was the only name that didn't appear. I knew it was dumb, and that Ryan didn't have access to technology in rehab, but I needed my best mate. Ryan would have known exactly what to do. This was his kind of thing. He was the one who usually pulled everything back together. If he'd been there, he no doubt would have had some sage words of wisdom to make me feel like I wasn't a total failure as a boyfriend.

I popped my phone in my lap and took a huge swig of my whiskey as I tried to channel my inner Ryan. What would he have told me to do if he'd been there? I peered at my phone as the answer became perfectly clear. Maybe I didn't know how to deal with the situation, but someone somewhere on earth did. I picked up my phone and consulted Doctor Google. My first search was 'how to support a partner after sexual abuse'. That seemed like a reasonable place to start. I read through pages and pages of case studies, general advice and medical articles on sexual trauma and how to support a rape survivor. I tunneled down the rabbit hole for several hours, and despite all the research I'd done, I still failed to find something that adequately addressed our particular situation. Ash wasn't only recovering from Dom's attack, she was also purging an entire decade of torture and abuse, along with bearing the burden of killing a man (albeit a shitty man), and none of the journals or blogs covered that.

- KAT McPHERSON -

I woke up at dawn with one arm wrapped around Mia, who had fallen asleep on my chest. My bladder was protesting, so I carefully returned Mia to her cot. I loved that little midget, but boy did she know how to drain my energy! I went for a pee and wandered out to the lounge room with the intention of watching a movie until breakfast since there was very little chance that I'd get back to sleep.

I grabbed the remote and turned to sit on the couch but was hit with a vivid flashback of my sexcapade with Beau.

"Ugh," I groaned with self-hate, "goddamn it Katherine, you've tainted the couch." I paced the room for a few minutes, ready for a rest but unable to place my butt on the sofa of shame. I stopped pacing and stared at my new nemesis. "Sorry sofa, but you have to go." I told it very politely as I plonked my tired bottom into Ryan's old leather armchair and pulled out my phone to list my traitorous piece of furniture on Marketplace.

I took a couple of pictures and then posted the ad, before scouring the internet for a replacement. I'd narrowed my selection down to a fairly long short-list and flicked on a movie as I pondered my forthcoming trip. Was I doing the right thing going back to work so soon? Should I have been leaving my newborn at a rehab centre? And what if I wasn't good at my job anymore? What if I let down the whole team? Then I'd be a bad employee as well as a bad mum.

By the time Mia and I pulled up at The Lodge, my stomach was churning with anxiety. I couldn't believe that in a few hours, we would be on different continents. Perhaps I should have said no to France. What if something happened to her and I was a two-hour train ride away?

"Maybe I should call Ritchie and cancel," I told Mia as I loaded her into the pram. She stared up at me happily with her big, chocolatey eyes. "Oh, stop looking so cute," I grumbled, pushing her towards the building. Ryan bounded out the doors before I'd even made it inside.

"Here's my gorgeous girls!" he called excitedly, picking me up and spinning me around. I gripped his shoulders tightly and laughed.

"You're in a good mood Mr McPherson," I said when he gently put me back down.

"Of course I am!" he said happily. "I get to spend two whole days with my daughter." Ryan helped me navigate the pram through the door and played with Mia while I signed in.

"Am I doing the right thing Ryan?" I asked, peering down at Mia as she laughed at his antics.

"I know this is hard, but it will be fine babe, I promise," said Ryan, taking the overnight bag off my shoulder.

"Yeah, it will be great," I agreed in an attempt to convince myself more than him. "I've got six bottles of breast milk in there," I said, pointing at the cooler bag stashed under the pram, "and a tin of formula in the nappy bag."

"Got it," he said with a confident smile. He threw one arm over my shoulder and gripped the pram with the other, then led us through to the lounge area. There were a couple of people sitting around, one of them was an old lady, who grinned ecstatically when she caught sight of us.

"Ah, this must be Kat," she said, standing up to greet us.

"Sure is," Ryan confirmed, "Kat, this is my friend Angelica."

"Lovely to meet you," I said, shaking her surprisingly strong hand.

"We've heard so much about you love," she replied with a welcoming smile, "it's great to finally meet you."

"Oh," I said, feeling a little embarrassed about what they might have heard about me.

"I'll put this in the kitchen for you love," said Angelica, taking the cooler bag from Ryan, as he pulled it out from underneath the pram.

"Thanks Angelica," Ryan said with an affectionate smile. It was lovely to see that he'd made some genuine connections during his time at The Lodge.

"She naps at-" I began to say when Ryan cut me off.

"Eleven and three," he said, proudly finishing my sentence. "Then down to sleep at eight, with a feed at eleven PM."

"Wow," I said, stunned that he'd already taken it all in.

"I've been listening and watching babe."

My heart melted. "I love you," I said, kissing him softly. Ryan leaned into me and wrapped his arms around my waist.

"Oi, oi!" cheered a handsome young guy who looked vaguely familiar. "None of that in here thanks," he said, punching Ryan on the shoulder.

"Thanks Rodney," Ryan said, rolling his eyes as he peeled himself away from me.

"Rodney?" I said stunned, as I realised who the guy was.

"And you must be Kat," he said, extending his hand.

"Yeah," I answered, shaking his outstretched hand as I cast Ryan a questioning glance.

"We've heard a lot about you, but he never mentioned how hot you are," Rodney said with a cheeky wink.

"Okay, that's enough out of you," said Ryan, elbowing Rodney away from me. "How about you go find Sloane for me?"

"Fine," said Rodney, "but before I go, I'd just like to remind you of the abstinence rule," he joked as he headed back out the door he'd just come in. Ryan and I both laughed and glanced bashfully at each other.

"So that's quite a turn-around," I said once Rodney had vacated the room.

"Yeah," Ryan said with a smile, "we're besties now. Didn't I tell you that?"

"No, I guess it slipped your mind with all the drama."

"Must have."

Within minutes, Rodney returned with an over-excited Sloane, who skipped through the door ahead of him.

"Hey Kat!" Sloane called as she frolicked excitedly towards me.

"Hi Sloane," I said with a smile that belied my anxiety.

"Excited?" she asked, giving me a hug.

"Yes and no," I answered honestly, as Ryan pulled Mia out of the pram and cuddled her gently against his chest. "Mia and I have never been apart, and soon we'll be in different countries."

"Not if you keep hanging around here," joked Ryan, showing me his watch. "You need to get going babe, or you'll miss the train."

I looked at Mia curled up in Ryan's strong arms. My chest tightened and I felt tears welling in my eyes.

"I can't leave her," I said, choking back the lump in my throat. Ryan's face softened with compassion, and he shuffled Mia around so that he could give me a one-armed hug.

"I've got this covered," he said, kissing the top of my head. "Mia will be fine, won't you Mia?"

"It's not Mia I'm worried about," I said glumly.

"You'll be fine too Mrs McPherson. In fact, you'll be more than fine. You'll be amazing," Ryan assured me.

"What if I'm not good at this anymore?"

"Babe, you're a phenomenal Creative Director. You're going to blow them all away."

"You're just saying that to get rid of me," I said with a sulky smile.

"Hey, if it was up to me, I'd lock you both in here with me until I leave, but you need to do this for yourself."

"When did you get so wise?"

"He didn't," piped up Rodney with a teasing grin, "he's just repeating what Byron said."

- RYAN McPHERSON -

I had to laugh at Rodney's banter. The guy had really lightened up over the last few days.

"I can't argue with that," I said, before turning my attention back to my stressed wife. "Babe, you're going to miss your train if you don't leave now."

"I know," she said, with tears sparkling in her eyes, "It's just so hard to leave her."

"I get it," I said, wiping a rogue tear off her cheek before it ruined her make-up. "Let's try a clean break." I suggested, turning to wave Sloane over. "Sloane, can you take Mia please?"

"Sure thing," she said, bouncing over.

"Now, mummy... give your daughter a kiss goodbye."

Kat nodded and bent down to plant a loving kiss on Mia's head.

"I'll see you in a few days beautiful girl," she said, running her hand softly down Mia's cheek.

"Well done," I said, planting a kiss on Kat's lips before handing Mia over to Sloane, who looked like she was about to burst with excitement. "Now, let me walk you out, while Sloane takes Mia for a play outside."

"Okay," she agreed reluctantly, keeping her eyes firmly trained on Mia.

"We'll be fine," I told her calmly as I guided her out of the living room.

"I know," Kat said tearily, "but I'm going to miss her."

I stopped walking and wrapped my arms around her.

"I know this is hard, but this is something you have to do for yourself. You're the strongest woman I know and I'm so proud of you for taking this opportunity."

Kat sniffed and looked up at me with smudgy make-up. "You are? You don't think I'm being a bad mum?"

"Of course not! You're an amazing Mum Kat, and by doing this, you're showing Mia that it's important to follow her dreams, no matter how hard it might be."

"Thank you."

I gave her a squeeze and then grabbed a tissue off the reception desk so I could tidy up her face.

"No need to thank me, it's all true." I dabbed the final splotch of mascara from under her eye and gave her a kiss. "You've got this babe. Now go kick some French butt." Kat nodded, hugged me, and then turned towards the door. She stopped at the threshold and turned back to me with a look of uncertainty. I smiled and gave her a reassuring nod. "You've got this," I told her confidently. "I love you."

"I love you too," she said with a nervous smile, before stepping through the door. I stood and watched her get in the car and, once she'd finally pulled away, I wandered back into the lounge room to see Rodney and Sloane huddled over Mia, who was playing happily on her play mat, which they'd set up on the floor.

"Do you honestly think we can do this?" Asked Rodney, as they stared at Mia.

"Of course, we can!" said Sloane confidently. "Angelica raised three of these, as well as nine grandchildren, I'm pretty sure we can handle looking after one little baby for a few days." I stood and watched the pair with amusement as they cooed and fawned over my daughter. Rodney stopped playing with Mia and sniffed the air at the same time as Sloane wrinkled her nose. "Phew, did you fart Rodney?" teased Sloane waving her hand in front of her face.

"No," he said defensively, "don't blame that stink on me. That's the kid. Maybe you should change her."

"What, just because I'm a woman, I'm the one who has to change the nappies?"

"Yeah," said Rodney with a shrug, "it's not exactly a man's job is it?"

"No, it's a parent's job," I said with a grin, stepping in to save them. "I've got this," I added, carefully lifting Mia off her play mat.

"Well thank fuck for that," joked Rodney with a sigh of relief, "I thought she was gonna make me clean up shit for a minute there," he said, nodding towards Sloane. I bounced Mia on my chest and laughed at the thought of anyone making Rodney do anything he didn't want to.

"You're such a baby," teased Sloane, "do you need Ryan to change your nappy while he's at it?"

"Fuck off," Rodney said with a smile on his face. I glanced at Sloane, and she was smiling too.

"You sure?" she prodded, "I bet Ryan would be very gentle with your cherries."

"Eww, there's no way I'd let that prick get anywhere near my cherries," said Rodney with mock disgust, "but I'd let you wipe my cherries any time you like popstar," he added with a cheeky wink in her direction. I expected Sloane to lose her shit at that point, but instead she giggled loudly, in a way that I'd never heard her laugh before.

"You wouldn't be able to afford my wiping services Rodney. I'm very expensive."

"I'm sure I'd find a way to cover it."

"Oookay," I said, deciding to put an end to their weird flirting before my breakfast made a reappearance, "I think that's probably all that I can handle of that," I said, riffling through the nappy bag for fresh supplies.

"Of what?" Asked Rodney, completely oblivious to how uncomfortable that moment had been to witness.

"Nothing," I said, shaking my head with a laugh. "I think I liked it better when they were fighting," I muttered quietly to Mia.

- KAT McPHERSON -

I was flabbergasted at the sheer size and opulence of Delfontaine Headquarters. Apparently, the precinct also accommodated Sandrine's home, but it was impossible to see any other buildings amidst the army of flat-topped Platane trees that guarded the commercial section of the estate.

The driver pulled up at the front of the steps and escorted me into the main reception area, where Ritchie was leaning against the tall desk, chatting to the receptionist as if they'd known each other for years.

"Tails," he called happily as he spotted me out of the corner of his eye. He muttered something to the receptionist and then came over to give me an enthusiastic hug. "How was your trip?"

"It was great," I said, excited to see him, "first-class was amazing."

"Our little treat to say thanks," he said with a wink as he took my suitcase from the driver and asked the receptionist to put it behind the desk. "We're so grateful that you've agreed to come back."

"Who's 'we'?" I asked, wondering whether he was just using the royal 'we' to sound more important.

"Nathan, Gaz and I," he said with a shrug, looking more like the old Ritchie, "and Sandrine."

"Oh," I replied with a nod. When had Sandrine become part of the 'we'?

"Has Nath filled you in?" he asked, guiding me out of the reception area and down a lavish corridor lined with gilt-framed mirrors.

"Yeah, as much as he could. I think I've got a good idea of what Ashley had in mind."

"I actually meant about their situ," Ritch said quietly, "but I'm glad he's covered off the work stuff too."

"Oh. Yeah, he did." I nodded solemnly. "Ash didn't sound too great to be honest."

"She definitely wasn't herself," he agreed with a concerned nod, "but Stoner seems to have it under control."

"And you seem to have everything under control at this end," I said, taking stock of this new, super confident version of Ritchie. He'd always been a confident guy, but this was different. It was as if he'd finally found himself. "You look like you're pretty comfortable here,"

"Yeah, I've got to admit Tails," he said mysteriously, as if he were about to reveal a huge secret, "I don't hate it here."

I laughed. "Well, that-" I said, interrupting myself with a shocked gasp when I turned a corner and came face-to-face with my ex-lover. "Beau!" I blurted awkwardly. The last time I'd seen him, he'd threatened me with a restraining order. "I'm sorry," I apologised quickly, at the memory of our last encounter, "I didn't know you were going to be here."

"It's okay," he said, with kindness in his eyes, "Ritchie told me you were coming."

I breathed a subtle sigh of relief as Ritchie beckoned Cody over to join us.

"Right people, let's get this show on the road," Ritchie said in his usual loud manner, except this time, he had a very professional and polished demeanor that I'd never seen in him before. He seemed to be taking to his new leadership role like a duck to water. So much so, in fact, that Nathan could be up for some stiff competition when he returned. "Cody, if you could show Beau and Tails to the board room, I'll let the Frenchies know we're here."

And there was that rough Aussie boy that I knew and loved.

Cody rolled his eyes and groaned, "Ritchie, how many times do I have to tell you not to call them Frenchies?"

"Probably another few thousand," Ritchie teased with a wink.

"I guess I should just be happy that you're not calling them frogs anymore."

"Exactly. Now stop dilly-dallying Codes and put the minions to work." Ritchie laughed jovially at his own joke as he strutted off down the big corridor to wherever the Delfontaine team were residing. He looked so comfortable in this setting that anyone would be excused for thinking that he owned the building.

"Welcome to life with Boss Ritchie," Cody quipped, with a game show style hand gesture, as we all watched the big, bald Aussie stride out of sight. "Follow me guys," he said, heading the other direction down the corridor.

"So, are we okay?" I whispered to Beau nervously, as we trailed along behind Cody, who was waving and chatting in French to every person we passed.

"Yeah," Beau nodded, but didn't look at me. "It's only a few weeks, so let's just push it aside and call it water under the bridge for now.

"For now?"

"That's the best I can do Kat."

"Okay," I agreed sadly. At least we weren't going to have an all-out brawl in front of our client.

"How was the train ride?"

"Pretty great! I've never traveled first class before."

Beau stopped walking and stared at me wide-eyed. "You got a first-class ticket?!"

"Didn't you?"

"No," he said sulkily, "I was slumming it in economy."

"Oh no," I said, trying to swallow back a smile. I wasn't sure whether it had been Ritchie or Nathan who'd been responsible for that little prank, or perhaps both of them in co-hoots, but it was sweet that they still had my back.

"Here's the boardroom," Cody said a little further up ahead, "Ah Sandrine," he greeted the unseen person nervously, as he stepped through the door.

"Bonjour Cody," said a sickly sweet voice with a smooth French accent. Her tone sent shivers up my spine.

"This is the rest of our team," we heard Cody say, before a short silence. "Err…" he stuck his head out of the door and desperately waved us in, "come on team, let's not keep Sandrine waiting."

Beau and I hot-footed it inside, where we were greeted with the sight of a well-preened, fifty-something woman who looked like a black-widow spider waiting patiently for her prey. Her tightly fitted black dress and six inch black Louboutins did nothing to dispel that very vivid comparison.

"Bonjour," she said, slinking forward to shake Beau's hand, as if she hadn't even seen me standing there.

"Bonjour Mademoiselle Delfontaine," said Beau with a childish grin, "je m'appelle Beau."

Sandrine let out a throaty laugh and tapped Beau on the shoulder.

"Oh, you flatter me, young man," she said with approval. "Where have they been hiding you?"

"In London," Beau said, his accent sounding uber-American, "they keep me locked away and only bring me out for special clients," he told her with a wink. The whole thing was so sickening I thought I was going to vomit. I'd never seen Beau flirt like that with anyone, so I had to wonder whether he was doing it purely for my benefit.

"Well, I have to say that Artemis seem to have very high standards," said the huntress, hungrily eyeing Beau as if she was about to devour him. Beau appeared to be pleased with the attention while Cody looked relieved that he was officially off the menu.

"I'm Kat," I said boldly, stepping forward with my hand outstretched, "I'm filling in for Ashley." Sandrine looked me up and down with an expression of indifference.

"Like a pussy cat?" she mocked, as if hoping to get a rise out of me. I stood my ground and kept my hand outstretched.

"With a 'k', like Kitty," I said, unphased by her attempt at intimidation. I held her stare and when I still didn't waver, Sandrine smiled and took my hand but didn't shake it. She held it firmly and kept her eyes trained on me.

"Bonjour Kat, I think you and I will get along very well," she said with a suggestive wink. I could have been imagining it, but it seemed as though she was flirting with me.

"I'm sure we will," I agreed with a tight smile, trying not to give her the wrong idea. Beau cleared his throat loudly as the French team began to trickle in. Sandrine finally let go of my hand and strode over to make the introductions. As the handshakes and double-cheek kisses began, I could feel the tell-tale tingling in my heavy breasts. My milk was coming in. I shook a few hands and then quickly excused myself to go in search of the bathroom.

I wandered the long, opulent hallways, but the place was like a labyrinth. I could feel the milk seeping into the breast pads so I stepped up my pace, thankful that I'd remembered to wear the pads today. Eventually I located the ladies' room and locked myself inside a very lavish cubicle. With my fancy electric breast pump packed safely inside my suitcase, which was down at reception, all I had to work with was the clunky hand-pump that I kept permanently stashed inside my handbag. I pulled out the contraption and sat on the toilet seat, noisily pumping my aching breasts, hoping like hell that no one came in whilst I was doing so. Motherhood was so undignified.

- RYAN McPHERSON -

When I brought Mia into group therapy there was such a fuss that. Twenty minutes into the session, Byron was still trying to get things under control.

"Come on folks," he called over the excited ruckus, "I know having Mia here is very exciting, but she'll be with us for a few days, so we have to find a way to concentrate in her presence."

"What if we all take turns?" Suggested Sloane, bouncing Mia against her chest. "I'll go first."

"She's not a fucking fairground ride Sloane," Rodney scolded from behind her. It was the first time I'd ever heard him call Sloane by her actual name. He bent down behind Sloane's shoulder, so his face was level with Mia's, and gently tapped Mia's little nose.

"No shit, cockrod," Sloane retorted, rolling her eyes. "You know what I meant."

Rodney straightened up and ran his hand through his hair with resigned exasperation. His demeanor had changed so substantially over the last few days, that it was hard to believe he was the same guy who'd tortured me for months.

"I think it's a great idea," chimed Byron approvingly. "You can rotate baby duties through the session."

"You don't want a cuddle, Byron?" Sloane asked curiously. All eyes turned to Byron.

"Err... no, I'm fine."

"Don't you like babies?"

"This session isn't about me Sloane," Byron said authoritatively. "Now can we please sit down and started?"

"Sure thing commander," Sloane said with a salute, as everyone else in the group took their seats.

"How about you give Mia back to her father for now?" suggested Byron with a smile. Sloane looked over at me as if only just noticing that I was standing there.

"Oh," she said with slight disappointment, "yeah, I guess that's a good idea." She handed Mia back to me and reluctantly returned to her chair, while I stood rocking Mia in my arms.

"Maybe you could start today, Slone?" Byron said, as Sloane cast her gaze back to Mia. "You seem very taken with Mia."

"She's so cute, how could anyone not adore her?"

"Very true," he agreed. "Do you think you'd like one of your own one day?"

"I guess so," Sloane said with a shrug. "I've never really thought about it before."

"You're in your twenties now so it's understandable that your biological clock might start ticking. How do you feel when you think about the idea of having a family?"

"Pretty sure I'd need a man for that," Sloane quipped.

"And how does it make you feel when you think about that?"

"About not having a man?"

"Or having one. You seem pretty comfortable being single, so I imagine for you, the bigger hurdle would be trusting someone enough to let them get close to you."

"Yeah. It's a little hard to trust people's motives when the media broadcasts your entire life, including your bank balance. You kinda get to a point where you accept that guys are only interested in your money."

"I don't think it's your money they're interested in," mumbled Rodney under his breath.

"You don't think there's a man out there who would love you for who you are?"

"How could they when I'm not who I am?"

"What do you mean by that?" Asked Byron, leaning forward in his seat.

"The person that everyone sees," said Sloane, "the girl on stage, she's not real. That's the girl that guys want and I'm not her, so how could they love me for me?"

"And the Sloane we see here... is she the real you?"

Sloane shrugged, "I suppose so."

"If you can let down your guard here, what stops you from doing that elsewhere?"

"There's no video cameras here. No technology. No one besides you guys to see me or judge me. But the real world isn't like that. In the real world, there's always someone watching."

"Is that why you admitted yourself to The Lodge? To get some privacy?"

"Maybe that's part of it."

"You're craving to be yourself, but you also desire human connection. You want to feel safe enough to drop the act and be real."

"Yeah."

"That's great Sloane," said Byron proudly, "thanks for opening up and sharing that with us. I really appreciate it. Is there a way you could replicate this environment in the 'real world' as you call it?"

"Not really. Not unless I lock myself in my house and frisk everyone at the door."

"I'd let you frisk me," piped up Rodney, "just give me a call and I'll make myself available for your frisking pleasure."

A few people laughed, but Byron looked annoyed.

"That's incredibly inappropriate Rodney," he said sternly. "Please apologise to Sloane."

"It's fine," interjected Sloane.

"No, it's not." Asserted Byron. "Rodney?"

"I'm sorry for being inappropriate," apologised Rodney.

"Apology accepted," said Sloane with a blush. Sloane caught my eye and I raised my brows questioningly. She shrugged as if she had no idea what I was asking, but then looked away quickly when she could see that I wasn't buying here innocent act. There had been some weird energy buzzing between the two of them for a few days. When had they turned from mortal enemies to potential love interests?

- NATHAN STONE -

The sun had risen and fallen again, and Ashley was still in bed, refusing to eat. It had become a one-in, one-out meal policy and even though I knew she wasn't going to eat it, I took in some dinner.

"Hey," I said quietly, as I crept into the dark room, grasping a bowl of vege stir-fry in one hand and a green smoothie in the other. "Dinner's ready."

"Thanks, but I'm not hungry," she mumbled from under the covers.

"You need to eat something."

"I can't."

"What about a smoothie?"

"No thanks."

"Ash…" I started to argue, before changing my mind. "I'll leave it here in case you change your mind," I concluded, carefully placing the bowl and glass onto the bedside table next to the unopened bottle of water I'd taken in earlier. "Can I at least talk you into drinking some water?"

"Okay," she agreed with a sigh, rolling over to face me. I couldn't make out her expression in the darkened room, but at least she was finally agreeing to something.

"Drink this," I said, as I cracked open the bottle and handed it over.

"Thanks," she said croakily, reaching for the water with shaky arms. She took a couple of small sips and handed it back.

"You sure you don't want more."

"No thanks," she said, rolling over and snuggling back down under the covers.

I sighed quietly and popped the bottle back onto the table. Perhaps she was avoiding me. Maybe her attack had changed her feelings and she didn't want to be with me anymore. Or maybe I was over-thinking it. I had no fucking idea. In fact, I had no fucking idea about anything anymore. Life as we'd known it, was over.

- RITCHIE CARLTON -

I took the team out to grab some dinner and explore Paris after work, but our outing was short-lived. After yet another exceptional French meal, we took a walk along the Seine and soaked up the magic of the river at night. The city lights twinkled over the undulating water and I could understand why they called Paris the City of Love. Despite the fact that the murky water of the Seine was as dirty as the Thames, the pretty riverbank had an air of romance about it. Amy would have hated it.

"Is that the end of our tour, boss?" Cody asked mockingly as our hotel came into sight.

"I hope so," said Tails, looking awkward, "I really need to pump."

"Pump what?" I asked with bewilderment.

She blushed furiously. "Umm…" Tails said, as her face turned the colour of a beetroot.

"Her breasts idiot," teased Cody, saving Tails from having to explain it to me.

"Oh," I said, understanding. "Well, you go do your thing love."

"Thanks Ritch," Kat said. "Night guys."

"I'll walk you back," Beau offered quickly.

"Oh, no, that's fine," Tails said, looking slightly panicked.

"You can't walk around Paris on your own at night," Beau pushed.

"What about the rest of our night out?" I asked, attempting to save Kat from being alone with Peterson.

"Actually," said Cody guiltily, "I'm supposed to meet Guillaume in an hour."

"Oh, for fuck's sake," I said with disappointment. "So, none of you are gonna come out and enjoy Paris with me?"

They all looked at me sheepishly.

"Sorry Ritch," shrugged Beau, guiding Tails in the direction of the hotel.

"What a supportive team you are," I huffed.

"So, does that mean I can go?" Cody asked hopefully.

"Fine," I sulked, "go and fuck your French fella."

"Thanks Rich," he replied, patting my shoulder with a grin. "I love you big guy."

"Fuck you," I said as he ran off to catch up with the other two. I looked around the buzzing street and spotted a little wine bar on the other side of the road. "That'll do."

I dodged the doe-eyed couples and young, drunk hipsters, and made my way inside the funky little bar. I found a seat at the window and texted Didier to see if he would come out for a drink. I wanted to pick his brain about the role. I had no intention of taking Sandrine up on her offer, but I wanted to find out exactly what I'd be turning down, before I did so.

As I ordered a drink my phone beeped in my pocket. It was a message from Didier to say he was on his way. I settled in with my glass of red and watched the people walk past. Amy would have enjoyed sitting next to me, taking the piss out of the lovely-dovey couples wandering hand-in-hand. Two drinks later, a familiar face strolled past the window.

"Didier," I called, rising from my seat to greet him as he entered the bar, "thanks for meeting with me."

Didier joined me at the table and shook my hand enthusiastically.

"Not a problem Ritchie," Didier replied, double kissing my cheeks as he gripped my hand. Kissing men was still way out of my comfort zone, but I was getting better at not showing embarrassment. "What did you wish to speak about?" He asked, as we both took a seat.

"Sandrine mentioned that you were retiring at the end of the year."

"That's right," he nodded stiffly.

"She offered me the role."

His brow furrowed and he took a sip of his wine.

"Oh, I see," he said, gently placing the glass back on the table.

"Sorry mate," I apologized, feeling awkward about bringing it up, "I didn't mean to over-step. I thought she'd talked to you about it."

"No, it's not that," Didier said, shaking his head. "Sandrine is free to replace me with whomever she wishes."

"You don't think I'd fit the role?" I asked with curiosity.

"On the contrary," he said with another shake of his grey hair, "I think you'd be perfect for the role."

"Then what's your hesitance?"

Didier sighed and glanced around the bar before leaning over the table.

"Your... relationship with Sandrine complicates things."

"Yeah, I get that."

"I don't think you do, mon amie," he said gravely.

"Why not?"

"Sandrine isn't what she seems."

"She's not a cold-hearted bitch?" I joked light-heartedly, but Didier didn't laugh. He pursed his lips and fixed his watery blue gaze on me.

"Sandrine is a woman who will do anything to get what she wants."

"Yeah, I'd figured as much," I agreed with a nod.

"She wants you Ritchie."

"But she knows I'm in love with someone else."

Didier laughed heartily, as if I'd just cracked a hilarious joke. "If you think that will stop her, then you're not the smart man I thought you were. If you accept this job, you will never get away from her. She would own you for the rest of your life."

- KAT McPHERSON -

I was infinitely thankful that Cody had walked back to the Hotel with us as I still hadn't told Ryan that Beau was there. I could only imagine what he'd think if I'd taken a stroll through Paris alone with the guy I'd cheated on him with. When I got back to my hotel room, I locked my door and let out a sigh of relief before heading straight to my breast pump to do a milk dump.

Once my boob was sufficiently fastened to the machine, I dialled the number Ryan had given me for The Lodge. I needed to talk to him before he somehow heard it through someone else. He wasn't likely to find out, but with the state of our luck over the past few months I wasn't willing to take the risk.

"Hey babe," Ryan said chirpily, once the office manager had retrieved him from his room. "How's Paris?"

"Amazing," I said. His voice was like home. "How are you two going? How's Mia?"

"She's great. She's right here. Say hi to mamma," he told our non-verbal baby. "No, she's not feeling talkative right now," Ryan joked. I chuckled half-heartedly, but my chest felt tight with a yearning to be there with them.

"I wish we could do a video call," I said sadly.

"Unfortunately they haven't created that technology for landlines yet."

"I miss you guys."

"We miss you too," Ryan said supportively. "But tell me all about your trip," he said, changing the tone. "I have so many questions. How was the meeting? Is the hotel nice? What's Sandrine like?"

I laughed at his enthusiasm. Ryan always knew how to cheer me up.

"Well, Sandrine is exactly how you'd imagine her to be and seems to have taken Ritchie as a trade-in on Nathan."

"Oh ouch. Is Ritchie okay?"

"He seems fine with the situation. In fact, I'd even say he's enjoying it. He's like a whole new Ritchie."

"Maybe sex-slavery is up his alley."

"I actually think he might be the one in charge to be honest. He seems to have the Black Widow wrapped around his little finger."

Ryan laughed at my description of Sandrine. "Is she really that bad?"

"She's worse," I said, sinking down onto the bed, engaged in my conversation. "And I think she was flirting with me."

"Can't say I blamer her," he teased.

"Seriously though Ry. I can't put my finger on it. She seems okay on the surface but there's something not right about her and I can't figure it out."

"Maybe you don't need to. If everyone is happy and safe, just let it be."

"Yeah."

"And how's the work?"

"Oh, the work itself is great. I'm loving it but…"

"But what?"

"Beau's here."

"What?" he asked through gritted teeth.

"They still haven't found anyone to replace him on the account, so Gaz insisted they put him back on it."

"Okay."

"There's absolutely nothing to worry about babe, I promise. We've agreed to keep things civil for work and that's it."

"Right," he said. His silence was making my stomach churn with anxiety.

"I'd never do anything to ruin what we've just got back. I love you Ryan and I know I made a massive mistake before, but that's exactly why I won't repeat that. Losing you was the worst thing that's ever happened, and I never want to experience that again. Please say you trust me," I begged.

"I do trust you Kat."

"Okay, but you've clearly got concerns."

"I absolutely have concerns," he admitted earnestly. "You're in the City of Love with that yankie prick, while I'm a continent away, locked in a rehab centre. It scares the fuck out of me." Ryan paused, and I could almost visualize him rubbing his face in the way he always did when he was stressed. "I trust you babe and I know that you won't let anything happen but that won't stop me from worrying about it."

"What can I do to make you feel better about it?"

"Nothing. This is my test of faith."

"If you think of something, please tell me, because I'll do anything to prove that to you."

"You don't have to prove yourself to me Kat. I love you regardless."

"I love you too."

At Ryan's end of the line, a muffled voice said something in the background.

"I've got to wind it up babe, but I promise I'll be fine. We've got this."

"We do."

"Chat tomorrow?"

"Yep, I'll check-in again in the morning."

"Great."

"I love you."

"I love you too. And so does Mia."

"Chat soon."

"Chat soon babe. Bye."

I hung up the phone and sat for a moment, praying to the Virgin Mary that nothing would get in the way of re-building my marriage. I let out a huge yawn and glanced at the bed. It looked super comfy.

I changed into my pyjamas and jumped into the cushy bed with a joyful giggle. It was big and soft, and I had it all to myself. I never thought I'd be quite so excited about sleep, but crawling into the massive plush bed, knowing that I wouldn't have to wake up until the morning, was my idea of heaven. I snuggled inside the covers and smiled contentedly. A full night of uninterrupted sleep awaited me.

Whoever coined the phrase 'slept like a baby', had clearly never had children. 'Slept like a log' was more factually accurate. And that was indeed the way in which I'd slept that night. I was down for the count until the early hours of the morning when my dreams were infiltrated by a warm, wet feeling coming somewhere from the real world.

My sleeping brain told me that I was relaxing in a spa bath full of hot chocolate, but my waking brain was alerting me to a different reality. I peeled my eyes open to discover that I was lying in a large pool of breast milk.

"Oh my god," I moaned, sitting up in the soaking wet bed. How would I explain that to housekeeping? I rolled out of the bed, stripped off the sheets and then climbed into the shower to de-stick myself. I'd have to find a manageable way to deal with my leaky boobs for the next few days. Evidently it wasn't just my heart that was missing Mia.

When I arrived back at Delfontaine headquarters, the receptionist showed me to the breakout room and I nearly fell over backwards when I saw the sheer size of it. Calling it a 'room' was a gross understatement, it looked more like a luxury studio apartment, or a movie set. The area was light and airy, complete with a large leather sofa; fully equipped kitchenette; oversized marble table punctuated with elegant high-back seats; and even a door that declared itself to be a unisex bathroom. I wandered around the room, awe-struck.

"This is bigger than my hotel room," I mumbled to myself as I meandered over to make myself a cup of tea in the pretty little kitchen. The kitchenette was fairly user-friendly, so it wasn't hard to locate what I needed, and I'd just poured the boiling water into a fine porcelain teacup when a familiar voice echoed from behind me.

"Hey Kitty-Kat."

I turned around with tea in hand to see Beau walking in the door. He hadn't called me Kitty-Kat since before our fight. Actually... he hadn't called me Kitty-Kat since the night of our affair.

"Beau. Hi," I answered, nervously jiggling the teabag up and down in my delicate cup. We'd barely spoken a word to each other since I'd arrived in Paris, and even then, it had been primarily work-related discussions. Being alone together in a room was a whole other level of awkward.

"How are you going with everything?" he asked with a smile, plopping his notebook down on the table. "Getting up-to-speed on the account?"

"Yeah, I think so," I said, still mindlessly agitating the teabag, "how about you?"

"There's a lot to cover but I think I've got a reasonable grasp on it," he answered with a shrug.

"Want a tea?" I asked, gesturing at the freshly boiled kettle. He eyed my cup of over-brewed English Breakfast and shook his head with a smile.

"I think I'll pass on the tea," he teased. I followed his gaze down to the dark brown liquid in my mug and immediately stopped jiggling the bag. "But I will make myself a coffee," he added, joining me in the kitchenette. I stepped backwards instinctively, so as to not be too close to him. I was still worried about the implications of us being alone.

"How are you coping being away from Mia?" Beau asked as he prepared himself a plunger of freshly ground coffee. He seemed genuinely interested.

"Honestly... it's hard," I said, adding some milk to my super-strong tea. "I've never been apart from her for longer than an hour."

"That sounds tough," he said, attempting his best to be empathetic about something he had zero experience of. "Where is she? With your parents?"

"No with Ryan at the Lodge."

"Oh," he said, as we made eye contact for the first time since he'd entered the room. The fact he was the reason for Ryan's incarceration floated unsaid through the air, like a fart in the breeze.

"It's good for them to have some quality time," I said quickly, taking a sip of my tea. I scrunched my nose in disgust at the bitter brew. "God, that's terrible," I said laughing and choking simultaneously. Beau laughed with me then took the cup out of my hand and tipped the offensive contents into the sink.

"Here, have some of this, he said, filling a second mug with the steaming aromatic coffee. "Coffee's better than tea anyway," he added with a wink as he handed me the mug.

"That's only because you yanks have no idea how to make a proper cup of tea," I retorted.

"And neither do you apparently," he teased with sparkling eyes, as he nodded at the abandoned teacup.

"That was only because you distracted me," I bantered, "you know that I'm normally a world-class tea maker."

Beau raised an eyebrow in intrigue and took a long sip of his coffee.

"I'm distracting, am I?" he asked provocatively.

"You...err..." I stuttered, unable to form a complete sentence.

"Good to see you two here bright and early," Ritchie chirped loudly from the door. I jumped away from Beau with a combination of surprise and guilt, spilling my coffee all over the white bench top.

"Shit," I muttered as I quickly cleaned up my mess. "Morning Ritch," I said, looking over my shoulder at him as I absent-mindedly mopped up the coffee.

"Carlton," Beau greeted Ritchie, taking the tea towel out of my hand as he did. "I've got this," he said with an amused smile as he nodded towards the brown puddle that I was moving around the bench top.

Ritchie plonked his stuff at the head of the table and joined us in the increasingly crowded kitchenette, forcing me to stand shoulder-to-shoulder with Beau. I stood rigidly, trying unsuccessfully to avoid my arm touching his.

"Since you guys all bailed on me yesterday, I've organized a team outing this afternoon," Ritchie said, continuing his chatter as he made his coffee.

Beau glanced at me sideways and shot me a sad smile. No words were exchanged but his eyes said it all. He missed me as much as I missed him, but our friendship could never be the same again.

- Chapter 4 -

Post-Paris Plummet

- RYAN McPHERSON -

I felt strangely conflicted about Kat's imminent return. On one hand, I was unbelievably excited about seeing her and hearing all about Paris, but on the other hand… I'd have to say goodbye to Mia. I'd really enjoyed having her at The Lodge with me over the last couple of days, so it was going to be difficult to let her go again.

I walked laps of the lounge, bouncing Mia on my chest, as I waited for Kat to arrive.

"I'm going to miss you young lady," I told my daughter quietly, as I kissed her on top of her delicate black curls. I smiled and ran my finger down her chubby cheek. There was no doubt my kid was going to be a stunner. With Kat's pretty face, my chocolate brown eyes and the beautiful caramel shade of her skin, Mia had the best of both of us. It was inevitable that she would be breaking some hearts later in life.

As I lapped up the last few minutes of alone time with my daughter, one of the orderly's showed Kat into the living room.

"Well, aren't you two a sight for sore eyes?" Kat said, running over to us with a huge grin on her face.

"We could say the same about you," I said with smile as I wrapped one arm around her waist. We cuddled together in a family hug, and I planted a firm kiss on her lips. "How was it?" I asked, handing Mia over.

"Busy, and amazing, and chaotic and absolutely fabulous," she said with a laugh, "but I missed this little lady and all I could think about was getting back here to you two," said Kat, rubbing her nose against Mia's. "How was everything here? Any problems?"

"She definitely missed her Mamma, but we had a great time together."

"Good," Kat said with a nod, cuddling Mia into her chest. "I'm glad you guys got some quality time together."

"She was pretty popular around here," I said, guiding her towards the sofa, "even Rodney helped out."

"Wow," she said, taking a seat.

"Was it good to get back to work?"

"It was," she said with less conviction than I would have expected. I sensed a 'but' coming.

"But?..."

"But I kept thinking about the moments I was missing with Mia."

"That's to be expected," I said, patting her knee, "especially being so far away from her."

"Yeah, I know, but that was only a few days. What happens when I go back to work full time?"

"You'll be able to see her every night and day once you get back to the office babe, and you can pop back here at lunch time if you're really missing her."

"True, but I just have to wonder whether I'm doing the right thing. We wanted a child for so long and now we've finally got one, I'm abandoning her."

"You'll be leaving her with her father every day. That's hardly abandoning her."

"I guess you're right."

"Of course I'm right," I said with a grin.

"It's really good to see your face," she said, leaning against me.

"Right back at ya," I said, hooking my arm over her shoulder. "Is everything okay with you?" I asked, taking stock of her unusual demeanor.

"Yeah... I've just been thinking about the Kelly situation."

My stomach dropped. I knew we'd have to revisit this conversation, but I wasn't quite prepared for it straight off the bat.

"Okay," I said, feeling anxious about how things were about to play out.

"I had a lot of time to think on it while I was away," she said, barely above a whisper.

"Amazing what some sleep can do huh?" I joked awkwardly. She smiled tightly and shuffled around to face me.

"This is going to sound crazy Ryan, but...I think you should try to talk Kellie out of having the abortion."

"Why?" I asked as quietly as possible, "she doesn't want to be a mum so that's kind of her call to make," I said, surprised by Kat's reaction, "I thought you were pro-choice."

"I am," she said, nodding her head. "It's not that, it's just..." Kat paused and rested her spare hand on mine, "it took us so long to get pregnant with Mia and I don't think I could go through that again."

"I don't understand what that has to do with Kellie."

Kat smiled and squeezed my hand tight. "Ryan, we always said that we wanted two kids, and my chances of getting pregnant again are only going to get worse with age," she said as her meaning began to sink in, "so what if…"

My jaw dropped. "Are you saying…"

Kat nodded, "this could be our only chance to have another child."

"But," I said in shock. It was certainly not the response I'd expected from her.

"I mean, obviously Kellie would have to be willing to go through with the pregnancy," Kat said quickly, "but what if she was open to it? What if *we* kept the baby?"

"You'd be okay with that?" I asked, stunned. I would never in a million years have expected Kat to make a suggestion like that.

"If she was happy for me to adopt the baby and be the mum, then I'd be very okay with that. This baby shares your blood Ryan, and Mia's. It will be connected to both of you and that makes it family regardless." She took a deep breath and wriggled closer to me. "I totally understand if Kellie doesn't want to do that. It's a massive thing to ask of her, but I think maybe it's worth asking. What do you think?"

"Well… I think…" I struggled to find the words, "I guess it can't hurt to ask."

"Really?"

"Yeah, I mean, if you're not up for another round of IVF, then maybe this is meant to be."

Kat nodded with tears in her eyes, "I think it is."

"But how will that fit in with you going back to work? Two kids under two will be a pretty big undertaking."

"I know, but that's something I'm willing to work out. Every bone in my body is telling me that this baby is ours."

"Okay but let's just take one step at a time. I can't contact Kell from in here, so you'll need to line it up for me."

"I can do that."

"Are you sure?"

"Absolutely," she said confidently. "I've loved getting back into work, but being away from you two made me realise that our family is more important than anything, and this might be our only chance to add to it."

I smiled and tucked a strand of curls behind her ear, convinced that no one had ever loved anyone as much as I loved her at that moment.

"I love you so much," I told her with my hand under her chin. "You are such an amazing woman and the fact that you see this as a positive thing just goes to show exactly how phenomenal you are."

"You don't think I'm crazy?"

"Of course I do," I teased with a smile, "but you're also the most amazing person I know."

"So, you think I can make all of this work?"

"I think we can make all of this work. We'll be in it together."

"We will." Kat paused and peered over Mia's head with a nervous smile. "I guess now is as good a time as any."

"You mean you want to call Kellie right now?"

"Yeah, why not?" she said with a shrug. "Are you having second thoughts?"

"I haven't had time to have second thoughts, I've only just had my first thought on it."

"I know, but we have to speak to her before her appointment."

"Right."

"It's just to make a time to chat."

"Okay. I guess the reality of the situation is freaking me out a little," I admitted. "I can't believe you're not freaking out."

"I've had a few days to sit with it."

"True."

"So... shall I call her?" Kat watched me through Mia's bouncy curls as I pondered the idea.

"This is fucking insane."

"Yeah," she agreed. "Is that a 'yes' then?"

I swallowed back the nervous lump in my throat and took a deep breath.

"Yeah," I confirmed. "Let's call her."

Kat squealed and jumped up and down with Mia in her arms, before running over to give me a kiss.

"Thank you," she said, her beautiful brown eyes sparkling with joy. I cuddled the two of them into my chest and then let out a loud, nervous laugh.

"Holy shit," I chuckled, "did you ever think you'd be asking another woman to have my baby?"

"No, but nothing in life has gone to plan over the last three months so nothing surprises me anymore."

- KAT McPHERSON -

The three of us wandered out into the garden so we could make our phone call in private. I couldn't believe what I was about to do but every fiber of my being told me that this was all meant to be. Ryan set up Mia's play mat on the lush green lawn while I stared at my phone with butterflies in my stomach.

"Kellie's appointment is on Monday, so it's now or never," Ryan said, picking up on my hesitancy.

"I know," I agreed, "what if this is a dumb idea?"

"Isn't it worth asking anyway?"

"I suppose so."

"If it's not meant to be, then she'll say no and we'll all move on with our lives, but at least we gave it a go."

"You're right," I nodded, dialling her number. My heart pounded as the phone rang.

"Hello, Kellie speaking." As soon as she answered the call, my voice faltered and I failed to respond. "Hello?" Kellie said at the other end of the line.

"Hi, Kellie, sorry," I spluttered, forcing the sound out, "this is Kat… Ryan's wife."

There was a pause at the other end of the line and I glanced at Ryan nervously. He nodded reassuringly.

"Ryan told you?" she asked timidly.

"Yeah, he did. Is there any chance we could meet up and chat?"

Another pause.

"Ummm…"

"I know this is weird, but we'd really like to talk to you about it," I pleaded, trying not to sound too desperate.

"Okay," she agreed reluctantly, "I've got a gap between classes this afternoon. Would 3:30 work for you?"

"Uhh, sure. Okay." I spluttered, not expecting to meet her alone, or so soon.

"Perfect. Are you able to get to Hoxton?"

"Yeah, I can do that."

"Cool. There's a café around the corner, I'll text you the address."

"Okay great," I said, feeling slightly nauseas. "I'll see you then." I hung up the phone and stared at Ryan in shock.

"This afternoon?" He asked, looking as stunned as I felt. "By yourself?"

"Yeah."

"Fuck."

"Yeah," I repeated. We stared at each other for a moment and then burst into nervous laughter.

"Holy shit, this is really happening."

"It is."

"Right… well, I guess we'd better make a game plan."

Ryan and I spent an hour coming up with a spiel and a general plan of what exactly I would be proposing to the potential mother of our child. By the time we were done it was getting late, so there was no point in me driving to Hoxton when the tube would take half the time. Mia and I said goodbye to Ryan and set out on our dubious adventure via the London Underground. I had severely underestimated how difficult it was going to be to navigate public transport with a pram, but we made it. Barely.

Somewhat frazzled and seriously doubting my sanity for wanting to take on a second child, I wheeled Mia's pram over to the table where Kellie was already waiting with a pot of tea and two cups.

"Hi Kellie, thanks for meeting me," I said, standing awkwardly in front of her.

"Honestly, I wasn't sure if I should," she admitted motioning to the seat across from her. "I thought maybe you wanted to beat the shit out of me, hence the public venue."

I laughed. "No, I'm not here for a fight."

She smiled with relief and peered into Mia's pram as I settled into my seat. "So, this is Mia?" Kellie asked, studying her child's half-sibling as she slept quietly. "She looks a lot like Ryan doesn't she?"

"Wait until she's awake and you see her eyes. She's the spitting image of him."

"So, you and Ryan are okay then?" Kellie asked, as she poured some tea into the spare cup for me.

"Yeah, we are," I said with a nod. "You guys can't change the past any more than I can."

She put the teapot down and scrutinized me for any signs of deception. "That's very cool of you," she said sceptically.

"I'm in no position to judge," I explained with a shrug, "I'm sure Ryan probably told you what I did?"

"Even so…" she trailed off. "What did you want to speak to me about then?"

I swallowed hard to dislodge the nervous lump that had wedged itself in the middle of my throat at some point along the Northern

Line.

"Ryan said that you don't want to keep the baby," I said diplomatically.

"That's right," she said, eyeing me warily.

"And that you've got an appointment booked for next week?"

"Yeah," she agreed again, then put down her cup. "Kat, you obviously have a question."

I nodded nervously. "I do," I said, taking another deep breath. "I know this is a really crazy thing for me to ask but... would you consider having the baby?"

Kellie raised one brow suspiciously. "Why? Does Ryan want to keep it?"

"Yeah, but-" I tried to explain before she cut me off.

"I'm sorry Kat, I can't do that," she jumped in, before I could even finish my sentence. "I'm not cut out for being a Mum and it wouldn't be fair to anyone for me to pretend otherwise."

"What if you didn't have to be a mum?" I asked desperately.

She froze. "You mean, like, put it up for adoption?"

"Sort of..." I said, edging my chair a little closer to hers. "What if Ryan and I raised the baby. I'd officially adopt it and you could have as much or as little to do with us as you wanted."

Kellie was visibly taken aback. "Whoa," she breathed, "that's not what I was expecting you to say."

"Honestly, it's not what I expected either, but it took so long for me to get pregnant with Mia and I had a few miscarriages before she came along. I don't think I could go through IVF again."

Her eyes dropped downwards as she ran her hand over her still flat stomach. "I didn't know that."

"Ryan and I really want another child. We hadn't planned on it quite so soon, but I think this could be our chance to do it without all the heartbreak." I twisted my hands nervously in my lap. "I guess it would be kind of like a surrogacy."

"Wow," she said, "I don't know what to say Kat."

"You don't have to say anything right now. Obviously, we'd make sure you're looked after, and we'd pay for it all. You wouldn't have to worry about anything financially."

"Okay."

"Look, I know it's a huge thing to ask and I don't want you to feel pressured, just please don't go to that appointment until you've had a chance to think it over."

Kellie nodded. "Okay, I'll have a think on it."

"Thank you," I said, feeling tears welling in my eyes, "thank you."

"I can't make any promises Kat. There are a lot of things to think about."

"I know, and I really appreciate you being open-minded about it. I really didn't know how you were going to react."

"Same here with the pregnancy. I actually tried to talk Ryan out of telling you."

"You did? Why?"

"You guys only just got back together, and I thought that something like this might break you up," she shrugged, "I didn't want to ruin his life for a second time."

"You didn't ruin his life, Kellie."

"I'm the one who gave him the drugs," she said shamefully. "I'm so used to fueling-up that I didn't think about whether or not he'd be able to handle it. I just assumed he'd be fine."

"He made his own choices."

"Yeah, but I was the devil on his shoulder."

I smiled and patted her hand. She might have been a party girl, but she had a good heart.

"You're really sweet. I can see why Ryan-" it was my turn to trail off. I couldn't bring myself to finish that sentence.

"This is weird huh?" she asked, sharing my awkwardness.

"Yeah," I said with a nod, "if someone had told me three years ago that my husband would be in rehab while I was asking his ex-girlfriend to have a baby for me, then I would have assumed they were on the same drugs that landed him in there in the first place."

Kellie laughed. "Yeah, it's a bizarre situation."

"Well... I'll leave you to it Kellie," I said, taking one last sip of my tea. "Thanks for hearing me out, and for not making me feel crazy for asking."

"You're not crazy," she said, squeezing my shoulder. "I actually think you're pretty fucking amazing. You've seen the positive where most women would have seen a disaster. It says a lot about you Kat. You see the good in things and that's not crazy."

"Thank you," I said, swallowing back hot tears.

"If I decide to do this, I know you'd be the best mum that this baby could ever ask for."

I nodded stiffly, concentrating all my energy on not crying.

"You've got my number now," I said, popping a fiver on the table to cover our tea, "so just call me once you've had some time to think it over."

"I will."

"And, if you need anything..."

"Thanks Kat."

- RITCHIE CARLTON -

Amy was waiting at my place when I arrived home from Paris, which was bitter-sweet since I had a semi-guilty conscience about spending the entire week shagging my client. Sandrine had already texted six times since I'd left her office and there were only so many ways that I could politely rebuff her offer. The constant buzz of Sandrine on my phone was a tangible reminder of my cheating. But was it really cheating if Amy and I weren't a couple?

I had boomeranged between guilt and apathy, the whole way home, but regardless, I was pleasantly surprised to be greeted by the sight of Amy standing in my kitchen wearing my old rowing T-shirt and a pair of my smallest rugby shorts. She looked hot-as-fuck.

"Taken up rugby have you?" I asked, dumping my bags in the middle of the lounge room floor.

"I was hanging out to get into your pants," she joked.

"You look hot," I said pulling her towards me by the waistband of the shorts, "but I do like you way better when you're naked."

"I was thinking the same about you," she retorted. I didn't need a second invitation. Within seconds I'd lifted her off the floor and we were madly snogging.

"Not that I'm complaining, but aren't you supposed to be at work?" I asked between kisses.

"I took the day off. I wanted to surprise you."

"Well consider me surprised," I said with a laugh as I lifted her up over my shoulder. I carried her up to the bedroom and threw her on top of the poorly made bed.

"You're wearing way too many clothes young lady," I joked making a dive for my rugby shorts. Feigning horror at the attack, she grabbed one of the pillows from behind her head and walloped me on the side of the face. "I think you need to be punished for that," I teased as I rugby tackled her.

"Oh really?" she challenged, as she wriggled out of my grasp, re-brandishing the pillow for a second attack.

"Oh, you're in so much trouble now." I scrambled for my own pillow so I could launch a defense. I hit her in the face with my pillow and then grabbed hers out of her hand. She squealed and laughed as I threw both pillows onto the floor. "Now," I said, pinning her hands over her head, "let's get you out of my pants."

"Please do," she answered as I whipped the shorts off in one swift move.

"Your turn," she said with a grin as I released her hands and allowed her to unbutton my jeans. Amy used her foot to push my jeans down to my knees, and we both laughed when my dick jumped out at her. "Well hello stranger," she joked as her eyes flashed with passion. We stared at each other for a moment and then she wrapped her legs around my waist.

"God you're gorgeous," I thought out loud.

"Ritchie, just shut up and fuck me."

"I can't help it. You're so fucking sexy."

"I bet you say that to all the girls," Amy answered with a wink. My stomach churned with guilt. She was right. I'd said exactly the same thing to Sandrine a few days earlier. I sighed and rolled off her. "What are you doing?" Amy asked in confusion.

"Aims, I've got something to tell you."

"Right at this moment?"

"Yes, I have to tell you now."

"Why? Can't it wait until after we've done this?"

"No, I need to tell you before."

"Fine, be quick then. What is it?"

"I shagged someone in Paris," I blurted. She sat up and stared at me silently. Not a word, not a breath, not a whisper. "I didn't plan it, but it happened," I added, desperately needing to hear some sort of response from her.

"Right," she answered with a nod, before climbing onto my lap. "Shall we do this thing then?"

I leaned back from her as she tried to continue where we'd left off.

"Did you hear what I said Aims?" I asked with frustration, holding her at arm's distance by her shoulders, "I shagged someone else."

"Yeah, I heard you," she sighed and climbed off the bed. "You're a free agent Ritch, so what else is there to say?"

"Wow. Seriously?" I asked indignantly.

"Yeah," she shrugged, "we're casual so I can't stop you from shagging other people." She didn't give a fuck. I'd prepared myself for her not to be upset, but the reality of her indifference was like a knife to my heart.

"That's all you have to say?" I asked, my pain turning to anger.

Aims glared at me with piercing eyes, pulling the shorts back on.

"What do you expect me to say Ritchie? Well done? Congratulations?" she snapped sarcastically. "You fucked someone else, what is there to say?"

"I don't know Amy, perhaps something to show that you actually give a shit," I shot back angrily. "Anything would be better than 'right'." I paused and waited for a response, but she remained silent. "Do you even care?"

"Of course I care."

"Really? Because you don't seem that bothered by it."

"Our relationship has been pretty clear from the start Ritchie. You don't owe me anything. We're not a couple, therefore you can shag whomever you like. End of story."

I dropped my head with sad acceptance. "I guess I was just hoping that I meant more to you."

"Obviously," she said snidely, "because your actions make that abundantly clear."

My head shot upward. "So, it does bother you then?"

"I guess it does," she conceded with a sigh. I felt my chest ease as hope flooded through my body.

"Does that mean we can talk about being exclusive?" I asked hopefully. Her jaw dropped and rage flared in her eyes.

"Is that why you fucked someone else? To trick me into committing to you?"

"Of course not," I assured her adamantly, "the Sandrine thing just kind of happened."

"You fucked Sandrine?" she asked, her eyes ablaze, "that's hardly just 'someone' is it?"

"Does it matter who it was?"

"It does when you're fucking our client Ritchie. And not just any client, it's a client that we're both working for, who also happens to have abducted and raped one of our best friends. I mean, seriously Ritchie, you couldn't honestly have expected me to be okay with you fucking Sandrine."

"I fucked Sandrine, past tense. It's not an ongoing situation," I said indignantly, as if that gave me the moral high ground.

"How many times?" she asked with anger flashing in her hazel eyes.

"Huh?" I grunted like an idiot.

"How many times did you fuck her Ritchie? Was it just once or did she lock you in her sex dungeon and abuse you too?"

"I never even saw the sex dungeon," I said huffily, avoiding the question.

"How many times Ritchie?"

"Well, that's hard to say," I spluttered, "a few."

"In the same session or was it spread out over days?"

"A few days," I mumbled before going on the offensive. "What the fuck is happening right now anyway?" I asked incredulously. "Why does any of this matter to you?"

"I'm just trying to ascertain exactly how much of an arsehole you actually are."

"Are you kidding me with this?" I growled, "I've spent two years begging for your commitment and you've constantly reminded me that we're nothing more than fuck-buddies. Why do you suddenly care now?"

"Because a random shag is one thing but taking our client as a second fuck-buddy... that's a whole different ball game Ritchie."

I rubbed my face to ease the pain that my brain was feeling from Amy's incomprehensible fuck-buddy rules.

"So, what are you saying?" I asked with a sigh.

"I'm saying we're done Ritch," Amy said definitively. "Our fuck-buddy agreement is over."

"Shall I call the lawyers so they can amend the paperwork?" I asked snidely.

"Bye Ritchie," she seethed, before marching out the door and slamming it behind her.

- RYAN McPHERSON -

Facing my demons during therapy sessions was one thing, but fighting them in my sleep was another. I knew I'd have to face all the gory details eventually, but that felt a lot easier to do during daylight hours. Sleeping had become so distressing that I spent my nights trying to keep myself awake, which also meant that I spent my days trying not to fall asleep. I hadn't had one decent night of sleep since I'd uncovered my childhood memories. The monsters came to life at night and there was no avoiding them in my dreams.

Having Mia with me for a few nights had been a good distraction that had enabled me to avoid sleep without even thinking about it, but now that Kat was back and Mia had gone home, it was once again mano-a-monster.

Normally I was the last one to leave the TV room, but tonight, Rodney had hung back too. I stared at the screen, not actually watching the crap reality show that was on, but not wanting to acknowledge his presence, in case he wanted to talk.

"You missing Mia?" Rodney asked casually, also staring at the screen.

"Yeah, I got used to having her around."

"I think we all did," he said with a surprising amount of compassion. "She's pretty cool for a baby," he joked.

"She is."

"It also would've made it a lot easier to avoid sleeping while she was around huh?"

My eyes darted over to him and then quickly back to the screen.

"Yeah," I agreed with a shrug. I figured there was no point in lying about it.

"The nightmares ease off eventually," he told me as offhandedly as if we were discussing football, "but they won't go away completely. That's why I started on the crack," he admitted as we both watched a bunch of plonkers competing for their fifteen minutes of fame.

"It happened to you too?" I asked, trying to sound like I didn't care about his answer.

"Yeah," he said, rubbing the back of his head, "show biz is filled with the sick fuckers. Everyone knows, but no one does anything about it because they're all in it together."

I stopped staring blankly at the television screen and turned to him with stunned horror. I wasn't surprised about his revelation; it was fairly common knowledge that pedo's roamed free in the entertainment industry; what I was shocked about, was the fact that he was opening up to me.

"Fucking hell," I said, lacking a better response.

"Yeah, it's pretty fucked up."

I swiveled around in my seat, dropping the pretense of watching the telly, as I looked over at him with complete understanding.

"Did your parents know?" I asked, genuinely intrigued about his past.

"They had no idea. I never told them, and they were too busy enjoying the royalty cheques from my TV roles to ever ask any questions."

"Shit Rodney, I never knew."

"Why would you?" he said with a shrug, "I haven't even told any of the therapists here."

"How come?"

"I dunno. I guess I figured if I didn't talk about it, I could pretend it never happened."

"So why are you telling me?"

"That's pretty obvious, isn't it?" he said gruffly.

"Yeah, I guess it is," I agreed. We both fell silent for a moment and let our eyes slide back towards the television.

"That's why I admitted myself in here," he said as some dickhead on the TV ate a cockroach for the sake of a few hundred quid. "Whenever the nightmares start again, I don't trust myself. I know I can't fall off the wagon in here, so I check myself in until they stop again."

"Are you going to tell Victoria?"

"I dunno. Maybe," he said, shrugging. "I wasn't going to, but I guess I might think about it now that I know…" he let his sentence trail off.

"You told your wife?"

"Nope," I said, running my hand over my head. "I don't know if I should with everything else that's going on."

"Would telling her help you?"

"I don't think so."

"Would it make a difference to your relationship?"

"Probably not," I answered, pre-empting the scene in my mind, "but she'll probably start to wonder what's going on when I wake up screaming every night."

"Then there's your answer," he concluded logically.

"Yeah," I agreed, "but maybe I'll wait for this baby drama to calm down."

He looked at me with intrigue.

"What baby drama? Is something wrong with Mia?"

"No, no, nothing like that. The chick that I was dating after Kat left… she's pregnant with my kid."

"Oh shit. So the saga continues," he said with an unprecedented show of empathy.

"Yeah, but that's not even the most complicated part," I said, relaxing into the conversation and strangely finding myself enjoying Rodney's company. "Kat wants us to keep the baby."

Rodney snorted in either shock or amusement, or possibly both.

"Mate, are you serious?"

"As a heart attack," I confirmed.

"Jesus. So, let me get this straight… your wife wants your ex-girlfriend to have your baby?"

"Yep."

"Buddy, your life is crazier than the plots of my show."

"I know," I said, nodding, "my life has been completely insane lately. But I promise you, before this, I was boring as fuck."

Rodney laughed loudly. "There are many things I'd call you McPherson, but boring isn't one of them." We shared a chuckle and with it, all of our previous hostility evaporated into thin air. It was hard to believe that a few weeks ago we'd been mortal enemies.

"I suppose no one can accuse me of being boring anymore," I agreed as our laughter subsided.

"So… are you going to confront your folks?"

I looked at him with horror. "I hadn't even considered it," I said with panic. "Do you think Byron and Victoria will expect me to do that for closure or whatever?"

"They'll probably suggest it."

"Fuck," I swore. If confronting my parents became the one thing that stood between me and home, then I'd have to do it, but that was far more than I could fathom.

"I guess that's one reason I haven't mentioned my thing," he said, turning back to the telly. "God that guy is a git," he said watching the wannabe celebrities try to outdo each other.

"What's the deal with you and Sloane?" I asked, changing the subject.

"There's no deal," he answered with a shrug.

I snorted with amusement. "If you say so."

"I do say so."

"Okay," I said, mimicking his shrug, "it's none of my business anyway."

His eyes darted up again to study me. "Why? Did she say something to you?"

"So, you do like her."

"She's okay for a stuck-up coke-head."

I grinned and sank back in my recliner. Who would have ever expected that I'd be witness to a rehab romance?

- NATHAN STONE -

I sat out on the balcony, wrapped in a blanket, staring into the darkness. I could hear the waves crashing against the shore, but I couldn't see them. The moon was covered by the clouds, so the inky midnight sky reflected down onto the ocean, creating an endless void of blackness. It felt fitting. Dark and ominous was the appropriate mood for my life at that moment.

I looked over my shoulder into the dark bedroom. Ash was still in bed and Fred was still standing guard. Or lying guard at least. The cat had gotten noticeably fatter over the last few days, so she was probably glad of the opportunity to laze around on the bed all day and night.

I sighed and picked up my phone. I needed to distract myself, so I scrolled through my Facebook feed of friends' parties, babies, and wedding photos. It seemed like the rest of the world was still functioning, while we were in stasis. Would things ever be normal for us, or were we destined to be stuck in an endless loop of drama and instability? As I pondered our fate, a notification popped up on my screen.

"What are you doing awake?" said a messenger bubble from Tails.

"Couldn't sleep. What about you?"

"Baby."

"Fair enough. How was Paris?"

"Interesting. How's Ash?"

"Not good."

"And how are you?"

"Not good either."

"Anything I can do?"

"Thanks, but I don't think there's anything anyone can do right now."

"Nath..." The dots flashed as Kat typed, but then they vanished so I tapped out my questions.

"How's Ryan? What's happening with him? Is rehab going okay?"

The dots vanished. Tails had probably fallen asleep, so I put my phone down and recommenced staring out at the dark ocean. What was I going to do?

"Sorry, had to switch sides," said a message from Tails, lighting up my phone screen. "Ryan is good. Rehab has been good for him."

"Good to hear."

"Nath, I know you're all the way down there, but you're not alone, ok?"

"Thanks Tails."

"Hey, Ritch is online. I'll make a group chat." I gave her a thumbs up and, after a couple of seconds, the group chat popped up on my screen. Tails had called it 'The Midnight Gang'.

"I do like a bit of David Walliams," I typed to no one in particular.

"It felt appropriate," replied Tails. "Has Amy gone home Ritch?"

"Yep."

"All okay mate?" I asked, sensing the hidden angst behind his single word response.

"All good. Just the usual. What about you? How's Ash?"

"About as good as she was when we left Paris."

"Shit," replied Ritch. "Happy to be back with Mia, Tails?"

When there was no response from Tails, I jumped in.

"She's probably fallen asleep."

"Yeah."

I closed the group chat and messaged Ritchie directly.

"What's going on?"

"Told Aims about Sandrine and it didn't go down well."

"Ouch. Salvageable?"

"No idea." The dots pulsated as Ritchie typed more. "Are you alright? Insomnia isn't a great sign."

"Well Ash has no problem sleeping. She's pretty much catatonic most of the time. It's me that can't sleep. I have no idea WTF I'm doing."

"I take it you haven't told Tails the full deets?"

"Nope."

"Maybe you should. She's a chick, she might be able to give you some advice."

"She's got enough to worry about."

"True," he agreed. "What about Amy?"

"Sounds like she's got a bit on her plate too [grimace face]"

"Harsh but fair [shrugging man]. So whatcha gonna do then?"

"I dunno. Just be here I guess. What are you gonna do about Red?"

"Get trashed."

"Solid plan mate [laughing face]."

- RITCHIE CARLTON -

When I rocked up to work on Monday morning, my head was pounding, and I stank of stale alcohol. I'd lost the entire weekend in a blur of drugs, alcohol and possibly sex. I knew I'd done something - or many somethings - but I couldn't grasp onto any tangible memories to piece it all together. There was something impalpable, yet undeniably sinister about my black-out. It was as if I'd been Roofied. I wasn't the sort of guy who ever over-indulged to the point of memory loss, yet I couldn't remember one single thing about my weekend.

I had vague recollections of talking to Sandrine, but everything else was lost in a hazy fog. I had the distinct feeling that I'd seen her in person, but there was no sign of her presence in my flat, and no evidence that I'd gone to Paris, so it was a mystery.

Needless to say, it had caught me by surprise when my alarm shrilled that morning. I'd been so hungover that I hadn't even thought to have a shower, I'd merely sprayed myself with deo and practically crawled out the door, still wearing the clothes I'd passed out in.

I slunk through the reception area and up to our secured floor hoping that no one would spot me. Today was the worst possible day for a hangover. I could barely see straight, let alone think straight, and with Nathan gone, the responsibility fell on me to brief the entire team on the outcomes from our workshops in Paris. Hopefully Gaz had informed the team of the Ashlan situation because I didn't want to deal with that calamity in my current state.

I tried to sneak quietly to my desk but was spotted by one of Ashley's designers.

"Hey Ritchie," she called, "how was the trip?"

I looked up and winced as my head rattled from the movement.

"Yeah good," I said non-committally, making a B-line for the safety of my desk. A line of coke would have been a welcome sight at that moment.

"Do you know when Ash will be in?" she asked casually, "we need her to brief us on the logo design."

My stomach churned. Partly from the hangover, and partly from the realisation that Gaz had left me to deal with Nathan's mess.

"Uhh," I muttered, avoiding eye contact, "we'll have a team meeting soon and go over everything then."

"Okay," she said, seemingly happy with my explanation, "thanks Ritch."

I threw my backpack under my desk and flopped into my chair with my head in my hands.

"Here," a glass of fizzing orange liquid appeared on my desk and I looked up to see Amy standing over me with a surprisingly sympathetic look on her face. "Drink that, it'll help."

I nodded obediently, and then knocked back the sweet drink. It didn't have quite the same effect as snorting a line, but it was good enough to take the edge off.

"Thanks," I said, wiping my mouth with the back of my hand.

"No problem." Amy stood and watched me pull myself together. "No one knows yet Ritch."

"Yeah, I got that impression," I said with a groan as I rubbed my aching temples.

"I think Gaz was hoping that Nath would change his mind and come back."

"Probably," I agreed, peering up at her through squinty eyes, "but unfortunately they're already in Cornwall."

"I heard," Amy nodded as she scrutinised my disheveled state. "Where the fuck were you this weekend Ritch? You were totally AWOL. I rang you like a million times."

"Yeah, I know, but I didn't see the point in answering since my whereabouts is no longer your business," I mumbled without thinking. It was a twatty answer and I knew it.

"God you're an arsehole," she snapped, backing away in response to my arseholey comment.

"Yeah, well I guess that's why you had to sort yourself out this weekend," I retorted harshly. I'd already started down the path of cuntdom so there was no point stopping it now. Maybe Alpha Male was still hanging around.

"Fuck you," Amy snapped before storming out towards the

elevators. Ah shit. I'd have to chase her. I stumbled out of my chair and jogged (in the loosest sense of the word), after her as she marched down the corridor.

"Aims wait," I called, as my head pounded in time with my feet, "I'm sorry," I apologised helplessly as I caught up with her and grabbed her arm. She turned towards me, unable to escape.

"What the fuck was all that about?" She seethed in fury.

"I don't know," I answered honestly, "I'm just angry. At myself. And Gaz. And you. But mostly me. I didn't set out to shag Sand…" I dropped my voice and looked around to make sure no one was within hearing distance. There were a couple of people loitering by the lifts, so I guided her further down the hallway to where there were no prying ears. "I didn't mean for it to happen, but once it did, I guess I was hoping it might make you realise that you want to be with me. It was stupid and I'm sorry that I put that back on to you. You've been upfront with me from the beginning, and it wasn't fair for me to expect anything more from you."

Amy sized me up, debating whether or not to accept my apology.

"What happened to you this weekend?" she asked curiously. "No actually, don't answer that. I don't think I want to know."

"I'm surprised it bothers you so much," I said with exhaustion. I rubbed my temples to try and ease the throbbing. "I'm trying to understand Aims, but I just don't get you. You don't want me, but you don't want anyone else to have me either. What am I supposed to do with that? How do I live a proper life when I'm floating in no-man's land?"

"I do want you," she said, holding my stare intensely as we stood face-to-face. I inched slowly closer to her, making her nose twitch at my stench. "You stink Ritch," she said, not unkindly. I didn't move. "Seriously Ritchie, you stink," she re-iterated as I slowly backed her up against the wall.

"You love it," I teased staring down at her, with desire flaring in my belly.

"Get away," she said making a feeble attempt to push me away. Her touch did nothing more than spur me on. Perhaps Alpha Male had decided to stick around after all.

"Not until you admit that you want to be with me," I taunted her as I reached up and put my hands against the wall so that my pits were on either side of her head. It was completely immature, but really fucking funny.

She covered her nose with revulsion, making me chuckle childishly. It brought back memories of pre-school when I used to pick on Sonia

Grey because I fancied her, which did make me wonder how my flirting techniques had regressed so badly.

"Very mature," Amy said rolling her eyes, "why don't you just hold me down and fart on my face?"

"Now there's an idea," I joked as I pretended to mull it over. I would have enjoyed messing with her, but she actually did look like she might puke from my stink. "So…?" I prompted, awaiting her declaration.

"So what?" she asked simply.

"So, are you going to admit it?" I asked teasingly.

Amy averted her eyes and took a deep breath. "Fine, you're right," she mumbled, still looking at the floor.

"Sorry? What was that?" I taunted with a grin of self-satisfaction.

"I said you're right," Amy replied, with a childish roll of her eyes.

I chuckled with superiority. "And what am I right about?"

"Don't be a dick."

"I'm purely seeking clarification," I said with faux innocence. Amy remained silent. "So?" I asked again.

"Fine," she said, clearing her throat self-consciously. "I do care that you slept with Sa- err – someone else."

"Which means what exactly?"

"I'm not going to say it Ritchie."

I frowned with frustration. I wanted to kiss her, but my desire to hear her to say the words far outweighed that need, so I stood my ground, silently cocooning her in my force-field of stench. At the exact moment that she looked like she was about to cave, the wall vanished from behind her.

"Oh fuck," I blurted as my hands momentarily floated mid-air. Why hadn't I noticed it was a door when I'd leaned against it?! With my entire body weight having been supported by said door, I fell to the floor, taking Amy down with me. I instinctively wrapped one arm around her back and used the other hand as a shock absorber against the hard floor. Amy grabbed me for support, and we collapsed on the floor wrapped around each other in a tangle of limbs.

We heard an explosion of laughter as we peered up to see Cody and the entire Dev team standing in the doorway of the meeting room, staring down at us in shock. Amy and I attempted to untangle ourselves as they all curled over in hysterics.

"It's not what it looks like," I explained, helping Aims to her feet.

"Yeah right," Cody teased, with glee. "Come on folks, it looks like these two need some privacy."

Once the crowd had dispersed and we'd straightened ourselves up, I turned my focus back to my non-girlfriend. I couldn't help but grin at her. She was so hot it should have been illegal.

"What?" Amy asked, cocking her head at my expression.

"I was just thinking," I muttered casually.

"Thinking what?" she asked.

"Thinking about how damn... unattractive you are," I teased with an evil smile. "Honestly, how do you even look at yourself in the mirror?" I joked with a laugh as she began punching me playfully.

"Shut up," she retorted, with a huge smile on her face, "you're pretty ugly yourself."

"So I've been told," I agreed with a chuckle.

"It looks like we still have an audience," Amy pointed out as she glanced over at one of the young client services girls standing at the elevators.

"Vicky or Nicky?" I asked quietly, unable to remember which of the bottle-blonde account managers she was.

"Ricky," Aims corrected me with a teasing smile.

"Ah yes. I knew it was one of the 'ickys'," I joked with a chuckle. "They all look the same to me."

"They all look completely different," she laughed.

"All I know is that none of them look like you," I said without thinking.

"Ritch..." Amy answered awkwardly. I knew she hated me saying things like that, but I couldn't help it.

"But only because they're all so much hotter than you," I added, wondering how I ever got sucked into this backwards relationship.

"That's better," she teased with an approving smile.

"So... are we good?" I asked uncertainly. She re-tied her hair while I patiently awaited her answer. Once her mop of thick, shiny, red hair was securely bunched on top of her head, she looked me in the eyes and nodded.

"We're good."

"Okay," I nodded with relief, "I think we should probably get back to work now."

"Right you are, boss," agreed Amy with a wink.

"I think we both know who's really the boss in this relationship."

- KAT McPHERSON -

On Monday morning, I was up at the crack of dawn, getting organised for my first day back at Artemis, and for Mia's new day-care arrangement with Ryan at The Lodge. Rehab was a bizarre place to leave my child, but the whole group seemed to have embraced Mia as their own and I got the feeling they all needed her, as much as I needed the babysitting.

It was a strange feeling to be heading back into the office after such a long time. Almost six months in fact. My world had changed so much since I'd last been inside that building, and being there made me feel like life was starting to regain some semblance of normality. Admittedly part-time hours were a far cry from the full-time career I had worked so hard to build, but still... it was a routine and I was using my brain again. I was a normal human adult, doing normal human adult things that didn't involve a baby. That's not to say that I didn't miss Mia. My heart ached when we were apart, almost as much as my boobs did, however going back to work had made me feel more like myself than I had in a long time.

I stopped outside of the big glass doors and took in the sight of the majestic building as it sparkled in the autumn sun.

"Hey Kat, you're back?" asked one of the Client Services guys, who was walking back into the building with a giant coffee in-hand. He reminded me of a young Nathan Stone.

"Hey Christian," I said, smiling as he gave me a quick hug, "yeah, just part-time."

"Awesome. Welcome back then."

"Thanks."

"You coming in?" he asked with a teasing grin, "or you going to stand out here and stare at the building all day?"

"I was thinking I'd just stand out here," I retorted, relaxing at the easy banter. "That still counts as being at work, right?"

"Does in my opinion," he chuckled, as I wandered inside with him. "Congratulations on the baby by the way. How's she doing?"

"She's doing great. She's amazing actually."

"That's awesome," he said patting my shoulder, "and how's Ryan? I heard you guys are back together?"

I'd forgotten that nothing was a secret at Artemis.

"Yeah, we are," I said awkwardly, tucking a wayward curl behind my ear. "He's good. He's only got a few weeks left in rehab and then he's back home."

"Great," he said, stopping mid-stride and looking as if he wanted to say more. "For what it's worth Kat, I would've punched Beau too. He was being a cunt."

"Oh," I said with shock at his blunt words.

"But I'm sure that's all in the past now," he said, waving his free hand in the air as if to waft away the bad vibes. "I just thought you should know that it wasn't an unprovoked attack. Ryan's a good guy."

"Thanks Christian," I said, as we arrived at the reception desk. "Anyway, I've gotta grab my new pass."

"Awesome," he said with a smile, "good luck with your first day back."

"Cheers."

Christian swiped himself in through the security doors and I turned to greet the receptionist, whom I didn't recognise.

"Hi, I'm Kat McPherson, I'm back from maternity leave today."

"Ah Kat, yes, you're on the Delfontaine account," she said, shuffling some papers behind her tall desk. "I've got your security tag here."

"Thanks," I said as she handed it over, along with a large envelope.

"That's an updated Non-Disclosure Agreement and your new contract. You can return those directly to HR once you've signed them."

"Okay thanks."

"Do you know where you're going?"

"The ninth floor I believe?"

"That's the one. It's a secure floor so you'll need to tag in again once you're up there."

"Okay, great." I swiped myself through the doors, and made my way upstairs. Everything was exactly the same, yet completely different. How was that even possible? I passed a few familiar faces and repeated the same answers to the same questions, which were generally, 'how's the baby?', followed by 'how's Ryan?'. Not one single person asked me how I was.

I was feeling a bit deflated by the time I made it up to the ninth floor. The second set of security doors slid open and the first face I saw was Amy's. We'd mended our bridges, but there was still a long way to go, so I wasn't entirely sure what to expect. I hesitantly stepped through the sliding door as she looked up from her desk and beamed at me.

"Kat!" she called, jogging in my direction. "Welcome back!"

"Thanks," I said, feeling reassured by her warm greeting.

"How are you feeling babe? A few nerves being back I imagine?"

"Just a few," I joked, heartened that at least one person cared about me.

"How did you go without Mia last week?" she asked, draping her arm over my shoulder.

"It was hard," I said, feeling immediately lighter, "not to mention all the breast pumping I had to do."

Amy threw her head back and laughed loudly. "I can't begin to imagine," she said with a smile. "And where is the young lady today?"

"She's with Ryan."

"They're pretty cool at The Lodge then?"

"Yeah, they've been very accommodating."

"Welcome to your new home," Amy said, guiding me to the desk opposite hers. "We're pod mates."

"And are you okay with that?" I asked warily. Aims looked guiltily down at her shoes and then peered up at me with big, sorrowful eyes.

"Kat... I'm really sorry I was such a bitch."

"You weren't a bitch," I said immediately.

"Yes. I was," she said firmly. "I was a massive bitch and I really hope that you'll forgive me so we can go back to how it used to be?" Amy bit her lip nervously as I plonked my bag onto my new desk.

"Aims..." I paused, "I'd love that."

She exhaled with relief. "You would?"

"Of course I would. I've missed you so much."

"I've missed you too," she said throwing her arms around my neck. "I'm so glad you're back! You, me and Ash will make an awesome team." Amy paused and looked at me with curiosity, "you are staying once Ash gets back, right?"

"I'm not sure yet."

"Well, I hope you do. It would be great to have all us girls working together." I smiled at her and sat down at my desk, trying to hide a huge yawn as I did so. Amy looked down at me and grinned. "Caffeine time?"

"I've already had one," I said, yawning again, causing us both to chuckle. "I didn't sleep very well."

Amy pulled her purse out from under her desk and patted me on the shoulder. "Then it's time for a top up. Come on boss, I'll shout you a coffee." We headed back downstairs towards the canteen and it almost felt like old times. "Been good getting back into work?" she asked with genuine interest.

"Yeah, it has. I'm starting to feel like myself again."

"That's good," she said winking, "because we've all missed you. It would be a shame if you came back as someone else."

- NATHAN STONE -

Another sun rise was upon us and very little had changed. It was as if we were caught in a vortex, where the days passed by while we were suspended in time. I glanced over at Ashley sleeping next to me, and hoped beyond logic that she'd wake up, jump out of bed and suddenly be normal again. I waited for a moment, wondering if maybe today was the day. But she didn't move.

I sighed and rolled out of bed, and as per our new daily routine, Fat Freddy plonked down after me, and waddled towards the laundry for her breakfast. I looked back at Ash, and then followed my chubby cat to her food bowl. I poured out some of her expensive food and patted Freddie as she chowed into it.

I stood up straight and stretched my back as I peered out the laundry window at the newly trimmed front yard. One positive that had come from spending so much time at the shack was that the place was looking better than ever. I'd finally had time to do all the jobs around the cottage that I'd been meaning to do for years.

"I guess I'd better call the in-laws," I told Freddy, who had practically inhaled her breakfast. "They'll be expecting an update."

- RYAN McPHERSON -

I stood outside of the Medical Directors office with my stomach twisting in knots. Tony had requested a private meeting, and I didn't know whether it would be positive or negative. With Mia staying at The Lodge, I hadn't had a chance to speak to Geoff so I had no idea what was happening with my case. Taking a deep breath, I knocked on Tony's door, silently praying that it would be good news.

"Come in," he called sternly. I gripped the brass door handle, and my stomach lurched as it turned.

"Hi Tony," I said formally, edging nervously into his office.

"Hi Ryan. Have a seat," he said, waving towards the chair in front of his desk.

"Thanks," I nodded, perching uneasily on the edge of the seat as he shuffled some papers.

"How's it going with your daughter here?" he asked casually, as if we were making small talk at the pub on a Friday afternoon.

"Uhh... it's really good," I said, wondering if Mia was the reason I was there. "Has someone complained?"

"No, not at all. In fact she's been quite the hit from all accounts."

"Oh good," I said with a sigh of relief. "So what did you want to see me about?"

"Well Ryan," he said, resting the papers on the desk in front of him, "from what I've heard, you've made a lot of progess. Would you agree?"

"Yeah, I feel like I've had a couple of big breakthroughs."

"And would you say that you've got to the heart of your drug dependency?" he asked, brows raised. My immediate response was to deny that I had a drug dependency, but then I caught myself and realised that denying it was part of the problem.

"Yes I do," I agreed with a humble nod. "I've discovered some underlying traumas that have been driving my decisions my whole life without me even realising it."

"Good to hear," he said with an approving nod. "And do you feel like you have worked through those traumas sufficiently?"

"Honestly... I don't know."

"Okay." He paused and scanned the paperwork again. "Do you think you've learned enough tools here to work through any issues that might arise on the outside?"

"Are you asking if I'm ready go back into the real world without going off the rails again?"

"That's exactly what I'm asking," he confirmed. I thought about it for a moment, surprised that he was trusting me enough to ask my opinion. When I still hadn't responded, he added, "let me put it this way... all of your therapists think you're ready to be discharged and I'd like to know if you agree with them. So what do you think Ryan, are you ready to go home?"

- KAT McPHERSON -

After a successful first day back at work, I was feeling elated but exhausted. Mia was down and I was re-heating a Marks and Spencer's meal when the door buzzer rang. I looked up with curiosity and answered the intercom before the noise woke Mia.

"Hello?" I said into the little white box.

"Hi Kat, it's Kellie."

My tummy fluttered with hope at the meaning behind her visit. I almost asked how she knew my address and then realised that it was a question I most certainly didn't want the answer to.

"Come on in," I said, buzzing her into the building. I greeted her awkwardly at the door and welcomed her into the apartment, secretly curious about which spots in my home she'd had sex with my husband, in case I needed to order any other new furniture. "Would you like a tea?"

"No, I'm fine thanks."

"Okay," I said ushering her through to the lounge.

"Where's Mia?" she asked, looking towards the nursery, which was a tell-tale sign that she was way too familiar with the layout of my house.

"She's asleep," I said, trying to push those thoughts out of my mind.

"Oh, of course." Kellie sat down on the sex sofa and I had to hold back a gag. I couldn't shake the image of Beau and a heavily pregnant version of myself, together on that couch in the most undignified of positions.

"What's up?" I asked as delicately as possible. I just wanted to hear her to say 'yes' or 'no' so that I'd know for sure and could plan for whatever future laid ahead of us.

"Kat, I've been thinking about what you said the other day," Kellie said, winding her hands together in her lap.

"Okay," I said, with nerves rising.

"I'm not cut out for being a Mum like you are," she said calmly, "it's not something that I've ever wanted."

"Okay," I replied, unsure which direction the conversation was about to go.

"And a full-term pregnancy is a big commitment for me right now."

"I see," I nodded with disappointment.

"But I also see how much you love being a mum and even though I don't understand it, it's something that I can't deny."

"I'm not sure I understand what you're saying," I said with confusion.

"I don't want to be a parent Kat, but I'd love to watch this child grow up," she said with a smile. "If you and Ryan are willing to let me be around as 'cool auntie Kellie', then I'd love to give you guys this gift." My stomach flipped with elation.

"Really?!" I asked in shock.

"Yes really. I want you to be this baby's Mum. You and Ryan are great parents and you'll be able to give it a stable life. It will be 100% yours and I won't interfere at all."

"Kellie... this is..." I was lost for words and tears sprung to my eyes.

"This is amazing," I said, jumping to my feet to give her a hug. "Thank you."

She was taken aback as I wrapped my arms around her, but after the initial shock had worn off, she softened and allowed herself be encased in my embrace. Tears streamed from my eyes and when I finally let her go, I saw that she had tears in her own eyes.

"Oh no, why are you crying?" I asked, wiping my cheeks dry.

"I don't know," she said with half laugh, "I seem to cry a lot lately."

"That's just the hormones," I told her softly as I wiped her tears away. "Your body will throw all sorts of weird and wonderful things at you over the next nine months."

"Well… eight months at least," she said with a sad smile. "Kat, I'm really scared."

"I totally understand, but we'll be here for you the whole time, so you won't be doing this on your own."

Kellie nodded and wiped her nose on her sleeve. She looked like a scared little girl and I suddenly had the weirdest maternal desire to take care of her as if she was my child too.

"I don't know what to tell my parents. I have no idea how they're going to react. I haven't even told them I'm pregnant yet."

"Maybe try telling them the truth," I suggested tactfully, "they might be shocked at first, but they'll come around."

"Yeah maybe," she agreed half-heartedly, "but what if they want to meet their grandchild? What if they try to stop me giving you the baby and want me to keep it?"

"Then we'll navigate that together," I said, squeezing her hand. "I mean it when I say that you won't be doing this alone Kellie. In fact, I can guarantee that you'll be ready to get rid of me by the time the baby arrives," I joked.

She laughed with a snotty snort. "Thanks Kat."

"Hey, you're family now, and family sticks together." I handed her a tissue, and she blew her nose loudly. "How about that cuppa now?" I asked, sounding eerily like my mother.

"That sounds nice."

- RYAN McPHERSON -

On Tuesday morning, I was playing Monopoly with my peculiar collection of new friends, waiting for Mia to arrive for her day at rehab daycare. The orderly came out to tell me I had visitors, and Sloane jumped with excitement.

"Ooh she's here!" she trilled, clapping her hands enthusiastically.

"Yeah, I must admit that I look forward to seeing that little poop machine every day," confessed Rodney with what appeared to be a blush.

"Oooh Rod are you getting clucky?" teased Sloane.

"So what if I am?" he asked defensively.

"Well, it makes you more likeable for one thing," she retorted with a cheeky wink, to which Rodney immediately blushed again. I shook my head with a smile. At some point those two would figure it out. They were the only people at The Lodge who didn't know they fancied each other.

The odd pair continued their banter, and I let out a chuckle as I headed to reception to greet my family. My grin widened when I saw my two favourite girls standing in the reception area.

"G'day gorgeous," I said loudly, putting on my best Aussie accent.

"It's like Ritchie's right here with us," Kat joked with a giggle, and then gave me a soft kiss on the lips. She was so happy and relaxed that I felt my body react to her touch. There was passion glimmering in her gaze, but there was very little to be done about it whilst I was in rehab.

"Enough of that, or you'll get us all in trouble," teased Sloane, and then ran straight over to Mia. "Hello Miss Mia," she cooed lovingly as she stuck her head into the pram, "we've been waiting for you girlfriend."

Kat laughed at Sloane's excitement. "Do you want to get her out for a cuddle?"

"Yes please," said Sloane, carefully extracting Mia from the pram. "There's that gorgeous face," she said, cradling Mia protectively in her arms. "Mind if I take her for a walk in the garden?"

"Not at all," said Kat with a smile, "I'm sure she'd love that."

We watched Sloane carry our baby away so lovingly that Mia could have been her own child. Rodney and Angelica quickly followed along behind her, while Kat and I giggled at the sight of the odd procession.

Once they'd left the room, we exchanged amused glances and

my stomach flipped at the adoring look in her eyes.

"Looks like it's just the two of us," I said with a nervous shrug, unsure why I was feeling shy around my own wife.

"Looks that way," she agreed with a cheeky smile.

"Have you got time for a cuppa before you go?"

"Actually I'd rather walk and a chat."

"Sure." I led her out to the Japanese Gardens. "You look tired," I said, pushing one of her auburn curls off her face.

"Yeah, I'm exhausted," Kat said with a smile.

"What's with the grin then?"

"Oh, I can't tell you exactly what's going through my head right now, or you'd be tempted to break the abstinence rule."

I laughed, squeezing her around the waist. "I love you so much."

"And I love you so much," she said, as her body sank against mine.

"I'm going to ravish you once I get out of here."

"I'll hold you to that," she giggled. We strolled across the little wooden bridge that ran over the koi pond.

"So, what else is on your mind?" I asked, reading between the lines of her frisky mood.

"I've got some good news."

"Okay…" I said warily, "which is what exactly?"

"Kellie came to see me this morning."

"Oh," I said with surprise. "What did she say?"

"She wants us to have the baby."

My heart pounded and I stopped in my tracks. "Really?" I asked turning to face her.

"Yeah."

"Oh my god," I breathed in shock, "we're having another baby."

"We are."

"Holy shit." Was I really prepared for a second baby when I'd barely had enough time with the first?

"She's nice Ryan."

"Who? Kell?"

"Yeah," she nodded, "I can see why you were attracted to her. I originally thought it was the boobs but… she's a sweet girl."

"I don't know that I'd call her sweet," I joked, thinking back to all our sordid sexploits, "but she's got a good heart," I paused and studied Kat's face. "So you really want to do this?"

"Yeah, I really do," she said with genuine excitement. "And I want to be there for Kellie. This is a huge thing for her and she's young. She's going to need our support. Will that be weird for you?"

"Probably," I said honestly, "but I'll just have to push past it."

"Good, because she's coming to see you today."

"Okay. Why?"

"I thought it would be good for you guys to talk before we all sign on the dotted line."

"That's a good idea babe."

"Are you sure?"

"Yeah, we probably need to chat."

"Thank you. You're amazing," she said giving me a lingering kiss that was laced with desire. I felt a little breathless from the intimate gesture and I stared into her hazel eyes.

"I was thinking the same about you," I said croakily, doing my best to calm my excited body. I pulled away from her and led her over to the red bench seat. "I've got something to tell you too."

"I bet it's not as good as my surprise," she teased.

"I wouldn't be so sure about that," I said with a grin.

"Really? It must be pretty amazing to beat my baby news."

"Well… I had a meeting with the Medical Director yesterday."

Kat leaned forward and looked at me curiously. "What about?"

"All of my counsellors feel that I've made great progress and they've agreed to waive the last couple of weeks of my sentence."

Kat looked at me agape. "So… does that mean…"

"I'm coming home next week!" I exclaimed excitedly.

"Really?" she asked, with tears welling in her eyes.

"Yes, really," I confirmed with a smile.

"Oh my god!" she squealed, throwing her arms around my neck as she burst into tears. "I can't believe it. You're finally coming home."

"I'm finally coming home." We held each other tight, and it felt like we were closer than we'd ever been… except that I was still holding on to one hell of a big secret. I pulled away from her and wiped the tears off her cheeks. "Only a week and we'll be starting our new life together."

- NATHAN STONE -

On Tuesday morning, we had a breakthrough. After a full week in bed, Ash finally got up. Freddy and I had gone through the motions of our usual daily routine, but that day, when I emerged from the shower, Ashley was awake.

"Hey," I said quietly, worried that I'd scare her.

"Hey," she answered without looking me in the eye. I threw my damp towel into the washing basket.

"Fancy a shower?" I asked, expecting her to refuse. "The water will still be hot."

She nodded her head, "sure."

"Great," I said with surprise. Ash looked weak and frail from not having eaten solids for a week, so I helped her into the bathroom and pulled out a fresh towel for her. "Just call if you need me," I said before leaving her to shower in private. I looked down at Freddy, who had resumed her position on the bed. "Wow," I told the fat cat. "Now all we have to do is get her to eat something."

I pottered in the kitchen to prevent myself from hovering around the bathroom door, but when I heard her return to the bedroom, I couldn't help myself.

"Can I get you some food?" I called cautiously.

"No thanks."

"Okay." I waited for her to come out of the bedroom, but she never emerged. I paced a few laps of the kitchen, wondering whether to go in and check on her. I finally decided that I should, and when I walked in, she was sitting on the bed wearing clean pyjamas and towel-drying her freshly washed hair. I approached her slowly to check the dressing on her shoulder.

"The wound's healing up well," I told her pointlessly as she stared blankly at the floor. "Should be able to get the stitches out by the time we get home."Ashley didn't respond so I finished re-dressing the wound in silence and then took the towel from her hands. "Let me dry it for you," I offered swapping the damp towel for a brush and the hairdryer. She nodded and let me blow dry her hair.

We didn't exchange any more words, but at least she'd left the bed for a moment. It wasn't a massive improvement, but it was an improvement none-the-less and I was willing to take any win I could get.

- RYAN McPHERSON -

"So how are you feeling about everything?" I asked Kellie as we walked laps through the gardens, trying to get Mia to sleep. In the harsh light of day our age difference was incredibly apparent and I felt more like her dad than her ex-lover.

"I'm petrified," she joked, running her hands subtly over her still-flat belly.

"That's understandable," I reassured her, deciding that it was better not to mention the gory details of the horror-show known as childbirth. Even witnessing it was scary enough, I couldn't imagine having to be the person pushing it out. "Is there anything we can do for you?"

"Not really. It's just a matter of coming to terms with the birth. I'm fine with the rest."

"Could you do an elective cesarian?"

"I could, but the recovery time is a lot longer."

"We'd cover you for that if you'd rather go that way," I said, seeing the fear in her eyes. "Whatever you need, we'll support you."

"Thanks Ryan. I'll think about it," she said with a nod as she peered down at Mia in the pram. "I think I must be crazy for doing this, but it feels like the right thing to do. You and Kat are such good parents. You deserve to have another baby."

I stopped walking and rested my hands on her shoulders.

"Kell... this is an amazing thing that you're doing for us, but if you have any doubts, please voice them now before it's too late. I don't want you to be locked into something you're not comfortable with."

Kellie smiled and patted my hand. "I'm not going to change my mind, Ryan. I want to do this. I don't know why... but I do. And yes, I do wonder what the fuck I've gotten myself into, but my heart knows it's right."

"As long as you're sure."

"I am sure, even though I think I'm mental for it."

I laughed and resumed my position behind the pram as Mia started to grumble.

"So, you're really okay with this?"

"Yeah. I'm not planning on having my own kids, so it will be nice knowing that there's a kid out there somewhere who shares my DNA."

"I thought you wanted to be around? What did Kat say? Cool

Auntie Kellie."

"I'm handing over all my rights Ryan," she told me seriously. "It will be written into the contract, so you'll be under no obligation to include me. It will be nice to be around, but who knows what might happen. You guys might want to leave London, or even go overseas and I won't get in the way of that. This kid will be yours in every sense, and if there's a little room for me to make an appearance in their lives then great. But if not, that's okay too."

"Wow. You know Kell," I said, throwing one arm over her shoulder, "you're one of the most paradoxical people I've ever met."

Kellie stared up at me blankly. "I don't know what that means."

I chuckled, endeared by her innocence. "It means you're a very complex woman and sometimes it feels like you're two completely different people."

"So... kind of like I'm schizophrenic?"

I threw my head back and laughed loudly. "No," I said, once my laughter had subsided. "Just that there's a lot more to you than meets the eye."

- Chapter 5 -

Emergence

- NATHAN STONE -

After the shower day, Ash had gone back to bed and spent another week sleeping. Or perhaps pretending to sleep. It was hard to tell. To pass the time, I'd been reading, researching and pottering around the house. Midnight texts with Kat had become a regular thing, as had my updates to the Grangers'. Obviously, I hadn't been entirely honest about Ashley's mental state. If I'd told them the complete truth, they'd worry about her even more, so I sugar-coated the situation. There was no point in making everyone stress.

I felt like I was failing Ash. After two weeks of trying, I was officially out of ideas. Our situation was looking bleak, and it had become abundantly clear that I was ridiculously under-qualified to deal with the situation.

I stood at the kitchen counter, staring out at the ocean as I prepared Ash another meal that she probably wouldn't eat. The sea was turquoise, and the rising sun was shimmering across the rippling water. Under any other circumstances, this would have been the perfect romantic getaway. I chopped some avocado into a bowl as Fred waddled in after finishing her breakfast. There was no denying that our Freddie was eating for six. Her belly was huge, and I suspected it wouldn't be long before we heard the pitter-patter of little paws around the house.

"At least you haven't lost your appetite," I said, giving her a quick pat, then washed my hands and resumed my pointless meal prep. If I couldn't get Ash to eat something soon, she would waste away. She'd already lost a fair amount of weight in the few weeks that we'd been at the shack and I dreaded the thought of her going back to the gaunt, skeletal figure she'd been during her Dom days.

I heard a noise in the living room and looked down at Fred, who was still sitting at my feet. I put down the knife and stuck my head around the kitchen wall to see Ash standing at the bookshelf, staring at the pink salt lamp. Her baggy jumper was hanging off her shoulder, revealing the top of her spine, which was beginning to protrude from her thinning body.

"Ash?" I asked, hoping that I wasn't having a stress-induced hallucination. She turned towards me and my stomach dropped at the sight of her face. In the bright light of day, it was clear how unwell she was.

"Hey," she said quietly. Her eyes were highlighted by dark bags; her face was pale as a ghost; and her cheeks were slightly sunken, making her look more like Skeletor than She-Ra.

"Are you okay?" I asked, slowly stepping out of the kitchen.

"Yeah," she said, with an actual, real-life smile. I was both elated and stunned. I hadn't seen her smile for so long that I'd almost forgotten what it looked like. It wasn't the same quality as her usual sparkly-eyed grins, but it was a smile none-the-less. Ash looked back at the lamp and pointed, "so, Mister Stone... under that well-polished veneer of yours, is a guitar-playing, hippie, surfer-boy."

I laughed at her unexpected change of mood, and scratched the back of my neck nervously. "Yeah, I suppose so," I shrugged.

"Maybe we aren't that different after all," she said, almost to herself. I didn't know how to respond so I just stood there, silent and awkward. "This place is amazing Nathan."

"I'm glad you like it."

Ash glanced around the bright room, with its random collection of shabby-chic furniture and eclectic beach art, none of which matched. She smiled again and then fastened her piercing green eyes on me. Her gaze was so intense that I almost felt naked under her stare. For the first time since her attack, I could see a glimmer of the old Ash in her eyes.

"This is the real you isn't it?" she asked, already knowing the answer. I nodded and exhaled, realizing that I'd been holding my breath for an entire fortnight. In fact, I probably hadn't breathed properly since the day we'd first run into Dominic at the hotel.

"Do you want some food?" I asked hopefully.

"That would be good, thanks," she said with a nod.

My jaw dropped, "really?"

"Yeah. What's on the menu?"

"I was just making you an avo smash," I said as I studied her warily, unsure whether to believe my eyes and ears. Was she actually back, or was I dreaming?

"Sounds great."

Ash took a step towards me. "Thank you for taking such good care of me Nath."

"It's been my pleasure," I said giving her a weird, awkward nod.

"Well, that's a blatant lie," she teased, laughing tiredly. "I know it hasn't been a pleasure for you, but I appreciate you giving me a safe space to fall apart."

"Ash…" I said, shaking my head, "you're the most important thing in my life - not that you're a 'thing' of course," I added quickly, "but… you know, you're important and nothing else matters anymore."

Tears sprung into her eyes and I stood glued to the spot, wishing that I could wrap her up in my arms. I was too scared to go near her, so I employed my default technique of tucking my hands into my pockets.

I bit the inside of my cheek and glanced out the sliding door to the sparkling ocean. I could feel the lump in my throat begin to rise as I fought off the unwelcome tears that were threatening to shed. I'd never been one to cry, but these past few months had turned me inside out.

Ash walked over and placed her hand on my cheek, "I love you, Nathan."

I swallowed down the lump and looked into her eyes, which were the only recognizable feature on her thin face.

"I love you too," I said in a croaky whisper, "and I want to help you through this."

She smiled faintly, "you already have."

- ASHLEY GRANGER -

I stroked Nathan's stubbly jaw as he stood with his hands wedged firmly in his pockets. His bloodshot eyes were studying me intently, like he was searching for a trace the person I used to be. He ran one hand through his ruffled hair and then placed it gently on top of my hand, still resting lightly on his cheek. Nathan looked broken. This whole thing had been hard on him, but he'd managed to keep it together and maintain enough strength to carry both of us. I didn't have the words to thank him for that, so I leaned my forehead against his.

"Thank you," I whispered.

"I don't know what else to do for you," he said with a crackle in his voice and his hand still resting on mine.

"Just keep being you," I said with tears in my eyes. Nath nodded and turned his head to kiss my hand, but besides that, didn't move a muscle. I knew he was being respectful of my space, so I closed the small gap between our bodies and gently threaded my arms around his waist.

He let out a long breath and wrapped his arms around me, resting his chin on my head as I leant my cheek against his warm chest. I could hear his heart pounding in a steady rhythm.

"I missed you," he said quietly into my hair, with a stifled sniff. I felt his Adams Apple move against my head and I looked up at him as a solitary tear rolled down his face.

"I'm back now," I said, wiping away the tear, "but I need to tell you what happened with Dom."

"Only if you want to."

"I need to," I said, choking back my own tears, "you need to know, because it might change your feelings."

"It won't," he answered softly but firmly. "No matter what happened with Dom, nothing will change my feelings for you."

I dropped my head against his chest again. He was impossibly sweet, and it was killing me. "That's easy for you to say now."

"Yeah it is," Nath said, taking my chin, "because it's true." He tilted my head upwards so that I was looking him in the eyes. "What happened in your flat has no bearing on our relationship, or on my feelings for you. You were forced into a horrific situation and whatever you did to survive… and whatever he did to you…" Nathan swallowed hard as more tears sparkled in his eyes, "it might break my heart to hear what you went through, but it won't make me love you any less. If you want to tell me what happened then I'll be here to listen, but don't tell me out of guilt. You have nothing to be sorry for."

"But I do," I said, fighting off my own tears. "Nathan, when Dom…" I paused and closed my eyes. It was such an uncomfortable thing to admit out loud. "When he…" I stopped as I stumbled over the words again. Saying them out loud would make the whole thing feel real.

"Hey," he said softly, "if this is too hard, just wait until you're ready."

"But I have to say this Nath."

"Okay."

"When Dom… did what he did… I…" I took a deep breath and looked him in the eyes, "I had an orgasm," I blurted with a cringe. I felt nauseated saying the words out loud but Nathan's face softened with a look of relief.

"Is that what you're worried about?" he asked, rubbing my arms gently.

I nodded and stared down at our bare feet. "I'm so sorry," I whispered.

"You don't owe me an apology for that."

"But-"

"No Ash. No more of this," he interrupted sternly. "Blaming yourself isn't healthy, especially when you didn't do anything wrong."

"But… doesn't it mean that on some level I enjoyed it?"

"Maybe your body did, but that's just a physical response," Nath said factually, "and it's common in those situations. It has nothing to do with enjoyment or pleasure, it's purely the body reacting to a physical stimulus," he explained as if he was quoting a textbook. I cocked my head curiously, wondering how he'd become such an expert on the matter. He blushed and gave a half-shrug, "I've been doing a lot of a research." I was both stunned and heartened by his dedication.

"You did research?" I asked breathlessly, struck by an overwhelming surge of love for the man.

"I wanted to understand and make sure I was doing everything I could for you."

Tears sprung into my eyes again, and I took his face in my hands.

"You're an amazing man, do you know that?"

"The He-Man to your She-Ra?" he joked sadly. I smiled, letting out a half-laugh/half-cry snort, as my tears broke free and began streaming down my face. Nathan pulled me close, holding me tightly while I cried into his chest once again. I was surprised I still had tears left after shedding so many already. I should have been shriveled up like a raisin. I wiped my eyes and peered up at Nathan, which caused my head to go dizzy. My eyes momentarily blacked out and Nathan grasped me tight as I swayed on my feet. "Are you okay?" he asked with concern.

"Yeah, just a head-spin," I answered, gripping his shoulders as the blackness cleared.

"Let's get some food into you before you pass out," he said as he herded me over to the dining table and sat me down.

"Yeah, I am pretty hungry," I agreed, feeling my stomach rumble. "I don't know how I managed to live on nothing for ten years. It's only been a few days and I'm about to pass out."

"Twelve days," Nathan said quietly.

"Huh?"

He cleared his throat, "we've been here for twelve days."

"We have?"

"Yeah," Nathan nodded with a smile.

"Oh my god," I said with surprise, "my parents must be freaking out."

"I told them you've been on heavy painkillers that make you drowsy."

"Perfect. Thanks. And what about Gaz? Was he pissed?"

"Not at you, no," he said with a strained smile, "he said you should take as much time as you need."

"Okay."

"Kesha's texted every day to check on you," he added. "She said they've got the same person to cover your classes as last time, so there's no need to go back until you're ready."

"Alright," I said, impressed by Nathan's PA skills, "thanks for taking care of all that."

"All part of the service," he joked.

"What about Jock?"

Nathan rubbed his neck. "Uhh…yeah… No."

"He knew Nath. He sent me a text when we were in Paris. Did you tell him?"

"Sort of."

"How do you sort of tell someone something like that?"

"That's a long story and I don't think you need to worry about it right now."

I eyed him skeptically, trying to deduce his meaning from the look on his face. "Okay," I agreed with a nod, "I'll take your lead there, but we're going to circle back to that later."

Nath nodded his head awkwardly and cleared his throat. "How about we get that food sorted huh?"

"And then I want to tell you everything that happened that night."

"Alright," Nath nodded and kissed me on the forehead. "I'm so proud of you."

- KAT McPHERSON -

The day had finally arrived! Ryan was coming home! It felt like Christmas morning and I all-but bounced out of bed. I felt like a Disney Princess, as I pranced around the house singing and dancing.

"Daddy's coming home today Mia," I sang to my daughter as she watched me, wide-eyed, from her bouncer as if I was a crazy person. Which essentially I was. I was crazy excited that I'd be bringing my man home after so long.

The house was looking great after my renovation rampage and I couldn't wait for him to see it. It felt like we really were getting a fresh start and nothing could have dampened my spirits. I poured myself a hot cup of peppermint tea as my phone vibrated excitedly on the kitchen table. I grabbed my cup off the bench and glanced over to see who was calling.

"Oh my," I muttered, when I saw Beau's name glowing on my screen. What on earth would he be calling for? We hadn't spoken one word to each other outside of work, and suddenly he was calling me on a Saturday morning? I popped my cup on the table and picked up the phone.

"Hey," I said warily.

"Hey Kitty-Kat," Beau replied in the same cheerful way he used to, back when we were besties. "How's your morning going?"

"Good thanks, and yours?"

"Great! Just on my way back from Water Polo," he said as if it was perfectly normal for us to chat on the phone.

"Cool. So... what can I do for you?" I asked, wondering if perhaps he was drunk because it was the only explanation I could think of.

"Oh, nothing," he said snapping out of his over-friendly tone. "I just wanted to call and say good luck for today. I know it's a big day for you guys."

"Oh. Wow. Thanks," I babbled, surprised at the purpose for his call. "That's really... nice of you."

Beau sighed heavily. "Look Kat... I never really apologised for my role in... well... everything. I'm not saying that your behaviour was okay, but I knew what I was doing when I slept with you and I'm sorry for being selfish."

"You don't owe me an apology Beau. I was the slutty one who cheated on my husband."

"Right," he said, seemingly stunned by my blunt response. "Well... anyway... that was all I called to say, so..."

"Thanks Beau," I said, jumping in as his sentence trailed off. "I appreciate the call."

"Yeah, sure, no problem," he said, and we both fell silent.

"Anyway..."

"Right. I should let you get ready."

"Yeah," I agreed. "I'll see you Monday."

"Yeah, see you then. Bye."

"Bye Beau." I hung up the phone and placed it face down on the table, then looked at Mia with disbelief. "Well that was unexpected."

- RYAN McPHERSON -

Saying goodbye to everyone at The Lodge was much harder than I'd expected. After nearly three months locked away with that rag-tag crew, we'd become more like family than fellow inmates. I did the rounds to say my goodbyes to the rest of the group, then grabbed my luggage and snuck out to wait for Kat in the reception area, with my two main partners-in-crime. I plopped down my luggage and turned to them with a sad sigh.

"I can't believe I'm saying this, but I'm going to miss this place," I said, taking another glance around the building that had been my home for the past few months.

"And I can't believe you're leaving," Sloane said, throwing her arms around my neck and squeezing me hard. "How am I going to stay sane without my rehab brother?"
I gave her a tight hug and patted her back in a brotherly fashion.

"You've got Rod now," I said quietly into her ear. She looked up at me and blushed, but didn't argue. "Come and see us when you get out yeah?" I told her sternly.

"Of course!" she said, quickly brushing a tear from her eye.

"You've got my number, so no excuses. Mia will need Aunty Sloane time."

"Deal boss," she agreed with a grin, finally releasing her grip on my shoulders.

"I can't believe they let you out early," Rodney teased, punching me hard in the bicep.

"They felt bad that I was showing you up," I bantered back.

"Sure mate, you keep telling yourself that," he said. I laughed and grabbed him in a headlock so that I could pull him in for a sneak hug. He tried to wriggle out of my grasp but I employed Ritchie's 'Carlton Crush' technique and secured him tightly. "Oi, get off me ya posh cunt."

"Not until you tell me you love me," I goaded him.

"Fuck off," he grumbled, as I forced him into a hug.

"Okay then," I said, before whispering into his ear. "How about you tell Sloane you love her instead?" Rodney pulled back from me and this time I let him go. He eyed me suspiciously, so I nodded encouragingly. "Take care of each other," I reiterated with a smile.

"Absolutely," Sloane said, casting a sideways glance at Rodney, who nodded in agreement.

"Sure," he said awkwardly as we saw my car pull-up outside. I studied their faces in turn, and a wave of sadness gripped me, so I embraced them both for one last group hug.

"Well... I guess that's it," I said, picking up my bags. "I'll see you guys on the other side."

- RITCHIE CARLTON -

Thank God for Saturday morning rugby with the Aussie boys. It was the only thing that had been keeping me sane since Nathan and Ash had fled to Cornwall. In the few weeks I'd been home, Sandrine had stepped up her recruitment campaign to relentless levels, while my non-relationship with Amy had hit an all-time low. Aims had come back to my house the night before for just long enough for us to fuck, then left immediately. I had no idea how to break the toxic cycle, or even if I really wanted to.

We'd been going through the motions of being fuck-buddies, but our friendship was strained. In fact, I wasn't even sure if we had a friendship to salvage. We'd always been so pre-occupied with playing our pretend couple game that it was hard to tell if there ever was a friendship to begin with. I was still dwelling on my failing psuedo-relationship as I jogged towards Regents Park for our pre-game warm-up session.

"What's up your arse today?" My lanky mate Wayne asked, as he sidled up next to me. Wayne had also been Nathan's physio since his car accident, which meant that most of our recent conversations had revolved around Stoner's recovery. I was surprised that his question was directed primarily towards my wellbeing.

"Nothing," I denied, knowing that he'd probably get distracted with our warm-up and stop asking questions.

"Come on mate, give me more credit than that. It's Amy right?" he grilled as he tossed the ball to me.

"Yeah," I sighed sulkily and threw the ball back to him. The woman was putting me in a serious funk. I had no idea how to handle the situation. Did I walk away or keep torturing myself just to spend some time with her?

"You looked pretty cosy last night."

I caught the ball and wondered whether it was worth mentioning my latest failed attempt to break up with her, but that would have been mortifying.

"Yeah, but that was only because she was horny," I admitted and kicked the ball in Wayne's direction. "She has me so tightly by the balls that I'm not even sure I still have any."

Wayne laughed in sympathy, forgetting that the ball was hurtling towards him. "Maybe you should go back to Paris and get your French lady to check for you," he suggested as he caught the ball a millisecond before it hit his face.

"I know you're taking the piss, but that's a very appealing idea right now."

Wayne tucked the ball under his arm and gave me his full attention, as if he was about to give me a counselling session.

"I don't want to sound like your mum, but if the Amy thing is making you this unhappy, then I think you need to end it mate," he said sagely.

"Yeah, I do," I agreed as the game whistle blew. It was time to get on the field and run off my rage.

- ASHLEY GRANGER -

Over breakfast, I told Nathan everything about the attack including my rose quartz defense, the belt handcuffs, the moment I stabbed Dominic and all the gory details in between. I hadn't expected him to take it as well as he did, and most certainly hadn't expected that telling my story would make me feel better, but it had done just that. Sharing the whole gruesome experience with Nathan had lightened my burden, and I even managed to almost eat an entire meal.

Nathan had gone all-out with my smashed avo and even sprinkled pumpkin seeds and fresh parsley on top. I'd woofed down my scrumptious meal, when I felt my stomach churn. I paused, fork-in-hand, to see if my final few mouthfuls would settle, but I could feel the bile rising in my throat.

"Are you okay?" Nathan asked, as I put down my fork abruptly.

"Nope," I said, quickly jumping to my feet with my hand over my mouth, hoping that I'd reach the bathroom in time. The second that I bent over the toilet bowl, my body began purging the meal I'd just eaten.

"Hey," Nath said quietly, rubbing my back with one hand, "you alright?"

"Yeah," I nodded, waving away his concerns. "I think my body just needs to re-adjust to eating solids again."

"Maybe we should have started with smoothies," he joked.

"Hindsight is 20/20," I agreed, wiping my mouth.

"Just like your dad's hearing," he joked. It sapped the small amount of energy I had, but I couldn't hold back a laugh. "Here," Nath said, handing me a glass of water.

"Thanks." I peered up at him with an embarrassed smile. "Sorry."

"Don't be sorry. It reminds me of our first date."

I sipped the water and smiled. "But I thought that wasn't a date."

"That was definitely a date," he said with a sexy grin.

"So why didn't you kiss me then?" I teased, handing him back the glass of water.

"Besides the fact you were chucking for half of it?"

"There was plenty of time before I started vomming," I said, climbing to my feet as he helped me up. "There were a few times I thought you were about to, but then you chickened out."

"Honestly… you looked like a deer in headlights every time I thought about it," he said with shrug, "plus you were drunk, so it didn't feel right."

"Ever the gentleman," I joked as he guided me out to the living room. I sat down on the huge sofa and tucked my scarred feet up underneath my bottom. "So, what's on the schedule for today boss?"

Nathan laughed, "I think we both know who's the boss around here and it's certainly not me."

"Aww has Freddie been bullying you?" I joked.

"Yeah, she's pretty demanding," he replied with a grin, "but I love her, so she's worth the effort."

My stomach did a little flip, so I leaned back against the cushions and studied his beautiful face. He'd done so much for me over the last few months that I didn't even know how to begin to articulate my gratitude.

"You must be going stir-crazy," I said simply.

"Yeah, I won't lie… I have been itching to get down to the beach." I peered out the doors to the crystal-clear ocean.

"It looks like a nice day out there," I said encouragingly.

"I'd love to get out for a surf, but I'm not sure how my knee will go. Or my hips for that matter."

"Well let's find out."

"You wanna go surfing?"

"Why so surprised? Can't women surf too?"

"Yeah of course, but I didn't think- I mean-" he spluttered, back-pedalling badly.

"It's okay, I don't surf," I laughed and gave him a cheeky wink. Nath rolled his eyes.

"Well, at least I know you're back to normal again," he joked.

I chuckled and studied his gorgeous but tired face. I had to ask him the question that had been playing on my mind since Dom had mentioned it in my flat.

"Did you and my Dad really plan to kill Dom?" I blurted. Nathan let out a shocked 'ha', at my question and ran his hand through his hair.

"Uhhh, yeah we did," he admitted sheepishly, "but don't get angry at your dad, it was all my idea. I wouldn't have got him involved but he guessed when we went to lunch that day and then I couldn't talk him out of it. I think he was just making sure I didn't get into any trouble."

"Right," I answered, feeling a little shell-shocked that Dom had actually been telling the truth about the murder plot. "So, I guess that's what you were discussing in the cellar at lunch that day?"

"Yep."

"And if Dom hadn't come after me, you guys were going to do this... when?"

"Geoff was going to do it while we were in Paris."

"Holy shit," I laughed in disbelief. My father had genuinely planned to physically murder my ex-boyfriend. I sat in stunned silence as I processed the news and Nathan edged cautiously closer to the sofa, looking like a dog who had been caught chewing the furniture.

"Are you okay?" he asked quietly, as he hovered nervously in front of me. "I mean... how do you feel about your boyfriend plotting a murder? I need you to know that it's not something I make a habit of."

"Well I'd hope not."

"It was the only solution I could think of where you'd be free and safe." Nathan watched me worriedly as I let out a big breath of air. It was an extreme thing for him to do.

"Are you angry?" He asked with a grimace.

"No," I said, looking up at him with complete adoration. "I think it was ... brave."

"You do?" He asked warily.

"Yeah, I do," I said, with a smile, "stupid... but brave and oddly sweet. I know you wouldn't make a decision like that without weighing up all the options first, so it shows that you must care about me a lot to do something that risky."

"Technically your dad was going to do the risky part," he joked, sitting carefully down next to me. "Ash... I care about you more than anything in the world. I'd do anything to protect you and if your dad hadn't figured it out, then I would have killed that prick without a second thought."

"You could have ended up in prison."

"It would have been worth it to see you living your life without having to look over your shoulder all the time."

"Nathan…"

"I love you Ash and your happiness means more to me than my own freedom," he said, taking my hand.

"Likewise," I said, interlocking my fingers with his. He held my gaze for a moment and then broke the silence.

"How did you find out about that anyway?"

"Dom," I muttered quietly, "he installed that app on your phone while you were in the hospital."

Nathan sighed and nodded his head. "Well that certainly explains a few things," he said, his eyes boring into mine. "I'm sorry you had to go through all of that. I wish I'd got to him before he got to you. If I'd acted quicker, he wouldn't have seen it coming."

"Somehow I don't think that's true," I told him as I stroked his stubbly cheek, "I think it was always going to be me versus him."

"I guess that's another way to look at destiny," he joked sadly.

"Hey, everything's good now and I'm fine. This is just another chapter that we'll have to leave behind."

"Yeah, I suppose."

"Anyway," I said chirpily, switching the mood, "the ocean isn't going to surf itself."

"And there's the awkward humour," he teased, releasing my hand. "Looks like you're 100% back to normal then."

"Go get into your wetsuit smartarse," I said, trying unsuccessfully, to shove him off the couch.

"Right you are ma'am," he joked in a bad American accent as he rose from the seat and saluted me. I laughed and saluted back before heading to the bedroom to change into my swimsuit.

Despite my accidental starvation diet, my bikini was fitting a little tighter than usual. My boobs were practically spilling out of the top and the shorts were very grippy around my tummy. I must have packed on a few extra pounds since I'd left Bali and not realised.

Feeling self-conscious about my plumpness, I pulled on a skirt and tee and returned to the living room.

"Okay, I'm good to go," Nathan said, emerging from the laundry with his wetsuit only half on. He was bare chested from the waist up and the arms of the wetty were hanging down by his legs.

"Oh my," I mumbled under my breath, as my jaw nearly hit the ground. It was the first time I'd seen his bare skin since we'd been at the shack, and I'd almost forgotten how amazing his chest was.

- NATHAN STONE -

"You might want to grab a hat, the sun can get pretty bitey down here," I said to Ash as I returned to the lounge room with a couple of beach towels and a bottle of sunscreen.

"I'll be fine," she said, staring at me with a strange expression. I studied her for a moment, trying to decipher the unfamiliar look on her pale face. Maybe she was trying to hold back another vomit.

"Are you okay?" I asked.

"I'm fine," she said with a weird shrug, "I just don't think I need to worry about the English sun after living in Bali for three years."

"Have you seen yourself lately?" I teased with wink, throwing her the bottle of sunscreen. "You should take a look in the mirror to check for a reflection, because you're as pale as a Cullen."

"Wow, comparing me to a vampire, you know how to make a girl feel special," she joked with sparkly eyes. Even though she was still a shadow of the old Ash, it seemed like she was finally back.

"Take it as a compliment," I said, shoving the towels into a rucksack. "Haven't you seen the movies? Apparently, all vampires are hot."
She laughed and started rubbing the sunscreen onto her arms.

"That's very true, and they sparkle in the sunlight."

"I think you'd be more likely melt in the sunlight at the moment."

"Hasn't anyone ever told you not to provoke a vampire?" she teased, slathering the sunscreen over her white legs, "it never ends well for the human."

"I'd be pretty safe. You're probably the only vegan vampire that ever existed."

Ash grinned, "that would be a good point if I planned to eat you, but I was thinking I'd turn you into a vampire. That way I could keep you forever."

"And pass up the opportunity to be with Edward until the end of days?" I joked, grabbing a cap off the hatstand.

"I'd choose you over Edward in a heartbeat."

"A heartbeat that we wouldn't have if we were vampires."

"Touché," Ash agreed with a smile. I plopped the cap onto her head and gave her a wink.

"You know you'd be stuck with me for eternity, right?"

Ashley's big green eyes peered up at me from underneath my huge cap. It nearly felt like we were back to how we'd been before the attack.

"If I had to live forever Stone, then I'd want you there to suffer along with me," she joked. I laughed, flicking her cap visor down over her eyes.

"It's good to have you back Chucky." Ash stiffened and re-adjusted the cap with a solemn expression on her face. The mood quickly shifted, and I froze in dread as I saw the spark quickly vanish from her eyes again. I had no idea what had triggered her, but something had flipped a switch. "Everything alright?" I asked worriedly. "Did I say something wrong?"

"No, sorry," she sighed, shaking her head. "Dom called me Chucky that night and it just…" she trailed off. What a fucking cunt Dom was.

"Hey," I said, sitting down next to her, "it's okay, I won't call you that again."

"It's not your fault," she said, patting my thigh, "he was trying to intimidate me but…"

"Yeah, that's pretty fucked up," I agreed, clasping my hands in my lap. "I guess I'll just have to stick to calling you 'babe'."

"I can live with that," Ash said with a sad smile.

"Okay," I agreed, noting her change of mood, "so what's that face about then?"

"It's just… I'm no better than him, you know?"

"Are you kidding me? How can you say that?"

"Nath… I took Dom's life and I actually feel pleased that I'm the one who did it. What sort of person would be proud of killing someone?"

"The sort of person that's fought to save her own life more than once," I told her sternly. "The sort of person that endured years of abuse and survived. The sort of person who never gave up when others would have. The sort of person that salvaged herself from a wreckage and built a new life from nothing." I paused and wiped a tear from her eye. "The sort of person that I'm in love with," I said quietly, as I felt my own tears threatening to fall. "You're amazing Ashley Granger, don't ever forget that. Besides… you did Dom a favour."

"How exactly did I do him a favour?" She asked with a smile, rolling her eyes playfully.

"If you hadn't killed the fucker your dad would have tortured him with a slow painful death," I joked grimly. A sparkle of the old Ash flashed in her eyes and I sighed shamefully. "I'm sorry I wasn't there to protect you."

"I love that you want to protect me, but I needed to save myself."

"I know," I agreed sadly, "you really don't need me at all do you?"

"Yes I do," she replied with big eyes, "I need you to love me."

"*That*, I can do," I told Ash with a confident smile. I'd never been so sure about anything in my entire life.

"Anyway..." she said, as she stood up, "...let's get down to the beach. I don't want to talk about Dom, he's already wasted two weeks of our lives."

"And the rest," I mumbled with a sombre nod.

We walked silently down the sandy track to the shoreline. The sun was shining brightly, warming the sand and our faces, but there was a slight chill in the breeze to remind us that were still in England. We stood and admired the water for a few minutes in companionable silence, then I pulled up my wetsuit and threaded my arms into the sleeves, as Ash stripped down to her bikini.

I tried my hardest not to look at her, but I couldn't help it, my eyes kept wandering back to her beautiful but very pale body. I wasn't super pleased that she'd lost so much weight over the last few weeks, but I had to admit that it did make her boobs look a lot bigger than usual.

She peered over at me and I quickly turned my attention to the zipper string at the back of my wetsuit.

"How do you think your knee will go?" she asked, dipping her toes into the clear blue water.

"Not sure to be honest," I said, picking up my board with a slight groan as I felt a twinge in my hip. "I'm also not sure about my hips."

"Don't push yourself."

"I won't," I said, as I threw my board into the water, "I'll take it slow, but you have to promise not to laugh at me."

"I can't make that promise," she teased.

"Smart arse," I called over my shoulder as I slid onto my board, enjoying the feel of the water rippling underneath me. It would be a miracle if my body was strong enough to get me to my feet, but I wanted to try anyway. I paddled out towards the break and waited for an easy wave. I needed to start small until I got my surf legs back. I caught a small barrel, but when I tried to make the leap to my feet, my body wouldn't let me do it.

I sighed in disappointment and paddled back out again. After a few failed attempts to get to my feet, I had to concede that I didn't have the strength or stability to get myself standing yet, so I decided to let it go and enjoy the paddle instead. Even though I wasn't surfing, it was nice to be back out on the ocean anyway. It had been a good twelve months since I'd last been out on the board.

I peered over my shoulder at Ash, swimming in the shallow water. She saw me looking and gave me two thumbs up. My heart surged. It was the happiest I'd been in a long time. The sun was shining, the water was crystal clear, and Ashley had finally come back to me.

- RYAN McPHERSON -

I carried Mia through the threshold of our building. I hadn't set foot in that place for months and, after so long, it was hard to believe that I was finally home. I was once again a free man and it felt damn good.

"Welcome home babe," Kat said as she unlocked the door to our flat, standing back to let me go in ahead of her. I stepped silently through the doorway and took stock of our home. It looked exactly the same, yet completely different.

"Wow," I said, popping Mia's capsule down on the floor, "it's good to be back."

"I've made a few changes," said Kat, following me inside, "go take a look."

I walked from room-to-room, soaking in the new vibes of my old home. It was our house, but better. Kat had upgraded some of the furniture and added more photos to the picture wall to include Mia.

"This is amazing babe," I told her with pride.

"I felt like this would help us with our fresh start."
I caught her eye and gleaned her unspoken meaning from the look on her face.

"I love it," I told her, sliding my hand around her waist and kissing her softly. She whimpered ever-so-quietly and wrapped her arms around my neck, returning my light kiss with a passion I hadn't felt in her for a long time. I pulled her body firmly against mine and almost forgot that our daughter was sitting in her capsule next to us, until she let out a cry to let us know that she was feeling neglected. "We'll resume that later," I said, peeling myself off Kat and kneeling down to Mia. "Feeling left out miss?" I asked gently bopping her little nose with my finger. She stopped crying immediately and stared up at me so lovingly with those big brown eyes of hers, that my heart practically melted.

"Actually, it's past time for her morning nap so she's probably tired," said Kat as I stood up with Mia cuddled into my chest. I looked from my beautiful daughter to my beautiful wife with a sense that life was finally perfect. I smiled cheekily at Kat and wrapped my spare arm around her waist so I could give her a slow, purposeful kiss.

"Well, that's mighty convenient," I joked huskily into her ear, as I rocked Mia in my other arm. Kat blushed and bit her lip as she watched me intensely. I pulled back from her with a grin. "I've got this covered, you go and relax."

"Thanks," whispered my gorgeous wife, with what appeared to be combination of love and lust sparkling in her hazel eyes.

I took my time with my Dad duties. It was nice feeling like a normal family as I changed Mia's nappy and coerced her to sleep. After several off-key bedtime songs, and a lot of back patting, Mia was settled, so I returned to the lounge room to find Kat leaning against the back of the sofa with a grin on her face.

"The kiddo is tucked in and fast asleep," I said, prowling towards her.

"Good job Super-Dad," she teased with a smile as she reached her arms out for me.

"Thanks, Super-Mum," I said, resuming our previous position.

"It's nice to have you home babe," she said, running her hand over my newly bearded face.

"It's nice to be home." I ran my thumb down her cheek and across her pink lips. Kat's eyes bore into mine and I suddenly felt overwhelmed with the intensity of my love for her. We leant in closer to each other and although our lips weren't quite touching, neither of us moved any further. I twisted one of the curls that hung by her beautiful face, enjoying the feel of her body pressed against mine. Eventually our lips closed on each others in a soft, slow kiss that was filled with so much emotion it was almost as intimate as having sex. I felt her hands slide gently around my waist with a touch so electric that it sent tingles through my entire body.

"I've missed you," she whispered seductively into my ear.

"I've missed you too."

"Maybe we should do something to rectify that," Kat suggested, letting her lips brush against mine again.

"Does that mean you're ready?" I asked, hoping that I wasn't mis-interpreting the situation.

"Oh, I'm very ready," she said, pulling my face to hers and kissing me hard to emphasize her point. We leaned against the back of the fancy new sofa, kissing and slowly rediscovering ourselves as a couple. Being together again felt incredibly different to before, yet also comfortingly similar. Reassuring in its familiarity, but tantalizingly transformed, as if we'd upgraded ourselves, and this was a new and improved version of us. As the heat kicked up a notch, we maneuvered ourselves gently over the back of the sofa, landing softly on the plump cushions.

"New couch, new memories," breathed Kat as we let our hands roam and explore each other's bodies. We weren't frantic or frenzied in our desire, in fact the whole thing was unhurried and purposeful. We slowly undressed each other and for a long moment, enjoyed the feeling of our naked bodies pressed against each other. I stared into Kat's eyes, with my hard-on pressed against her pubic bone and she arched her hips to take me in.

"Are you sure?" I asked, hoping like hell that she was, otherwise I'd have to sort myself out. She smiled and kissed me provocatively.

"I couldn't be more sure," she answered, wrapping her thighs around my waist to pull me into her. We both sighed with relief as I slid into her. It felt like coming home.

"This is amazing," I told her with a breathless chuckle as we moved against each other. Kat gave a husky laugh and ran her hand along my jaw. I grabbed the back of her head and crushed her mouth to mine. She fervently returned my kiss and, as our bodies squeezed tightly together, my angle changed slightly. I felt her heart pound faster against my chest and when our hips met again, I hit a magic spot deep inside her. Kat let out an automatic moan of pleasure. She laughed and pressed her face into my neck to stifle her noises, but the movement made her muscles clench, which pushed me over the edge too. "Shhh," I said as we both giggled and groaned like we were fumbling teenagers fooling around in the back of a car, "we'll wake Mia."

I grasped Kat's hips tightly, trying hard to control my volume as my whole body surged with relief. We heard Mia stir from the nursery and we both froze to see if it was going to turn into a full-blown cry. We waited, frozen mid-coitus, but there was no further sound from her room. I pulled Kat's body tightly against mine not wanting the feeling to end. She draped her arms around my neck, and softly nuzzled my chin with her nose.

"Whoa," I sighed with satisfaction, and kissed her hard with my remaining energy.

"Whoa is right," Kat chuckled in agreement, leaning her forehead against mine. I let my fingers trail across her back languidly as we laid together, exhaustedly reveling in the feeling of being connected in the most intimate of ways. "I've missed this."

"Me too," I sighed happily as Mia cried out in earnest. "Oh well. Duty calls," I said, peeling myself off my super sexy wife.

"Yes it does," she agreed, "but I've got this one babe, she's going to need a feed."

I glanced very unsubtly at her boobs and noticed that they looked ready to burst.

"I guess she will," I agreed with a teasing wink as I offered her a hand up. She slapped me playfully as she stood, so I grabbed her and hoisted her up over my shoulder with her bare bottom pointing in the air.

"What are you doing?" Kat asked with a squeal as she grappled for something to hold on to.

"Home delivery," I joked, carrying her into the nursery.

"This is very undignified," Kat argued. I laughed and carefully swept her down from my shoulder, placing her gently into the armchair. I then draped a blanket over her lap to offer the illusion of propriety.

"Is that better?" I asked teasingly as I gave Kat a quick but firm kiss on the lips.

"Much," she said with a smile, watching me contentedly as I scooped Mia carefully out of the cot and placed her into Kat's arms.

"There you go ladies. Bonne appetite Miss Mia." I stroked her little head and then squeezed Kat's shoulder. "Is Mummy hungry too? Shall I get some food sorted?"

"Mummy is starving. Food would be great."

"Your wish is my command."

- KAT McPHERSON -

As I sat with Mia clutched against my chest, I could hear Ryan clattering in the kitchen, humming 'Our House' to himself. I smiled and stroked Mia's hair as she drank. In that moment, life felt perfect.

Once I'd finished feeding Mia, I propped her safely on my shoulder, threw the blanket around both of us and joined Ryan in the kitchen. My stomach flipped at the sight of his gorgeous bare torso as he grated a carrot. I was disappointed to see him wearing shorts, but the fact that he was standing in our kitchen after so long was enough for me. I watched him lecherously, and he grinned when he looked up and caught me perving.

"All done?" he asked, eyeing the large gap in the front of the blanket where my naked flesh was on display.

"We have one happy camper," I said, gently patting Mia's back to burp her. "What are you making?"

"Burritos," he said with a wink, "but if you keep standing there semi-naked, then I'll never get them made."

I laughed and blushed at the attention. "Am I too distracting for you?" I teased dropping the blanket completely.

"Phew," he said, rubbing the back of his head with a shy smile, "get some clothes on woman, or I'll end up with permanent damage," he joked, doing a readjustment jiggle.

"Fine," I said turning my naked bum in his direction, "I'll go get dressed if that's what you want."

"Oh, you already know what I want, but unfortunately it's not a baby appropriate activity," he said, with a sexy rumble to his tone that made heat flare in the pit of my belly. In my pre-baby days, I would have jumped on him then and there. I looked over my shoulder and let my eyes roam over his newly toned chest.

"So…" I said, not sure what I was attempting to say. I swallowed down the lump of desire that was rising in my throat. "I'm going to have a shower," I concluded with a nervous smile before retreating to the bedroom, leaving the blanket abandoned on the floor. Why did I suddenly feel like a nervous teenager around my own husband? Surely the time to be coy would have been before we'd had sex?

I popped Mia in her bouncer and positioned her on the bathroom floor so I could watch her while I showered. I let the water wash over me and calm my excited body. The memory of our session was burned into my mind like a flare gun in the dark night. It had been like a super-charged version of our previous sex life and it had somehow shifted our relationship to a whole new level. I felt like we were us, but better. And Ryan's skills had certainly levelled up too. Not to mention his new shredded figure. I just wanted to sink my teeth into that chest of his.

"Your Daddy is way too hot for his own good," I told Mia factually, but she didn't seem bothered by my candidness. As much as I loved that little caramel bundle, Ryan and I needed some time to reconnect, and I couldn't figure out how were we going to do that when we only had an hour here and there during Mia's nap times. I peered over at my gorgeous little poop machine. "I think we might invite Auntie Rosie down for a visit," I suggested to my daughter. "Would you like to spend some time with your Auntie Rosie?"

"Are you talking to me?" asked Ryan as he popped his head in the bathroom door. "I like Rosie a lot but I'd rather spend time with you," he joked, as he let his eyes wander over my wet body.

"I was talking to Mia," I said, trying to ignore his smoldering stare.

"Good conversation?" He teased.

"I was just telling her that I'm going to ask Rosie down to babysit so we can have some alone time," I said as he began to strip off his clothes. "What are you doing?"

"I'm getting in there with you," he said, opening the shower door.

"I thought you were sorting food."

"I was, and now it's ready whenever we are… which I predict will be at least fifteen minutes," he joked, hungrily eyeing my naked flesh.

"But Mia's right there," I argued. He looked over his shoulder and then let go of the door.

"That's easy to fix," he said, turning her bassinet the other way around. "Problem solved, now she can't see anything." He once again reached for the shower door.

"She can still hear."

He sighed and smiled patiently, then vanished out of the bathroom. In a matter of seconds, he returned with the portable speaker and his phone. He popped the speaker next to Mia and tapped at the phone screen. Meditation music echoed through the bathroom, creating a health spa kind of vibe. Ryan left his phone on the bench and looked back at me with his sex eyes.

"Sorted," he purred, climbing, uncontested, into the shower with me. "Now, I believe we have some business to attend to," he whispered into my ear as he let his fingers trail over my wet skin.

"I believe we do," I muttered back, enjoying the feel of his hands all over my body. He grabbed my bottom and lifted me up as if I weighed nothing. "Wow," I said, pleasantly surprised by his new-found strength.

"If you think that's 'wow', just wait until I get started," he said, sliding into me and taking my breath away. My chest was pounding again. Even though we'd already done this once, I still felt nervous about having sex with him. So much had happened in the time we'd been apart, that it almost felt like I was having sex with a stranger.

I held tight to Ryan as he tried his best to keep his balance on the slippery shower floor. The hot water rained over us and I enjoyed the feel of his wet naked body as it slid against mine. The steam rose around us as we gripped to each other, puffing and panting in a combination of excitement and exhaustion. We were both determined to finish the job properly without having to relocate, so Ryan leaned me up against the wall and repositioned himself. With the extra support we were able to get some momentum and it didn't take long before we both threw our heads back in silent pleasure, trying not to alert Mia to our activities.

"Oh my god," I exhaled, with my thighs still wrapped firmly around his waist.

"How was that for our second time back?" he asked under the barrage of water.

"That was amazing babe," I said looking into his loving eyes, "I'm particularly impressed that you didn't collapse."

"Me too," he admitted with a laugh.

"You've definitely buffed up while you've been away.

"No more dad bod here," he joked, "so don't even think about stuffing me full of baked goods."

I laughed and kissed him hard as he lowered me back to the ground.

"Don't worry babe, I've got better things to do than baking."

"You sure do," he said with a smile as the warm water sprayed down around us. I snuggled into his chest and squeezed him tight. I couldn't believe he was finally home and we were together again. Ryan sighed happily and rested his chin on top of my wet curls. "Mmm... this is heaven."

- RITCHIE CARLTON -

Our game progressed as expected, given that we were playing the Romanians. Those guys were all tiny and notoriously easy to defeat. It was a total massacre and we'd scored two tries and a goal before the first quarter had ended. I'd successfully executed my second try for the game, and amongst the cheers, Wayne tapped my shoulder and nodded towards the other side of the field. I looked over my shoulder and saw Amy standing at the sidelines.

"Amy?" I said, bewildered. In the entire two years that we'd been hanging out, she'd never once come to watch a rugby match. "What the fuck is she doing here?"

"Maybe she's making an effort," Wayne suggested with a shrug.

"Better watch out for flying pigs," I joked as the rugby ball flew at my head. "Fuck," I blurted in pain as the damn thing hit me square in the nose. I grasped my nose as the pain left me disoriented.

"Blood rule," called the ref as I heard people beginning to fuss around me.

"Are you okay mate?" Wayne asked as my eyes came back into focus. Blood was flooding down my hand and dripping off the end of my elbow.

"It looks worse than it is," I answered in a nasal voice.

"Ritch!" called Amy, running into the middle of the field to where I was standing.

"Hey," I said, pinching the bridge of my damaged nose to stem the bleeding.

"Are you alright?" she asked, peering under my hand to inspect the damage.

"I'm fine," I said, brushing her hands away, "stop fussing."

"Carlton, you're sitting out for the next quarter," called coach.

"But I'm fine," I argued, sounding like Steve Urkel.

"No arguments Carlton. Off," he bellowed.

I sighed and nodded, letting Amy guide me over to the sidelines, whilst I kept a firm hold on my nose. She riffled through her bag and pulled out a travel pack of tissues.

"Here," she said, handing me one, "this should help."

"Thanks," I muttered, holding the tissue to my nose and tilting my head upwards in the hope that gravity might assist. The game resumed and, a few tissues later, the bleeding finally slowed. I mopped up the last of the blood from my nose and shoved the wad of bloodied tissues into the side pocket of my rucksack. I stretched out my back and then glanced down at Amy, who had barely said a word. We stood in awkward silence for a moment, a state to which both of us had become quite accustomed of late.

"Thanks for the tissues," I said, breaking the silence.

"No problem."

Another silence.

"Soo…" I ventured cautiously, "what brings you to Regents Park on a Saturday morning?"

"You," she answered simply. "I thought it was about time I got to a game."

"Right," I said with a nod, and turned away to focus on the game. I could sense her stewing silently beside me, but I didn't know what else to say. Amy shoved her hands into her pockets and kicked at the grass.

"I thought you'd be happy about it," she mumbled. "I'm sorry if I encroached, I honestly thought I was doing something nice."

I peered at her from the corner of my eye. "It was nice," I said, staring at the field pretending to watch the game, "but I wish you'd told me you were coming, so I didn't get distracted by a hot redhead and end up copping a ball in the face."

"Sorry," Amy laughed. I looked over at her with a smile.

"You wanna grab a pub lunch after the game?"

"Yeah," she said with a nod and a smile, "that would be good."

- KAT McPHERSON -

Our first day together as a family passed blissfully. We reveled in each other's company, doing all the things that normal families did every day.

"Maybe you should give Nath a call," I suggested to Ryan, as we packed the picnic basket for our outing to the park. "I'm sure he'd like to hear from you."

"Yeah, I wasn't sure if I should call or not. Do you think they want some privacy?"

"Babe, it's been two weeks since the attack. I think they'd both be happy to hear your voice right now."

"I would feel better knowing they're both okay," he said with a nod.

"Go do it now, I've got this sorted," I said, nodding at the food piled on the bench."

"Cool, thanks." He disappeared into the lounge to get his phone, while I returned to the lunch prep. I hadn't even finished packing the picnic when Ryan returned to the kitchen. "It rang out," he said with disappointment. "So did Ashley's."

"They're probably down at the beach or something," I said, cheerily. "Try again after lunch."

"Yeah," he agreed, sliding his phone into his back pocket, "and in the meantime, we'll devour this amazing feast," he joked, eyeing all the gourmet supplies I'd bought for his return home.

We finished packing up our luxury lunch and piled everything into Mia's pram, then walked down to the park at a leisurely pace, enjoying the Autumn sun. The leaves had begun to fall, but the wintery chill hadn't yet set in, so it felt like London was being gifted with an extended summer.

We found a nice shady spot under a big sycamore tree, and I smiled contentedly as I watched Ryan playing blissfully with Mia on the blanket. We were finally together as a family, and it was better than I ever could have imagined. It was daunting to think that we'd be adding another child to the mix soon - it would be challenging having two kids under two - but I knew with every fiber of my being, that our new baby would only multiply the joy. In twenty-four hours Kellie would be coming for lunch to sign the paperwork and our crazy, hypothetical idea would become reality.

"Can you believe that there'll be four of us next year?" I said, leaning back to rest my head on Ryan's legs.

"Not really," he said, as he reached down to play with a strand of my curls. "It's hard to believe that it's actually going to happen."

"Yeah, I know," I said, tickling Mia's tummy as she laid between us, cooing happily. "I was half expecting Kellie to change her mind."

"Me too, but she seems genuinely happy about it."

"Hmm… maybe we shouldn't count our chickens until the paperwork is signed tomorrow," I said, with slight dread. "It's too late for her to terminate, but she could still decide that she wants to keep it."

"I don't think that's going to happen babe."

"It's not likely, but it's a possibility. I'll withhold my excitement until she signs that contract."

"Fair enough," Ryan agreed, sitting up to give me a kiss, "but I'll still put a bottle of champers in the fridge to be on the safe side."

"Sounds like a plan," I agreed with a smile. "Are you excited?"

"I very much am," Ryan said, grabbing a couple of grapes out of the picnic basket, "but I want to enjoy being the three of us before we turn into four."

"Yeah."

"What do you think you'll do once Ashley gets back? Are you going to stay on at work, or do I need to resign from my position as house husband?"

"I don't know, what do you think?"

"I think it's entirely your call babe," he said, taking on a slightly more serious tone, "I'd be happy being a stay-at-home dad and I'll support you one hundred percent if you want to go back to work permanently; but if you'd rather be at home, then I'll start looking for a job. Either way, we're a team and we'll make it work."

I smiled and stroked his stubbly cheek. "How did I get so lucky to end up with someone like you?"

"If you want to get even luckier, we can head home and put Mia down for a nap," he joked, bending down to give me a soft, teasing kiss.

"Tempting," I said with sly smile, "but I think we should make the most of the nice weather while we can."

"Ooh I didn't know you were an exhibitionist," Ryan teased as he wrestled me playfully.

"Stop," I said with a giggle, batting him away, "we'll squash Mia."

He looked over his shoulder at Mia, who was still lying on the blanket unscathed and completely obvious to our antics.

"She's fine," he said with a laugh, as he rolled off me and helped me sit upright. My core strength was certainly not what it had been before having a child. Ryan's big chocolate eyes bore into mine and warmed me from the inside out. "I'm so happy I have you."

"And you'll never lose me again, I promise," I said, tightening my grip on his hand. "I'm all-in Ryan, and I'll spend the rest of my life making sure that I don't fuck this up again."

"Me too," he said cupping his spare hand around my face. "Maybe we should renew our vows?"

"Really?"

"Yeah, I mean… maybe we'll wait until the next one is born so they can be part of it too," Ryan said, "but, what better way to mark our fresh start than a big party?"

"I love it," I said with excitement, "does that mean I get another diamond?" I teased with a wink.

"You're the money-earner now, so that's up to you."

"So, I am," I agreed with an evil smile, "In that case, I shall have the biggest diamond money can buy."

We both laughed and then Ryan's eyes darted over my shoulder at something in the distance.

"It's Ritch and Aims," he said, nodding in the direction he was looking.

"I thought they'd broken up."

"They'd have to be a couple in order to break-up," Ryan said with a shrug as he waved at the dysfunctional pair. "But whatever they are, they look quite cozy."

- RYAN McPHERSON -

"Ritch, Amy!" I called, waving excitedly at our friends.

"Hey! Mac Daddy is out of jail," Ritchie joked cheerfully. He trotted over to us with Amy in tow. I stood up to greet them with hugs and back slaps, as Kat climbed to her feet to join us, bouncing Mia in her arms. The next round of greetings and hugs concluded before we split into pairs. Ritch patted me on the back emphatically, "well look at you outside in the real world. How does it feel to be a free man?"

"Fucking amazing," I said with a laugh.

"I bet."

"And what about you guys," I asked quietly, nodding in Amy's direction, "I thought you ended it."

"I'm working on it," he admitted sheepishly.

"I see," I said, feeling sorry for the big guy. "So, how's the Delfontaine account going?" I asked, changing the subject.

"Yeah, pretty good mate," he said, gratefully embracing the new topic of conversation. "It's amazingly under control. Your wife has been a lifesaver," he said loudly, peering around me to get Kat's attention.

"Oh, I've hardly done anything Ritch," Kat said with blush, "I'm sure Ash will do a much better job once she's back."

"I'm hoping we'll have both of you on it," said Ritchie with a smile, "you'd be an unstoppable team."

"We'd also be a very expensive team," Kat said with a wink.

"Maybe," said Ritchie with a wink, "but I expect Ash will need to ease back into it anyway so I don't see why you couldn't job share to begin with."

"Okay you two," interrupted Amy, "that's enough shop talk for a Saturday."

"Fair enough," agreed Ritch. "What are you going to do with yourself mate? You going to take up Gaz on his offer to find you some work?"

"That all depends on what the missus decides to do," I joked. "If she decides to stay on at Artemis then I'll be Mr Mum. It's cheaper than putting Mia her into daycare, and when the second one arrives-"

"What?!" Ritchie cut me off. "Is Kat pregnant again?!" he asked with surprise.

"Ryan, I thought we weren't going to tell anyone yet," Kat scolded.

"Sorry," I said with an apologetic shrug, "it just slipped out."

"You're pregnant?" Amy asked Kat with a wide grin.

"No, I'm not pregnant, Kellie is."

Amy and Ritchie both glanced at us in confusion. Their eyes darted between Kat and I in stunned silence, unsure whether to offer congratulations or commiserations.

"Kellie's pregnant and the baby is mine," I explained, "but she doesn't want to keep it so it we'll be keeping it and Kat will be the adoptive mother."

"Oh wow!" blurted Amy with shocked excitement. "I can't believe it! That's amazing guys!" Amy flapped around hugging us both and Ritchie slapped me on the back with slightly less enthusiasm.

"Congrats mate," he said with a forced smile, "I'm really happy for you guys." He didn't seem happy, but it looked like he was trying his best. Ritch glanced at Amy, then let his eyes hover over Kat and Mia with a look of sadness.

"Sorry man," I apologised as I realised what was going through his mind. "This must be hard."

Ritchie quickly snapped out of his funk and etched a massive smile onto his face.

"Of course it's not!" he declared jovially, "it's amazing! You guys deserve a win or two. I couldn't be happier for you."

"Thanks Ritch."

"Honestly man," he said, with a genuine smile, resting his hand on my shoulder, "I'm glad that everything is finally working out for you."

"You guys want to join us?"

"Nah, we're heading to the Red Lion for a pub lunch and a chat," he said with a meaningful look.

"Ah… I get you."

Ritchie nodded solemnly and glanced over at Amy.

"Come on Aims," he announced loudly, we should leave these lovebirds to enjoy their family time." We said our goodbyes and watched them walking awkwardly together.

"Do you think they'll be okay?" Kat asked.

"I'm not sure," I said, giving my troubled mates one last glance.

"Is it weird that I feel bad for being happy when our friends are struggling?"

"If it is then we're weirdos together," I joked, squeezing her shoulder. "But we've done our hard yards so it's our turn to be happy and we can't tone that down to save other people's feelings."

"True," she agreed, looking up at me adoringly, "this is our happily ever after."

"Sure is," I said with a grin, kissing her gently.

"But still… it's horrible seeing our friends having a hard time."

"Speaking of which," I said, pulling out my phone, "I might quickly try Nath again." I dialled Stoner, but it rang out, as did Ashley's. "Still no answer."

- RITCHIE CARLTON -

Seeing the McPherson's together was bittersweet. They were radiating joy and contentment, which made me unbelievably happy because they deserved it, but it also made my heart ache for what I didn't have. I felt bad that I hadn't been more enthusiastic for them, but the moment I'd seen them sitting on that picnic blanket, I knew I had to break it off with Amy. All I could think was 'that should be us'.

I peered over at Amy as we walked in silence. The lightness that had started to return at the field, had been annihilated by our chance meeting with the McFamily unit. I was the one making things awkward, but I didn't know what to say. There was no point in pressing her on the marriage and kids issue as she'd already made it perfectly clear where she stood on that matter.

When we arrived at the pub, we ordered drinks and sat down at the bar while we decided on food. Amy peered at me sideways a few times, but I pretended to be engrossed in the menu.

"Are you okay Ritch?" she asked on her third glance. "You've been quiet since we left the McPherson's."

I sighed and nodded. "Do you want to join me for a fag?" I asked, gesturing to the balcony. "I could do with a smoke."

"Sure," she shrugged. I rose silently and ducked outside onto the balcony. Despite the fact that the traffic noise echoed up from below, the silence between us was excruciatingly painful. I handed her a cigarette and then lit it for her. She filled her lungs full of smoke and I sucked on my own tube of tar, while I waited for the words to form themselves. "Thanks," Amy said shuffling on her feet.

"No worries," was all I could think to say and then there was silence. We both said nothing. Not a peep. We just stood silently without saying a word. I knew it was up to me, but the only words left to say were the ones that I couldn't bring myself to utter. I peeked over at her quickly and she looked so uncomfortable that jumping over the railings might have been a preferable alternative to standing in silence with me.

"So, what's going on Carlton?" she asked, eyeing me suspiciously as she puffed on her cigarette.

"The thing is…" I began nervously, "seeing Kat and Ryan with Mia, and hearing they've got another one on the way…"

"It makes you want it more," she said apologetically.

"No," I said with a sigh, "it just made me realise that life keeps moving on while we're stuck here in this holding pattern." Amy dropped her gaze and studied her shoes. "The longer we do this Aims, the further away my dream gets. I love you and I want to have that with you, but you've made your stance clear."

"I don't want to be the person standing in the way of your dreams Ritch."

"I know," I said, not entirely sure what we were agreeing on. "So, where do we go from here then?"

"That's entirely your call Ritchie," she said with a smile. "Where do you want it to go from here?"

"I guess we go back to being friends."

"Okay," Amy nodded and stubbed out her fag. "Friends it is," she said sadly. I smiled, flicked my ciggy butt over the railing and closed the massive gap between us.

"Hi. I'm Ritchie," I said reaching out for a handshake. Amy looked at my hand with a cheeky smile.

"I'm Amy," she responded as she shook my hand. "Do you want to be friends?"

"Friends," I agreed with a mixture of grief and relief. Re-grief perhaps?

"Any chance we could have one more night together before we go back to friends?" she asked hopefully. "I was kind of planning a surprise for you tonight."

I took a deep breath, wanting to make a clean break, but knowing I couldn't resist. "Okay," I confirmed with a nod, "one more night."

- NATHAN STONE -

We hung out at the beach for a few hours, sunbathing and splashing in the cold water like children. It was a huge step forward and it almost felt like we were back to normal.

When we eventually returned to the shack, we heard a pained mew coming from inside as we stopped to brush the sand off our feet. We looked at each other and quickly ran into the house to check on Freddie.

She wasn't in her basket, so we darted through the old cottage trying to figure out where the sound was coming from. I finally found Fred in the guest room, curled up on the bed with three tiny kittens snuggled up at her belly, hungrily feeding.

"Awww, they're so cute," Ash said, looking at me in awe.

"Yeah, they are," I agreed with a smile, even though in the back of my mind I was wondering how to get the blood stains out of my expensive linen bedspread.

Ash jumped excitedly. "Two more to go!"

"Should we help her?" I asked. I hadn't gotten around to reading any of the literature that the vet had given us.

"Calvin said that she'd do most the work for herself," Ash said recalling our conversation with the vet we'd nick-named 'Calvin', "so I guess we just wait."

"Should I get her some water or something?"

"Yeah probably," Ash said with a shrug, "with everything that happened I never had a chance to read the leaflets."

"Me either."

Fred yowled loudly and we both cringed with sympathy.

"You're doing great Freddie," Ash told the cat proudly.

"Is this what Mia's birth was like?"

"No, this is much cleaner and quieter," Ashley laughed.

"Cleaner?" I asked, eyeing the mess on the bedspread. "I guess this is a good way to ease me into it then," I joked without thinking. Ash peered sideways at me with a curious look on her face and I realised that we were still a long way from the baby discussion. "I mean… you know… if we ever decided…" I let my words trail off and turned my attention back to Freddie who was mewing loudly.

A slimy little ginger blob popped out from beneath her tail and she began licking at the kitten, cleaning off all the slime and blood. Ash gagged and turned a sickly shade of green before quickly fleeing into the guest bathroom with one hand on her stomach and the other over her mouth.

"Are you okay?" I asked after her, a little concerned that this was the second time she'd vomited, that day.

"Yep," she called from the bathroom, heaving loudly, "that just…" she paused for another wretch, "that just grossed me out a bit."

"You got through the birth of a human child but *that* grossed you out?" I teased, as I stuck my head into the en-suite. Ash peered up at me pasty-faced.

"Yeah, but Kat wasn't licking the placent-ugh," she wretched again and stuck her head back into the toilet for another vomit.

"I think we need to get you to a doctor."

"I'm fine," she said, flushing the toilet, "I think I stressed out my body by not eating for so long."

"Maybe," I said unconvinced, "or what if you got tetanus from Dom's pocketknife or something?"

"I'm sure they would have covered that at the hospital," Ash said, hauling herself off her knees, "but if it makes you feel better, we could consult Doctor Google."

"Well, I am an expert researcher now," I joked, rubbing her back, "but that's not going to get you out of a doctor's visit. We can't take the risk, we've got no idea what sort of germs could have been on that blade. He could he have stabbed a million people with it for all we know."

"Okay, point taken," she agreed, raising her hands, "and you're actually freaking me out, so I'll go see my Doctor when we get back to London, if you promise to stop talking about it."

"Deal," I said smugly, "now you go rest, while I sit with Freddie."

"I don't want to abandon you guys at the crucial moment," she argued, splashing some water on her face, "What if something goes wrong with the last one? Calvin said it probably wouldn't survive."

"We'll be fine Mrs Stone," I joked with a smile, imitating Dr Klein. "I have it all under control, I promise. Now go lie down and before you know it, we'll be the proud grand-parents of five healthy fur-babies."

"Oh god, how did we go from parents to grandparents?" she joked with a laugh.

"We can't steal the parenting thunder from Freddie, she's the one doing all the hard work."

"Good point."

"Right," I said, guiding her out of the room, "off you go young lady, I've got a baby to deliver." I sent Ash to lie on the lounge, then perched myself on the edge of the bed to keep Freddie company while she delivered the final kitten. I'd mentally prepared myself for the thing to die, but when the little grey blob came out unbreathing, I had to do something. I gave Freddie a chance to do her thing, but she was getting increasingly distressed when her baby still hadn't taken a breath. I patted Fred and grabbed the slimy grey bundle. I needed to get its heart pumping, so I wrapped it in a flannel and began rubbing its chest firmly.

"Come on little guy," I muttered under my breath, whilst continuing my compressions.

"Everything okay in there?" called Ash from the other room.

"It's not breathing."

I heard Ash come into the room, but I was so focused on saving the kitten that I barely noticed her. The chest compressions weren't working so I did the only thing I could think of and started giving the sticky little blob mouth-to-mouth.

"Come on buddy, breathe," I urged him as I tried another set of delicate chest compressions. The limp little body gave a slight shudder as if it was trying to come back to the world, so I blew a few more breaths of air into its tiny mouth. After the third one we heard the faintest of mews as its chest started rising and falling gently.

"You did it Nath," Ash sobbed from behind me. I looked over my shoulder at her with a relieved smile.

"He's not out of the woods yet, but at least he's breathing," I said, giving the baby back to Fred so she could finish cleaning it. Fred nuzzled the little grey ball and soon enough it was making as much noise as its siblings. I wiped my mouth with the back of my hand. "Well, that was gross," I said as Ash rubbed my shoulders, "but totally worth it."

Ash planted a kiss on the top of my head. "You're a hero Grandpa Stone."

- ASHLEY GRANGER -

Once Fred and all five of her babies were snuggled up in their basket, Nathan stripped the guest bed and put on a load of washing, while I got lunch started.

"Well look at you go, Mr Mum," I teased when he finally joined me in the kitchen. Nath smiled with triumph.

"I told you I wouldn't be a dead-beat dad."

"You're gloating again," I said with a smile.

"So I am," he agreed, stretching his back. "What should we do now then? I feel like we should be cracking a bottle of Champagne or something."

"Then maybe we should," I said with a shrug, "you know... for Fred."

Nathan grinned. "Done," he said reaching for the champagne flutes. "How about you go and relax on the couch for a while. I don't want you pushing yourself too much until we know what's going on with you."

"Ooh I like it when you boss me around," I joked, patting him on the bottom.

"Really?" he said with a disbelieving laugh, "because I seem to recall getting slapped in the face the last time I tried to give you orders," he teased. I shot him a pretend scowl.

"You deserved it."

"Yeah, and to be honest, I didn't entirely hate it," he joked with a wink. "Now, maybe you should give your parents a call."

"Actually, that's a good idea."

"I'm full of good ideas," he said, grinning. "Your phone is charging on the corner table next to mine."

"Thanks," I said, heading out to the lounge room to locate my long-forgotten device. Both our phones had notifications glowing on the screens. "You've had a few missed calls from Ryza," I called out to Nath, "so have I. Do you want to give him a call back to make sure everything's okay, or should I?"

"Oh shit, he's home today," Nath said, appearing with an ice-cold glass of bubbly in each hand. "I'll call him while you call your parents."

"Okay, can you tell him I'll call him later?"

"Sure," he said with a smile, giving me a gentle kiss on the top of my head as he handed me one of the glasses, "Champagne for the lady."

"Why thank you sir," I said, as I stopped fussing with my phone and took the glass of champers from his outstretched hand. I clinked mine against his.

"To Fred," Nathan said with a smile.

"And to you, for saving little Shadow."

"Shadow?" Nath ruminated over the name. "I like it," he concluded with a smile. "But it's all in a day's work for He-Man," he joked as we sipped our bubbles. "Now, call your mother, woman," Nath teased with a cheeky grin.

"Gunning for another slap are you?"

"Only if it's a slap on the arse."

"I'm sure we could arrange that," I said, lightly smacking him on the bottom with my spare hand. I unplugged my phone and wandered out to the balcony to call my parents. The sky was blue, and the ocean was sparkling. I closed my eyes and revelled in the salt air. There was something about this particular beach that soothed my soul. I took a big gulp of my champers and popped the frosty glass down on the coffee table so I could dial my mum. I paced the balcony as I waited for her to pick up.

"Ash," Mum said worriedly down the phone line.

"Hey Mum," I said, ceasing my pacing to lean against the railing.

"It's so good to hear your voice," she said, sounding teary. "Are you okay love?"

"I'm fine Mum," I said reassuringly, "I was a little shaken up, and the pain killers knocked me out, but I'm okay now."

"Thank god," she breathed with relief. "I know Nathan is taking good care of you, but we were so worried." I glanced over my shoulder, at Nathan chatting on his phone inside. He was a good man, and he was mine. "How are you doing?" Mum asked comfortingly.

"Mum…" I said, stepping backwards so I could sink down onto the day bed. "I killed Dom."

"We know," she said in that caring way that mums do, "Nathan told your Dad. And we're both pleased that you killed him before he killed you."

I felt tears welling in my eyes. "But now I've killed a man."

"Dom doesn't count as a man love," said my Mum sternly. "He was a monster, and you did what you had to do."

"I know. But I'll still have to live with it for the rest of my life."

"Just like you've had to live with the memory of what he did to your Mia."

"True," I agreed. "Will it ever go away?"

"Probably not," Mum answered bluntly, "but it will get easier to cope with. Dom's finally gone Ash, and you've got Nathan now. You'll put this behind you."

"I hope you're right."

"Of course I'm right," she said confidently.

"Thanks Mum," I said with a smile, "and how are things there?"

"We're fine. Jock's been around a couple of times."

"Has he?" I asked with surprise, glancing back inside to Nathan.

"Yes, he wanted to check in on us to see how we're doing."

"Okay..."

"He's such a thoughtful boy and he's very worried about you. He seems to blame himself for the attack, but I don't know how he could possibly think-"

"Mum, could we not talk about it?" I interrupted, swallowing the lump in my throat.

"Sure honey."

I closed my eyes and let the ocean breeze carry away my sins.

"I love you mum."

"I love you too sweetheart, and so does your father," she said, sniffing back tears. "It's over now, so we can all sleep easy." And that was the truth of it. With Dom dead, we could finally lead normal lives again. No more looking over our shoulders or watching for shadows in the dark. With Dom dead, we were all free. "I know what happened was awful and I certainly wish you hadn't had to go through it," she said gently, "but I'm so proud of you love."

"Thanks Mum."

"Do you want to speak to your father?" she asked curiously, "he's out in the garden somewhere, but I can go find him for you."

"Yeah, that'd be nice."

"Okay, let's see if I can find him," she joked. I heard the sound of the back door opening. "Will you and Nathan come and see us on your way back from Cornwall?"

"Of course," I said.

"We'd love to see you both."

"It will be more than two of us. Freddie just had kittens, so you'll get to see the newest members of the Stone clan too."

"You're a Stone now are you?" Mum teased.

"You know what I mean."

"I certainly do," she replied smugly. "I certainly do."

- RYAN McPHERSON -

I pushed Mia's pram with one hand as we strolled down the tree lined footpath, sipping our takeaway coffees. The path was speckled with sunlight as it shone through the leaves of the shedding trees. Kat looked beautiful in the mottled light and the expression on her face mirrored how I felt. Life was good. No, life was great. This was a fresh start and this time we'd do it right. My phone chimed in my back pocket and Kat took the pram so I could answer the call. I looked quickly at the screen and grinned

"Nath," I said happily, excited to speak to my best mate

"Hey Ryza, it's damn good to hear your voice man."

"Likewise," I told him, feeling relieved that he sounded happy. "How's everything? How's Ash? I heard your message. Are you okay?"

"We-" he choked on his words and stopped talking. He cleared his throat and lowered his voice before continuing. "We're okay now. It was pretty dark for a while there, but it looks like we're through the worst of it now. She seems... better."

"I'm sorry I wasn't there for you brother."

"You were there. I was channeling my inner Ryan the whole time."

"Like a 'What would Ryza do' sort of thing?" I joked.

"Exactly," Nath laughed. "You're the new Jesus."

"I always knew I was special," I chuckled.

"How about you? I bet it's good to be out?"

"So good," I agreed with a smile, shooting Kat a cheeky wink.

"Glad to hear it."

"When are you guys back?" I asked, taking a loud sip of my coffee.

"Not sure," Nath said quietly, "today's the first day she's been out of bed so we might need a few more days here."

"It was pretty bad huh?" I asked, sensing his anguish through the phone line.

"Just a sec," he said as I heard the muffled noises of him relocating. Nathan exhaled slowly. "Dom raped her Ryza."

My stomach dropped and I stopped walking.

"I didn't know," I muttered breathlessly, concerned for Ash.

"I swore Ritchie to secrecy. I didn't want you guys to worry."

"Fuck," I whispered. Kat looked at me questioningly, but I shook my head and sat down on the nearest park bench.

"She doesn't want her parents to know, so please don't mention it," he said in a low tone.

"Of course not."

Nath let out a huge sigh, "I don't know what to do for her. She seems good today, but what if I do something to trigger her? I don't think I could deal with another two weeks like we've just had."

"Nath..." I said, letting my thought trail off as I heard him sob quietly.

"Sorry," he apologised with a sniff.

"No apology required mate." I paused and searched for some words of comfort. I'd never heard him so broken.

"Fuck's sake," he swore through sniffs, "I've kept it together for two whole weeks and now that things are better, I'm falling apart."

"That happens," I reassured him with a shrug.

"What do I do now? Just act like everything is normal?"

"I actually have no idea," I admitted, looking up at Kat, as she joined me at the bench. "Do you want to talk to Kat?"

"Nah, I'd better get back out there," he said, as if we were talking about a sports game.

"Okay," I nodded, "if you need anything just call."

"Will do."

"We're all here for you guys."

"Thanks Ryza."

"Take care man." Kat looked at me expectantly as I hung up the phone. I put down my coffee and draped my arm over her shoulder. "Things aren't good."

- NATHAN STONE -

I ditched my phone onto the bed and pressed the heels of my palms into my leaky eye sockets. Now wasn't the time for me to fall apart. I still needed to keep it together until Ash was out of the woods

"Pull it together Stoner," I told myself sternly. With my hands still glued to my face, I took a deep breath and then rubbed the last of the tears off my cheeks. I opened my eyes and paused with my hands mid-air, when I saw Ash standing in the doorway, looking heartbroken. I sat gaping at her in panic, not knowing what to say that would explain my current state. Our eyes remained locked for a moment, until Ash ran over to the bed and threw her arms around my neck.

"I'm so sorry," she whispered into my ear as she gripped me tightly. "I never meant to put you through this."
The breath I'd been holding, escaped in one long exhale as I relaxed into her embrace.

"I'm the one who should be sorry," I said, wrapping my arms around her as she crawled onto the bed next to me. "I'm supposed to be the strong one. I've let you down."

Ash took my face in her hands. "You haven't let me down," she said adamantly, through a sheet of her own tears, "and you *have* been the strong one Nathan. You've been my strength for two weeks now... but you don't have to be strong anymore, okay? Let me be here for you now."

"I don't know how to do that," I muttered, gently resting my hands on top of hers.

"Then let me figure it out," Ash said, as she pressed her lips firmly against mine. It was the first time our lips had touched since the attack. The intimate gesture caused another wave of tears to escape down my face. They merged with hers, and the salty liquid pooled around our lips. Ash sat back and ran her fingers over my wet cheeks. "I love you, Nathan. I'm so sorry I've done this to you."

"You haven't done anything to me babe," I said, sliding my hands down her arms. "Dom did this."

- KAT McPHERSON -

Since Ryan had gotten home, we'd been very conscientious about making up for all our lost sex time. We had been acting like overzealous honeymooners, but unfortunately, sex was a lot harder to come by with a baby to look after. Rosie was on her way down to London to babysit for the night, but it didn't feel soon enough.

Our trip to the park had worn Mia out, so we put her down and once again took the opportunity to get hot and heavy. Things had just started to get interesting when the intercom buzzed loudly.

"Oh shit, that will be Rosie," I said breathlessly, pushing the curls off my sweaty forehead. "She's early."

"Oh fuck," Ryan sighed with a mixture of pain and disappointment as I climbed off him.

"Sorry sexy, we'll save this for later," I said with a wink as I straightened my dress.

"What am I going to do about this?" he asked, gesturing towards his rather large erection.

"I don't know," I said, heading over the intercom, "but you'll have to figure it out quickly. I buzzed Rosie in and went out to meet her at the front door to buy Ryan some time. "Hey Rose," I said, as I opened the door to see Ritchie standing in the hallway. "Oh, hey Ritch. Sorry, I thought you were my sister," I said with a blush, as I quickly straightened myself up, hoping he hadn't noticed my flustered state.

"She must have let her looks slide since I last saw her then," he joked, rubbing his bald head. "I hope this isn't a bad time?"

"Not at all," I lied awkwardly. "Come in," I said, stepping back to let him in the door. Ritchie stepped inside and gave me a quick peck on my flushed cheek. "Fancy a cuppa?" I asked as he eyed me with amusement.

"I'm dying for a coffee, but I should've rung first," Ritchie apologised knowingly. "I think I'll take off and leave you guys to it."

"No, Ritch, honestly, it's fine," I stuttered, embarrassed that he knew what we'd been up to. "Is everything okay?"

"Oh, it's all good mate," he answered lightly waving away my concerns, "I was just trying to kill some time."

"Are you sure?" I asked, patting his muscly arm.

"Absolutely," he declared over-enthusiastically.

"So… you're okay?"

"I'm fine," he said with a nod as his sparkling eyes flickered down the hallway behind me, "but we can chat about this later. I think you have some more pressing business to get back to," he added with a wink. I blushed harder. "We'll take a rain check on the coffee huh? I'll shout you one on Monday, and you can fill me in on your sexy weekend."

I laughed with embarrassment and gave him a hug.

"Ryan will be disappointed he missed you."

"I get the feeling he'd be more disappointed if he was forced to see me right now," Ritchie joked. "I'll see you at work love."

"Thanks Ritch," I said, as he stepped back out the door, "but honestly, if you need to chat, I'm always happy to listen."

"I will definitely take you up on that at a more appropriate time," he said, punching me gently on the arm before letting himself out the main door.

I smiled to myself and closed our door, then ran eagerly towards the bedroom to continue what Ryan and I had started. As I passed the lounge room door, a pair of strong arms grabbed me around the waist and lifted me off the floor. I squealed and giggled as Ryan swept me up into his arms.

"Shh… we don't want to wake Mia," he whispered, carrying me over to the couch and placing me down gently. He looked me up and down with disapproval. "I'm going to need to you remove your dress ma'am," he joked in an over-accentuated American accent.

"Of course, officer," I said, playing along, "anything to help the pursuit of justice," I added, quickly stripping off my dress. Ryan maneuvered himself on top of me, straddling his thighs over my waist so I was anchored to the couch. He towered over me, and a wave of lust shot through the pit of my belly. He was like a work of art. I reached out to feel his newly sculpted chest, but he intercepted my touch and secured my hands above my head. I was completely at his mercy. His eyes sparkled with pleasure which sent a shiver of excitement through my body. My reaction spurred him on and as he gripped my wrists tighter, I wriggled unconsciously beneath his grasp. His new assertive confidence was an immense turn-on

As I writhed beneath him, my sexy husband finally bent down to kiss me but stopped just before his lips reached mine. He was teasing me, and after already having one interruption, I didn't know if I could take much more of it. Ryan kept a tight hold on my wrists with one hand while he let his other hand slide over my body. His fingers trailed across my thigh to my hip and up over my stomach. His mouth was still hovering above mine as his wandering hand worked its way upwards. He gently squeezed my breast and a spasm of pleasure shuddered through my entire body. My gasp was stifled as his lips finally closed over mine and I was in a state of total ecstasy. With a particularly athletic move, Ryan relocated his knees from outside my legs to in between my thighs and before I had time to process his maneuver, he slid easily inside me.

I let out a breathless moan and our eyes locked onto each other. It almost felt as if I could see right inside his head. Our instincts took over and we were no longer in control of our bodies.

Ryan exhaled deeply and wiped the sweat from his forehead. My breasts were pressed tightly to his chest and I could feel myself getting close just as the door buzzer interrupted us for a second time.

"Noooo," growled Ryan as we both hopelessly ceased our efforts.

"That probably is Rosie this time," I panted with my legs still tightly wrapped around him.

"I don't suppose we could leave her waiting out there for another five minutes, could we?" he joked, with a dash of frustration.

"I suppose not," I agreed, feeling an unspeakable sense of loss as he peeled his body off mine. The buzzer sounded again, and I sighed loudly as I retrieved my dress from the floor.

"So close," I muttered, pulling my dress over my head as Ryan climbed into his shorts and did his best to hide his even larger erection.

"Here," I said, throwing him one of the cushions, "that should do it."

"Yep, super subtle," he joked as I left him in the lounge room.

"Hello?" I said into the intercom.

"What took you so long?" said Rosie in a huff at the other end of the line, "buzz me in already woman." I buzzed her in and went to meet her at the front door. I laughed as I watched her, laden with bags and gifts, fighting to get in the front door.

"Need a hand?" I teased, as the big wooden door banged shut behind her.

"Hey babe," Rosie said puffing from the exertion. I grabbed one of the bags for her and she gave me an awkward sideways hug, around her huge load. "I brought presents."

"I can see that," I laughed, giving her a hand to get them inside. "How was the drive?" I asked, kissing her on the cheek.

"Eww, sweaty Betty," she joked light-heartedly as she wiped my sweat off her cheek. Drive was good, the traffic was heavy but moving." We lugged all the bags into the apartment and Rosie straightened up to stretch her back. "Now where's my adorable niece?" she asked, dumping her handbag on the kitchen table.

"She's down for a nap," I told Rosie as she headed into the lounge room, where Ryan was sitting on the new sofa with the cushion placed strategically over his lap. He was doing his best to act natural, and he might have been somewhat convincing had it not been for the fact that he was wearing his T-shirt inside out.

"Oh," Rosie said with a laugh as she caught sight of my disheveled husband, "hi Ryza, good to be home?"

"Very good to be home thanks Rosie," he said from his awkward position on the couch. By that point it seemed fairly obvious why he hadn't stood up to greet her.

"Anyway…" Rosie said, eyeing us both with amusement, "I could do with a nice long walk after that drive. Mind if I wake up Mia and take her down to the park?"

"Yeah, that's fine," I said, avoiding eye contact with Ryan.

"Yeah, that'd be great," he agreed, scratching his face nervously. "She's due to be up soon anyway."

"Great!" said Rosie, quickly fleeing the room with a mocking grin. Ryan and I exchanged embarrassed glances and sniggered silently.

- RYAN McPHERSON -

Kat packed Mia's nappy bag and walked Rosie and Mia to the front door.

"We'll be back in about an hour," said Rose, pointedly, "then you guys can fuck off to your hotel."

"Thank you," said Kat with a grin, closing the door behind them. She returned to the lounge room with a smoldering look in her eyes.

"Looks like we're finally alone," I said, as she stalked over to the couch.

"So we are," she agreed, pulling the cushion off me and throwing it onto the floor. "What do you think we should do?" Kat slid onto the couch and straddled my lap.

"I'm sure we could think of a few things," I said, running my hands down over her bottom and then up her smooth thighs.

"What about this?" She slid her hands over my shoulders and planted kisses down my neck.

"Yep, that's pretty good," I said croakily. "How about this?" I asked, as I snuck my fingers underneath her dress.

"That's definitely something to consider."

"You're so hot," I said, crushing her mouth to mine as she wriggled the waistband of my shorts downwards to extract my excited cock. I moaned as her hand squeezed firmly around me. Then I returned the favour by letting my fingers roam in her underwear.

"I can't believe we're actually alone," she said huskily.

"And we can be as loud as we want," I said, before grabbing her bottom and pulling her down onto me. Kat moaned loudly and gripped the back of my neck, squeezing her body tightly against mine. I was so close that I was worried I'd go before her. I did my best to slow myself down, but her movements were about to send me over the edge so I grabbed her hips gently. "Slow it down for a minute," I pleaded breathlessly as I concentrated on not blowing my load.

"Okay," she panted, biting her bottom lip, as she slowed her movements, "I'm really close."

"Me too," I whispered, regaining some control over my body, "let's just take a breath." She nodded her agreement, but as I re-adjusted my grip on her bottom, I felt my penis hit the sweet spot. Kat threw her head back and her whole body shuddered in pleasure, which was all it took to shatter my last shred of self-control, so I went with her. We both moaned loudly, allowing ourselves to enjoy the thrill of being unrestricted and uninhibited. After a few minutes of ridiculously vocal releases, we looked at each other and laughed. "Well at least we were efficient," I joked, running my hands up and down her back.

"That was definitely a record," Kat agreed, leaning against my chest.

"Too fast?"

"Not when you kick goals like that."

"I do my best coach," I joked with a groan as she wriggled off me. "Shall we go for round two or wait until we get to the hotel?"

She grinned at me and shrugged. "I think we might be mixing up our sports metaphors," she joked with a wink, before running towards the bedroom. I stared after her, wondering what she was doing. She stuck her head out of the bedroom door. "Are you coming, or do I need to call in a sub?" she asked as her dress flew out the door. I jumped into action and immediately started peeling off my inside-out clothes.

"I'm in coach."

- RITCHIE CARLTON -

The clock hit 5pm when I rocked up at Amy's place for our last night together. I looked at her spare house key in my hand and sighed. This would be the last time I'd use it. I turned the key and let myself in.

"Hi," I called into the quiet flat as I made a b-line for the kitchen to sort us some drinks.

"Are you coming in?" she called from her bedroom.

"Just grabbing some drinks," I said, pouring a couple of large glasses of whiskey as I heard her voice echo down the hallway.

"Be quick or I'll have to start without you."

"Okay fine," I conceded as I grabbed the drinks. I heard a breathy groan coming from the bedroom. "Are you okay?" I asked, plodding down the hall, with a glass of whiskey in each hand.

"I'm very okay," Aims called back huskily. My cock jumped involuntarily at the tone in her voice, and I sighed at my inability to resist the woman. She was clearly up to something, and it was no doubt filthy as fuck which, normally, would have excited me, however in the midst of my midlife crisis, it felt like she was rubbing salt into my wounds.

"Close your eyes," Amy instructed me as I began to push open her bedroom door.

"Okay," I agreed, curious about the sexy surprise she had in store.

"No peeking," she told me cheekily.

"And ruin the surprise?" I replied with a distinct lack of enthusiasm, despite my growing boner. I stepped carefully into the room with my eyes tightly shut and heard movement coming from the direction of her bed

"Okay, you can open them," she announced proudly. I opened my eyes to see Amy standing in front of me, dressed in a black leather corset thing with a hole in the crutch.

"Holy shit." I blurted in shock, knocking back one of the glasses of scotch in one gulp. She had converted the entire room into a torture chamber that, I imagined, would have matched Sandrine's sex dungeon. She'd even set-up a brutal looking rig on her bed. "What is this?" I asked putting the empty glass on her dresser.

"I thought we could do something a little different," Aims replied with a shrug.

"A little different?!" I retorted with a nervous chuckle, "Aims, this is more than a little different. This is more like a scene from Fifty Shades."

"Yeah exactly," she agreed proudly, "since you hooked up with Sandrine, I thought you might be into this. Besides, it could be fun."

"If by fun you mean painful," I joked, feeling uneasy about her plans, "and I never got into SM stuff with Sandrine, I think that was special for Nathan."

"Come on Ritch, be adventurous," she chided, pulling me towards her bed.

"Nah, I'm not really into this shit," I admitted awkwardly, attempting to back away. It was way too much for a naive Aussie boy, "I kind of prefer my sex to be more pleasure than pain."

"What if you use it on me?" she laughed. "You can tie me up and do whatever you want to me."

"Okay," I answered dubiously, "so you want me to like… whip you and stuff?" I asked, sculling the second glass of whiskey as quickly as the first.

"I want you to do whatever you want with my body. Just go mad. The kinkier the better," Amy replied with excitement as she ran over to grab a whip that looked like a cat of nine tails. "Try it," she suggested, holding it out to me.

"I'm not going to hurt you Aims," I told her firmly as she took the empty glass from my hand and attempted to replace it with the whip.

"But I want you to."

I gently pushed the leather contraption back at her, wondering what the hell had gotten into her.

"I appreciate the thought, but no," I declined tactfully. "I don't find abuse sexy."

"It's not abuse if I've asked you to do it," Amy answered with a shrug. How could she be so fucking blasé about something like this?

"There's a fine line," I argued, unwilling to hold the sadistic looking whip. "Sorry Aims. You know I normally play along with you, but I'm just not comfortable with this."

"You're serious aren't you?" she asked with genuine surprise.

"Yeah, I am," I agreed with a nod, surprised that she was surprised by my reaction. "In fact… I think I'm gonna go."

"What?" Amy breathed in shock, "this is supposed to be our last night together."

"I'm sorry. I just, can't be here right now," I told her, backing out the door. "I'll see you on Monday."

- KAT McPHERSON -

The hotel suite was amazing. I'd read all the reviews before I'd booked it but, being London, I hadn't expected it to be quite so opulent. Standard hotel rooms in our city were usually just a dinky little room that was only big enough to fit a double bed and a tiny bathroom, but this one was a full suite, complete with a little lounge area.

"Wow," said Ryan, as he put our suitcase down at the door and looked around the suite. "You went all out babe."

"I figured since we're having a night off we might as well make the most of it," I said, as he disappeared into the bedroom.

"You should see the size of this bed," he called. I joined him in the bedroom and laughed as he leapt onto the King-Sized bed. Ryan rolled onto his side and posed like a male model. "We're officially off-duty," he said suggestively.

"So we are," I replied with a grin, crawling onto the huge bed with him.

"What will we do with all this free time?" he said, grabbing me around the waist.

"Sleep?" I suggested with a giggle. I wrapped my arms around his shoulders as he playfully nuzzled my neck with his stubbly chin.

"There will be no sleeping in this bed," he teased, peering down at me with his big brown eyes. I could have easily lost myself in those eyes. He sighed happily and ran a finger over my cheek. "I feel like we've been apart for a lifetime."

"We kind of have," I agreed, blissfully trailing my fingers down his muscular back. "I guess we'd better make up for lost time," I added with a cheeky grin. I grabbed the bottom of his shirt and pulled it up over his head.

"Hmmm," he chuckled, "that sounds like a challenge I'm willing to accept." We stripped off our clothes in record time and, with a wicked smile, Ryan pulled the covers up over our heads, so we were cocooned inside the crisp white linen sheets. I giggled happily and pulled his face towards mine for a kiss. I ran my hands over his smooth back, enjoying the feel of his solid muscles, while Ryan ran his fingers up the sides of my hips. His touch was so gentle, that it made my hair stand on end. When his palm brushed against my nipple, goosebumps erupted all over my body. He chuckled with pride and repeated the action, evoking a fairly similar response from me the second time around.

"How am I going so far?" he whispered quietly in my ear, as he lightly kissed my neck. More goosebumps exploded across my skin.

"You're going pretty well," I replied breathlessly.

"Just 'pretty well'?" he asked with a husky laugh, smiling down at me from inside our blanket tent. "Well, I'd better try harder then," he joked, pressing his body firmly against mine. I could feel his penis between my legs and a fire ignited in the pit of my belly.

Ryan leant down and kissed me, subtly rubbing his hard cock against my clit as he did so. Little sparks exploded all over my flesh and I immediately spread my thighs and pulled him into me, needing to feel him inside me again. Without missing a beat, Ryan moved steadily on top of me and my hips rose to meet his. We both puffed and panted as our bodies ached for more of each other. My nails dug into his bottom with desperation to envelop him completely, and when he gave a little moan of pleasure, I lost all self-restraint.

With all the heavy breathing, our cocoon was rapidly steaming up, so we were forced to discard the sheets altogether.

"Phew," Ryan breathed, as he flung the covers off the bed with one hand, whilst still gripping me tightly with the other. Our sweaty bodies were stuck firmly together as we inhaled the fresh air with relief. We both laughed, and then Ryan held my eyes with a smoldering gaze. My stomach fluttered. He was so fucking sexy. "Now, where was I?" He asked with a grin, moving his hips around to find the exact spot.

"Right… about…" I paused as he made another small adjustment, "…there," I answered with a nod, as he hit his target. How was it possible that he had gotten so amazingly good at this?

- RYAN McPHERSON -

Our bodies were sprawled lifelessly across the bed after our first session of the evening. We were spent, breathless, and apparently hungry. My stomach rumbled loudly, and we both giggled like children.

"I think it might be time for some food," I chuckled, sitting up and rubbing my empty belly.

"Sounds like it," Kat agreed with a smile, rolling languidly onto her side. Her cheeks were flushed, her lips were bright red, and her hair was so frizzed up that she could have been an extra in 'Hair'. She was beautiful. I would have fucked her again if I wasn't so hungry and busting for a wee.

"Shall we order room service?" I suggested, as I jumped off the bed and ducked into the bathroom to relieve my aching bladder.

"Sounds good" she called, over the sound of my pee. I returned to the bedroom to see my hot wife lying naked in the bed, perusing the room service menu.

"Made your decision?" I asked, as a cheeky idea hit me.

"It all looks so good."

"How about you go make use of that spa bath while I sort the food?"

"Ooh, there's a spa bath?"

"There is indeed."

"I'm not going to turn that down," she said with a grin, handing me the menu. I grabbed her around the waist and gave her a long kiss.

"Go relax in that tub and your dinner will be ready when you get out," I said with a wink.

"You're not going to join me?"

"Maybe," I teased, slapping her bare arse, "but I've got a few little surprises of my own to organize first."

"Very mysterious," she joked, before strutting towards the bathroom. "But don't leave me waiting for too long."

"I won't." I watched Kat disappear behind the bathroom door and waited to hear the sound of running water before I ducked into the sitting room to call room service. I rang down and ordered the 'Lover's Platter' which included a bottle of bubbly; a feast of Asparagus, Mozzarella and prosciutto parcels; Oven baked oysters, thyme stuffed lobsters; and chocolate fondue with whipped cream and fresh strawberries for dessert. With the food ordered, I pulled on my pants and grabbed our empty ice bucket.

"Just popping out quickly," I called to Kat.

"What are you up to," she asked from the bathroom.

"Like I said, it's a surprise," I replied. "Back in a sec." I grabbed the key card and ran, shirtless, down to the ice machine in the hallway to fill our ice bucket. Once I was back in our suite, I left the full bucket on the coffee table and snuck quietly into the bathroom. Kat was lying back amongst the bubbles, eyes closed, with one leg draped over the side of the bath. I grinned to myself and crawled silently across the floor so that I was kneeling beside the big bath. Positioning myself at the best possible angle to avoid alerting her to my presence, I slid my hand into the warm water and ran my fingers over her clit. She jumped with surprise and her eyes flew open, but I just smiled and continued with the task at hand.

"Just lie back and enjoy it," I told her, gently pushing her shoulder back down with my spare hand. Kat nodded and relaxed her head against the bath with a smile as I let my fingers roam between her thighs. She moaned quietly and arched her back when my exploration ventured deeper. My movements were slow and gentle, but I could see her chest rising and falling as her breathing sped up. She moaned again and pushed her hips up towards my hand so I increased my strength and speed until she came with a loud moan.

"Oh my god," she breathed, after taking a moment to recover. "That was certainly a nice surprise."

"That's only the beginning, I said, as we heard a knock at the door. "And there's the next one." I added with a grin. "Stay here and recover. I'll call you when I'm ready."

- RITCHIE CARLTON -

By the time I got home, I felt completely deflated. How the bloody hell had Amy made the drastic leap from our amorous, but fairly vanilla sex life, to me brutalising her? I mean, what the actual fuck was going on with her? She'd always been a bit kinky, but tonight she'd taken it too far. There had been something different in her tonight. Something hard and quite frankly scary. It was as if she was in self-destruct mode and wanting me to press the 'start' button. I wasn't willing to do that. If she wanted to spiral, I wasn't going to help her do it.

I poured myself a bourbon and settled on the couch, when my phone vibrated on the coffee table. I glanced down at the screen to see Sandrine's name again. If she thought I was going to answer her call on a Saturday night, she had another think coming. I let the phone ring out as I sculled the rest of my drink and re-filled my glass, without a second thought for the French Millionaire.

Amy on the other hand, was a lot harder to stop thinking about. Tonight, was the first time I'd ever said 'no' to her and, although I felt like shit, I was proud of myself. Perhaps I was beginning to reclaim my balls after all. I took a long sip of the burning liquid, and nearly choked on it when the sound of my doorbell buzzed loudly through the silent room. I wiped my face clean and brushed down my sullied T. shirt, composing myself enough to deal with my uninvited guest. I wasn't in the mood for a visitor, so I snuck over to the door to peer out the keyhole. I wanted to see who was interrupting my wallowing before I decided whether to answer.

"Ritch?" Amy's voice called quietly from the other side of the door. I stepped carefully backwards with the intent to pretend I wasn't home, but in doing so, stood on a creaky floorboard and alerted her to my presence. "Can you at least open the door?" she asked patiently. I debated for a second, then sighed, and clicked open the door. My chest thudded at the sight of her but I stood my ground and leaned firmly against the door-frame to prevent her coming in. "I'm sorry," she whispered quietly as I stood with my arms crossed, silently staring at her, "I didn't mean to freak you out with all that." Without uttering a word, I stepped back from the door to let her in. She slunk past me and into my lounge room, where she spotted the bottle of Makers Mark on the coffee table. "Mind if I have one?"

"Sure," I agreed with a shrug.

"Thanks," she replied awkwardly. I watched as she poured the bourbon with shaking hands.

"What's going on with you Aims?" I asked, once she'd knocked back the entire glass in one go.

"I'm fighting a lot of demons right now," she answered, topping up my glass, before re-filling her own.

"They must be some fucking big demons," I muttered without thinking. Amy stared down at her feet shamefully.

"They're not small," she agreed, with her gaze still on the floor. She looked so fragile and child-like that I couldn't stay angry at her.

"Is this anything to do with that guy who killed himself?"

"Not really," Aims answered quietly, peering up into my eyes.

"So, is it about us going back to friends?"

"No," she said with a subtle shake of her shiny red hair. "But I am really sad about that."

My chest thudded violently in my chest. She was even more

beautiful without that tough exterior of hers. Her vulnerability made her twenty times sexier than usual, but I had to stay strong.

"You know I'm in love with you right?" I asked point blank, "if we kept this going, I'd need some sort of commitment from you."

"Don't do this tonight, Ritch," she pleaded quietly.

"Why? Because you might actually say yes?" I pressed with slight annoyance.

"No," she replied, "because I'll just break your heart again."
I rubbed my face with frustration.

"What would be so bad about being a real couple? Why are you so against it?"

"Tonight's not the night Ritch," she answered softly, "let's just enjoy our last night together." She stared up at me with tears in her eyes and my heart wrenched. I'd never seen Amy even close to crying before.

"Okay," I agreed with a nod. I had no idea how to respond to her open show of emotion because she'd never shared her feelings with me before. "Am I allowed to give you hug?" I asked awkwardly. She nodded with a sad smile, so I scooped her up in my arms and she melted into me. I revelled in the feel of our embrace… until she began kissing me feverishly. "Whoa," I said, peeling her off me and holding her at arm's length, "that escalated quickly."

"Sorry," Amy apologised sheepishly, staring down at the floor.

"I wish you'd just talk to me about whatever this is."

"I can't."

"Why not?"

Amy sighed, turned away and poured herself another glass of Maker's Mark. She sipped her drink slowly, as if biding her words.

"Ritchie…" she said, looking up at me before letting her sentence trail off.

"What is it?"

Amy turned away again and finished the glass of amber nectar. I watched silently as she popped the glass back down onto the coffee table and paced the room.

"There's some stuff in my past… bad stuff… that I've kept buried for a long time."

"Okay," I said, encouragingly, trying to decipher what she was saying.

"Some recent events have brought it up again and I don't really know what to do with it."

"And you don't feel like you can talk to me about it?"

"Ritchie, I love you, but you have serious broken wing syndrome. If you knew about this, you would just want to fix me and then you'd never move on with your life."

My heart pounded in my chest as I heard her say the words 'I love you'. None of her other words even registered.

"You love me?" I asked, stuck on those three little words.

"Yes Ritchie, I love you," she said, sliding her arms around my neck, "but I don't need you to fix me."

"So, what do you need from me then?" I asked, swallowing back the lump in my throat as she ran her hands up my neck and then down to my chin, pulling my head closer to hers.

"I need you to have sex with me one last time," she whispered into my ear. My heart sank and a sad sigh escaped from my lips.

"You know I can't say no to you," I said, holding my arms out to the side so she could remove my shirt. She threw my shirt onto the sofa and slowly kissed my bare chest. I lifted her off the ground, despising myself for being so weak. I was nothing more than Amy's sex toy, and although I would regret my decision in the morning, tonight I'd play my part.

- KAT McPHERSON -

I heard Ryan chatting with the room service guy as I dried and moisturized myself, concentrating on my stretch-marked hips and stomach. My poor belly had been stretched beyond capacity and while the marks seemed to be fading slightly, I had a feeling they would remain as a permanent feature on my body. I dried my hair and slid into one of the big fluffy bathrobes, tying the robe around my waist. I joined Ryan in the lounge room, where he'd set up a veritable feast on the coffee table.

"Wow, this is impressive," I said, squeezing his shoulder as he finished arranging some flowers in the center of the platter. He looked up and grinned proudly, pulling a bottle of bubbly out of the wine chiller.

"My way of saying thank you for being such an amazing wife," he said with a wink. He opened the bottle with loud pop, and poured a couple of glasses, handing one to me. "Here's to us," he said clinking his glass against mine.

"To us," I agreed with a smile, "and to new beginnings."

"Damn straight."

We sipped our champers, and I eyed the amazing spread.

"So, what do we have here then?" We sat down on the cushions he'd placed around the coffee table, and then Ryan talked me through the menu, feeding me a piece of each item as he did. It was very romantic, and all the food was delicious. Once we'd devoured our meal, I leaned back against the sofa feeling very content. "That was a wonderful surprise," I said, with a full belly. "Thank you."

"There's still one more surprise to go," Ryan said as he raised his eyebrows and glanced at the bucket of ice. "It's time to show you what I'm planning to do with these," he joked, pulling out one of the ice cubes. "Get ready for a chilling ride," he said as he slid the ice cube up my thigh. The chill took my breath away, especially when he kept going right up underneath my bathrobe.

"Oh," I gasped as the ice cube reached its destination.

"This should cool you off a little," he teased, maneuvering the ice in the most distracting way. I gripped the sofa cushion and moaned as he worked his icy magic. It was a combination of pleasure and pain, but it was exquisite.

When the ice cube began to melt, Ryan grabbed a couple of others. He deposited one where the previous one had been and then slipped the other under the collar of my bathrobe, running it over my already excited nipples. I moaned and pressed my body into his cold hands. My heart was pounding so fast that I thought it would burst out of my chest. I needed him and it couldn't wait. I threw off my bathrobe and pushed him backwards onto the cushions. I didn't have time to remove his shorts, so I pulled out his cock and pounced on him.

"I need you now," I told him, giving him no choice in the matter.

"I'm all yours," he said with a grin, as I began grinding myself urgently on top of him. Ryan rubbed my breasts and within minutes I was climaxing loudly.

When my orgasm subsided, he still hadn't come, so I grabbed a piece of ice and ran it slowly over his body as I continued riding him. As the ice explored his body, I felt his cock jump inside me, and I knew he was close. Feeling a little naughty, I slipped my hand behind me and ran the ice underneath his balls.

"Holy shit," he yelped with surprise, nearly throwing me off his lap when I slid it down towards his bottom. "Jesus babe," he said, failing to disguise the fact that he was verging on blowing, "warn a guy before you do tha-". He failed to finish his sentence as his body ignored his protests and surged with relief. "Fuuuuuck," he moaned, unable to articulate anything else. I laughed and sat for a moment while he recovered.

"You can't tell me you didn't enjoy it," I teased, carefully rolling off him.

"It was okay," he agreed with a blush.

"Just okay?" I asked, scooping up a handful of ice, "would you like to re-think that?"

Ryan laughed and grabbed the entire ice bucket.

"Do you really want to start a fight you can't win?" he asked with a cheeky grin.

"Who says I won't win," I retorted, throwing my handful of ice at him.

"Oh, I promise you won't win," he said, rapid firing a few ice cubes in my direction. I squealed and ran into the bedroom. "Just wait until I pin you down and really go to town with these," he laughed, running after me.

- RYAN McPHERSON -

I chased Kat to the bedroom, gripping the ice bucket in one hand, whilst stripping my shorts off with the other. In my haste, the damn shorts got tangled around my ankles and I nearly fell head over heels.

"Shit!" I swore, reaching for the door frame with my spare hand. I managed to steady myself and detangle one foot from the offending shorts.

"Everything okay there slugger?" Kat asked, giggling at my accidental comedy skit. Slapstick humour hadn't exactly been the vibe I was aiming for. With my shorts still hanging lifelessly around my left ankle, I looked up to see Kat lying naked on the bed with a huge grin on her face. The sight of her body took my breath away. My wife was a million shades of hotness.

"Wow," I sighed with a smile, feeling like the luckiest man on earth.

"Is there another half-time show, or are you going to get to work with those ice cubes?" she teased. I threw a handful of ice at her and put the bucket down on the bedside table so I could free my trapped ankle.

"You'll be begging for mercy woman," I joked, tackling her playfully. She squealed with laughter as I grabbed her around the waist and rolled on top of her. Our lighthearted wrestle came to a sudden halt when I felt a painful twinge in my back. "Ugh," I groaned, grasping my back like an old man.

"Are you okay?" she asked with concern, as I flopped back on the bed in pain.

"I think I put my back out when I tripped over my shorts," I admitted with humiliation. Kat snorted loudly in amusement.

"Oh no, you have an old man injury."

"Glad this is entertaining for you," I replied dryly.

"Roll over and I'll see what I can do for your back old man."

"Why? What are you going to do to it?"

"Don't be such a baby," she said, rolling her eyes, "I'm going to give you a massage. Now roll over."

"Okay," I agreed obediently, and rolled over to lay flat on my belly. She knelt over me and, perching carefully on top of my bottom, she started rubbing my back.

"Oh god," I groaned into the pillow as Kat pressed her knuckles into my lower back.

"Is that a sound of pleasure or pain?" she asked with amusement.

"Both," I exhaled with another moan, as her elbow dug into my spine. That much was true. Due to her pleasantly tortuous massage, I was sporting the boner to shame all boners which, incidentally, was adding to my discomfort. With Kat sitting on my bum, my poor cock was being crushed into the mattress in a painful yet strangely satisfying way.

"Maybe you should call me Christian Gray," Kat joked with a wicked chuckle as she continued assaulting my back muscles.

"Actually, I think you'd be able to teach him a thing or tw-owie," I grunted as she interrupted my sentence with another painful poke.

Kat erupted into laughter. "When did you start saying owie?" she teased amidst her laughter.

"Since you took up a job as a dominatrix."

"I've never heard a grown-man say 'owie' before."

"Well now you have," I replied dryly, concentrating on not saying it again. "You're enjoying this aren't you?"

"I'd be lying if I said I'm not."

"You won't be laughing when I refuse sex," I said breathlessly, feeling like I'd been punched in the kidneys.

Kat laughed, "as if you'd ever turn down sex for the sake of your pride."

"That's true, but I might not be capable of having sex again after this massage."

"You really need to woman-up girlfriend," she joked, rolling off me, "but lucky for you I need to pee." Kat patted me on the butt as she climbed off the bed. I groaned in relief, extricating my dick from the dent it had imprinted in the mattress. I rolled over and flopped back on the bed feeling amazingly agile again. I was impressed that her sadomasochistic massage had actually worked. Kat returned to the bedroom and stood in the doorway stark naked. Her figure had changed since having Mia, but I loved it even more now.

"God you're gorgeous," I sighed, as I studied every inch of her beautiful body.

"I'm glad you approve," she teased with a smile as she glanced at my rather obvious hard-on. "Does that mean it's game on?"

"Oh, it's on, like Donkey Kong."

- NATHAN STONE -

The following morning, I woke up to find Ashley's side of the bed empty. It was the first time since we'd been at the Shack, that she'd woken up earlier than me. In fact, it was only the second time in our entire relationship that I'd slept longer than her.

I stretched my back and rolled out of bed, straightening up my boxer shorts which had twisted around overnight causing the center seam to squish my bollocks. That was the exact reason I normally slept naked, but until Ash gave me a sign that she was ready for nudity then I'd keep myself covered up.

I pulled on a T-shirt, ducked into the en-suite for a pee, and then wandered out to see where Ash was. I peeked my head into the lounge room, but she wasn't there. Through the sliding glass doors, I spotted her sitting out on the balcony, curled up on the big daybed. She hugged a mug of coffee, as she stared out at the ocean, looking super cute with her hair tied up in a messy bun on top of her head. Her baggy woollen jumper had slipped down on one shoulder again and she was still wearing her fluffy purple bed socks. I smiled and watched her for a few minutes. The breeze was gently blowing her hair and the orange light from the rising sun was making her face glow in glorious colour. She looked deep in thought, as she stared out over the blue water.

I smiled contentedly and left Ashley to her thoughts. After checking on Freddie and the kittens, who all seemed happy in their makeshift bed in the laundry, I grabbed myself a coffee and joined my gorgeous girlfriend on the balcony.

"Are you okay?" I asked quietly, sticking my head out the door.

Ash looked up and smiled. "Yeah, just thinking."

I sat down next to her and draped my arm over her shoulder.

"Thinking about what exactly?"

She took a sip of her coffee and leaned into me.

"I don't want to go back to London," she said quietly.

"Me either," I said, breathing in the fresh salt air.

"It's so beautiful here, I wish we could stay forever," she mused sadly.

"We could if you wanted to," I said with a shrug.

Ash laughed, "yeah if we didn't have to live in the real world. But unfortunately, we must get back to work."

"Must we really?"

She wriggled around so that she was facing me. "What do you mean?"

I took a long sip of my hot coffee and then put my mug down on the coffee table.

"I have enough money to keep us both, we could live like this forever."

"We can't do that Nathan," she said, rolling onto her knees. "What about the Delfontaine account?"

"Ritchie and Kat seem to have it under control," I reassured her with a smile. "Seriously Ash, this whole thing has put life into perspective."

"Are you honestly suggesting that we quit our jobs?"

"Well, I'm suggesting that you could think about it," I said with a cringe, worried how she was going to take my news. "I've already quit."

She cocked her head with a look of disapproval. "Tell me you're joking Nath."

"I can't," I said bluntly. "They no longer need me on the Delfontaine account, so I resigned."

"Why?" she asked, gripping my hands, "because of me?"

"No," I reassured her with a smile, "this just helped me re-assess my priorities."

"I don't get it Nathan; your job is everything to you."

"No, you're everything to me."

Ashley stared at me flabbergasted. "But-"

"I mean it Ash, you're the only thing in my life that's real, and this whole situation made me realise that I've spent my entire life in a land of bullshit and manipulation. I spin shit to my clients to get million-pound contracts and then we spin more shit to make customers buy stuff they don't really need. I don't think I want to do that anymore."

"But you worked so hard to secure the Delfontaine contract, and you're willing just to hand it over to Ritch?"

"I already have," I said with a shrug, "and he's doing a great job." Ash stared at me agape and I rubbed my face with shame. "Sorry babe but I'm not changing my mind. I've been a vacuous human for the past 36 years and I've done some disgusting things in the name of work.

My life was shallow until I met you."

"I think you need to give yourself a little more credit than that."

"Why?"

"Because you're a good man Nathan. You've achieved so much."

"Yeah," I huffed with amusement, "I got handed part-ownership of a company, and then I fucked my way into winning a cosmetics client who pay us to tell insecure women that they need to look better."

"Nathan…"

"It's okay," I said, rubbing her arm with a smile. "I know I sound insane, but I'm actually more clear-headed than I've ever been in my life. This is my dark night of the soul, or a mid-life crisis if you will, but it's my turning point. It's taken me a long time to get here, but I've finally realised what life is all about… and it's not my job."

Ash held my hand. "I get what you're saying, but I don't think we should be making big decisions like that while we're recovering from major life events."

"It's already done, but I'm not going to make you give up your job if that's not what you want," I told her earnestly. Ash sighed and peered up at me with loving eyes.

"It's really tempting, but we should think it through properly."

"So that's not a 'no' then?"

"It's a maybe," she said with a smile. "Nath I can't think of anything better than moving down here with you, but I don't want to make a decision like that right now. Let's go home, try to get back to some sort of normal life and then see how we feel in a few months."

"Get back to a normal life?" I asked with a laugh. "That would imply that we had a normal life to begin with."

"Okay… well… let's attempt to lead a normal life like normal people for a few months," she corrected herself with a grin, "then if we don't like being normal, we can revisit this discussion."

"Deal," I agreed, "but can we at least stretch this holiday out for another week?"

Ash laughed and patted my chest. "I can pretend to be a basket case for one more week."

"No need to pretend," I teased with a cheeky wink.

"Ooh, you're getting brave Mr Stone. No more walking on eggshells then?"

"Nah… no more Mr nice guy," I said, as Fred escaped her rabble of noisy babies and sat down in front of us looking weary. "How are you going Freddie?" I asked, patting her head gently.

Ash patted Fred too. "The poor thing looks exhausted."

"Well, it can't be easy being a single mum of five," I said, barely able to believe that I was now the proud owner of six cats. "I bet she'll be happy having me home to help with the grandchildren," I joked climbing off the day bed and picking up my coffee. "Come on Freddie, let's sort out these kids of yours."

- ASHLEY GRANGER -

I watched Nathan lead Fred inside, and then sat for a moment, staring out over the water. Could I really quit my job and move to Cornwall? Did I even want to give up work? How would in I feel in another few months knowing that I'd given up my dream job? I shook my head. No. It was totally crazy. I couldn't do it.

I gulped down the last of my coffee and followed Nathan inside, thinking about what life would be like if we didn't return to London. As I pondered our possible future by the seaside, I ambled over to the bookshelf to browse through Nathan's book collection. His library was fairly eclectic, ranging from Harry Potter, John Grisham, Robert Kyosaki, Leo Tolstoy and even the Twilight series, which was an interesting surprise; but there was one book hidden in between two Tom Clancy's that I hadn't spotted until now. I stopped and cocked my head as I saw my favourite book of all-time, tucked right back in the shelf.

"Celestine Prophecy," I mumbled with surprise.

"What are you looking at?" Nathan asked, sneaking up behind me like a ninja.

"Oh shit," I swore with a fright.

"Sorry, I didn't mean to scare you."

"I didn't hear you come out," I said with a laugh as I pointed at the book in question. "Is that yours?" I asked curiously.

"Celestine Prophecy?" he said, popping his mug down. "Yeah, it's a bit random, but I really like it," he said with a blush, "I love the whole idea of following the flow, you know? Noticing the synchronicities and all that."

"Me too. It's actually my favourite book."

"Then, I'll read it to you," Nathan said, reaching over me to pull the book off the shelf.

"You want to read to me?" I asked with a surprised smile, wondering how this sweet man of mine could have ever been a player.

"Yeah," he said, looking down at me with a childlike smile. I watched him with intrigue as he backed away from me and sprawled length ways onto the massive sofa. "Come on," he said, patting the cushion beside him. I tilted my head with amusement.

"I know I say this all the time, but you continually surprise me Nathan Stone."

"Well, I should hope so," he said, beckoning me over, "I'd hate to be predictable."

I snuggled up next to him and he propped his left arm on the cushions so he could hold up the book. I rested my cheek on his warm chest and sighed happily as the sun began to shine through the double-doors. The thin white curtains fluttered gently in the breeze and Nathan leaned his cheek against my head, tracing his fingers up and down my spine as he began to read.

I draped my arm over Nathan's stomach and closed my eyes, listening to the soothing sound of his voice, backed by a symphony of waking seagulls and softly crashing waves. After a few chapters, I opened my eyes and peered up at my beautiful man, watching his face as he read animatedly. My heart fluttered in my chest. We hadn't been together for that long, but it was as if we'd never not been a couple - as if my life hadn't existed before Nathan Stone.

I reached up and lightly touched his face, running my thumb along his stubbly jaw, before tracing my fingers down the side of his neck. He stopped reading and gazed down at me with a smile that sent butterflies fluttering in the pit of my belly.

My breath caught in my throat and my eyes flicked down to his lips. With my hand resting on the back of his neck, I pulled his face to mine. The kiss was light and uncertain at first, but his soft lips were so inviting, that I went back for another more purposeful, kiss.

I ran my hand up the back of Nathan's neck and re-adjusted my position so that my chest was pressed against his. Still holding the book in one hand, he reciprocated my kiss apprehensively. I could feel his heart pounding, but he was holding back.

With my lips still against Nathan's, I took the book out of his hand and let it plop it onto the floor behind me. Nathan's eyes studied me intensely as I slid my hand underneath his T-shirt, running my fingers around his waist and up his back. His breath faltered as I gripped the bare skin on the back of his shoulder. He pulled away from me.

"Ash," he breathed hesitantly, holding his hands out to the side so as not to accidentally touch me.

"It's okay," I assured him, running one hand through the back of his hair as he studied my face with a penetrating expression.

"Are you sure?" he asked worriedly. I stared up at his handsome face and nodded, pushing the hem of his T-shirt upwards to emphasise my point. Nathan lifted his arms obligingly, so I pulled the shirt over his head and threw it onto the floor. I ran my fingers over his solid abs, but Nathan intercepted my touch and firmly secured my hand against his chest. "Are you really okay with this?" he asked, still unconvinced. I looked him in the eyes.

"I'm very okay with this," I reassured him, extracting my hand from underneath his palm so that I could remove my sweater. His eyes widened as I stripped off the baggy jumper and dropped it onto the floor on top of his tee, leaving myself naked from the waist up. I gently trailed my hands across his chest, and Nathans eyes lingered over my bare breasts. He gulped loudly.

"What about... you know... everything?" he asked as he ran his hands lightly up my arms, before holding me firmly at a distance.

"I'm fine Nathan, I promise."

"Are you absolutely sure?" he asked, with his hands still planted on my shoulders.

I smiled. "Just shut up and kiss me, Stone."

Nathan grinned and released his grasp on my arms, running one hand into my hair, and the other down my back. He pulled me in close and kissed me gently at first, but then he began to relax and let his instincts take over. I gripped my hands tightly around his back and we sank down into the big sofa, entwined around each other. He rolled us over so that he was on top. With all of Nathan's previous injuries, it was the first time that we'd ever found ourselves in that particular position and the feel of his warm body on top of mine sent a wave of urgent desire through my body.

"Is your knee okay?" I asked, barely removing my mouth from his.

"It's fine," he said breathlessly, hooking his fingers into the waistband of my pyjama shorts.

"And everything else?"

"All good," Nathan answered as he slid my pyjama's down as far as he could reach without interrupting our kiss. I grabbed the elastic on his boxers and used my foot to push them all the way down his legs. He kicked them off from around his ankles as I quickly wriggled out of mine. Finally free of our clothing, we both paused for a moment, breathless. He looked down at me and stroked my hair. "Are you alright?"

I smiled and nodded. "Yeah, I am," I said, hooking my right leg over his bottom and noticing, but not caring, that I still had my socks on.

Nathan nodded almost imperceptibly, and let his body sink down onto mine. I wrapped my other leg around his waist and lost my breath for a second when he slowly entered me. His movements were careful and measured, and he watched me intently to make sure that I was okay. I tried my best to maintain eye contact, but it felt so good that I couldn't keep my eyes open. I let out a silent gasp of relief and bit my lip, dropping my head back against the cushion. I dug my fingers into Nath's shoulders, straining my hips towards his, as he moved steadily on top of me. The moment was deliciously intimate, and it felt almost therapeutic, as if with every movement Nathan made, he was erasing Dom.

We clung to each other like our lives depended on it, as the world outside began to wake. All that mattered was the two of us. Nathan rested his forehead on my shoulder and the sound of his breath in my ear sent goosebumps across my flesh.

A moan escaped my lips and he squeezed me tight, making a little adjustment with his hips that set off a bonfire in the pit of my stomach. My whole body was ablaze, and every single hair on my flesh was standing on-end. I moaned again, unable to control myself. I was hanging right on the edge, but I still wasn't ready to jump. I'd never experienced anything like it before, and I didn't want it to end.

I was so overwhelmed that I felt tears forming behind my eyes. I quickly buried my face into Nathan's neck, so he didn't see my tears of emotion and mistake them for tears of distress. My nails dug deeper into his back as I wrapped my legs tightly around him. He groaned quietly and I could tell he was getting close too, but he was reigning himself in. He grabbed my hips to prop my bottom up and, for a second, I was left breathless as he sank further into me. My body began to tremble, and I moaned loudly as my brain exploded into a million pieces. Nath groaned and gripped me tight, setting off another round of explosions in my body as he shuddered with pleasure.

"Oh my god," I breathed in ecstasy as the waves of my orgasm crashed over me.

"Holy shit," Nath agreed breathlessly. He grasped me tight and began to slow down his movements, then eventually relaxed and rested his hips against mine. I squeezed my thighs around his waist one last time, not ready for it to be over, then I finally released my vice-like grip, sliding my sock-covered feet down his legs. I hooked one ankle around his thigh and rested the other one next to his foot, then flopped back and ran my shaking hands through my sweaty hair.

"Well, that was unexpected," Nathan said, shifting his body weight to the side so that he didn't squish me, "I think I'll read to you more often."

"You weren't joking about blowing my mind," I laughed, pressing my palms against my eyes to make sure all the tears were gone before he noticed.

"Yeah, it wasn't a bad effort considering."

Keeping my eyes closed for a moment, I let my hands flop against the cushion above my head. I opened my eyes to see him studying me intently.

"You're going to ask me if I'm okay, aren't you?" I teased with a tired smile.

He blushed, "I was… but I won't now."

I ran my hand down his face, "I'm okay. In fact, I'm better than okay."

"So that didn't trigger anything?"

"It just reminded me of exactly how much I love you."

- RITCHIE CARLTON -

It was late morning by the time I peeled my tired eyes open to find Amy still lying asleep next to me. She had reluctantly agreed to stay over for our last night together and it was the first and only time in our entire relationship – if you could call it a relationship - that she'd ever stayed an entire night. I rolled onto my side and watched her sleeping. God I was going to miss her.

"Are you watching me sleep?" she mumbled tiredly, with her eyes still closed.

"I only just woke up," I said, feeling bashful about being caught out. Amy's eyes peeled open and she gave me an awkward half-smile.

"So…" she said, rolling onto her back and stretching languidly, "should we go for one last round before I leave?"

"I was hoping maybe we could talk."

"About what?" she asked with slight confusion. "I thought we'd covered everything already," she added as she trailed her hand down my bare stomach. I groaned with annoyance and rolled out of bed.

"I can't do this Aims," I said, pulling on a pair of boxers, "if you're not going to talk then I think it's probably best if you go."

"Okay fine," she said, nodding obediently, "I'll be on my best behaviour." I looked over my shoulder distrustfully, but Amy smiled reassuringly and patted the bed. "Sit down and tell me what's on your mind."

"I have a few things on my mind," I said patiently, as I perched on the edge of my bed.

"Have you changed your mind about ending this?" She asked hopefully.

"No Aims," I grunted with exhaustion. How could she not understand? "The only thing that would change my mind is if you agreed to commit to me."

"I'm as committed as I get Ritch," she replied tersely. "I've never even considered seeing anyone else."

"You're missing the point. I'm thirty-seven. My younger sister already has two kids, and my younger brother is getting married at the end of the year. I'm in London doing… whatever it is that we're doing here."

"We may not be a normal couple, but you've got me Ritch."

"But I want to marry you, Amy. I want to have kids and raise a family together, not spend the rest of our lives in this holding pattern."

"I can't give you that," she answered quietly.

"Can't, or won't?"

"Won't."

"Why not?" I asked with exhaustion, "you said you love me."

"I do love you Ritch."

"So, what's the problem then?" It was hard not to take it personally.

"There's a lot of stuff about my life that you don't know," she told me quietly.

"Then talk to me about it for fuck's sake," I pleaded desperately. "All I've ever wanted is for you to let me in."

"I can't," she sighed, shaking her head regretfully.

"You mean you won't," I said, picking up on her earlier semantics.

"Yes."

"Why not?!" I repeated frustratedly, feeling like we were going around in circles.

"All you need to know is that I'm damaged goods Ritchie. I'm not wife or mother material."

"That's such a crock of shit," I hissed angrily, "you're just too gutless to give this a proper chance."

"How dare you. You know nothing about my past and what I've been through."

"Of course I don't, because you never fucking tell me about it," I snapped aggressively. "You make all these excuses but the truth is, you're just too scared to let me in."

"That's not fair."

"Isn't it? I guess sex toys don't need an opinion do they?"

"Fuck you Ritch," she replied coldly with tears in her eyes.

"Yeah. Fuck me…" I mocked with frustration, standing up from the bed, "…because that's all I'm good for right?"

"Of course not," she replied quickly, reaching out for my arm. I let her take my hand and she smiled mischievously, "but you are very good at it," she added with ill-timed humour. I pulled my hand from hers and stepped away from the bed.

"We're done here," I told her bluntly.

"What?" She asked in shock.

"If you can't commit then we have nothing more to say," I said firmly. "I think you should leave."

"You don't mean that," she informed me indignantly.

"Yes, I do," I replied coldly.

"But what about our final goodbye shag?"

"Last night was it, Amy. We're done."

"I think we should park this and have some breakfast."

"No more parking," I muttered, grabbing a T.Shirt out of my dresser.

"What are you doing?" Amy asked as I headed to the door, shrugging into my tee.

"I'm leaving," I answered simply. "I love you Aims… but I'm done. Just let yourself out when you're ready." Without looking back, I marched out the door and down the stairs, grabbing my keys before I walked right out of my flat. I felt broken but relieved. It wouldn't matter how much more we talked about it; I couldn't play out the charade anymore. I was a thirty-seven-year-old man, with no wife, no kids, and an extended family who lived on the other side of the world. I didn't want to spend another two decades blowing cash on drugs and alcohol just to fill a family-sized hole in my heart.

When I returned to my place hours later, I was relieved to see that there were no signs of Amy's presence, besides my spare key sitting on the hall-stand. As I stared at the key, I felt a kind of twinging in my chest and decided to flush it out with some Bourbon. I knew I'd made the right decision in breaking things off with Amy, but that knowledge hadn't helped it hurt any less. Gentlemen Jacks' seemed like the only logical solution to combating the swelling pain in my heart. Not bothering with a glass, I grabbed the bottle off the shelf and swigged it.

I glanced at all the missed calls from Sandrine and contemplated calling her, but it would take a few more bourbons before talking to Sandrine seemed like a good idea. I put the phone down and forced away the urge to distract myself with the sexy French nymphomaniac.

Breakfast, lunch and dinner, consisted solely of Jack Daniels, so by the evening, I'd started feeling much better. Or more to the point, I'd stopped feeling, period. The warm amber liquid had numbed my mind and, to a certain extent, my body too. As a consequence,

I'd wasted the entire day slumped on my couch, playing Grand Theft Auto, pretending that I wasn't wallowing in self-pity. It was surprising that I could even see the screen, so the fact that I'd managed to play a reasonable game was damn near a miracle.

I don't know when exactly, but at some point during that time, the sun had set outside in the real world and the silvery moonlight now spilled in through the windows. The blue flickering light emanating from my over-sized TV screen, was the only source of light inside the otherwise darkened apartment.

I glanced over at the empty bottle of Jacks lying abandoned on the cushion. Being a big guy, I'd always been able to put away the drinks, but knocking off a bottle of high-quality bourbon was quite a spectacular effort, even for me. It was a certain bet that tomorrow would hurt even more than today had.

With a groan, I heaved my body forwards to check the time on my phone. It was already midnight, but instead of getting up and going to bed, I started scrolling through my social media feeds. I looked at my sisters' page and flicked through the cute pictures of my nieces at the beach and their happy family photos, bathed in the light of the Australian sunshine. After switching over to my brothers account and seeing all their wedding planning excitement and engagement party photos, I made a snap decision. I jumped onto an airline website and purchased a one-way plane ticket to Perth. The second that I'd hit the purchase button, a feeling of relief had washed over me.

I booked it for late November so that I could get back in time for my brother's buck's night and all the pre-wedding festivities. Despite the fact that my split-second decision only left me about three months to wind-up my current life and prepare for my return to the land down under, I felt a strange sense of calm wash over me. Rather than feeling daunted, I felt excited. I would miss this crazy town, but moving home felt right. I hadn't realized until that moment, how much I'd actually missed home. I'd gone back nearly every Christmas, but a few weeks a year wasn't much in the grand scheme of things.

I leaned back against the couch and closed my eyes with a contented sigh. I was going home.

I must have drifted off, because the next thing I knew, my phone alarm was blaring loudly next to my head. I opened my eyes and squinted as I waited for them to focus in the light of day. In last night's bourbon haze, I'd failed to close my curtains, so the Autumn sunlight was streaming in the windows. I rubbed my eyes and silenced the screaming alarm, not quite ready to come to a sitting position. I didn't feel hungover, which meant that I was probably still drunk.

"I'm going home," I blurted happily to myself as I stared up at the roof. I felt a surge of joy rush through my body at the thought of what laid ahead. "I come from the land down under," I sang loudly, "where beer flows and men chunder."

I laughed at myself and drunkenly rolled off the couch onto my knees, in an attempt to get moving. It was odd that I felt so lighthearted given the events of the previous day, however that was just further reassurance that I'd done the right thing. The real test would be seeing Amy at work. It was all well and good to be chirpy whilst alone in my flat, but it would be an entirely different ball game to see her in person.

As it turned out, coming face-to-face with my ex-non-girlfriend was even more difficult than I'd originally anticipated. I arrived at the office in good spirits, showered, shaved and dosed up on a pleasant cocktail of Berocca, Hydralyte and Codeine. I swiped myself into our secured floor and, as the door slid open, Amy was standing on the other side of it looking as gorgeous as ever.

"Oh hi, hey, I didn't expect to see you here yet," I babbled nervously as I maneuvered my way around her scrumptiously tempting body. "You're here earlier than usual."

"Yeah, I had some work to get done," she said, edging her way out of the door with her back pressed against the metal frame.

"I thought we were on-track?"

"We are, but Kat's got us under the pump to get the ad concepts ready for when Ash gets back," she said with a forced smile.

"That sounds accurate," I joked half-heartedly, "Tails is a bit of an over-achiever."

"She is," she replied, clearing her throat, "Well… I'm going down to grab some coffees for the team. Do you want anything?"

"Nah I'm good, thanks mate." The 'mate' part had kind of slipped out accidentally, but it hung awkwardly in the air between us. I'd never called Amy 'mate' in the history of our entire friendship. I cringed and stepped backwards stiffly, hoping against logic, that she hadn't noticed.

"Okay," she said with a cute frown. My eyes darted everywhere but her face as I tried to stop myself from looking at her. It reminded me of an eclipse. Amy was the sun, and I was my 9-year-old self, failing to avert my eyes.

"Cheers though," I said with a shrug.

"No worries."

We shared a momentary awkward silence and then disappeared in opposite directions. I waited for the door to slide closed behind me and then let out a loud sigh as I rubbed my bald head with frustration. The next three months were going to feel like three years.

- KAT McPHERSON -

The weekend had been so lovely that it was excruciatingly hard to go back to work on Monday morning, especially knowing that Ryan was lying naked in our bed, while I was standing squished up against strangers on the crowded tube. The previous week, I had greatly enjoyed being back at work, but now that Ryan was home, it felt slightly less appealing. Perhaps I'd suggest reducing my hours a little more.

Ritchie had arranged a WIP meeting for the team leads at 9am, so I didn't have much time to dwell on the fact that my sexy husband was waiting for me at home. When I got up to the boardroom we had aptly dubbed 'the padded cell', no one else had arrived yet. I flicked on the lights and the eggshell covered walls came into full view. The windowless room had originally been intended as a sound studio, but now that we had a full production hub on the second floor, it had become redundant.

Needless to say, it was a far cry from our luxurious meeting room at Delfontaine headquarters. I filled the kettle and set up some mugs on the tiny bench top. After spending three solid days together, I knew how each of the boys took their coffee and we'd all gotten into a good groove as a team. As usual, Beau was the next person to arrive, followed closely by Ritchie, who looked like he'd had a very rough weekend.

"You alright Ritch?" I asked, adding an extra teaspoon of instant coffee into his cup.

"Big weekend," he said with a grimace.

"Here," I said, handing him his super strong coffee, "this will help."

"Thanks," he said gratefully, taking the warm mug from my hands. He took a long, slow sip and then eyed me with amusement. "So lady, are you gonna to spill the beans on your sexy weekend?" he teased, nudging me with his elbow.

"A lady never tells," I joked, glancing at Beau with embarrassment.

"Well, it looked like Ryan had been giving you a good workout," Ritchie said, laughing as loudly as his head would allow him.

"Ritchie," I scolded warningly.

"Oh, come on Tails, no need to be shy around here," he said, oblivious to the awkwardness he was creating between Beau and I. Suddenly it dawned on him why I was being weird, and his eyes darted between the two of us. "Oh," he said simply, before falling silent. With the most perfect timing, Cody pranced into the room with a box full of croissants.

"Breakfast is served," he declared, flamboyantly placing the box in the middle of the table.

"Ooh, pain au chocolat," I said, excited at the sight of the French baked goods, and also pleased for the distraction they had provided. "They'll go well with our coffee," I added, pointing towards the little sink area where I'd lined up our mugs.

"I thought it might be a nice reminder of Paris," Cody joked as he headed to the bench to grab his coffee. I picked up one of the chocolate croissants and it was still warm. I breathed in the fresh-baked smell and my mouth started to water. It was a beautiful moment between me and my breakfast.

"Yuuuum," I sighed in pleasure as I took a massive bite of the flakey pastry. We devoured our croissants and commenced our meeting.

Tired after my weekend of amorous sex, I zoned out as Ritchie talked through the agenda items. I still felt totally shattered from my athletic weekend. It had been a long time since I'd had that much sex, not to mention the fact that I'd had a baby in between. My whole body felt tender in places I'd forgotten I had. I yawned and stretched my aching muscles.

"You okay?" Beau mouthed silently from across the table.

"Yeah," I nodded, standing up to stretch my back.

"You right Tails?" asked Ritchie, pausing his discussion.

"Sorry, I just need to stretch my back," I said, feeling sheepish that I'd unintentionally interrupted the meeting.

"Probably pulled a muscle from all that weekend exercise," Ritchie teased with a wink, using air quotes on the word 'exercise', which invoked a snigger from Cody. Beau, on the other hand, looked pained. I blushed furiously and, at a loss for a decent comeback, I rolled my eyes melodramatically and returned to my seat. "Right, so how about we leave social media for now and take a look at the web content?" continued Ritchie, steering the conversation back to work. The meeting moved on, and by the time we wound up, my back was as stiff as anything. I stood up and couldn't help but wince as my muscles screamed in pain. Beau noticed straight away.

"Need a massage?" he asked with a cheeky grin. I was surprised he was being so flirtatious after everything that had happened. Especially in front of witnesses.

"I'll be fine," I answered with a raised eyebrow, before grimacing in pain again.

"Right you, on the sofa," he said pointing at the couch.

"What?" I asked laughing.

"You're having a massage. No arguments."

"Really Beau I'm fine. It'll ease up," I argued.

"You're moving like an old lady Kitty Kat, now go sit on the couch." I laughed nervously and glanced over at the other two. Cody was busy packing up his things so wasn't really paying much attention, but Ritchie was watching us with extreme interest. "Just do it missy or I'll carry you there," ordered Beau. I shrugged and, with a sigh of resignation, got settled on the sofa as Beau sat down behind me.

"Ouch!" I wailed with a twinge of pain as Beau pressed hard on my back.

"Sit still woman."

"I can't. That hurts."

"Of course, it hurts. You're completely knotted up."

"Can't you just go a little softer?"

"Do you want me to fix it or not?" he asked, as we bantered in the same relaxed way we had done before we messed up our friendship.

"Beau, I assume you're going to pull together that website copy for me?" asked Ritchie from behind us.

"Will do," barked Beau dismissively. There was a tense silence for a moment. I couldn't see what was passing between the two boys, but the tension was hanging so thick in the air that I could feel it.

"Tails could I have a word?" Ritchie asked in his authoritative, 'don't fuck with me' voice.

"Sure," I said amenably as I heaved myself up from the couch.

"I guess I should get back to work then," muttered Beau as he climbed to his feet and began gathering his things from the table.

"I guess you should," Ritchie agreed brusquely. He watched Beau like a hawk and waited until he'd left the room before he spoke. "What are you doing Tails?"

"What do you mean?" I asked with genuine confusion.

"With Peterson."

"I'm not doing anything with Beau."

"There was some serious flirting happening there."

"That wasn't flirting," I said defensively, "we're just getting back to being friends again."

"Kat if you believe that then you're deluding yourself," Ritch said firmly but kindly. "Peterson is trying to win you back and if you're not careful, you could end up ruining your marriage for good."

"That's a bit extreme Ritch. You know I wouldn't do anything to risk my marriage again."

"I know that, but I don't think Peterson does. He's still in love with you and he's not the sort of guy to give up easily."

"He's not in love with me Ritchie."

"Yes, he is, and you know it. It's fucking obvious to anyone with two eyes." Ritchie was right. It was obvious and I had made it worse by entertaining Beau's attention.

"Maybe," I said, too embarrassed to admit it. I'd have to undo this mess before it got out of control. "Ash is back next week so she can pick up all the Beau related work."

- RITCHIE CARLTON -

I had no idea where Kat's head was at, but I wasn't going to let her get away with that behaviour. It wasn't my business, but she and Ryan had a good thing going and I wouldn't let her fuck that up for a douchebag like Peterson.

"Does that mean you're staying?" I asked, hoping that I could give Gaz some good news, when I broke my bad news.

"Yeah, I'm going to stay."

"That's great news Tails!" I said emphatically slapping her on the back.

"But I want to drop down to part-time so I can help Ryan."

"Not a problem."

"So, I'll only work from ten until two, every day."

"Fine with me."

"And trips abroad won't really be an option."

"Okay."

"Really?" she asked dubiously.

"Yep."

"That seemed way too easy."

"Tails, you're not leaving and that's all that matters."

"Okay. Great," she said with a grin. "Can we start that as soon as Ash gets back?"

"Sure thing," I agreed, relieved that I didn't have to tell Gaz we were losing Kat too. "I'm gonna go tell Gaz the good news." We parted company and I ventured up to Gaz's glass tower to give him the best and the worst of it. "Gaz, can we talk for a minute?" I asked, sticking my head around his open office door. I knew better than to interrupt him without an appointment but when his door was open it was usually fairly safe to enter.

"Sure mate," he said looking up from his computer and waving me in. "What's up?"

I sat in the chair opposite him. "Kat's decided to stay on."

"Fantastic!"

"But she'll go to part-time when Ash gets back."

"Fine with me," he said with a nod. I faltered for a second and then steeled myself for the conversation I knew I had to have.

"Nathan and Ashley are coming back next week," I told him without further explanation. I'd hoped that he'd catch my drift without me having to say anything more, but he peered over the top of his glasses and then slid them off his nose.

"And?" he asked sternly.

"And… well… I was hoping that maybe Nath would be coming back to lead the account," I said, trying not to sound as nervous as I was. Gareth cleared his throat and folded his hands together on the desk.

"Why would he do that?" he asked me suspiciously. "Nathan quit the account remember?"

I sighed and flopped back in the chair. "Yeah I know, but the thing is Gaz," I said keeping my cool, "I'm not really cut out for this Client Partner thing."

"What makes you say that? From what I've seen, you're doing a fantastic job."

"Yeah, I'm not saying I can't do it," I said with a grimace, "I'm saying I don't want to."

Gaz took a breath and leaned back in his chair too.

"I see," he said simply. He studied my face and pondered my question for a moment. "Are you doing this for Nathan or yourself?"

"For both of us," I answered honestly, "but mostly myself."

"You don't want the promotion?"

"I don't want the promotion," I assured him, taking a deep breath for courage. "In fact… I won't be needing a job here at all. I'm moving home Gaz."

"What? when?" he asked with a well disguised panic.

"At the end of November, when I go home for my brother's wedding."

"So that's it? You're giving it all up to move back to the most isolated city in the world?"

"I am," I told him with unwavering certainty. "It's time for me go Gaz. Besides this job, there's nothing left for me here. I need to go back to Perth and settle down."

Gareth rubbed his face as he processed my news. I watched him intensely, willing him to give the job back to Nathan. After a moment he sighed and looked up.

"Well, I guess it only makes sense to hand the job back to Nathan then," he agreed reluctantly.

"Thank you, thank you," I said with relief.

"Does anyone else know?" Gaz asked with a raised brow.

"Not yet."

"Good, let's keep this quiet for now huh? I'd like to have a transition plan in place before we announce it."

"Sure thing."

He nodded gratefully and then a semi-smile crossed his thin lips.

"Ritchie, your departure will be a big loss to Artemis. And to me. I feel like I've watched you grow up over the years. It won't be the same around here without you."

"Thanks Gaz."

"But for what it's worth, it sounds like you're making the right decision."

"Cheers, I appreciate your support."

"I've got some contacts in Perth if you'd like me to reach out for you?"

"Thanks Gaz, but I'd rather do this on my own."

"I understand," he said with a smile, "but please use me as a reference. I'd love to see you succeed over there."

"Thanks, that means a lot," I said shaking his hand. I left Gaz's office feeling lighter than I had in a long time. That was the hardest job done so everything else would be a breeze from there. I pulled out a crumpled piece of paper from my pocket and ticked the first job off my list. Next one was to organise a shipping container. No stress, I could have that done before lunch. I smiled and shoved the list back into my pocket.

"Too easy," I said to myself, bounding happily downstairs when my phone buzzed in my pocket. I pulled it out and glanced at the screen with a heavy sigh. It was Sandrine again. Didier wasn't wrong when he said that she didn't give up.

I ignored the call and shoved the phone back into my pocket. That was a drama I could leave for another day.

- Chapter 6 -

The return of Ashlan

- ASHLEY GRANGER -

Mum descended upon us the second we walked through the door at my parents' place.

"How are you doing honey? Are you okay?" she asked, hugging me tight. "We've been so worried about you."

"I'm good Mum," I said, extracting myself from her firm embrace, as Nathan popped the cat cage down next to the hall stand. She looked me over, still grasping my arms tightly, a doubtful expression on her face. "I had a few rocky days there at the beginning but I'm fine now," I assured her.

"Hi Mary," Nathan said, stretching his back. Mum released me immediately and ran over to give him a hug.

"Oh Nathan, how are you love?" she asked him, studying his face in the same way she had done mine. She patted his cheek affectionately. "You look tired sweetheart," she concluded with concern.

"Yeah, I'm pretty exhausted," Nathan admitted, looking completely at ease with my mums show of affection, "but I'll be fine."

"Geoff's out in the garden if you want to go see him."

"Thanks, I will," he said shooting me a warm smile that melted my insides. He gave my arm a quick squeeze, and then strolled down the hallway and slid out the patio door. We watched Nathan leave and, as if sensing the lack of his presence, the kittens began mewing loudly in their cage. Mum turned her head and noticed the cage for the first time.

"Are these my fluffy little grandchildren?" Mum joked, bending down to look inside the cage.

"Apparently we're the grandparents, so you're their great-grandmother," I teased.

"Oh, they're so beautiful," she said, ignoring my teasing, "are you keeping them all or do you need to find them new homes?"

"I think Nath would like to keep them all, but it's not very practical in the apartment."

"We'll take a couple of them," Mum said, sticking her fingers through the bars to play with the ginger and white striped kitten we'd dubbed Garfield.

"Really?" I asked with surprise. For my entire life, my mother had never let me have a pet. "I didn't think you would be the cat type."

"I'm not usually, but look at those little faces," she said in the sort of tone one would use when talking to a baby.

"Don't you want to check with Dad first?"

"No, he'll go along with it whether he likes it or not."

"Are you really sure? You've never wanted a pet before."

"That's because I've always been too busy to worry about looking after animals," she said, peering up at me over her shoulder, "but now that you're off living your life, and we're both retired, it would be nice to have some extra energy in this house."

"Oh mum," I said, giving her a hug as she straightened up, "I love you."

"Does that mean you'll let me keep a couple?" she asked, taken aback by my overflow of emotion.

"You'll have to ask Nathan, but I think he'd be pleased to keep them in the family. We'll be keeping Shadow though. He's the little black one."

"He's very cute."

"Nathan saved him," I told her proudly. "He was stillborn, and Nath did cardiac massage and CPR until he started breathing."

"Well, your man is the total package isn't he?"

"He really is," I agreed. Mum smiled contentedly and looked me up and down again.

"You've lost weight," she said abruptly, ending our nice moment.

"Yeah, I've been sick Mum," I said a little too snarkily. "I think the painkillers have been irritating my stomach."

"Okaaaay," she agreed dubiously, "as long as you're not starving yourself again."

"Nathan wouldn't let me do that," I laughed. "He was practically trying to force feed me once I started keeping food down again."

"He's a good man," she said, guiding me through to the kitchen. "I'm so glad you have him honey."

"Me too."

"He's the one isn't he?"

I blushed and bit my lip, "I'd like him to be."

"He already is," she said certainly, as she flicked on the kettle.

I shrugged and sat down at the bench. "It's too early to say that. We're still so new."

"That doesn't make your feelings any less," she said knowingly, pulling out a couple of mugs. "Your father and I had only known each other for three months before he proposed to me."

"That's still longer than we've been together," I said loudly, so as to be heard over the boiling kettle.

"I thought you two were together before his accident?" Mum asked, pouring the boiling water into our mugs.

"No, we'd been hanging out a lot, but we weren't a couple."

"So, what was he doing at your house so late that night?"

"That's a very long and complicated Dom-related story."

"Does the same go for why Jock was there too?"

I blushed, bristling at the mention of Jock's name. I still had a lot of unanswered questions about Jock and how he knew about the attack.

"Yes," I answered eventually.

"In that case, I think I'd rather not know," she said, handing me one of the mugs.

"Probably best," I mumbled, cuddling the warm mug of tea. She ducked into the walk-in pantry and pulled out a jar of chocolate biscuits.

"They're vegan," she said pointedly, pushing the jar right in front of me.

"Thanks mum," I said, sipping my tea.

"Eat," she ordered, nodding to the biscuits. I conceded to her demand and pulled a cookie out of the jar. I took a tentative bite to see if it would stay down and, when it did, I took another, larger, bite. "I'm proud of you sweetheart," she said with tears in her eyes.

"For eating a biscuit?" I asked with a mouth full of chocolatey crumbs.

"No," she laughed, "for keeping your head held high. You've had a tough run and you've come through it with grace and dignity."

"Thanks Mum," I said with a wavering voice, feeling emotional again.

"I'm sorry you had to go through all that with Dom, but I'm glad that it's finally over."

"Yeah," I agreed, clearing my throat as I dunked the remainder of my biscuit into my cuppa. "Me too."

"I just wish your father had gotten to him first."

I looked up at her, stunned. "You knew about that?!"

"Not until after the attack," she admitted, "but I dare say I probably wouldn't have stopped him if I'd known."

"Mum!"

"Well, it's true," she said defensively. "That monster is finally down in hell where he belongs. But then… I suppose it wouldn't have been right for your father to kill him," she said rationally, "…you had to be the one to do it."

My jaw dropped at the blasé way in which my mum was discussing murder.

"What do you mean?"

"Ashley, you're a stubbornly independent woman. Can you imagine how you would have reacted it you'd found out that your father and your boyfriend had swooped in and saved the day?"

"Fair point," I said, unable to disagree with her logic, "but no one should have killed anyone."

"I think that's a matter of opinion," she answered primly sipping her tea. "You really have found your happy ending with Nathan. You know that don't you?" she asked, patting me on the arm.

"I hope so. I guess I'm just waiting for the other shoe to drop. Some days I think this must all be a big prank because he's too good to be true."

"Don't ruin it honey," she said disapprovingly, "this is your time to be happy, so just accept it with gratitude. Don't sabotage yourself."

"I'm trying not to."

"You've been through hell and back Ashley, so now God is making it up to you."

"I'd really like that to be true."

"It is true. It's your time sweetie. You get to be happy now. This is your fairy-tale ending."

- NATHAN STONE -

I wandered out into the massive garden to look for Geoff. I hadn't seen the backyard on our last visit, since Geoff and I had spent most of the time down in the cellar plotting a murder. The term 'backyard' wasn't substantial enough to describe the outdoor area. The huge property was well maintained and very impressive, accommodating a large pond, a fruit orchard, a rose garden, and a greenhouse full of vegetable beds, which is where I found Geoff, bent over some spinach.

"Hey Geoff," I called from the doorway of the greenhouse.

"Is that hotshot I hear?" Geoff joked, peeking up from behind his veggies. He beamed. "Good to see you lad," he said as he climbed to his feet and dusted himself off.

"And you," I said, as Geoff wandered over to shake my hand, eyeing me expectantly.

"How is she?"

"She's…" I thought about my words for a moment, "much better."

"Good." He nodded with approval. "And how are you?"

"I'm fine," I said, touched that they had both checked in on my wellbeing too.

"You look tired," he said gruffly as he patted me on the shoulder.

"It's been a rough couple of weeks," I admitted with a nod while he stared me down with his intimidating all-knowing judge look.

"There's more to the story isn't there?"

"Yeah."

"But you're not going to tell me, are you?"

"No."

Geoff nodded, smiled and gripped my shoulder. "Thanks for looking after our girl, Hotshot."

"I'll always look after her Geoff," I told him sincerely. "No matter what."

"I don't doubt that lad," he said with another smile. "Now, onto other matters… shall we go down to the cellar and choose a bottle?"

"Actually Geoff," I said, feeling butterflies take off inside my belly, "there's something I'd like to talk to you about before we go inside."

"Oh, yes?" he said with interest as his eyebrows rose in the center like two hairy caterpillars greeting each other. "What's that?"

"Well…" I said, in a very drawn-out fashion. This was it. This was the moment I'd spent two weeks of long, lonely days and nights rehearsing for. I took a deep breath to steady myself. "Geoff, I know this is a bit old fashioned, but I'd like your permission to propose to Ashley."

It was blunt but to the point. I'd rather hoped to recite the eloquent speech I'd prepared, but those were the words that exited my mouth instead.

"Wow," Geoff said looking shocked. The caterpillars were now both looking downwards towards his nose.

"I admit we haven't been together for very long, but I love her, and I can't imagine my life without her," I babbled, suddenly remembering some of the speech. I swallowed hard, and nervously awaited his response, too scared to make another sound. Eventually the caterpillars rose to their hind legs and Geoff smiled broadly.

"Of course, you can propose to her lad," he laughed. I breathed a silent sigh of relief as he slapped me on the back and then pulled me in for a tight, soil-covered hug. "You're the best thing that's ever happened to her Nathan. She lights up when she's with you and I wouldn't dream of standing in the way of that."

"Thanks Geoff."

"So, when are you planning on popping the question?"

"I'm not sure," I said self-consciously, "I'm waiting for my mum's old engagement ring to come back from the jeweller. I sent it off to be re-set for Ash."

"Well, that's a great idea," he said approvingly, "I'm sure she'll love it."

"I hope so," I said with a nervous smile, "assuming she says yes."

Geoff laughed jovially and clapped me on the back so hard that I almost fell face forward into the garden bed.

"She won't turn you down Nathan," he said reassuringly. "Come on, let's go crack a bottle of Bollinger to celebrate."

"I'm afraid that will have to wait for another time, Geoff. I'm driving us home."

"Why don't you two stay the night?"

"I'd love to, but we've got to be back at work in the morning."

"I thought you'd quit."

"I had," I agreed with a nod, "but your daughter called our boss and un-quit me."

Geoff laughed loudly and slapped me on the back. "Welcome to life with my daughter."

- RITCHIE CARLTON -

It had been hard keeping my news to myself for an entire week, but soon I'd finally be able to tell my friends that I was leaving. Everything was locked in. My resignation was done, the shippers were booked, and I'd already started sending my CV out to local agencies at home. The next thing on my list was to tell my parents.

When the clock hit midnight, I dialled them on Skype. It was 8a.m. Perth time so they would have been awake for at least an hour.

"Ritchie," said my mum excitedly, popping up on my screen with a close-up view of her face.

"Hey Mum," I said, with a laugh. "You don't need to sit so close to the camera, you know?"

"Oh hush," she tutted with embarrassment, as she leaned back to a more reasonable distance, allowing her poufy ginger bob to come into view. "It's good to see your face love."

"Yours too."

"You look pale," she said, squinting her blue eyes as she scrutinized me through the screen. "Well... paler than usual at least."

As a family of redheads, none of us ever got particularly tanned. We were basically Australia's answer to the Weasley's... except that there were a lot less of us, and we weren't magical.

"I live in England Ma. This is as tanned as I get over here."

"Just as well you'll be back in Oz for Chrissy then," joked my dad, as his scruffy red hair appeared behind my mother. "We can't have our oldest son turning into a sickly Pom."

"Hi Dad."

"Hey mate, how's life on the wrong side?" he asked, pulling up a seat next to Mum.

"It's okay," I said unconvincingly.

"And how's that lovely-looking bird of yours? Angie? Have you locked her down yet?"

I grimaced at the harsh reminder. "Amy... and we actually broke up," I said as unemotionally as possible.

"Oh love, I'm so sorry," said Mum sympathetically.

"Thanks Mum, but it was me who pulled the plug," I paused for a moment, "I'm moving back home."

Mum shrieked with joy. "Oh, my boy is finally coming home!"

"Great news son. It'll be good to finally have the whole family back together. When are you back?"

"November. I decided to come back in time for Seans Bucks' Night."

"He'll be stoked," chirped Dad.

"We should make it a surprise for the others," suggested Mum.

"Good thinking Pammy," agreed Dad, tapping his nose, "that'll be a riot. I reckon we could make your sister cry," he told me with a wink. Mum slapped his arm and rolled her eyes.

"What do you think love?" Mum asked me. "Would you like to surprise them, or do you want to share your news?"

"I don't mind."

"Let's keep it a surprise then."

"Okay."

"Is there anything you need us to do for you at this end?" Dad asked.

"Nah, I've got everything covered, I think. I just need a place to crash for a couple of weeks while I sort out my housing situation."

"Of course you'll stay with us!" declared my mother melodramatically.

"There's no rush for you to find a place mate, you're welcome to stay here for as long as you need."

"Thanks guys," I said with a yawn. "Hey, I'd better get to bed. I've got work in the morning."

"No worries, mate," said Dad with a nod.

"I'll start clearing out your old room," Mum offered excitedly.

"Thanks Ma, but please don't go to too much trouble for me."

"I'll go to as much trouble as I like, thank you very much."

"Okay," I laughed, raising my hands in surrender at my firecracker of a mother. "Love you guys."

"We love you too sweetheart."

"I'll call again in a few days."

"Okay son, chat soon," said Dad.

I closed my laptop with a content smile. Everything was lining up perfectly.

- KAT McPHERSON -

After another night of vigorous bed-related exercise, I woke up to the smell of bacon, wafting into the bedroom. I opened my eyes and glanced over to Ryan's side of the bed, which was empty. I smiled and stretched, then rolled out of the bed, pulling on my dressing gown before following the yummy smell out to the kitchen.

"Good morning," I said, smiling at my gorgeous husband, who was cooking up a storm at the stove-top.

"Good morning," he said, looking up with a grin. "You hungry?"

"Sure am," I answered, wandering over to give him a quick kiss. "Smells amazing."

"I figured you'd need a good feed after last night," he teased with a wink.

"You're definitely giving me a good workout," I agreed. "This baby belly will be gone in no time."

"I like your curves," he said, slapping me playfully on the bottom, as I bent down to kiss Mia in her bouncer. "This isn't quite ready yet, so why don't you feed her, while I finish it off."

"You hungry miss?" I asked Mia, pulling her out of the bouncer and resting her against my chest.

"There's a pot of peppermint tea on the table for you," said Ryan, stirring the mushrooms in the frying pan, while I settled down at the table to feed Mia.

"Wow, you really are spoiling me," I said, helping Mia latch-on. "Is this the sort of service I can expect if you decide to be a full-time stay-at-home dad?"

"That really depends," he teased, popping a plate of toast onto the table, "we may need to discuss some alternative forms of payment if this becomes a long-term situation."

"I'm sure we can come up with something."

Ryan poured me a cup of tea and headed back to the stove.

"How you feeling about today?" he asked scooping the bacon onto a serving plate. "Excited to be taking a step back or are you feeling a bit weird about sharing the job with Ash?"

"Actually, I'm quite looking forward to sharing the job."

"Really?" he asked with a raised brow.

"Yeah. I'm happy to be spending more time with you guys."

"Okay. For argument's sake I'll believe you, but if you do change your mind, that's okay. I don't have to go back to work if you'd prefer to be full-time."

"I can't see that happening. I think balancing the workload between the two of us will give us the best of both worlds."

"As long as you're sure.," he said sceptically. "Gaz has given me a couple of contacts, so I'll give them a call this week if that's your final decision."

"It is," I said with a smile, switching Mia over to the other boob, while Ryan served up our breakfast feast. "This looks amazing." Once Ryan had piled up my plate with a Full English breakfast, I ate one-handed while Mia finished her feed. "Hey, why don't you come into work with me this morning? Nath and Ash will be back and I'm sure everyone would love to see you."

"I'm not sure I'm ready to show my face there yet. Especially not with Beau around."

"He's fine now."

"He's fine with you," Ryan said with one brow raised, "but I nearly killed him. He won't forget that quickly, and neither will I." Ryan was trying to keep a neutral expression on his face, but his jaw was clenching ever-so-slightly. Ritchie had been right about the Beau thing. No matter how strong Ryan and I grew, Beau would always be an issue. "Babe, I love your optimism, but I won't play happy families with Beau after what went down. Regardless of whether he forgives me, I'll never forget that he broke our marriage, and I certainly have no desire to be friends with the prick again."

"So where do we go from here?"

"You and I get on with our lives as we have been, and he gets on with his. There's no need for our paths to cross outside of Artemis."

"Okay," I agreed with a humble nod. "I'm sorry I ruined us."

Ryan looked up from his breakfast with a solemn expression.

"Honey, you need to let that go," he said, clinking his fork down onto the plate. "We're fine now, we've moved past it."

"I know," I said, removing Mia from my boob and resting her over my shoulder, "but the fact is that it's going to make things awkward now that Beau and I are working together."

"Yes, it will," he agreed bluntly, "but I trust you."

- RYAN McPHERSON -

We finished our breakfast without another word about Beau, and Kat went off to get showered and ready for work.

"Right Miss Mia, what are we gonna do today?" I asked my daughter as she cooed happily in her bouncer. I bopped her on the nose and began clearing the table. "Maybe we'll go for a walk. You enjoyed the park, didn't you?" I chatted to Mia while I tidied up, and had the whole kitchen looking spotless by the time Kat emerged from the bedroom looking super-sexy in her black button-down dress. "Wow," I breathed, pausing my bench-wiping mid stroke.

"Does it look okay?" she asked nervously. "It's a lot tighter than it used to be."

"You look hot," I said, restraining myself from running over and stripping the dress off her.

"Really?"

"Babe, you look amazing."

"Good, because I don't have time to get changed." Kat got herself organised and Mia and I waved her goodbye from the front step, then went back inside to prepare for our outing. The catch with having a baby, was that I could no longer simply walk out of the door, like I once had. It took twenty minutes to pack up the nappy bag and make sure there was milk, water, baby wipes, spare clothes, nappies, bags, disposable changing mat and pretty much everything including the kitchen sink.

Once I'd completed that particular parental challenge, we were finally ready to leave the house. I pushed the pram down our street, and a tall, well-dressed bloke walked past us, doing a double take as he saw Mia in her pram.

"Mia?" he asked with surprise. My head whipped around, and I held him in a suspicious stare. "And I guess that makes you Ryan?"

"Yes."

"I didn't realise you were out of rehab."

"Just got home," I said sternly, wondering how the fuck this guy knew so much about me. "How do you know my daughter?" I asked with a polite smile, "does your wife go to the same mother's group or something?"

"Err... no. I'm an old friend of Katie's," he said awkwardly, giving Mia a gentle pinch on the cheek. I watched him with a raised brow.

"You know my wife?"

"Yes. I'm Xavier Brownlough," he told me meaningfully. My jaw dropped, as I realised exactly who the man was. "I take it you know who I am then?" he asked calmly.

"I know you attempted to steal my wife," I replied stiffly, debating whether to punch the mother fucker.

"I was in love with her, yes," he admitted with a nod, "...but I didn't try to steal her from you."

"Right," I answered sarcastically, clenching my fist in anticipation, "you just proposed to her for the fun of it."

"She told you about that?"

"She sure did."

"Look Ryan...I'd be lying if I said I didn't want Kat back, but I also want her to be happy, and I want what's best for Mia, so if that means you two staying together then I'm okay with that."

"Well thanks for your blessings," I sneered sarcastically.

"I'm sorry, I didn't mean for it to come out like that," he said, running his hand through his perfect, shiny hair. The guy looked like one of those Ken Dolls from the nineties.

"Okay," I answered, dubiously, "and what brings you down to London?"

"Work conference," he said with a shrug.

"Not my wife?"

"No, but I thought I'd drop in and see her while I was here. That's where I was heading." When I stared at him blankly, he shrigged and said, "Shirley gave me the address."

"Of course she did," I replied, rolling my eyes at my meddling Mother-in-law. "Kat's at work right now."

"Oh right," he answered with disappointment, "I didn't realise she'd gone back to work already. I probably should have called first."

"Yeah," I said, feeling a strange sort of respect for the guy. He seemed like a decent bloke... outside of the fact that he'd tried to steal my wife. "I'll let her know you stopped by."

"Thanks."

"No worries," I nodded. We stood in awkward silence. "Kat speaks highly of you," I said, breaking the silence.

"That's surprising given what I did," he said with self-depreciating snort.

"I imagine she's already made you feel sufficiently guilty for that mistake."

"She did a pretty decent guilt trip, yeah."

"My wife is a formidable woman."

"That she is," he nodded with a sad smile. "Can you tell her I'm sorry? I never meant to make life harder for her."

"I think she knows that," I said kindly, "but I'm happy to pass it on." Mia began to whine in her pram. "I'd better keep moving before the boss fires me," I joked.

"Sure, sorry to hold you up."

"Not a problem," I said, continuing on my way.

"You're a lucky man Ryan," Xavier called after me. "Make sure you treat her right and don't be an idiot like me and let her go. She's one of a kind."

"She sure is," I agreed. "Take care Xavier."

- ASHLEY GRANGER -

And just like that, after three weeks away, we were back at Artemis. I stared blankly into space as Ritchie debriefed us on the status of all the current Delfontaine projects. Normally I would have been eager to hear all about it, but I was finding it hard to muster enthusiasm. Perhaps it was because I'd been unwell since the attack, or maybe work didn't feel as important after facing another life-or-death situation, but whatever the reason, I was starting to think that Nathan could be right. Maybe we should escape the rat race and move down to Cornwall.

I scribbled random notes, as Ritchie began a run-down of the website requirements, and halfway through his summary my stomach lurched with the familiar warning of an impending vomit.

"Sorry Ritch, excuse me for a minute," I said, abruptly standing up and fleeing from the padded cell, in the direction of the bathroom. I ran to the toilets as fast as my wobbly legs would carry me, and quickly locked myself in a cubicle. I was kneeling on the cold floor, vomiting unceremoniously into the toilet bowl when I heard the main door squeak open.

"Are you okay babe?" Amy called into the ladies' with concern. I tore my head away from the bowl momentarily and flicked the lock to let her in.

"I'm still not right after the attack. I've been vomming every d-" the last of my breakfast forced its way out of my stomach before I had the chance to finish my sentence. Amy rubbed my back, as I heaved violently.

"Try sipping some water," she suggested, handing me an ice-cold bottle of water.

"Awesome thanks." I flushed the toilet and rinsed my mouth with the water. "I think the worst of it's over," I told her as I took a large gulp of the water.

"How about you stand up for a bit?" she suggested. My knees were sore from being on the cold, hard tiles, but I wasn't sure if I could trust my stomach enough to move out of the cubicle yet.

"I would, but I'm too scared it will make me hurl again."

"Okay, well at least sit for a while," she said, flipping the toilet seat down for me to sit on. "Do you think you could be preggers?"

"Nope," I shook my head adamantly as she helped me to the seat, "I've got an implant."

"They're not completely fail-safe Ash," she said with a grimace.

"But they're pretty reliable, I mean… that's their sole purpose for being right?"

"Mmm hmmm," Aims said agreeably, "and they last, what, three years?"

"Yeah."

"So... when did you get it?"

I thought for a moment. I'd had it put in just before I went to Bali so that was… oh shit. My jaw dropped.

"Just over three years ago."

"Hmmm…" Amy said, "and you've been vomiting for at least, what... three weeks?" she guesstimated fairly accurately. I nodded silently. "And when was you last period?"

"Ummm…" I cast my mind back over the past month, trying to remember the last time I'd had to buy a pack of tampons. I looked up at Amy in shock. "Oh shit," I muttered quietly, "I haven't had my period since the week before Nathan came back to work."

"That was about two months ago," Amy said. I did the math in my head. It had been three weeks since Dom's attack, and Nathan and I had been together for at least a month before that. Amy was right. That was nearly two months ago. So much had happened since Nathan and I had gotten together that I hadn't even noticed my lack of period.

"Oh my god," I said breathlessly, "I'm pregnant." We fell into an unusual silence, staring at each other like stunned mullets. What was Nathan going to say? Our relationship was still so new, was he ready to be a dad? We'd only just started to find some normalcy after all the drama we'd been through. My stomach lurched as a sick realization hit me. "Aims, what if it's Dom's?"

Her face fell, but she smiled and knelt on the floor in front of me, taking my hands in hers. "He didn't… you know… finish the job though right?"

"No, he didn't but what if…"

"The chances are low Ash."

"But it's still a possibility," I said with despair. "Not only do I have to tell Nathan I'm pregnant, but I can't even tell him with certainty that it's his baby." Silent tears rolled off my cheeks as I succumbed to the brutal reality of my situation.

"Hey, listen to me," Amy said, cupping my face with her hand, "everything will be okay, I promise. Nathan will be there for you no matter what and we don't even know if you're definitely pregnant."

"Well… there's only one way to know for sure," I whispered. "I need to get a pregnancy test," I said gulping down another mouthful of water. The cold liquid hit my stomach almost instantly and set off another wave of nausea. I jumped quickly off the toilet seat and stuck my head back into the bowl.

"Okay, perhaps, you stay here, and I'll run down to the chemist," Amy suggested.

"Yep," I spluttered between wretches.

"I'll be back in five. Try not to lose your stomach lining while I'm gone," she teased, closing the stall door so I was left to hurl in solitude.

I didn't need a test to confirm it, I already knew the answer. I was pregnant. I hadn't thought about it until that moment, but my body felt exactly the same as it had the last time. The vomiting, the tiredness, the big boobs, the dizziness, the mood swings, and the constant tears… it all made sense.

How was I going to tell Nathan?

- RITCHIE CARLTON -

Sans Ashley, there wasn't a lot of point in continuing our meeting, since it was primarily to get her and Nath back up-to-speed.

"I think we should probably leave it there for now," I told the group. "We'll reconvene this afternoon. There are still a few details I need to iron out anyway. Nath could you hang back please?" I asked in my most business-like manner as the others vacated the room. "We've got a couple of things to go over."

"Sure," he said with a grin, waiting for the last of our colleagues to exit. He glanced around to make sure the room was clear and nudged my arm. "Leadership becomes you, my man. That was very professional."

I chuckled half-heartedly with the burden of my news weighing heavy on my chest.

"Not for much longer," I said, deciding to get straight to the point.

"What do you mean?"

"You're getting the job back."

"What? Why? Did Gaz agree to that? He seemed pretty serious about dropping me as Client Partner."

"Yes, Gaz agreed – reluctantly," I said honestly, "but the thing is Nath…I'm moving back to Perth."

Nathans' jaw dropped and he looked momentarily stunned into silence. "Are you serious?" He asked after a brief silence.

"Serious as a heart attack," I confirmed.

"Why mate? When? You can't really want to leave London. Is this because of Red?" He asked in one long sentence, without taking a breath.

"Like I told Gaz… it's time." I explained calmly. Nathan sank back in his chair.

"Well… I can't say I'm happy about it, but if you're sure that's what you want then I'm happy for you."

"Thanks man," I said with a grateful nod. "I've never been more sure about anything in my life."

"Yeah, you do look disgustingly calm about it."

"Because it's the right decision, and I've been putting it off for too long. I'm almost middle-aged and I'm still partying like a twenty-year-old. It's time for me to go home, find myself a nice Aussie girl and settle the fuck down."

"I go away for three weeks and everything changes."

"Life goes on right?"

"Sure does," Nathan agreed, standing up to give me a hug. "I'm proud of you man. That must have been a tough decision to make."

"It was, but I know it's the right one."

"Of course it is," he agreed with a proud smile. "I'm going to miss you Ritch."

"I'm gonna miss you too Stoner," I said, punching his arm so as to avoid any major displays of emotion.

"So how much longer have we got you for?"

"Until November," I said apologetically. I felt like I was abandoning him, but I had to get on with my life and that was never going to happen whilst I was living in London.

"Well I'd better start planning a leaving party for you then."

"It's gonna take you months to plan a leaving party?"

"Well, it has to be the party to end all parties mate. This is going to require precision planning."

"You and Ash will have to come down under for a visit," I suggested hopefully.

"Too right we will," he joked, retuning my arm punch. He paused and studied me knowingly, "have you told Red yet?"

"Nah, not yet."

"And you don't think you should have told her first?"

"She's not my girlfriend dude, I don't owe her any explanations," I said coldly.

"I suppose not," he said with an empathetic shrug. "And how did you things end with you-know-who?"

"Interestingly," I admitted.

"What does that mean exactly?"

"Didier is retiring at the end of the year and she wants me to take over his job."

"She what??" he asked, stunned. "Ritchie, that's a killer opportunity."

"Yeah, except it comes with certain 'conditions', if you get my drift."

"I do," Nathan nodded with complete understanding.

"The woman that I'm in love with won't commit to me and one that I'm trying to keep my distance from is pushing for a commitment that I don't want."

"That's certainly a conundrum," Nath agreed with a nod.

"The quicker I get out of this town the better," I said with a chuckle. Nathan sighed and scratched the back of his head. There was something troubling him and it had nothing to do with my news. "What's up Stoner? That look isn't because you're gonna miss me, so what's on your mind?"

"Truthfully… I don't think I want the job back."

"What do you mean? This company is your life."

"Not anymore. I've asked Ash if she'll move down to Cornwall with me."

"Shit, really? So, you'd just give up everything to move down to the beach? That sounds like a very Carlton thing to do," I teased. "What did Ash say?"

"We agreed to give it a month before we make a decision."

"Sensible."

"But what do I tell Gaz? I can't accept the job if we decide to do a runner in a month. I think I need to turn it down."

"Eek, that's gonna be a fun convo."

"Are you offering to tell him for me?" he asked with a mischievous grin.

"Fuck no! That's on you man."

- ASHLEY GRANGER -

Amy was back with the test before I'd even finished vomming.

"You still alive in there?" she joked upon her return.

"Barely," I replied exhaustedly. She laughed and opened the test kit, unnecessarily reading the instructions out loud. "Aims, I get it. I pee on the stick, it's not that complicated."

"Geez, a thanks would've been sufficient," Amy retorted good-naturedly, "but since you're hormonal and in the midst of a personal crisis, I'll let you get away with it. Here…" she said, shoving the stick at me, "…now pee on it smart-arse."

She closed the cubicle door and I picked myself up off the floor to use the loo as it was originally intended. I pulled the cap off the test and weed on the little white stick of fate. Once the stick was sufficiently peed upon, I exited the stall, and placed it flat down on the sink, as per the instructions. Amy and I both took a seat on the bench while we awaited the result.

"Do you think you'll keep it?" she asked curiously. We seemed to have agreed that I was indeed, pregnant. The test was merely a formality by that stage. I sighed and bit my lip as the emotion began to rise.

"Yeah, probably, but either way, I'd like to keep this quiet for now." I admitted, letting my tears shed freely without even attempting to hide them. Amy jumped off the bench and wrapped me up in her skinny little arms.

"Whatever happens, you won't be alone," she said, stroking the back of my hair as I cried on her shoulder. I gripped her tightly until my sobs subsided. "Do you want to talk about it?" she asked gently.

"I wouldn't know where to start."

"Then just say whatever comes out first," Amy suggested quietly as I peeled myself off her. She wet a hand towel and dabbed my cheeks with the cold wad of paper. "Sometimes saying it out loud makes the memory less painful."

I took a deep breath and nodded. "I was prepared for him to kill me. I'd kind of always been waiting for it to happen, but the sexual stuff - I just wasn't expecting that. I don't know why. He raped me the first time I left him, so I should have seen it coming but-"

"No one can ever see something like that coming Ash."

"I should have," I replied adamantly. "I guess I just somehow thought being with Nathan made me safe, but instead that was what drove him to do it. I feel tainted now. Like I'm permanently dirty, you know."

"Yeah I do."

"You do?"

"More than you know," she said with her eyes full of understanding. We sat silently for a moment, until Amy broke the silence. "Ash, I'm going to tell you something that I've never told anyone before."

"Okay," I nodded, sensing that something profound was passing between us.

"My stepdad was like Dom. I grew up watching him beat the shit out of my mum."

"I'm so sorry Aims."

"No pity Ash. I'm only telling you this so you know that I understand exactly what you're going through."

"Alright."

"My mum was a nurse and she worked the night shift, so every night, from the time that I was about four, he would wait for her to leave and then come into my bedroom. At that point he was just grooming me, but then by the time I was six it was actual sex. Well… rape to be exact."

"Oh my god," I breathed sorrowfully, feeling my stomach lurch with disgust at the thought of anyone doing that to a six-year-old. "What happened? Did he ever get caught?"

"Not exactly," she replied with a dark chuckle, "one night, when I was sixteen, I hid the butchers knife under my pillow and waited for him to come into my room."

"And you killed him?"

"No," Amy answered with a shake of her head, "no, I cut off his cock," she said with an evil grin. I was so shocked I burst into laughter and she giggled morbidly along with me.

"Seriously?"

"Yep."

"So, what happened after that?"

"I threw his dick out my window and he jumped out after it. We never saw him again after that. I guess he knew he'd have to explain what had happened."

"Oh my god, did you tell your mum?"

"Nah. I couldn't tell her the real story, it would've broken her heart. I told her that he'd attacked me and I stabbed him in self-defense. Since there was no evidence to the contrary, that was what they wrote in the police report."

"Do you think he's still out there?"

"I don't know, probably, but at least he won't be raping kids."

"Yeah," I agreed, stunned.

"Anyway, enough of my sad story…" she said, changing the subject, "if you were a hundred percent sure that the baby was Nathans, would you want to keep it?"

"Yeah, I would, but I don't know if Nathan would agree."

"I think he would surprise you."

"I guess he is pretty clucky over the kittens… but kittens are quite different to an actual human baby."

"Ash, stop it. That man has done a lot of things out of his character since he met you."

"Well, that's certainly true."

"Face it. You, my tall friend, are a Stone-tamer."

"I guess we're about to find out if you're right." Nathan had continuously surprised me since we'd met, but parenthood was a huge step, especially only a few months into a relationship, and even more so when the paternity of said child was under contention. I studied Amy's face and noticed that she wasn't her usual bubbly self.

"So what's going on with you?" I asked suspiciously.

"What do you mean?" Amy asked innocently.

"Somethings not right with you."

She sighed. "Ritchie's done with me."

My jaw dropped. "And you hadn't told me because…?"

"I figured you didn't need any more drama," she said, glancing down at my stomach, "but I guess drama always finds you huh?"

"I guess it does," I agreed, resting my hand on her shoulder, "but no matter what's going on, I always want to know if there's something big happening for you."

"Thanks babe," she said, squeezing my hand.

"So, are you okay?" I asked, worried about my stoic friend.

"Yeah," she said with a shrug, "it's been coming for a while, so I've been mentally preparing for it."

"And how do you feel about him walking away for good?"

"Sad," she replied honestly, "but I won't stop him. He deserves better than I can give him."

"I don't know about that," I argued, "he's in love with you Amy, all you have to do is love him back."

"No, he wants a family and I can't give him that," she said dismissively. "Anyway lady, it's been way over three minutes now. It's time to find out if you're a mamma," she teased with a smile. Butterflies fluttered in my stomach. Amy jumped off the bench, gave me a hug, and then picked up the stick without looking at it. "This is the moment of truth Ash," she said, handing me the test. I grasped it and took a deep breath. Once I'd seen the result, there would be no turning back.

We looked at each other silently for a moment, and then finally let our eyes drop to the result window. There it was…a little blue 'plus' sign. That confirmed it. I was knocked-up.

- NATHAN STONE -

"Holy shit." I swore with excitement as my phone beeped with a text message.

"What's up?" Ritchie asked.

"Ash's ring is ready," I told him quietly, as we gathered our things from the boardroom table.

"Wow. So, it's really happening then?" Ritchie asked with both shock and awe as we wandered out into the main office.

"Hopefully," I replied nervously. "Assuming Ash will have me until the end of time."

Ritchie laughed loudly. "Stoner, like I've been telling you since Ash started here… the woman is madly in love with you."

"I guess we'll find out soon enough," I answered with a deep breath, "I was thinking I'd go all-out and book us a weekend in Monaco next month. Maybe have a quiet lunch at Café De Paris."

"Sounds like you've got it all planned out. There's no way she will say no." I knew he was right, yet that didn't stop me from being damn nervous about it. "Speaking of which," Ritchie asked, glancing over at the bathroom as we walked past, "is she okay? She's been in there a while."

"Yeah, she has." I agreed, stopping to peer back in the direction of the toilets. "She hasn't been well since the attack, but she's refusing to go see a doctor." Red emerged from the bathroom looking like an undercover agent. "Is she okay?" I asked her, as she attempted to sneak quietly past us.

"Uhh…yeah. Just women's stuff." Red answered evasively as she dashed back to her desk.

"Women's stuff?" I mumbled to Ritchie, with a shake of my head.

"Beats me mate. Women are a mystery to me," Ritchie replied with a shrug. He sighed and peered over at Amy as she sat down at her desk on the other side of the room. "I was really hoping she'd call my bluff and finally commit," he admitted with a shrug as we continued towards our desks, "but I can't pretend anymore. I'm getting old. I want to settle down and have kids you know?"

"Yeah," I said, as something stirred in the pit of my belly. Ritchie and I both looked at each other.

"Ashley's not Up Duff is she?" he asked, apparently having the same thought as I was.

"Nah, I doubt it," I said unconvincingly.

"You sure?" he prodded, "because her melons are huge."

"Don't talk about my girlfriends' melons," I snapped in annoyance, ditching a paper wad at his head.

"Sorry dude," he apologised sincerely, dropping his files down on his desk, "but you've got to admit, it makes sense." My brain began whirling at a million miles an hour. Ash and I had been officially together for about two months and besides that couple of weeks after her attack, there had never been a break in our sex life. Surely, she would have said something if she thought pregnancy was likely? "You're weighing up the possibility, aren't you?" Ritchie asked with a sly smile as he watched me with amusement.

"Nah. She's not preggers man, she's got that implant thing," I told him confidently.

"If you say so mate," Ritchie placated me with a shrug.

"It's probably just a stomach bug," I concluded as I reached my desk, not entirely believing my own prognosis. I sat down and pondered the possibility. Ritchie had been right about a lot of things lately, could he have been right about that too?

Ashley finally returned from her extended visit to the loo, exchanging a conspiratorial glance with Red as she sat down at her desk. I watched her like a hawk as she sank quietly into her chair on the opposite side of our workstation.

"Are you okay?" I asked, when she offered no explanation for her absence.

"Uhh… yeah, fine," she said uncertainly, peering around her big screen.

"You fled a project meeting to be fine, did you?" I asked as she continued pretending to work.

"No, I fled the meeting to be sick," Ash answered primly, "but now I'm fine."

I gave her my 'cut the bullshit' look. "I'm calling my doctor," I said, picking up my desk phone to make my point.

"Put the phone down," she said with amusement, "I don't need to see a doctor."

"Ash there's clearly something going on with you," I said, putting the receiver back in the cradle.

"Yes, there is," she agreed, "but now isn't the time to talk about it." She went back to her pretense of working and stared intensely at her computer screen as if it would make me go away.

"Either you tell me what's going on or I'll call the doctor," I threatened. Ash rolled her eyes and sighed like an exasperated a teenager.

"You really can't wait until we get home?" she negotiated. The woman was so fucking stubborn.

"No, I want to know what's wrong."

"Fine," she huffed, standing up and looking around the busy office. "In here," she ordered as she pulled me off my chair and into the empty meeting room.

"What on earth is going on?" I asked as she closed the door behind us.

"Well, this is not how I was planning on telling you but…" she took a deep breath, "…I'm pregnant Nath."

I stared at her agape. "What?"

"I'm pregnant," she repeated, "I just did a test in the bathroom." She pulled out a little white stick from her back pocket and showed me the blue plus sign.

"Wow," I breathed, staring between the stick and her stomach. I had no idea what to say.

"Yeah," Ash said with a nervous laugh as she shoved the test back into her pocket and shuffled awkwardly on her feet. "Nath…" she hesitated, "it could be Dom's."

"Do you think that's likely?" I asked as tactfully as possible.

She sighed and sank to the nearest seat. "It's not likely," she said bleakly, "but there's a possibility, and we wouldn't know that for sure until the baby was born."

"Oh, okay," I said, feeling lost for words. I was a little disappointed that I hadn't had the chance to propose before knocking her up - assuming it was me who'd done the knocking - but nothing about our relationship had been traditional, so it seemed fitting to do it all backwards. Ash bit her lip and looked up at me uneasily.

"So, how do you feel about all of this?" she asked worriedly. "If it's yours…, are you okay?"

"I'm fine, are you okay?"

"I'm fine," she paused. "And if it's Dom's?"

I crouched down in front of her chair and grasped her hands gently as she twisted them in her lap.

"Listen," I said, tucking a strand of her hair behind her ear and cupping her chin in my hand. "Maybe this isn't what I'd had in mind, but our relationship has been crazy from the beginning, so it would be weird if we started doing things the normal way. You're the best thing that's ever happened to me Ash and it makes no difference to me who's baby you're brewing in there," I rested my hand on her stomach. "You're my family now, you and this baby. No matter what."

"You're ready to start a family?"

"I am," I answered with joy as I stood up, scooping her into my arms as I went. "We're having a baby Ash. We're going to be parents, of a little non-furry human person," I said kissing her firmly on the lips as she wrapped her arms tightly around my shoulders.

"We are," she said with tears in her eyes. "So, you really want to do this?

"Yes, I do and I'm so fucking happy."

"Really?"

"Did you honestly think you'd be able to get rid of me that easily Granger?" I teased, putting her feet gently back on the ground.

"Well, I wouldn't have blamed you if you'd wanted to walk away."

"I'd be a fucking idiot if I walked away," I told her with a content smile. "Holy shit," I said, running my hands over my face as the reality began to sink in. "What are your parents going to say? Are they going to freak out? Your Dad is going to kill me isn't he?"

"They worship the ground you walk on Nathan, I can pretty much guarantee that they'll be annoyingly excited unless…"

"Unless it's Dom's," I said, finishing her train of thought.

"If this baby comes out with black hair, then I'll have to tell them what happened."

"Let's just cross that bridge if we come to it."

"Okay," she agreed, with tears shimmering in her eyes, "but can we keep this quiet for a while?"

"Sure," I agreed, wiping a tear from her cheek. "Hey, it'll be fine, I promise."

"What about your Mum?" she asked, "I haven't even met her yet."

"So, let's do that. Why don't we go see her on Saturday?"

"That would be good," Ash nodded.

"First problem solved," I joked. "So, how far along do you think you are?"

"This might be wishful thinking, but I have a feeling I was already pregnant when I went up to Framlingham."

"We'd only been together for what… three weeks then?"

"Yeah, but it felt exactly like the last time. I was so emotional that I thought I was having sympathy hormones for Kat but maybe…"

"Maybe we hit a home-run straight off the bat," I joked, feeling elated, yet shell-shocked.

"Yeah."

"How do we find out?"

"I go to the doctors. If we did get it first go then I'd be about eight weeks and they might be able to do a scan."

"And if we didn't?"

"Then they wouldn't bother with a scan."

"Okay, so first step is to find out if we can get an early scan?"

"Yep," she agreed with a smile that quickly faltered.

"Wow," I said in a daze, "we're really doing this."

"Yeah, we are," she agreed, biting her bottom lip.

"We're having a baby," I laughed with a mixture of excitement and nerves.

Ash nodded, "we're having a baby," she confirmed with a smile. I grinned at her mischievously and pulled her closer.

"If we weren't at work, I'd jump on you right now."

"Well, I did give you the option to wait."

"You did," I agreed, stepping back from her to thwart my building excitement. "Does that mean it might be time to revisit our discussion about moving to Cornwall?" I asked hopefully.

"Yeah, maybe," she nodded uncertainly. I ran my hand gently over her stomach, blown away by the fact that my child, biological or not, was growing in there.

"I can't believe I'm going to be a father."

"You're going to be an amazing dad Nath," she said, resting her hand over mine.

"And you're going to be an amazing mum."

"I guess I should book that appointment with my doctor now," she joked.

"Let me make a couple of calls first."

Ash rolled her eyes and laughed. "You have a guy who can find you an OBGYN too?" she teased.

"Actually, I do," I said with a wink. "Leave it with me."

- RITCHIE CARLTON -

Nath and Ash snuck out of the boardroom and slunk back to their desks looking suspicious. I caught Nathans' eye and raised a questioning brow. He shrugged, looked around and then came over to my desk.

"What's going on?" I asked as he rested his butt on my desk.

"Ash isn't well so I'm taking her to the doctors."

"Okay," I agreed, still unconvinced by his explanation. "Everything alright?"

"Yeah, we just need to make sure it's nothing sinister after Dom's attack."

"Fair call mate," I said with a nod. "I've got things covered here."

"Awesome, thanks." He trotted off and went straight out the security doors. I peered over at Ash with amusement. "Aren't you supposed to be going with him?"

"He's got to make a couple of calls before we go," she said with a guilty shrug. One talent that Ashley Granger did not possess, was lying convincingly.

"Righto," I said, deciding that it was none of my business. I got back to work and watched as Nathan faffed over Ash. There was definitely something fishy going on but I figured they'd tell me when the time was right.

"Back shortly," Nath said as they passed my desk.

"No wuckers," I nodded, and busied myself with the ever-growing list of Delfontaine tasks. That was another situation I'd have to face. I'd told Sandrine I'd think about her offer, but I had no intention of taking her up on it. Now I'd have to tell her that I'd already booked a ticket home. She was not a woman who was used to being turned-down. Unlike myself, the news would not go down well. But Sandrine could wait. The next person I'd have to tell was Amy. I glanced over at my ex-non-girlfriend and took a deep breath. It was now or never. With butterflies in my belly, I approached her desk.

"Aims?" I said, steeling myself for the conversation.

"Uh-huh?" she replied, without looking up from her screen.

"Can we grab a drink after work?"

"What would be the point of that?" she asked unemotionally, still pre-occupied with her work.

"I'd really like to chat."

"About what? I thought you'd already said it all."

I sighed and swung her chair around so that she was facing me.

"There's something I need to tell you."

"You've got my attention… so tell me."

"I don't want to talk about it here."

"Fine," Amy agreed reluctantly.

"Five o'clock at the Horse and Cart?"

"Sure," she said with an unenthusiastic shrug.

"Thank you."

"Is there anything else?"

"Err… no. I guess I'd better get back to work anyway. I've got a phone conference with Sandrine in five minutes."

"Well, you'd better not keep the Black Widow waiting," she said snidely, and turned back to her screen.

"I don't exactly have a choice. She's my client."

"I'm aware of that," Amy said through clenched teeth. I sighed, cursing myself for getting involved with Sandrine Delfontaine.

"I'll see you at five?"

"Yeah," she answered without looking up.

- ASHLEY GRANGER -

I could feel my nerves rising as we sat in the obstetricians waiting room. Dr Judith Nolan was one of London's most sought after obstetricians but thankfully Nathan's physiotherapist, Wayne had used his connections and gotten us to the top of her list. I handed back the half-completed paperwork to the receptionist feeling deflated. I couldn't fill out any of the paternal information they'd asked for, and it made me feel awkward beyond belief.

"You okay?" Nathan asked, squeezing my leg as I sat back down next to him.

"I'm fine," I lied blatantly. "I'm just nervous. What if I'm only a few weeks along? We won't know whether the baby is yours until it's born."

"Ash, listen to me," he said, wriggling around in his seat and taking both my hands in his. "Whatever the case may be, this child will be mine. Genetics are irrelevant."

"But they're not irrelevant," I argued stubbornly, not acknowledging his beautiful comment. "They want all the paternal details for hereditary conditions and stuff. I won't be able to answer any of those questions if it turns out to be Dom's."

"Babe," he said in a calm voice, "if this baby turns out to be Dom's, will you still love it?"

"Of course I would," I said without a second thought. "I'll love this baby no matter what."

"And so will I," he answered with a smile, "and that's all that matters."

I smiled and wrapped my arms round his neck in an uncomfortable sideways hug. "I love you Mister Stone."

"I love you too Mrs. Stone," he answered, giving me a soft kiss. I laughed at his joke and he looked at me with confusion. "What?" he asked with a puzzled look on his face.

"You just called me Mrs. Stone," I said with a chuckle.

"I did?" he asked with a disbelieving grin.

"You did," I teased.

"Well maybe Calvin was onto something, because you definitely have a Mrs. Stone vibe about you."

"Ashley Granger?" Called a short, smartly dressed woman.

"Yes, I'm Ashley Granger," I said, waving one hand in the air.

"Are you sure about that?" Nathan joked with a wink. I smiled, rolled my eyes and jumped to my feet so quickly that I nearly gave myself another head spin. Nathan gripped my arm tight to stabilize me.

"Do you want me to come in with you?" he asked.

"Of course," I said, surprised that he'd think I wouldn't want him in there.

"Hi Ashley, I'm Judith," the doctor said, reaching out her hand to shake mine.

"Hi Judith, thanks for seeing us at such late notice," I said with a smile.

"Not a problem, I owed Wayne a favour anyway," she joked.

"This is Nathan," I said, waving my hands towards Nath, who was standing behind me.

"Hi," Nathan said succinctly.

"Lovely to meet you both," Judith said, shaking Nathans's hand. "Follow me." We both nodded and followed Doctor Nolan down a hallway and into her consultation room. Besides a curtained area off to the side, it looked more like a lounge room than a doctor's office. "Have a seat," Judith said to us, gesturing to the tub chairs positioned in the middle of the room.

"Thanks," we said in unison and settled into the cushy chairs. The Doctor sat down in the large armchair opposite us and glanced over the paperwork. I saw her eyebrow flicker at the empty gaps I'd left.

"So…" she said as she continued to read, "you're not sure how far along you are?" she asked tactfully as her eyes darted over the page.

"Err… that's right." I replied awkwardly. "Is there any way of finding out?"

"At this stage, we usually just calculate it from the date of your last period," she replied apologetically, "so if you skipped your last one, then I'd suspect you're at least one month in."

"Okay, but the things is…" I said, finding it hard to say out load. I peered at Nathan, and he understood my silent plea immediately.

"Ash was attacked about a month ago," Nathan explained, throwing me a comforting glance, "and she's worried that the baby might not be mine."

"I see," said the obstetrician kindly as a look of comprehension crossed her face. "In that case, we can take a look with the ultrasound. If you're any less than six weeks, we're not likely to see anything."

"Okay," I said eagerly, "let's do that please."
Nathan squeezed my hand supportively.

"Sure," she said, rising from her seat, "just pop yourself up on the bed and I'll get the machine set up. I looked at Nathan for reassurance and he nodded, encouraging me over to the bed. I was so scared the baby would be Dom's, that I felt almost paralyzed. I was unbelievably thankful to have Nathan there with me. He helped me up onto the paper lined vinyl and I wriggled noisily to get comfortable. "Okay, lift your dress up please love," the doctor prompted, throwing a sheet over my legs for the appearance of propriety. I pulled up the hem of my dress, feeling my stomach churning with nerves as the doctor squirted freezing cold gel all over it. I looked sideways at Nathan as the obstetrician rolled the cold wand over my belly. He smiled and draped his arm over my shoulder.

"No matter what happens, we're in this together okay?" He said, taking my hand with his spare one. I nodded silently, unable to speak, and Nath planted a firm kiss on my forehead. "I love you," he whispered quietly.

"I love you too," I said, resting my head against his arm.

"And there's your baby," the obstetrician announced happily. My heart jumped into my throat and Nathan squeezed my hand tight.

"You can see it?" I asked hopefully.

"I sure can," she answered with a smile. "They don't look like much at this stage, but do you see that little jellybean shaped blob there?" Nathan and I both leaned closer to the screen to get a glimpse of the shape she was pointing to. "That's your baby."

"Wow," Nath said, looking down at me with tears sparkling in his eyes.

"So does that mean I'm more than six weeks along?" I asked anxiously. It was the only answer I cared about.

"Well, the machine will calculate your estimated conception date, but from the looks of this I'd say you're about eight or nine weeks."

"Oh, thank god," I exhaled loudly, as tears rolled down my cheeks in streams. "It's yours," I said through the tears. I hadn't even registered that I was crying until Nathan took my face in his hands and wiped my wet cheeks.

"It was mine either way," he said, kissing me softly.

- KAT McPHERSON -

Our floor was unusually quiet when I arrived at work. Ritchie, Beau and Cody were hauled up in the boardroom having a conference call with Sandrine; the development team were brainstorming in the break-out room; and Ashlan was nowhere to be seen. Without any of their leads, my design team were all quietly working behind their big silver screens. I wandered over to Amy's desk where she was sitting, brows furrowed in concentration.

"Hey Aims," I said, popping my bag under my desk. "Where's Ashlan? I was hoping to see them."

"They had to duck out," she said, looking up from her computer with a smile.

"First day back and they're already slacking," I joked.

"You just can't find good help these days."

"Apparently not," I chuckled.

"They should be back soon. How was your morning?"

"Lovely actually," I said with contentment. "I could really get used to part-time work."

Amy winced slightly. "Enjoy it while you can."

"Why? What's going on?"

"I have a sneaking suspicion that you might be needed full-time again." I eyed her suspiciously.

"Where's Ash and Nathan?"

"I honestly don't know."

"But you know something."

"Do I?"

"You're being very annoying."

"Thank you," she teased with a grin. "Anyway... I was thinking the three of us girls could go out for lunch together. You in?"

"Sounds perfect." I set to work on my rather long to-do list, and didn't stop until around midday when Ashlan finally entered the building.

Amy nodded towards the security doors as Nathan guided Ash through the door in a very protective and gallant fashion. Ash looked gaunt but tanned, like she'd been shipwrecked on a tropical island for three weeks, rather than recovering from an attempted murder.

"Ash!" I called, with a wave, jogging towards her until I felt my weak pelvic floor straining under the pressure. I stopped dead in my tracks, concerned that I was going to pee myself, while Ash closed the gap between us.

"Hey," she said with a huge smile, wrapping me up in her tall, bony frame, "it's good to see your face."

"And yours," I said, giving her a squeeze, "how are you?"

"I'm okay," she nodded. "How's Mia?"

"She's great," I said, keen to hear all the goss, as I moved over to Nath. "And how are you, Mr superstar boyfriend?"

"I'm okay too," he chuckled giving me a hug. "What about you Mamma Bear? How's life with your husband back home?"

"Tiring," I joked with a wink. "So where have you guys been?"
The pair exchanged a quick glance.

"I had to go back to get my stitches out," Ash said casually.

"Cool," I said with a shrug. "Can Amy and I steal you away for a girl's lunch?"

"Sure," Ash agreed with a smile, "I'd love to."
Twenty minutes later, we were sitting in GBK, munching on burgers.

"So…how's Ashlan?" I asked Ash curiously. "All well with you guys?"

"All good," she shrugged. "We're just doing our best to get back to normal." Amy and I looked at each other and laughed.

"Normal?" I teased. "Do you guys even know how to be normal?"

"Not really," she said with an embarrassed smile, "but we're trying it out for a little while."

"Well, that will be interesting to watch," Amy replied with a grin.

"No doubt the boys will start another betting pool," I joked, before taking a huge bite of my burger.

"Odds on them making it less than a week," Amy said, grabbing a chip off my plate.

"Another betting pool?" Ash asked with a confusion. "Meaning there's already been one?"

"Err... yeah, quite a few actually," Amy admitted. "The boys have been taking bets on you guys since you first arrived at Artemis."

"I thought you knew that?" I said, having just assumed that she'd been privy to the fairly overt goings on.

"Of course I didn't know that!" Ash exclaimed, looking mortified. "What have they been betting on exactly?"

"Various things," Amy shrugged.

"Such as?"

"Umm... how long it would take you two to hook up; how many times you'd get caught snogging in the office; how long it would take for Nathan to fuck it up; how long before..." Amy listed, counting all the bets on her fingers.

"Stop," Ashley said, holding up her hand to silence Aims. "Let me get this straight... you guys have been betting on the intimate details of my life for the last six months?"

"We have," Amy confirmed.

"Hey," I interrupted defensively, "I haven't had anything to do with this."

"But you knew about it," Amy dobbed. Ashley's green eyes turned on me with a piercing stare.

"Yeah, I knew about it," I admitted sheepishly, "but in my defence, I thought you knew too."

"Pathetic," Aims teased, rolling her eyes at my lame excuse.

"At least I didn't profit from our friends," I said with a teasing glare.

"You were making money off us?!" Ash asked Amy, nearly choking on her vege burger.

"Only a little bit at the beginning," Amy explained rationally, as if that made it okay, "I was asked to stop placing bets due to my close personal friendship with both of you."

"How much?" Ash asked, looking insulted.

"A hundred and fifty quid."

"Seriously?! On which bet?"

"How long it would take for you two to hook up," Aims said.

Ashley looked flabergasted. "So, when you and Ritchie organised that night at Club Bordello...?" Ash trailed off as Amy grinned. "You little fuckers," Ash said, throwing a chip at Amy.

"Before you get angry..." Amy said, laughing, "We used the winnings to pay for your room."

"Still not okay," giggled Ash, hurling a few more chips at Amy. "I can't believe you did that! How embarrassing."

"But totally worth it right?" Amy asked, catching one of the airborne chips and shoving it in her mouth.

"You've got me there."

"See... we did you a favour," Amy rationalised. "I think the pot's up to three hundred quid now."

"For what?" Ash asked, stunned.

"For how long it will take Nathan to pop the question."

"Oh my god," Ashley gasped dramatically, "there's something seriously wrong with you people."

"Be careful what you say honey," I warned her with a grin, "you're one of us now remember?"

"So, it would seem," she said with a resigned sigh.

- RYAN McPHERSON -

I heard the front door unlock, so I grabbed Mia and opened the inside door for Kat. The door swung open, and Kat stood with her key held mid-air.

"Have you been standing there waiting for me to get home?" she asked with a smile, kissing Mia's head.

"I might have been keeping an ear out," I admitted, giving her a kiss. "How was your day?"

"Interesting. How was yours?" she asked, taking her shoes off and hanging her handbag on the coat rack.

"Also interesting," I said, heading through to the kitchen to put Mia back into her bouncer.

"Sounds like you have a story to tell," she called.

"I certainly do."

The smell of my freshly cooked pasta wafted out from the oven.

"Smells great in here!" she said, following me into the kitchen.

"Dinner is ready and waiting my lady." I ushered her to the table and pulled out her chair.

"Why thank you my lord," she said with a little curtsey, before taking her seat.

"I've made a lasagna," I said, wandering over to the oven to check on my masterpiece.

"I didn't know you could make lasagna."

"Either did I. The internet is a wonderful thing."

Kat laughed, and patted Mia's head as she played in the bouncer beside her chair, while I carefully removed the giant lasagna from the oven. "Was that your interesting story?" she teased.

"No," I joked, pulling a face at her, "my interesting story is that I met Xavier today."

"You what?!" she asked, eyes bulging. "As in my ex Xavier? From

Framlingham?"

"Is there another Xavier?"

"Not that I'm aware of," she chuckled nervously. "How did that come about?"

"He dropped in to see you," I said casually, as I sliced up the lasagna.

"Here? At our home?"

"Yep. Well, not here exactly, we'd just left for a walk, and he was on his way over."

"How did you know it was him?" she asked, looking very uncomfortable at the idea of Xavier being around.

"He recognised Mia."

"Oh. That's impressive given he's only met her a couple of times." She fell silent for a moment as the information sunk in. "What was he doing in London? How did he know where we live? Why was he coming to see me?"

"He's here on a work conference," I said, dishing a big slice of lasagna onto her plate, "your mum gave him our address; and I think he was just coming to visit. He asked me to apologise to you."

"For what?"

"For being a dick, I guess," I said with a shrug, "he seems to feel quite bad about putting you in an awkward position."

"Well, that's one way to put it."

"That was me paraphrasing. I think what he actually said was something along the lines of: 'I didn't mean to make her life harder.'"

"Right."

"He seems like a decent guy."

"Sure," she said, with a strange look on her face. "Are you saying you liked him?"

"Yeah, sort of. I mean... apart from the fact that he kissed you and proposed to you while we were still married."

"Apart from that," she teased, shaking her head with a confused smile.

"I totally would have understood if you'd left me for him," I teased her, "certainly much better than getting left for Peterson anyhow." Kat stared at me with disbelief. "What?" I asked with a shrug.

"I can't believe you're joking about that."

"Monty Python babe," I said, punching her arm playfully.

"What does that mean?"

"Always look on the bright side of life."

- RITCHIE CARLTON -

I glanced at my watch again. It was quarter past five, and Amy still hadn't arrived. I ordered drinks anyway, and as I made my way back to the table, I saw Amy walk through the door. My anxiety melted away and my body relaxed.

"You came," I said with relief.

"I nearly didn't."

"Well, I'm glad you did," I said, ushering her into the booth.

"What did you need to tell me?" She asked, sitting down opposite me.

"Before I tell you my news… I have to check one last time."

"Check what?"

I pulled the ring out of my pocket. "Amy…" I leaned forward over the table, "would you ever consider marrying me?" I asked, opening the ring box. Amy answered my question when she sighed and rolled her eyes. I nodded and retracted my hands. "I'll take that as a no?"

"You already know the answer Ritchie."

"Yeah, I do," I agreed, closing the ring box, "but I had to make sure, otherwise I would've regretted this."

"This? Ritchie, you're being weirder than usual. What's going on?" I took a deep breath and leaned back in my chair.

"I'm moving back home Aims."

Her jaw dropped and she looked as stunned as if I'd slapped her in the face.

"Why?" she asked simply.

I shrugged. "Without you, there's nothing left for me here Amy. I want to settle down and have kids and if that's not with you, then I'd rather go home and be near my family."

"But what about your promotion?"

"It doesn't matter."

"What do you mean it doesn't matter? Does Gaz know you're leaving?"

"I resigned last week."

She sat back in her chair and raked her fingers through her hair.

"You've worked so hard for this. How can you walk away from your career when it's just starting to take off?"

"Success doesn't mean anything if I have no one to share it with."

She dropped her hands into her lap and sighed. "When do you leave?"

"November."

"Seriously?"

"Yep," I nodded, "there's no point in dragging it out. I'm going home for my brother's wedding as planned, but I won't be coming back."

She sat silently for a moment. "I can't believe it," she said quietly.

"Not really much point in staying anymore."

She fell silent for a minute while she sipped on her pint, then put the glass down and looked me in the eyes for the first time since we'd sat down.

"I don't want you to go Ritch."

"So, marry me then."

"I can't do that," she said shaking her head. "I can't be the only reason you're leaving?"

"No, but you're the only reason that matters."

"That's not fair Ritchie," she said sternly, "you've built a whole life here that has nothing to do with me."

"True, but I've only stayed this long because I had you."

"What about Nathan, and the rugby guys, and the rest of the crew?"

I smiled sadly. "I'll miss all of them, but they're not what's been keeping me here. I have a million reasons to go home Amy, but none of them matter if you ask me to stay." I paused and waited for her to say something, but she remained silent. "Give me a reason to stay Aims." I pleaded desperately.

"I can't," she replied coldly, "and quite frankly," she said, rising from the table, "it's really unfair of you to put that responsibility on me. If you stay, do it for yourself, not me. You're the one who said it Ritch, we're done here. Stay or go, it's got nothing to do with us," she plonked a fiver on the table. "Either way… you need to grow the fuck up and make a decision on your own." Amy grabbed her handbag and slung it over her shoulder. "Consider this our last goodbye Ritchie," she said before turning on her heel and storming away.

I sat and watched her leave with a distinct lack of emotion. We were done, that was it. I hated ending it like that, but I didn't have the energy or the inclination to chase her.

I leaned back in my chair and sipped my beer, glancing at the ring box sitting on the table. I put down my glass and flicked open the lid, eyeing the delicate diamond ring with disgust. The time had come to sell that fucking thing.

- NATHAN STONE -

As Ash pottered in the kitchen, I peered out the full-length window at Holland Park. The sun was beginning to set, and there were a few families enjoying the final moments of the day together. In seven months, that would be us. Ashley, me… and our baby. Holy shit, we were having a baby. In less than a year I'd be a Dad. I did a quick calculation in my head and, depending on how far along Ash was, it would be either March or April when the baby arrived.

"If you're two months into this pregnancy," I said, turning back to Ash as she pulled a couple of clean plates out of the dishwasher, "then our baby could end up with the same birthday as me."

Ash looked up from the dishwasher and froze, plates in hand. "Oh my god," she whispered in horror. "I don't even know when your birthday is. We're having a baby and I don't know one of the most basic things about you," she said with alarm.

"April 17th," I told her calmly, taking the plates out of her hand and putting them down on the bench. "And we have plenty of time to learn all the things about each other."

"So, you're an Aries?" she asked, in typical Ash style.

"Yes, I'm a stubborn sheep."

"But I'm a Pisces," she said as if it was a matter of national importance. "That's fire and water, it's not a great match Nathan."

I laughed affectionately. "Look at me, my little fishy," I teased, as panic flashed in her eyes. I took her beautiful face in my hands and kissed her gently on the lips. "We've defied all the odds in our relationship thus far, are you really going to let the stars get the better of us?"

She peered up at me and smiled, "you have all the answers Mr Stone."

"Except the answer to your birthday," I joked.

"Why don't you test your psychic skills and guess," she teased.

"Okay, well you're a Pisces, so I'd say March. Maybe the 2nd?"

"February," she said with a grin, "…the 22nd, but that was an impressive guess."

"I had a feeling there was a two in there somewhere. See… now we know each other's birthdays," I told her smugly, "and I also know that your favourite alcoholic drink is vodka soda because it has no calories; and you like your lattes with either coconut or almond milk because soya tastes gross. Your favourite colour is turquoise, and your eyes turn almost that exact shade when you wear that colour. I know that you bite your bottom lip whenever you're nervous, or excited, and no matter what oil you're wearing, you always smell like a warm spring day. You love the city, but when you're at the beach you truly come alive, and whenever you're in the sunshine you take a moment to close your eyes and enjoy the feel of it on your face. I know that you prefer to floss your teeth with those little plastic stick thingies, even though it makes you feel super guilty about ruining the planet, and I know that you look the most beautiful first thing in the morning when you've just woken up. I know that you dance around the kitchen when you think I'm not watching, and that you sing out loud when you have your headphones on because you forget that people can hear you. I know that you're determined, driven, resilient and tough-as-fuck. And I know that I'm a better person when you're around," I paused and smiled, watching tears glisten in her eyes. "Do you need me to keep going? Because I have plenty more."

"No," she said breathlessly, "that was pretty good."

"Pretty good? That was fucking awesome," I joked, knowing that there was one more thing I had to add. It wasn't how I'd planned to do it, but as I looked into her eyes, I knew it was time. After all, right was better than perfect. "But I haven't mentioned the most important part yet," I said, taking her hand as I knelt down on one knee, wishing I had the engagement ring in my pocket. "I also know that I love you, and I want to spend the rest of my life discovering all the stuff I don't know about you yet," I paused and swallowed hard. "This is not how I'd planned to do this but... Ashley Jane Granger – see I also know your middle name," I teased, "will you please marry me?"

Ash stared at me with wide eyes and the tears that had been shimmering under the surface finally broke and rolled delicately down her cheeks.

"Really?" she asked, biting her bottom lip.

"I know we haven't been together for long, but I want to spend the rest of my life with you Ash. Our relationship has been crazy and chaotic, and we've lived through more shit this year than most people experience in an entire lifetime, but the main thing that it's taught me, is that I don't want to live without you." I paused and waited for her answer, but she didn't say anything. "So, what do you think Granger? Do you want to be Mrs Stone for real?"

- ASHLEY GRANGER -

I stared at Nathan in shock as he knelt in front of me. I couldn't believe that he was proposing. It was like a dream.

"Wait," he said, not giving me a chance to answer his question. "Hold that thought, I'll be back in sec."

"Okay," I said with a stunned laugh as he jumped up and ran out of the room. I couldn't believe he'd just asked me to marry him. I mean… I knew he was happy to commit to parenting a child together, but I'd never dared to imagine that the un-tameable Mr Stone would want to get married.

"Right, let's try that again," Nathan said as he returned to the kitchen. "And this time I'm going to do it properly," he said resuming his position on one knee in front of me. My heart flipped inside my chest as he opened his hand and held up a little blue box. "Ashley Granger, will you be my wife?" he asked, lifting the lid of the box to reveal a wave shaped ring with a huge princess cut diamond in the middle of it. It was more like a work of art than a piece of jewellery.

"Yes," I said, dropping to my knees to join him on the floor. Nathan beamed with joy, and pulled the ring out of the box.

"Well then fiancé…consider yourself locked in," he said as he slid the massive diamond ring onto my finger. A waterfall of tears sprung from my eyes. Maybe it was the hormones, but now that I'd started, I couldn't stop. "You okay?" he asked, and wiped the tears from my cheeks. I nodded but I couldn't speak so he gave me a lingering kiss that sent shivers all over my body. I was terrified, ecstatic and relieved at the same time. Nathan leaned back to look into my eyes.

"I've put a ring on it, so now you're stuck with me," he joked.

I took his face in my hands, "there's no one else I'd rather be stuck with." I planted my mouth on his and slid my hands around his neck, running my fingers through his hair. Nathan's warm tongue explored mine, and he wrapped his hands around my waist, pulling me into him. As much as I hated to admit it, being in his arms made me feel safe and protected. I'd spent my whole life trying to be tough and independent, relentlessly attached to my stubborn belief that I had to take-on the world alone, but Nathan had shown me there was a better way to live. He'd shown me that I didn't have to do it on my own.

"I love you so much," he breathed into my ear, before trailing kisses down my neck.

"I love you too," I said with a shiver, as my skin tingled with goosebumps. Our kiss quickly escalated into a steamy moment, and I slid my hand down between our bodies. I reached into the front of Nathan's jeans and he let out a quiet moan as my hand rubbed against his flesh.

He fumbled around with the endless floaty fabric of my dress until he found his way underneath it and ran his hands up my thighs. He subtly shifted my g-string to one side as I unzipped his jeans and, with my dress billowing over us, I lowered myself onto him, clutching his shoulders tightly, as we both moaned. Fighting with the fabric on my flowy dress, Nathan tried to slide his hands around my hips, but the dress kept getting in the way.

"This has to go," Nath said as he whipped my dress up over my head and spread it out over the tiles, like a blanket.

"Then I'd better even it up," I said, as I returned the favour by removing his shirt.

"You're so fucking sexy," he whispered breathlessly into my ear, rolling us over, so that I was lying flat on the makeshift rug, with him on top of me.

"So are you," I said kissing him hard, and wrapping my thighs firmly around his waist, feeling every inch of him inside me. We completely lost track of time as we clung to each other, moving fluidly, like we were one body. Nathan groaned and tilted his hips upwards at just the right angle. "Oh my god," I gasped, letting my head drop backwards against the cold tiles, "you're so good at this."

"We're so good at this," he joked between moans. He repeated his hip movement and I whimpered with pleasure as the sensation pushed me over the edge. A huge orgasm crashed over me, and Nathan let himself go, moaning loudly as we grasped each other tightly. "We'll probably have to leave this part out of our engagement story when we tell the kids," Nathan joked with a croaky laugh as he looked down at me through the frame of his scrumptious biceps.

"Kid's plural?" I teased breathlessly, still gripping to his muscly back. "Does that mean you want more than one?"

"At least two," he puffed with a grin, delicately brushing a strand of wayward hair off my face. "Being an only child was lonely."

"Yeah, it was," I agreed, "but I did get really good at playing on my own."

"You'll never need to play alone again," Nath said as grin spread across his lips, "but if you do, I want to be there to watch."

I laughed and ran my finger along his square jaw. "I think that could be arranged," I said, taking his face in my hands. I opened my mouth to say something but then stopped, unsure how to articulate all the emotions I was feeling.

"What's on your mind?" he asked, twisting my hair around his fingers.

"I don't know," I said with a bewildered smile, "nothing and everything at the same time. Does that make any sense?"

Nathan smiled, "strangely... it makes perfect sense."

– Chapter 7 –

Discovery

- KAT McPHERSON -

I kissed Ryan goodbye and strutted down my street, glancing over my shoulder at him as he stood at the front door bouncing Mia in his arms.

"I love you," I called with a wave.

"We love you too," he called back, waving Mia's chubby little arm for her. I grinned and popped in my earbuds, stepping up the pace so that I could get to the tube on time. It was wonderful to have such a leisurely start to my working day. Life was finally back on track and, in fact, almost better than it had been before all the drama. I waltzed into the office at 10am, feeling incredibly content with my life.

"Morning Boss lady," I greeted Ash chirpily, as I plopped my handbag down on my desk. Ash looked up from her computer and her serious expression turned into a smile.

"Hey my lovely," she said. "How's your morning been?"

"Beautiful. How about yours?"

"Hectic," she said, looking slightly frazzled. "Amy's not in today so I'm covering her workload."

"Is she sick?"

"I don't know," Ash said, leaning back in her chair, "she hasn't called in sick, and her phone keeps ringing out."

"That's not like her."

"No, it's not," she agreed. "Normally she'd at least text. She must be really unwell."

"She's probably switched her phone to silent so she can get some sleep," I said, thinking no more of it.

"Yeah, I guess," Ash shrugged. "Hey, would you mind staying back a bit today? We've got so much to hand over and I'm feeling a bit overwhelmed with it all."

"Sure."

"Thanks," Ash said with a grateful smile, "I really appreciate that."

"No problem." She looked drained. "Beside the workload... how are you doing?" I asked, concerned.

"I'm fine," Ash answered automatically. I raised my brows

disbelievingly. "Just been feeling a bit off-colour," she explained apologetically.

"Okay," I said mockingly, unwilling to accept her lame answer, "and how are you really doing?"

She looked up with an embarrassed smile and sighed. "I'm okay," she assured me with a nod. "I wasn't for a while there, but Nath got me through it."

"I'm glad he's been there for you."

"Honestly Kat, I don't know how I would've got through this without him." Ash ran her hand through her sandy blonde hair and a huge diamond sparkled in the fluorescent light.

"Holy shit," I said, grabbing her hand to get a closer look at the ring. "Is there something you need to tell me?"

"Oh… yeah," she said with a blush, and then shrugged as if it was no big deal. "Nathan proposed last night."

"Oh my god!" I squealed leaning over the desk to throw my arms around her neck. "Ashley, that's amazing! Congratulations!"

"Thanks," she said with a blush. "I wanted to tell you and Amy at the same time, but I guess I'll just have to fill her in later."

"I won't say a word," I promised, with a grin. "But as soon as you've told her, we're starting on plans for your hen's night."

"Oh my gosh, Kat, slow down. We haven't even set a date yet."

"I can't believe you're being so calm about this."

"I guess I haven't had much time to process it," she said with an awkward smile. "Hey, would you and Ryan like to come over for dinner tonight? It would be great to catch up properly. I feel like so much has happened for all of us, and we haven't had a chance to debrief."

"We'd love to."

"You don't want to check with Ryza first?"

"No, he's been dying to see you guys, so I know he'll be keen. Besides, it'll be good for him to get out of the house."

"How's he enjoying being a house husband?"

"He seems to be loving it."

- RYAN McPHERSON -

I was standing at Mia's change-table in a poop-stained t-shirt, cleaning her up after a literal shit-show. She'd just let rip, the biggest poo explosion of the century, which had leaked right out of her nappy and soaked the two of us in runny, stinky, yellow shit.

"Right," I said, cleaning the last of the offensive liquid out of her various cracks and crevices, "I think we've got it all." With one hand still planted firmly on her chest, I wadded up the pile of dirty baby wipes and shoved them into a disposable nappy bag, one-handed. I bent down to grab a fresh nappy from the shelf underneath the change table when I felt warm liquid dribbling onto my head and down my face. Horror washed over me as I realised what was happening.

"Dude," I wailed with disgust, as I used the clean nappy to wipe the pee off my face. "That's not cool!" I looked up at Mia just in time to catch her last dribble of wee with my eye. "Ugh," I cried, grabbing my eye with the nappy hand as the acidic pee stung my eyeball. Thankfully, the nappy had been more absorbent than I'd expected based on past experiences, and the wee from my face had soaked into the fabric enough not to add to the stinging in my eye. Mia giggled at my antics.

"This isn't funny, devil child," I teased, tickling her chubby belly. The stinging had begun to subside, so I pulled the nappy off my face and squinted my damaged eye open. "At least you didn't blind me," I told her, ditching the nappy into the nappy bin. "Shall we try that again?"

I managed to clean us both up with no further dramas, but I was well and truly ready to get out of the house. I glanced at the big, glowing elephant clock on the nursery shelf. It had been the longest day ever and it wasn't even lunch time. I needed a dose of adult life to help me recover from the baby assault. I shot Kat a quick text to see if they'd all come out and meet me at Costa Coffee so that I didn't have to face the rest of Artemis just yet.

"Right munchkin," I said, lifting Mia off the change table, fresh, clean and poo-free, "Daddy needs a coffee."

- NATHAN STONE -

After a busy morning, Ritchie, Kat, Ash and I, all took a wander down the street to meet Ryza for a well-earned coffee-break. With almost the whole team back on-board, the Delfontaine account was full steam ahead.

"I can't believe you proposed," said Kat, as we trailed a little behind Ritchie and Ash, who were a few paces ahead of us, deep in conversation.

"I know right?" I agreed with a grin. "Who would have thought."

"Not me," she teased, nudging my shoulder with hers, "but I'm really proud of you."

"Aww shucks, Tails, you're making me blush."

"I mean it Nath, you've really grown up this past six months."

"I guess it had to happen at some point," I joked with a grin. "Just a pity that it took a couple of life and death situations to get me there."

"Hey, whatever it takes," she teased. I pushed her playfully and she stumbled, face first, into Ritchie's broad back. "Ouch," she laughed, rubbing her nose with a wince.

"You right there love?" Ritchie asked, helping her regain her balance.

"You've got a hard back Carlton," she said, giggling despite her damaged nose.

"That ain't my only hard body part."

"Eww," said Ash, smacking Ritchie's arm, "TMI big guy."

"Let that one slide," I warned Ritchie, as he opened his mouth to retort with some sort of reference to being big, "she's my fiancé now remember?"

"Fine," agreed Ritch with a childish grin.

"Hey Ritch, have you spoken to Amy today?" Kat asked, once she'd recovered from her face-plant.

"Err… no," he said, glancing at Ash for help.

"They had a pretty big row last night," she explained on his behalf.

"She stormed off and I haven't heard from her since," added Ritchie.

"What happened?" asked Kat, "I thought you guys were okay?"

"Uhh, yeah… we were."

"So, what happened?" I asked, unable to stop the words.

"I asked her to marry me again." We all fell silent, resisting the urge to facepalm. "We're really done," Ritchie said sadly. "I'm definitely going home."

"Hey Strangers," called Ryza, breaking the tension as he pushed the pram in our direction, waving excitedly.

"Hey babe," said Tails, running over to give her family hugs and kisses. Ash grinned at the sight of our other best friend and, hot on Kat's heels, she ran over and threw her arms around Ryza.

"God it's good to see you," she said, squeezing him tight. "I've missed you."

"You too," Ryan said, leaning back to look her over. "Are you okay? You look thin. Have you been eating?"

"I'm fine Mum," she teased with a smile, stepping back from Ryan.

"Err… I'd say you're more than fine," interrupted Tails, grabbing Ashley's hand to show Ryan the engagement ring. "She's going to be Mrs Stone."

"Holy shit," said Ryza, taking a closer look at the ring, then peering up at me with a mixture of shock and pride. "I'm impressed Stoner."

"Had to lock her in so she wouldn't leave me," I joked, with a wink at my fiancé.

"Understandable," Ryan teased. "Congrats guys. That's awesome news," he added, ducking around Ash to shake my hand. After finishing off the handshaking and hugs, Ryza looked around the group. "No Amy?"

"She's away today," said Kat.

"Not well?" he asked.

"We're not sure," I chimed in.

"I'll go check on her after work," Ash suggested. "I know she acts tough, but she loves you Ritchie, so she's probably devastated that you're leaving."

"You're leaving?" Ryan asked Ritch, with surprise.

"Yeah," said Ritch.

"Let's go get those coffees," I suggested. "We've got a lot to catch you up on."

"Sounds like it," said Ryza.

We found a table, ordered our coffees and settled in. It almost felt like old times as we gossiped and caught up on all that had happened over the past few weeks. Months in Ryza's case. It was a pity that Red was missing or it would have felt like life was completely back to normal.

"She's probably just taking a day to gather herself," said Ash, trying to put a positive spin on Amy's absence. "She really does love you Ritch."

Ritchie snorted with amusement. "She's got a funny way of showing it."

"Come on Ritchie, you know what Amy's like," said Kat, "she's not good at emotions."

"That sounds familiar," I said, shooting Ash a cheeky wink.

"Very funny," she replied, rolling her eyes.

"Here Ash," Ritchie said, pulling a key out of his pocket. "This is Amy's. You might as well take this with you tonight."

"Are you sure Ritch? You don't want to give it to her yourself?"

"Better to have a clean break."

"Okay."

"Why don't we all go grab a beer after work?" I suggested cheerfully, "it'll get your mind off things Ritch."

"That's a great idea!" Ryan agreed, slapping Ritchie on the back. "Boys night on the town."

"Yeah, why not," shrugged Ritchie. "It's been a while."

- ASHLEY GRANGER -

After work, I caught the tube out to Amy's place. It was nice to sit in a public space without feeling the need to look over my shoulder. I hadn't noticed my absence of fear until that moment, and it finally occurred to me that I was really, truly free. My life was now my own, and I'd never have to be scared for my life again. I relished the feeling for the whole tube ride and walked to Amy's apartment with a smile on my face, remembering a time when I wouldn't have been brave enough to walk alone, out in the open.

I pressed the buzzer, but there was no answer so I buzzed again. Maybe she was still in bed. I pulled out my phone and rang her, but it diverted straight to voicemail.

"Hi this is Amy, leave a message."

"Aims it's me, I'm outside your place. Are you okay?" I asked the voicemail before hanging up. A bad feeling started to form in the pit of my stomach. Something wasn't right. I pressed the buzzer again but there was still no answer so I wandered down to the footpath to see if I could glimpse inside her window. Since her flat was on the third floor, I couldn't see anything. I turned to leave, before remembering that Ritchie had given me his spare key.

"Bingo," I said with triumph, as I pulled the key out of my handbag. I let myself in the main door and climbed the stairs to her flat, stopping to knock on her door just in case.

"Aims it's Ash." I called through the door, but there was no response. Why did I have such an awful feeling lurching in my stomach? "Amy?" I called again, before letting myself in. "You home?" The flat was unnervingly quiet. "Aims?" I called again, as I wandered through her silent apartment, "are you here?"

There was no sign of her in the lounge room or the kitchen, so I checked her bedroom. Nothing. She must have gone out. I popped Ritchie's key on the hall stand on my way out, when I noticed an envelope with my name on it. I plucked the envelope from the stand and found several more behind it. Nathan, Kat, Ryan and Ritchie. There was one for each of us. Perhaps she'd arranged a going-away party for Ritchie.

Curious, I peeled open my envelope to reveal a letter. I began to read the handwritten note and the world ground to a screeching halt...

Dear Ash,

I'm so sorry.

I know you'll probably blame yourself for this, but please don't. There's no way you could have seen this coming, and even if you had… there's nothing you could have said or done to stop it, so quit beating yourself up about it.

You are an amazing, beautiful, loving woman and even though we've only known each other for six months, I feel blessed to call you my friend.

You're the only person in the world that will be able to explain this to Ritchie. Please look after him for me, and make sure he finds a nice Aussie girl who will treat him well.

You will be an awesome mum, Ash. I'll be watching over you with a smile as you cruise through the challenge of parenthood as gracefully as ever.

My time has ended, but yours is just beginning. There are so many wonderful things in store for you, so make the most of every day. You're free Ash, never forget that.

I wish I was as strong as you, but I couldn't live with the pain anymore. I don't have the strength to go on. It hurts too much. Perhaps it's the cowards' way out, but it's the only way to make it stop.

I love you heaps girl. Keep being awesome.

Big kisses,
Aims xx

The letter slid out of my hands and floated to the floor as I stood in shock and disbelief. Surely that couldn't mean what I thought it meant. I looked towards the closed bathroom door.

"Amy?" I called in desperation, "Aims are you in there?" I called again as I strode to the bathroom and pushed open the door. Despite having read the letter, my brain wasn't prepared for the sight that awaited me. The air drained from my lungs when I saw Amy's body lying lifelessly in a bath full of bright red water.

"Amy!" I screamed in horror as I sprinted over to her. "No, no, no!" I wailed frantically trying to wake her up. "What did you do?" I sobbed angrily as I searched her cold neck for a pulse. I couldn't feel a heartbeat, so I put my cheek to her mouth and felt a very faint stir of breath on my skin.

I breathed air into her lungs and then pulled her arms out of the water so that her slashed wrists balanced precariously on the rim of the bath, above her heart-line. There was still a light but steady flow of blood dripping from the massive gashes that spanned the length of each of her forearms.

"Stay with me Aims," I pleaded as I scrambled for towels to wrap her wrists. "What did you do?" I asked again, as if she would respond. She was so pale that her skin almost looked blue. "Please, please, please, keep breathing," I begged her lifeless form, as tears flowed from my eyes. "Come on Aims, wake up," I pleaded attempting more CPR even though I had no idea what I was doing.

I grabbed my phone and dialled emergency, having vivid flashbacks of the last time I'd had to use that fucking number.

"Stay with me Aims," I instructed her desperately, gripping her limp hand as the phone rang.

"Hello, what emergency do you require?" asked the man on the other end of the line.

"Yeah Hi, I need an ambulance…" I told the operator urgently, giving him all the details. "You need to hurry, I don't think we have long." I hung up the call, hoping like hell that the ambulance would get there in time.

"Fuck," I gasped, choking on my tears. The reality of the situation began to hit me. I might lose Amy. I continued breathing for her and in each break, I took stock of the scene in front of me. There was blood smeared everywhere - thick, dark blood. It was all over Amy; all over me; all over the floor and the bath.

"What were you thinking?" I asked her, peeling a strand of her wet auburn hair off of her face. "Why would you do this to yourself? What am I going to tell Ritchie?"

My insides began to crumble. I needed Nathan. I hit the speed dial on my phone with a shaky, bloodied hand and flicked the phone to speaker so that I could continue administering my version of CPR.

"Hey babe," Nathan greeted me happily. The sound of his voice nearly brought me undone.

"Nathan, I need you," I croaked urgently, trying desperately to keep it together for a little while longer.

"Are you okay?" he asked with panic.

"I'm safe, just grab Ritchie and get over to Amy's," I implored him desperately, as I choked back my tears. I couldn't fall apart yet. "Please hurry babe."

- NATHAN STONE -

Ash hadn't even hung up the phone before I'd sprung into action.

"What's happening?" asked Ritchie as I grabbed my keys and clambered out of the booth.

"Something bad," I said, pulling at Ritchie's shirt as he stared at me in a daze. "We have to go now Ritch."

"Go where?" he asked in confusion, trying to climb out of the booth after me.

"To Amy's," I said gravely. At hearing Amy's name, Ritchie hurdled over the table and followed me quickly out the door with no further questions. We hurried down the footpath and jumped into my car without uttering a word.

"Any idea what's going on?" Ritchie asked, once we were on our way, speeding through the streets of London.

"No idea but Ash said she needs me, so it must be bad."
He sighed and nodded his head in agreement.

"Shall I tell Ryan not to come?" Ritchie asked, gripping tightly to the armrest as I took a left turn with a little too much speed.

"Yeah, good thinking," I said, expertly navigating my sports car through the backstreets of Clapham. "But don't tell him there's a drama. Say something's come up and we have to rain-check. I don't want him or Kat stressing."

"Roger that," Ritchie said, as I wove my way around the evening traffic, something in my gut told me that every second counted.

"She said she was safe," I told Ritchie as we roared through a quiet, tree-lined street, "but she sounded really shaken up, so it's hard to tell."

"At least we're not going to a hospital this time," Ritch joked. "I don't think I could handle another one of those visits."

"Let's not tempt fate," I said, screeching around another corner. We were almost there, but my anxiety levels were through the roof. "Can you dial Ash?" I asked Ritchie, throwing him my phone.

"Sure." He dialled Ashley's number and a loud dial tone echoed through the small car as the phone connected to the Bluetooth. Ash didn't answer and eventually it rang out.

"Try again," I said, weaving through a street full of double-parked cars. Ritchie dialled again and it rang out. "Fuck," I swore, wracked with panic, "why isn't she picking up?"

"She's probably got her phone on silent or something," Ritchie said calmly, "but we're only a few blocks away so just chill."

"That's a physical impossibility right now," I said, having flashbacks of the night I'd walked into Ashley's bloodied flat. "Ritch, I have a really bad feeling about this."

- KAT McPHERSON -

I arrived home to the alluring scent of aftershave, wafting through the door.

"I'm home," I called, letting myself into the flat.

"We're in here," Ryan called from the lounge room as I popped my handbag on the kitchen table.

"Hey, you two," I said, sticking my head around the lounge room door, where Ryan was playing with Mia. My breath caught in my throat at the sight of him. He was wearing the burgundy Versace shirt that I'd bought him for our first wedding anniversary, and it hugged his body in all the right places. "Wow, I haven't seen you in that shirt for years," I said, biting my lip at the sight of my sexy husband.

"It hasn't fitted me for years."

"Well, it fits perfectly now," I said, running my hands over his shoulders. "In fact, it fits so well I want to take it off you."

Ryan chuckled and kissed me softly. "That will have to wait until I get home," he said, peeling my hands off his body, "I'm late to meet the boys."

"I suppose I could let you out on good behaviour for one night," I teased.

"How kind of you," he laughed.

"I'll be ready and waiting for you when you get home," I joked, stepping back from him.

"And I'll be looking forward to that," he said with a wink as he bent down to get Mia from her bouncer. "Night, night gorgeous. Be good for your mummy." Just as he lifted her up, Mia projectile vomited all over his shirt.

"Oh no!" I said with a laugh as Ryan stood frozen in shock.

"That's one way to say goodbye," he joked, as I took Mia from him.

"That's three for three today. She's pooped, peed and now chucked on me."

"The glamorous life of a house-husband," I teased. "You get cleaned up, I'll sort this one," I said, carrying Mia into the nursery while Ryan trotted off to the bedroom to change. "Right my little spew-monster, let's get you cleaned up."

- RYAN McPHERSON -

I shrugged into a clean shirt. It wasn't as impressive as the Versace one, but it was passable. I heard a beep come from the dresser, and it took me a moment to realise that it was my phone. I'd gotten so used to not having one, it was taking some time to get back into the swing of technology again. I left my shirt half buttoned and checked the text.

'Sorry man, we have to raincheck – something urgent came up.'

My heart sank. Boys' night was off. As much as I hated to admit it, I'd really been looking forward to it. I put the phone back down and wandered out to the nursery, where Kat was tidying up the final remnants of Mia's stomach eruption.

"Looks like you ladies have got a hot date tonight after all," I joked, leaning my shoulder against the door-frame. "Boys night got cancelled."

"Oh babe, I'm so sorry," Kat said, throwing the dirty jumpsuit into the laundry basket. She popped Mia back into her bouncer and came over to give me a hug.

"All good. It means I get to spend the evening with you," I said with a shrug, standing upright as she slid her hands around my waist.

"I know you were looking forward to it," she said, her eyes darting to the 'v' where my buttons had been left undone, "but I'm sure we could find a way to make up for it."

I laughed as she walked her fingers up my bare chest. "Actually," I said, resting my hand on top of hers to stop it wandering across my skin, "I was thinking that maybe I'd take you two out for dinner."

"Like a real date?"

"Exactly."

"Well, I wouldn't say no to that."

"Great!" I said, grabbing her hips and turning her around. "Go get dressed and I'll look after little miss."

"Ooh, I like it when you're bossy," she teased, as she looked back over her shoulder with a cheeky wink.

"Go now, or we'll never get out of here," I said, slapping her gently on the arse as she walked away.

"You sure I can't entice you to come and help me?"

My whole body reacted to the smouldering look in her eyes. I looked down at Mia in her bouncer and then back at my sexy wife who had already stripped off her shirt. My eyes darted back to Mia as my brain calculated a solution whereby, I could have sex without feeling guilty. But that seemed impossible. Kat vanished into the bedroom and, two seconds later, her shirt flew out of the door.

"I'm waiting," she called, as her bra followed quickly behind. I bit my knuckles and cast my gaze back down to my daughter.

"Sorry kiddo," I said, as I scooped up Mia in her bouncer, and placed them both carefully down next to the bedroom door. "I'll pay for your therapy when you're older," I promised her, kissing her quickly on the forehead before darting through the door to see Kat lying naked on the bed.

"Hey there sailor," she said, beckoning me over.

"Totally worth the psychologists bill," I joked, quickly dispensing of my trousers before crawling onto the bed on top of my half-naked wife. "You're wearing way too many clothes," I said, unbuttoning her trousers.

"I was thinking the same about you," she said with a smile, pulling my shirt up over my head.

"And now you're wearing just the right amount." I ran my hands over her breasts and, much to my surprise, a small amount of milk dribbled out of her nipples. "Oh," I said, with surprise as her hands flew over her boobs.

"Oh my god," she said, blushing, "maybe I'm not wearing quite enough clothes."

I laughed and ran my finger over her cheek, "you're perfect."

Kat started to wriggle out from beneath me.

"I think I'll put a bra on," she muttered awkwardly. I rolled off her so she could get up.

"Babe, it's fine," I assured her, grabbing her hand before she climbed off the bed.

"No, it's embarrassing," she said, unable to make eye contact with me. "I have no control over my body anymore and it's mortifying."

"I love your body," I said, pulling her towards me, "your body is amazing. It made that little angel out there." I pointed towards the door to where I'd left our precious child for the sake of getting laid. "She may need a lot of therapy to recover from the amount sex she's heard us having, but if wasn't for this body," I said, sliding my hands around Kat's waist, "then we wouldn't have her."

Kat stared into my eyes and smiled.

"That's beautiful... but I'm still putting a bra on," she said, jumping up and rummaging through her underwear drawer.

"I'll take you any way you come."

She turned and raised a brow, with a naughty glint in her eye.

"And I'll come any way you want me to."

- ASHLEY GRANGER -

I was still attempting CPR, but Amy's skin grew paler and paler. I was too scared to stop so I just kept going until I eventually heard the ambulance siren out the front of Amy's flat.

"Thank God," I sighed with relief.

"Hello?" One of the paramedics called in the door.

"In here!" I shouted from my position on the floor. I was too scared to stop CPR in case it was the only thing keeping Amy alive. The paramedics ran into the bathroom and surveyed the gory scene.

"Are you okay love?" the man asked me, checking me over as the woman ran quickly to Amy's other side.

"I'm fine," I assured him as he helped me to my feet, "please just help my friend." The man glanced over at the woman and my heart dropped as I saw the look they exchanged.

"I'm sorry, but she's gone," the woman apologised.

"What do you mean?" I asked stupidly, even though I knew exactly what she meant.

"She's dead," the woman said apologetically.

"No!" I wailed as tears streamed relentlessly down my face. "Do something! You have to save her!"

"I'm sorry love, but she's gone. There's nothing we can do for her." The woman told me gently.

"No, Amy," I sobbed helplessly. "How could this have happened? Why didn't I see it coming? How could she have done this to herself?" I wailed inconsolably. The woman pulled out a plastic sheet from her medic bag while the man attempted to calm me down. "Please just check her again," I pleaded, as the woman unfolded the thick black plastic. "She was breathing. I felt her breath."

"I'm sorry," the man said, grasping my arms to keep me stable, "but that's called agonal breathing. It happens right at the end." I knew what he was saying was true, but my mind was fighting the information.

"But…" I muttered, letting my sentence trail off as I watched the woman pull the plastic sheet over Amy's body. After everything we'd all been through over the last six months, I wasn't willing to accept that this was the way it would end for Amy.

"Ash?!" Nathan's voice called frantically from the front door.

"Nath!" I sobbed in relief and dashed out of the bathroom door.

Nathan ran towards me and I hurled myself into his arms weeping inelegantly into his chest.

"What's going on?" Nath asked calmly, gently stroking my head as I sobbed loudly. "Are you okay?"

"There's been a fatality," said the male medic, emerging from the bathroom, as Ritchie appeared behind Nathan.

"What do you mean fatality?" Ritchie asked the guy, before turning to me. "Ash… where's Aims?"

"I was too late Ritch," I told him through a heavy sheet of tears. Ritchie's face turned ashen and a look of disbelief contorted his features. He peered into the bathroom and saw the plastic sheet.

"No!" he cried, shoving everyone out the way as he dove for the plastic.

"Ritch," Nathan called in shock as the lady tried to intercept Ritchie. She wasn't quick enough to stop him and he grabbed the sheet. The thick black plastic, slid off the bathtub to reveal Amy's lifeless, blood-drained body.

"No!" Ritchie howled, jumping into the tub to scoop her up in his arms. Tears streamed from my eyes as I witnessed Ritchie falling to pieces. It was the most heart-wrenching moment I'd ever witnessed in my life. "Amy, wake up. Please wake up," he pleaded desperately, hugging her limp body tightly against his chest.

"She's gone sir, there's nothing we can do now," the paramedic told him calmly. Nathan held me tightly as we watched the scene unfold. Ritchie, sat in the bath, soaking wet, with Amy in his arms.

"Please go help him Nath," I begged quietly as the two paramedics exited the bathroom to give Ritchie some privacy.

"See if you can get him out of that bath," the guy said quietly to Nathan, patting his shoulder.

"Okay," Nathan agreed, looking down at me sadly. "Are you okay?" he asked, squeezing my shoulders.

"I'm fine," I said with a nod, "Ritchie needs you right now."

- RITCHIE CARLTON -

I bawled loudly as I clutched Amy's dead body against my chest. Somewhere in my mind I was waiting – hoping – that she would open her eyes. I couldn't believe she was dead. Surely it couldn't be real. I was convinced that at some point I was going to wake up and realise it was some kind of fucked up dream. Like when Nathan thought Ash was dead. Amy would wake up and be fine and we'd live happily ever after like Nath and Ash. Or maybe this body was just a stunt-double and the real Amy would jump out from behind the door or something. But it couldn't possibly be real. That wasn't an option. She couldn't be dead. She couldn't be gone.

"Come back to me Aims please," I cried pitifully into her wet hair, "I love you. Please don't leave me."

"Ritch," Nathan said quietly, gently putting his hand on my shoulder.

"I'm not leaving her Nathan," I told him without looking up.

"She's gone mate," he said, sitting on the edge of the bath, "you've got to let her go."

"No," I argued, squeezing Amy tighter, "she's going to wake up Nath, just like Ash. She's gonna be fine. This isn't real."
Nathan gripped my shoulder tightly.

"I know you want to believe that – we all do – but she's gone Ritchie." His words cut through my brain fog and pierced me right in the heart. I sobbed loudly and rocked back and forth with my dead non-girlfriend in my arms.

"Go," I told Nathan firmly, as more tears rolled down my cheeks.

"I can't leave you like this Ritch," he said softly, "I'm going to sit here with you until you're ready."

"Fine," I snorted stubbornly as snot, tears and water all blended together on my face. How could the universe be so cruel? I closed my eyes and rested my chin on Amy's head. If her body hadn't been so cold and limp, I could have almost convinced myself that she was still alive.

"I love you," I whispered to her sadly, as I began to come to terms with the fact that she wasn't going to wake up, "I'll always love you."

"Sir?" A voice asked from somewhere in the real world. "The coroner is here to move the body."

"Please, just a bit longer," I begged, squeezing my eyes shut tightly. Maybe if I wished hard enough this would all go away. A chill ran through my body and I realised that I was shaking so badly I was almost convulsing.

"We need to get you out of there," replied the voice softly, "I'm sorry."

"Can we have another five minutes?" asked Nathan, rising from his perch.

"Okay," the lady relented, "but only five minutes, then we really need to clear out of here."

"Thank you," said Nathan as he rested his hands on my shoulders again. "Okay bud, it's time to say goodbye."

"I can't."

"You can," he told me firmly. I opened my eyes and looked up to see a man standing at the bathroom door with the word 'CORONER' emblazoned on his jacket. This really was the end. Amy was dead and she wasn't coming back. "Come on, let's get you out of there," said Nath, offering me a hand.

"Okay," I agreed calmly. I kissed Amy's head one last time and then rested her gently against the edge of the tub before stepping out onto shaky legs. Nathan gripped me firmly so that my numb legs wouldn't collapse beneath me. The paramedic handed Nathan a thermo-blanket, which he wrapped around me before guiding me out into the lounge room.

"The paramedics want to check you over before they go," he told me as I sat staring vacantly at nothing in particular.

"Okay," I agreed again. I didn't care. They could do whatever they wanted to do. Nothing mattered anymore. Amy was dead. Amy was fucking dead and it was all my fault.

- NATHAN STONE -

As the paramedics saw to Ritchie, Ashley called me out into the hallway. She was gripping a pile of envelopes in her hands.

"I found these Nath," she said showing me the envelopes, "she left one for each of us." Ash handed me an envelope with my name on it and I stared at it with apprehension.

"Is this…?" I asked, letting my words trail off.

"Yeah," she breathed with a nod. "There's one for Ritchie too, but I think maybe it's best if you give that to him," she said, passing over the second envelope.

"I can't believe Red's gone," I muttered, running my hand nervously over the top of the envelopes. Ash brushed her hand along my jaw and looked deep into my eyes.

"You're allowed to cry Nath. It's okay to be sad."

I cupped my hand over hers and then kissed her fingers.

"There will be time for that later," I said, peering over my shoulder at Ritchie, "but right now he needs me to be strong."

She nodded with complete understanding. "The cops are downstairs," she said threading her fingers through mine, "they want statements from us."

"Okay, I'll let him know."

"I'll go do mine now. That should buy you guys some time."

"Thanks," I said, giving her a tender kiss before she let herself out of the flat. I stared down at the envelopes in my hand and took a deep breath, carefully opening mine as best I could with shaking hands. I pulled out the letter and unfolded the crisp white paper.

Dear Nath,

Where do I even start? You, my dear slut-bag, are one of the best mates I've ever had. You're one of the few people in the world who I trust unconditionally, and probably the only person who has never been afraid to call me out on my bullshit.

It's been an honour being your friend dude. I got to watch you grow from the man-whore of Artemis, into one of the best men I've ever known. I know you're probably rolling your eyes right now, but I mean it. You're a good guy Nath, so continue being the noble man that you have become. Own it and embrace it. Your new life starts here.

You've proven yourself to be a worthy boyfriend for Ash, and I know you're going to be a great father to this baby too. I have no doubt that you'll do your own Dad proud.

I'm trusting you to keep an eye out for my boy. He's going to need you Nath. Please look after him for me and make sure he goes back home to his family where he belongs. Don't let him stay in London and wallow.

I'm so proud of you Nath. And I'm pleased that one of us finally got our shit together. Take care of yourself and your new family. They're your world now.

Love you mate,
Love Red xx

Silent tears streamed down my face as I read her words. I still didn't understand why she'd done what she did, but given that she'd left suicide notes, it was clear that she'd had no doubts about it. I wiped the tears off my face and shoved both envelopes into my back pocket. This wasn't the right moment to give that letter to Ritchie.

"Hey man," I said to him, resting my hand on his shoulder, "you doing okay?"

"Not really," he said sadly.

"Yeah, me either," I told him, pulling up a seat next to him.

"I can't believe she's actually gone."

"Yeah, me either," I repeated, leaning my elbows on my thighs, "it fucking sucks."

"Sure does," he agreed, rubbing his bloodshot eyes. "I mean… was her life really that bad? I don't get it. I know things weren't perfect, but I didn't realise I'd broken her."

"Red was already broken Ritch. She was damaged long before you met her."

Ritchie sobbed and dropped his face into his hands.

"It's all my fault."

"It's not your fault man," I said, patting his back, "if there's one thing I can tell you for sure, it's that Amy loved you and nothing you did could have pushed her to this. This was all her." Ritchie nodded and continued weeping into his hands. "Hey, I know you don't want to think about this right now, but we have to go make statements for the cops."

- KAT McPHERSON -

I rolled onto my side and smiled at my sexy, sweaty husband as he laid sprawled on the bed beside me. He'd become so self-confident since we'd split, it almost felt like I was married to a completely different man. I took a moment to appreciate his muscular new figure and then rested my head on my hand.

"Would you be upset if I said that I didn't feel like going out?" I asked, hooking my leg over his. Ryan laughed and ran his hand up my thigh.

"Not at all, I was kinda thinking the same thing," he said, trailing his fingers up and down my side. "Shower, movie and uber eats?"

"Sounds perfect to me."

"I'll check on Mia while you shower."

"You're not going to join me?"

"As much as I'd love to... I need a rest," he admitted with a laugh. "I know I've trimmed down, but I still have my limits."

"Slacker," I teased, climbing off the bed, "but I'll concede. I haven't had this much action since we first started dating. I expect there's a UTI on the horizon for me."

"Sounds fun," he joked, as I strutted to the bathroom. "You women get all good stuff huh?"

"We sure do," I called back to him, flicking on the shower. I let the hot water wash over me, and my aching body relaxed from head to toe. If anyone had told me a few months ago that I'd be this hot-to-trot, I would have laughed in their face. After the destruction of my downstairs department, I'd thought I'd never want to have sex again.

"So how is it working with Ash?" Ryan called from the bedroom.

"It's little intimidating if I'm being honest," I replied, as he stuck his head inside the bathroom door with Mia cradled against his bare chest. "She really knows her shit."

"That's true," he agreed, "but so do you."

"Not like she does," I disagreed, lathering some shampoo into my hair. "Ash takes it to a whole new level. I'm not even sure why she didn't go for a partner position. She could run rings around some of the guys I've worked for."

"I think she was happy to get back into work after so long away."

"Yeah," I agreed, rinsing off the lather. "I can see why you guys won the McEwan pitch though. I don't feel quite so bad about losing to Mareechi's now that I know how talented she is."

"And what about Beau?" he asked, trying to look casual. "How is that going?"

"You have nothing to worry about, babe. We're keeping it friendly, and as of yesterday I've handed everything Beau related over to Ash."

"Okay," he said, sounding skeptical. I stuck my head out of the shower door.

"I know it's a weird situation, but I promise you, on Mia's life, that I won't let anything come between you and I Ryan, but if you'd prefer me to quit, I'll do that."

"I don't want you to quit," he said, stroking my wet cheek. "You love your job."

"I do. But I'd give it up if you asked me to."

"I'll never ask you to do that. We're in this together babe. I trust you."

"Thank you."

"Now, I'm going to leave you to shower while I get this young lady a bottle." He gave me a wink over his shoulder as he retreated from the steamy bathroom. I finished washing my hair, then shaved my legs and gave myself a face scrub. When I finally emerged from the shower feeling fresh and clean, I grabbed my trousers off the floor and pulled them over my naked bottom. There was little point in getting properly dressed, since I planned on removing them again very shortly.

- RYAN McPHERSON -

I gave Mia her bottle and then changed her nappy. She'd be nodding off to sleep in no time, and then I'd be able to ravage my wife again.

"You're getting very good at being Mister Mum," Kat joked, appearing stealthily at the doorway.

"Yeah, I quite enjoy it to be honest."

"Does that mean you don't want to go back to work?" she asked, joining me by the cot.

"No, I still like our part-time plan," I said, wrapping Mia in her swaddle.

"Cool. Did you call that contact of Gaz's?"

"Sure did. I'm meeting with him next week."

"Oh babe, that's great! Why didn't you tell me?"

"We've been kinda busy since you got home."

"Good point," she said with a smile, leaning over to look at Mia, before turning back to me with a mischievous grin. "Fancy getting busy again?"

"Absolutely," I agreed with a wink. Mia was beginning to doze off, so we both gave her a kiss goodnight and crept quietly out of the nursery. Kat peered over her shoulder and then took off running towards the loungeroom. I quickly caught up to her and grabbed her in a gentle rugby tackle which sent us tumbling to the floor. We giggled like children and from our awkward position on the new rug, I proceeded to strip her naked.

"This is the second time I've had to get you out of these pants tonight," I chuckled.

"So it is," she answered with a grin, as she unbuttoned my jeans. "Guess I'd better avoid wearing those in future."

"No, I like taking them off you."

"In that case, maybe I should wear them more often," she joked from beneath me, using her foot to push my pants down to my knees.

"Definitely." We stared at each other for a moment, and then Kat wrapped her legs around my waist. "God you're gorgeous."

Kat smiled naughtily, then grabbed my bare bottom and pulled me downwards. We both groaned with pleasure, and held eye contact, as I moved steadily on top of her. Even at a slow pace I was getting carpet burn, but it was worth it.

- RITCHIE CARLTON -

Even though I'd spent nearly an hour holding Amy's lifeless body in my arms, it was too hard to comprehend that she was really dead. My brain seemed to have disconnected itself by the time the lady-cop returned with our typed statements.

"Mr Carlton," said the female officer, as she handed me the final clipboard. "I need you to read and sign your statement," she told me, nodding at the clipboard I was now grasping tightly in my hands.

"Thanks," said Nathan on my behalf, while Ash rubbed my back supportively.

"Yeah, sure," I agreed, glancing down at the paper, unable to tear my eyes off the first line.

INCIDENT TYPE/OFFENCE: SUICIDE.

Suddenly the whole situation became too much for me to handle. How was I supposed to do this? I was using all my energy to keep myself together so if I had to re-live the whole thing again, I'd probably fall apart. Without a word, I dumped the clipboard on a vacant chair and wandered straight out the exit. I needed to get outside for some fresh air. I had to pull myself together.

What the fuck had happened? How had things gotten so bad? Why hadn't she just talked to me? What the fuck had she been thinking? I took a few massive breaths of the fresh air and looked around the bustling street. People were living their normal lives, while my entire universe had shattered. How could the sun still be shining, or the trees swaying in the breeze, when the woman I loved was lying dead in the mortuary? The pain hung heavily in my heart. It was my fault. Our fight must have pushed her over the edge. Why did our last words to each other have to be angry ones? I would have given anything to kiss her and tell her that I loved her.

The weight of my emotion got the better of me, and I leaned my hands against my knees as I swallowed back my tears.

"Come on Ritch, get your shit together," I told myself firmly before forcing my body to an upright position. I began pacing up and down the footpath, trying to make sense of everything that had happened. None of it was computing. What the fuck had happened? Why had Amy killed herself? She'd had issues, but had they been that bad that taking her life seemed like the only choice? There were so many questions buzzing through my mind, that I couldn't think clearly. "Pull it together Ritchie."

"Yeah, get your fucking shit together and stop acting like a pussy," I heard Amy's disembodied voice say from somewhere in the depths of my mind. My frustration finally overflowed.

"Fuck you," I growled with rage at the imaginary voice. "Did you do this to punish me?" I wailed, before kicking the rubbish bin with all my strength. Being at a police station I'd expected the trashcan to be bolted down, so I recoiled in surprise when the fucking thing crashed to the ground with a huge bang. "Why did you have to leave me?" I asked pathetically, as I dropped to my knees on the dirty pavement.

"Ritch?" Nathan called from behind me, as I attempted to pick up the scattered rubbish. "You alright mate?"

"I kicked the bin," I replied as if that would answer his question. Nathan picked up the bin and I quickly wiped the tears from my eyes before he saw them. I shoved the litter into the bin piece by piece, and Nathan knelt down to help me dispose of the remaining evidence of my destructive behaviour. He patted my back, looking as though he was about to hug me.

"Ritchie," he started and then stopped. It was clear he had no idea what to say, which was fine by me, because I had no idea how to respond.

"Sir?" The same officer asked, from the doorway. Nathan and I both looked up at her, still on our knees in front of the rubbish bin as if we were praying to the lord of litter. "We really need you to sign that statement," she said, holding out the clipboard.

"Fine," I nodded, as I rose to my feet with a deep sigh. I took the clipboard from her hands and, without reading over it, I flicked to the back page and signed my name. "Done," I replied, handing her back the folder.

"You don't want to read through it?" she asked disapprovingly.

"I know what it says," I answered coldly, trying to hold back another bout of tears.

"Okay," The woman nodded understandingly and retreated inside. Once Nathan and I were alone, he rested his hand on my shoulder and cleared his throat.

"Here," he said handing me an envelope with my name on it. My chest flipped at the sight of Amy's swirly handwriting.

"Is that...?" I asked, unable to finish my sentence.

"Ash found them at Amy's place."

"Them?"

"Yeah," he said with a crackle in his throat, "there was one for each of us."

I wiped my nose with the back of my hand to stop myself from crying again.

"Thanks," I said, carefully taking the envelope from his outstretched hand as if it was made of glass. I stared down at the envelope, tracing the letters with my finger. Emotions began to rise in my chest, knowing that Amy's hands had touched the paper.

"I'll give you a moment," suggested Nath quietly.

"No," I answered quickly, "I don't want to read this here." I needed to be somewhere peaceful and beautiful to read Amy's last words to me, not standing in the doorway of a cop-shop.

"Okay," he agreed with a nod, "do you want me to take you somewhere?"

"No thanks. You should take Ash home. I'm going down to Postman's Park."

"Alright, as long as you're okay," Nath nodded, eyeing me with concerned skepticism.

"I'm fine Nath," I said, patting his shoulder, "I'm not gonna top myself."

His face turned stern. "That's not funny."

"It wasn't meant to be," I said with a shrug. I could see he was genuinely worried about me so I patted his arm with reassurance. "I promise you don't need to worry about me."

"Okay," he conceded, "but call me if you need me."

"Will do," I agreed before jogging off towards the tube station.

- ASHLEY GRANGER -

I watched Nathan watching Ritchie jog away from the police station. I was worried that he hadn't let himself grieve yet. He'd known Amy longer than anyone else and they'd been really close, so it would have to come out at some point. I just hoped that would be sooner rather than later. He waited until Ritchie was out of sight, and then turned back to the station to see me standing at the glass doors.

"How are you coping?" he asked, wandering over to join me.

"I've been better," I admitted, winding my hands around his waist. "What about you? You've been very calm through all of this."

"Babe," he said, pulling me in close, "after everything that's happened, I don't think anything can really shake me anymore."

"I suppose not," I agreed.

"And how are you feeling physically?" he asked worriedly, "you know, with the pregnancy."

"I'm fine, I'd actually forgotten in amongst all this drama."

Nathan leaned down to kiss me and then rested his forehead against mine.

"I can't believe she's gone," he said quietly, with a crackle in his voice. A tear rolled down his cheek, so I squeezed him tighter.

"Me either," I said, taking his face in my hands as he let his grief begin to show.

"She knew what she was doing Ash," he said, gripping my waist. "She sat down and wrote those fucking letters and then killed herself." He sniffed loudly as I wiped some of the tears off his cheeks. "Why would she do that?"

"I don't know," I admitted, "I know she had a lot of issues, but I never would have imagined that she'd do this."

"I guess you never really know what's going on in someone head."

"I guess you don't," I agreed as we held each other. We stood silently for a while, processing the traumatic events of the day. The warmth of his body was comforting so I closed my eyes and held him tight. It was all so surreal. "We should go tell Kat and Ryan," I said after a while. "I need to give them their letters."

Nathan leaned back and studied my bloodied outfit.

"Are you sure you're up to doing that right now?"

"They should know sooner rather than later."

"True," he agreed, stepping back and taking my hand. "I'll need to tell Gaz too, but that can wait until tomorrow." He cast his eye over my blood-stained clothes. "You want to go home and get changed first?"

I followed his gaze and glanced down my sullied outfit. "No, I'd rather get it out of the way. The longer we leave it, the harder it will be."

"Thirty minutes won't make a difference."

"Maybe not," I agreed, "but once I get home I won't want to leave."

"Okay," he nodded and kissed me on the top of my head, "let's do this then."

- KAT McPHERSON -

Ryan and I were lying naked on the lounge room floor, debating our possible dinner choices, when we heard the buzzer ring.

"Shit, who would that be?" Asked Ryan as he climbed to his feet and pulled on his jeans.

"No idea," I said, as he wandered out to answer the intercom.

"Hello?" I heard Ryan say out in the hallway.

"Hey man," came Nathans crackly voice through the intercom, "can we come in?"

"Sure," Ryan said, buzzing him in. He stuck his head into the lounge room and scooped his shirt off the floor. "Get dressed, it's Ash and Nathan."

I was already two steps ahead of him and was in the process of buttoning up my trousers again. I threw on my T-shirt and joined Ryan in the hallway as he swung the door open to reveal the pair, looking broken and bedraggled.

"Oh my god," I gasped. Ashley was covered in blood.

"Ash are you okay?" Ryan asked, quickly checking her over.

"I'm fine," she said with a stiff nod, "it's not my blood."

"Let's chat about this inside," Nathan said, herding us inside.

"What the hell happened?" Ryan asked, stunned.

"I think it's best if we sit down," Nath suggested, rubbing Ashley's arms protectively.

"Okay, come on through." I waved them into the lounge room.

"Shall I make some tea?" Ryan asked, as we exchanged concerned glances.

"Not just yet," Ashley said quietly, "there's something we need to tell you."

Ash guided me to the new sofa, and indicated for me to sit. I nodded and sank down onto the cushy lounge as she perched on the edge of the armchair opposite me.

"What's going on?" Ryan asked, joining me on the couch.

"There's no easy way to tell you this…" Nathan said, sitting awkwardly on the arm of the chair Ash was in.

"Tell us what?" Ryan asked with confusion. Nathan and Ashley looked at each other gravely, and I saw tears spring to both their eyes.

"What's going on guys?" I asked with a sinking feeling in the pit of my stomach.

"Amy's…" Ash said, unable to complete her sentence. She choked back a sob and my chest tightened with anxiety.

"Amy's what?" I asked quietly, looking between her and Nathan for an answer. Ash shook her head and closed her eyes.

"Amy's what Nathan?"

"Amy's…" Nathan began to say.

"Amy's dead," Ash blurted abruptly. An ice-cold chill ran through my body.

"What?" I said breathlessly as the air evacuated my lungs.

"What do you mean?" asked Ryan.

"She's gone," Nathan said, squeezing Ashley's leg. "She killed herself. Ash found her this afternoon."

A wave of goosebumps erupted across my flesh, and I gripped Ryan's hand. "Oh my god," I said one milli-second before wails of grief erupted violently from my chest. Ryan wrapped his arms around me, and we held each other tight.

"What did she – I mean – how did she do it?" He asked, through his own tears.

"She slit her wrists," Nathan said through clenched teeth.

"Does Ritchie know?" I stammered.

"Yeah. He and I arrived just after the paramedics," said Nath.

"Is he okay?" I sniffed between sobs.

"Not really, but he's doing as well as can be expected," Ash said, snuggling into Nathan.

"And are you okay?" I asked Ashley, "it must have been awful finding her."

"It was," Ash said. Her voice cracked and a tear rolled down her cheek, "but I'm fine."

I stood up and gave her a hug, starting a chain of group hugs.

"Why would she do that?" Ryan asked once we'd done the rounds.

"She had some stuff going on," Ash said, as she peeled away from me to fish around in her handbag. She pulled out a couple of envelopes and straighted up. "She left us all letters," she said handing them to us. I let go of Ryan and took my letter from Ashley's hand. "I'll go put that tea on," she said, motioning for Nathan go with her.

The two of them scuttled out to the kitchen while Ryan and I looked at each other, and then down at the letters in our hands. I felt numb with shock.

"On the count of three?" Ryan asked with a lop-sided smile.

"Yeah okay," I agreed with a deep breath.

"One… two…" Ryan paused, "…three," he said as we both opened our envelopes together. I unfolded the paper with a shaky hand and read through her curly writing.

Hey Hot Mamma,

Please don't waste your tears on me. I've been an awful friend to you. I know that we put it behind us, but I wish I could go back in time and change my behaviour so that we never had that fight in the first place.

I hate that I let you down the way I did. The way I treated you is one of my biggest regrets. I hope that over the last few weeks, I've been able to heal some of the damage that I've done. I wish I'd had more time to make it up to you.

I should never have given up on you Kat. You've never once given up on me, no matter how hard I've pushed you away. I missed you so much while we were apart and that's on me. Having you back in London and being able to spend time with you has been one of the highlights of my life… and I can say that with confidence given that it's about to come to an end.

You're a great friend, a great mum and a great wife, so don't ever forget that… even if there's some know-it-all bitch telling you other-wise. You are everything you need to be, and you are worthy of this beautiful life that you and Ryan are creating together.

I know you won't be able to understand what I'm about to do, but I love you Kat. You're my family and I'm sorry that I lost sight of that.

Take care of yourself and your growing tribe. I'll be keeping an eye on you all from wherever I end up.

Love Aims x

With tears in my eyes, I gently placed the paper down on the couch and looked at Ryan as he stared intently at his letter. His jaw clenched on off as he carefully folded up the paper and slid it back inside the envelope. He looked up at me, almost surprised to see me there.

"You okay?" I asked, rubbing his leg gently. He shook his head stiffly.

"Not really," he said through gritted teeth, "how about you?"

"Not really."

- RYAN McPHERSON -

I held Kat tight, and we cried in each other's arms. I felt more than grief, I felt rage too. Amy's letter had made me angry more than anything. I stroked Kat's hair as she cried, and did my best to quell my unresolved feelings.

"I don't get it," Kat said between teary sniffs. "Why would she kill herself?"

"Amy had a lot of issues babe."

"I know, but I can't imagine her doing something like that."

"You don't have to imagine it," I said through gritted teeth, "you're living it." I leaned back and looked her in the eyes. "Amy killed herself babe. She's gone."

Kat sobbed loudly, so I pulled her into me again and held her while her tears flowed. It sounded harsh, but she had to face reality. Sugar-coating Amy's selfish choice wouldn't help anyone. I ran my thumb across Kat's cheeks to wipe her tears.

"I might grab Ash some clean clothes," Kat said, smiling sadly.

"Good idea. Maybe we should invite them to stay for dinner. We could order Indian."

"Sounds good," she agreed, climbing to her feet, "but maybe you should go get Ritchie."

"Yeah," I agreed, running my hands through her hair. "Would you be okay if I invited him to stay here for a few days? I don't think he should be on his own."

"I was going to suggest the same thing."

"Cool," I said with a sad nod.

"I love you, Ryan."

"I love you too."

"I'm so glad I have you. Please don't ever do something like this."

I rose to my feet and cupped Kat's face in my hand, looking deep into her eyes.

"Babe, I would never leave you like that."

She nodded, and more tears dripped down her cheeks. She wrapped her arms around my waist and snuggled her face to my chest.

"I don't know what I'd do without you."

"I'll do my best to make sure you never have to find out."

- RITCHIE CARLTON -

I ran all the way to Postman's Park and collapsed onto the wooden bench that I'd sat next to Amy on many times before. I let my breath slow back to normal as I took in my surroundings. The park was peaceful and quiet enough to hear the wind rustling through the leaves. I'd always imagined that one day Amy and I might have gotten married there if I'd ever managed to talked her into accepting my proposal.

I glanced down at the envelope in my hand and slowly ripped it open. The sight of her handwriting on the paper, made my heart wrench in my chest and I gritted my teeth as I read her last words.

Ritch, I'm sorry.

I'm sorry for everything.

I'm sorry for our fight; I'm sorry for all the shit that I've put you through over the years; and I'm sorry for what I'm about to do... but mostly I'm sorry that I could never show you how I really feel about you. I know it seems a bit pointless now, but I need you to know that you will always be my one true love Ritch.

I'm sorry that I couldn't love you in the way you needed me to, but please know that I've loved you with everything I've had to give. You've been the best thing in my life, and I wish I could have loved you in the way you deserve to be loved. Thank you for being you and thank you for loving me so whole-heartedly, despite the fact that I was a total bitch to you at times.

Please know that my decision to do this has nothing to do with our dramas. If anything, it's because I want the best for you. I want you to find a gorgeous woman who will give you everything you've ever wanted, and more. Go back to Perth and make beautiful babies with someone who can be a good wife and mother. When you do, know that I'll be looking down on you with love, joy and nothing but good blessings.

Please don't be sad, be reassured in the knowledge that I'm at peace with this decision.

There's a lot of stuff from my past that I was never able to tell you, but if you want to hear it, Ash can fill you in. I don't want my last words to you to be tainted with the sordid details of my shitty childhood.

I will be with you forever my gentle giant.

Yours Always
Aims xx

I dropped my head into my hands, crunching the paper against my face. How could she? How was I supposed to move back to Australia with all this weighing so heavy on my heart? What did she expect from me? How could she have been so fucking selfish?

I sat on that park bench and sobbed for a long time. So long that the air greeted me with a bitter autumn chill that cut straight through my damp hoodie, and the sky had turned pastel with the impending sunset. I shivered but didn't leave. I couldn't. Once I got up and left this park, I'd have to go back and live in a world without Amy. I was lost so deep in my grief that I didn't hear Ryan approaching.

"Need some company?" he asked, making me jump out of my skin.

"Ryza? What are you doing here?"

"Nath and Ash are at ours and I thought you might need to talk," he said, throwing a jacket over my shoulders, "and Kat thought you might need a jacket."

I smiled sadly. "Thanks."

He took a seat next to me on the bench. "I'm really sorry man."

"Yeah," I grunted, "there's nothing we can do about it now."

"No, there's not."

"She wrote me a fucking letter and everything," I said, holding up the crumpled, snotty, tear-stained letter.

"Yeah, me too," he said, pulling out his crisp, clean envelope and tapping it against his leg.

"Did it make you feel better?" I asked, rubbing my nose with the back of my hand. He cleared his throat and passed me the letter.

"Honestly… it just made me angry," he said bluntly.

"Yeah, I know that feeling," I said, eyeing his letter as he held it in front of me.

"I think you should read it," he said, pushing it at me.

"Why? I was barely able to read my own letter."

Ryan opened the envelope and pulled out the letter. I watched him with curiosity as he unfolded the paper and began to read it aloud.

"Dear Ryza, I know this has been a tough year for you, but I need you to know that I'm unbelievably proud of you." He choked on a lump in his throat and wiped his eyes quickly before reading on. "Despite everything that's happened, you've knuckled down; taken responsibility and faced your demons. What you've achieved in your time at The Lodge has been nothing short of super-human." His voiced cracked but he read on. "It's been a long, rocky road, but you've blossomed into a strong, confident, amazing guy, and you need to give yourself credit for that. You've bloomed, when many would have shrivelled and died."

"Stop," I put my hand over the letter, "I don't get why you want me to hear this."

"Just let me finish," Ryan said firmly, removing my hand from the piece of paper. I nodded silently and he continued reading. "It's been an honour to be part of your journey Ryza, and I know that once you get out of rehab, your life will be as beautiful and happy as you've always planned," he ceased reading and looked at me sideways, waving the letter with well controlled rage, "she wrote this fucking thing when I was still in rehab," he said dropping the letter in my lap. "She knew what she was doing, she'd been planning it for weeks," he said with a disgruntled chuckle. "What she did had nothing to do with you Ritch, and nothing to do with your fight. Amy was… troubled." He paused and I stared at the words on the paper unable to read them. "She planned it all Ritch. She organised all of this and then she let Ash come over to find her body," he added with disdain. "She didn't care how this would affect any of us. She was in such a dark place that she couldn't see through her pain. There was no way any of us could ever have understood or known what she would do."

I let his words sink in for a moment as I ran back over our last few weeks together. In retrospect, her strange behaviour finally made sense.

"Thanks Ryza."

"No thanks required," he said, patting my back again. "Now, let's go home."

"I don't want to go home."

"I mean my home," he said with an empathetic smile. "You're staying with us for a while."

"Am I?"

"You sure are," he said standing up with groan, "we want as much Uncle Ritchie time as possible before you fuck off back to Oz."

He offered me a hand up and, as I stood, I felt my cold bones creaking.

"Geez, I'm getting old," I said, stretching out my aching body.

"As are we all my friend," Ryza joked with a smile. "Come on, let's go. We're ordering Indian and I don't want Nathan scoffing all the Papadums before we get there."

- NATHAN STONE -

Kat had successfully put Mia down to sleep, and Ash was in the McPhersons shower de-bloodying herself, while I set the table in preparation for our feast. The food was starting to get cold, but in the light of the day's events, I doubted that any of us would be particularly hungry anyway.

"Should I put it in the oven?" Kat asked, eyeing the pile of plastic takeaway containers, as she joined me in the kitchen.

"Nah, we can reheat it once they get here if we need to."
At that moment, we heard the front door click open. We both looked up and waited for the guys to appear in the kitchen.

"Look who I found," Ryan said light-heartedly as Ritchie followed him through the door. Ritch looked worse than he had when he'd left the police station. His face was blotchy and expressionless with dark bags well-entrenched under his bloodshot eyes.

"Oh Ritchie," Kat breathed with relief, as she ran over to him and threw her arms around his waist. "Are you okay?" she asked with her face planted against his large chest. Their height difference was so extreme that it would have been a funny sight had it not been for the grim circumstances.

"As well as can be expected," he said, accepting Kat's embrace and gently patting her back as she gripped tightly to him. He caught my eye and I gave him a solemn nod. He returned my nod as best he could with Kat still clinging to him like he might disappear if she let him go. She was still gripping him tightly when Ash came out of the bathroom wearing fresh clothes, and towel drying her hair. She stopped when she saw Ritchie standing in the kitchen.

"Ritchie," she said in almost exactly the same tone as Kat had done, "feeling any better?"

"Not really," he said grimly. Kat finally let go of Ritchie and stepped back so Ash could take over the hugging duties. Ash hung the damp towel over the back of the nearest chair and wrapped her arms around Ritch.

"I'm so sorry," she whispered quietly, as Ritchie held her tight.

"You've got nothing to be sorry for," he told her firmly, as tears streamed down both of their faces. I could feel my own tears threatening to shed at merely witnessing the emotional scene, so I busied myself with laying out the cutlery. It was impossible to believe that Amy was gone. Hadn't we endured enough suffering already? But this was, by far, the worst of all our recent ordeals. This time we'd actually lost one of our own. How were we going to get over this one? It seemed like every time we recovered from one drama, another one occurred to destabilise us again.

Kat tucked herself under Ryan's arm and we all watched silently, unable to tear our eyes away.

"I should have got there sooner," Ash argued tearfully, gripping the back of Ritchie's bloodied shirt.

"There's nothing you could have done love," he said, pulling away from her to look her in the eyes. "You did everything you could Ash, you can't blame yourself for this." He stared at Ash intently when she looked as if she was going to argue the point. Ritchie's piercing stare had the intended effect, and Ash nodded silently. They both hugged again, and more tears flowed all-round.

"Anyone hungry?" I asked, once we'd all collected ourselves.

"Not really," said Ryan, resting his hand on Ritchie's shoulder, "but we should probably eat anyway huh?"

We all took our seats, and as Ritchie sat down, a loud crunching sound emanated from his bottom.

"Oh," he said, standing up and pulling two crumpled pieces of paper out of his pocket. "I forgot about those," he added, trying to flatten them against the table. "I take it you've all read yours?"

"Yep," I said, lining up the takeaway containers along the middle of the table. I placed one in front of Ritchie. "And a bucket of Vindaloo," I joked with very little enthusiasm. Despite the lack lustre delivery, my joke resulted in an eruption of laughter from around the table. I think everyone must have been so delirious that it somehow seemed funny. I stopped in my tracks, surprised by the favourable reaction, and then found myself laughing along with them.

We served up the food and ate our meal with an almost normal level of banter and chatter. In that moment it felt like nothing had changed. Ryan poured drinks for everyone, and when he attempted to hand Ash a glass of wine, I watched to see how she would respond.

"No thanks Ryza," she said with a smile, "I'm fine." She was trying to act casual, but it wasn't commonly accepted for people not to drink in our little circle.

"Don't be silly," he said with a wave of his hand, "I'm the sober one here." He plonked the glass in front of her and Ash smiled politely.

"Thanks," she said, but made no move to drink the wine. I decided that it was best to create a distraction before anyone noticed that she wasn't drinking. I pulled my neatly folded letter out of my pocket.

"I thought it might be nice if we all read out our letters," I said, holding mine up in front of my face, "would anyone like to hear mine?"

The chatter stopped and everyone looked at me as the reality of the situation returned.

"I don't think I could read mine out loud," said Kat, but I'd like to see yours. Shall we do a swap instead?"

"Sure," I agreed, putting my letter on the table as she ducked off to collect hers from the lounge room.

"I'm not ready to read the others yet," Ritchie said, pushing his two crumpled letters towards the middle of the table, "but here's mine and Ryan's if anyone wants to read them."

Ash looked at Ritchie's pile. "Hold on to yours Ritch," she said, pushing it back towards him, "I think you should wait until you're ready to share that." Ritchie nodded and put his letter back in his pocket as Ash picked up Ryan's.

"You want to read mine?" she asked Ryan, passing him her pristine envelope.

"Yeah," he said with a sad nod, "that would be good, thanks."

- ASHLEY GRANGER -

Ryan began reading my letter before Kat had even returned to the table. Ritchie quietly munched on his Beef Vindaloo, deep in thought as the rest of us read the swapped letters. Silence descended upon the group as we each processed Amy's words. After a brief moment of hush, Ryan cleared his throat and looked up at me, holding my letter in the air.

"Ash," he said loudly and slowly. I peered up at him and, seeing the look on his face, it dawned on me what he was about to ask. "You're pregnant?"

I'd forgotten Amy had mentioned the pregnancy in my letter. Nathan glanced at me with raised brows, waiting for my lead.

"Uh... yeah," I said with a blush.

"What???" Kat squealed with excitement, clearly not having reached that part of Nathan's letter yet. In response to the abrupt noise, a whine echoed from the direction of the nursery. Kat dropped her voice immediately and paused to see if the whine would turn into a cry. When it seemed certain that Mia had fallen back to sleep, Kat broke the silence. "Guys, that's amazing! Congratulations," she said jumping up to give me a hug.

"Well that explains the engagement," Ryan joked as he clapped Nathan on the back in a congratulatory fashion.

"Actually, I ordered the ring a while ago," said Nathan, shooting me a shy smile. "And I even got permission from Geoff."

"You did?" I asked, unable to stop a smile from spreading across my face.

"I sure did. In fact, I had the whole proposal planned out, but then you beat me to punch with your baby news," he teased.

"Well, congrats guys," said Ryan happily. "That's great news."

"Thanks Ryza," I said, taking another quick glance at my gorgeous fiancé. He smiled and winked as the conversation continued.

"It's your turn for a dad bod now," Ryan teased Nathan.

"Not likely," retorted Nath, fake punching Ryan in the gut as I peered over at Ritchie who sat quietly at the end of the table, trying his hardest to look happy. He looked over and caught my eye, forcing a smile to his face, and we exchanged an understanding look. I could feel his pain combining with mine and I had to swallow back a new lump in my throat. It was hard to feel cheery when Amy wasn't here to join in the excitement.

"Why didn't you tell us?" Kat asked, still buoyant from our news.

I could feel the sorrow welling in my chest again and I was positive that I'd burst into tears if I attempted to talk. I tore my eyes off Ritchie and looked to Nathan for help.

"We only just found out," said Nath, putting his arm around my shoulder as he jumped to my rescue.

"So how far along are you?" Kat asked, with great interest.

"About eight weeks," Nathan answered for me again. Kat's eyes bulged out of her head and all three of them stared at us with blank expressions, clearly trying to do the maths in their heads.

"Wow, that was fast," said Ryza. "You're only a few weeks behind Kelly," he added with surprise.

"Yeah, we got it first go," Nathan confirmed with a proud shrug. He was attempting to be cool about it, but he really did seem very pleased with himself. I rested my hand on his leg and his fingers intertwined mine.

"Well mate, at least you know you've got good swimmers," joked Ritchie, finally breaking his silence.

"Yeah, if we keep going at this rate, we'll have enough of them to fill out the Junior Premier League," teased Ryan. Everyone laughed except for Ritchie and I, who both smiled half-heartedly. He kept looking at me as if he wanted to ask me something.

"How did Amy know?" Kat asked quietly.

"We did a test at work yesterday," I said sadly, choking back that annoying lump. "She was the one who figured it out."

We all fell silent at the mention of Amy. I looked over at Nathan and I could see the pain in his eyes too. He smiled sadly at me and then peered down at his glass. He picked it up and held it out in front of him.

"To Amy," he toasted, handing me a spare water glass to toast with, "life will not be the same without her."

"To Amy," we all repeated solemnly. Ritchie skulled his drink and stood up abruptly.

"I need a shower," he said, looking down at his dirty jumper.

"Sure man," said Ryan, "you know where everything is."

"Cheers," said Ritch, quickly vacating the room. We all looked at each other, unsure how to make the situation better. We were in unchartered territory now. We'd made it through a lot of shit together, but we'd never lost one of our own before.

"It'll take time," said Nath, nodding reassuringly at the rest of us. "We just have to give him some time."

- RITCHIE CARLTON -

I sat on the bed, wearing nothing but a towel as I stared at Amy's letter. The words "Ash can fill you in', were all I could focus on. What were the demons from Amy's past that had stopped her from marrying me and why had she felt comfortable enough to tell Ash but not me?

I pulled on the T.shirt and tracksuit pants that Ryan had left out for me. They were way too short, but at least they weren't covered in blood. I studied my reflection in the mirror and would have laughed if I hadn't been so depressed. I looked ridiculous. I needed my own clothes. I shoved the letter into the pocket of the sweatpants and grabbed my wallet and keys.

"Any chance someone could drive me home to get some clothes?" I asked, walking out to the kitchen to model my absurd new look. The whole group laughed as I did a little twirl in Ryan's clothes.

"I'll take you," said Ash, rising from her seat.

"Cool, thanks," I replied with a nod.

Nath stood up and gave Ash a kiss. "Drive safely."

"I will," she assured him, stroking his cheek. "We'll be back shortly."

We drove in silence for a short while, until I worked up the courage to ask the question that had been on my mind.

"Ash," I said slowly, as I pulled the letter out of my pocket and placed it on the armrest, "Amy said you know some stuff about her past and why she..." I trailed off, unable to say the words.

Ash nodded knowingly. "Yeah, she asked me in my letter, to tell you about it."

"What happened to her?"

Ash concentrated on the road as she told me all about Amy's childhood. As she spoke, pain gripped my chest. It explained so much of why she'd been the way she'd been and even why she'd killed herself. A childhood of sexual abuse was a big burden to bear.

"Why didn't she tell me herself?" I asked, gripping my chest to try and ease the pain. "I could have been there for her. I would have understood. I wouldn't have put so much pressure on her to commit. Things could have worked out completely different."

"I don't think she knew how to tell you Ritchie."

"That's unfair." My soul ached so much, it was tangible. I felt like my heart was going to burst out through my ribs like that scene out of Alien. Amy's death, Amy's life, and the fact that she hadn't told me about any of her trauma... all of it hurt beyond words. What was I supposed to do with that knowledge? Was Amy expecting me to move on as if nothing had happened? Why couldn't we have a happy ending like Ash and Nath? How could our story end like this? Where was I meant go from there?

The only thing I knew for certain, was that my life would never be the same again.

- Epilogue -

The last goodbye

- RITCHIE CARLTON -

The crowd milled around out the front of the funeral parlor, as I hid inside, waiting nervously for people to gather for the service. I'd never been to a funeral before, and it was horrible that my first one was the woman I'd been in love with. I peered out the door and spotted Ryan standing with the rest of the crew. I hovered furtively, waving to get his attention and I eventually caught his eye. He excused himself from the others, who were deep in conversation, and subtly stepped backwards, quietly peeling away from the group.

"Hey man," he said, giving me an awkward hug, "how was the viewing? How are you holding up?"

I shrugged and ran a hand over my shiny, bald head. "She looked so real," I told him with disbelief, "I was waiting for her to wake up and shout 'just kidding'," I added, mimicking Amy's Welsh accent with a sad laugh. "Honestly Ryza," I said with a long sigh, "I don't know if I feel better or worse after seeing her like that."

"I don't know what to say Ritch," he said, patting me on the shoulder, "I can't even imagine how I'd feel if that was Kat." I nodded in appreciation and looked over at the rest of our group amongst the growing crowd. Nathan was the only person I knew who'd pay for someone else's funeral. He had to be the anonymous donor. "You okay mate?" Ryan asked with concern.

"Yeah, just something weird happened."

"That seems to be that standard state of play these days," he joked.

"I spoke to Amy's mum about giving her money for the funeral," I confided in him, "and she said that someone's already paid for the whole thing."

"Who?"

"She didn't know," I said with a shrug, "they wanted to remain anonymous, so she'd assumed it was me."

"It was probably Nathan," Ryan said, tilting his head towards Nath who stood, brows furrowed, with one arm draped protectively over Ashley's shoulder.

"Yeah, I expect so," I agreed with a nod. "Amy's mum doesn't have a lot of money and Nathan knew that. I can't let him do that though. I've got a good nest egg saved up so I'm gonna pay him back."

"I don't think that's a good idea Ritch. You know what Nathan's like. He won't want you to know that it was him." Ryan paused and looked around at the lavish funeral home. "He obviously wanted Amy to have a nice send-off, so just let him have this one.

"I can't let my best friend pay for my girl-err- Amy's funeral," I protested in a hissed whisper, realising that I couldn't even call myself Amy's boyfriend.

"Why not?" he asked with a shrug. "She was his friend too."

"But-"

Ryan held his hand out to silence me.

"Ritch, Nathan loves helping. It's his way of showing that he cares," he said, cutting me off, "and you'll need your nest egg to set yourself up when you get home."

I was about to debate his point further, but we were spotted by Ashley who came running towards us, followed closely by Nathan while Kat and Mia trailed along behind them.

"Ritchie," Ashley breathed, throwing her arms around my waist as she pressed her face against my chest. I was taken aback for a moment, but quickly softened as Ash held me tight. I sighed sadly and wrapped my arms around her, resting my chin on her head as I closed my eyes to thwart the impending tears. "We're all here for you Ritch," Ash said quietly, "just let us know what you need."

I unfurled my arms and leaned back from Ashley, gently resting my hands on her shoulders.

"All I need is to have you guys here with me," I said, patting her shoulders reassuringly.

Kat handed Mia to Ryan so she could get in on the hugging action. Ryza propped Mia up against his shoulder and jiggled her gently, while his wife tucked her tiny frame inside my enormous one.

"I'm so sorry Ritch," she said, engulfed in my embrace.

"It is what it is. There's nothing we can do now besides move forward."

Kat peered up at me through her shiny curls and smiled woefully. She looked like she was about to burst into tears.

"Love you Ritch," she squeaked with a nod as she peeled herself out of my arms. Ryan draped his free arm around her, allowing Nathan to step forward and give me a man-hug.

"Just say the word if there's anything we can do Ritch," he said patting me on the back.

"Actually, there is one thing," I said, glancing guiltily in Ryan's direction.

"Sure thing," Nath said following my gaze to cast Ryan a questioning look. He glanced between Ryan and I, as we conducted our silent conversation. "What's going on?" Nathan asked suspiciously. Given that he'd once asked me to cover up a murder, he probably expected something extreme and/or illegal.

I reached into my back pocket and pulled out the cheque that I'd written. He watched me with curiosity as I slowly unfolded it and held it out towards him. When he didn't take it, I shoved the cheque into his hand.

"I want you to have this," I explained as he stared at me with confusion.

"What's this for?" Nathan asked, when he finally looked down at the paper.

"The funeral," I answered with a meaningful nod.

"I don't understand. Why are you giving me a cheque for the funeral?"

"Look Stoner, I appreciate the gesture," I said as the rest of the group looked on, "but I need to do this for her."

He stared at me with his mouth agape.

"Ritchie," he said, attempting to hand me back the cheque, "I have no idea what you're on about."

"The funeral Nathan," I said, with impatience as I pushed the cheque back towards him, "I know you paid for it."

"But I didn't," he argued, trying to slide the paper into my palm.

"Oh, come on Stoner," I laughed, pulling my hand away so he couldn't pass it back to me, "who else would anonymously pre-pay for a lavish funeral?"

"I don't know but it wasn't me." Our friends looked doubtfully at each other as if having some sort of silent vote about whether Nath was telling the truth. Ash smiled and raised one of her thin brows at Stoner.

"You know this has Nathan Stone written all over it right?" she teased.

"Honestly babe, it wasn't me," he said earnestly, before addressing the whole group. "I would have happily paid for it, but I can't take the credit for this one. It was probably Gaz."

"Yeah maybe," I said, unconvinced.

"You really think Gaz would do that?" Kat asked, unconvinced by Nathan's protestations.

"Not really," Nath answered honestly. "It's not exactly Gareth's style, but who else does Amy know that has a spare ten grand to drop on a funeral?" Ryan opened his mouth to answer but Nathan cut him off, "besides me," Nath clarified, knowing what he was about to say.

Ryan shut his mouth and his eyes drifted over to the building behind me. We all followed his gaze towards the door, as the funeral director stepped outside. I watched him approach with a feeling of dread in my belly. His presence meant only one thing.

"Ritchie and Pallbearers, could we have you inside please? We're ready to start." Nathan and Ryan nodded at the man and I had to take a deep breath to calm myself. Ryza and Kat exchanged Mia again, and Nath looked to Ash for reassurance, while I stood alone, without my partner in crime to comfort me. Despite the fact that I wasn't alone, I felt lonelier than ever.

Nathan and Ryan ushered me towards the door and I knew there was no avoiding what was coming. As much as I wanted to believe it wasn't real, there was no escaping the fact that it was time for me to say my final goodbye.

Amy's funeral passed in a blur. I spent the whole time concentrating so hard on not crying that I had couldn't tell you much about any of it. I wanted to be strong, but I hadn't realised how hard that was going to be. The moment I saw the coffin being carried down the aisle with Ryan and Nathan at its helm, my brain vacated my body. It was real. Amy was dead and she wasn't coming back.

The pain was too much to bear, so I let my mind drift off to more pleasant thoughts of life in Oz while the service continued somewhere in the real world. In a few months, I'd be back home in Australia and this nightmare would be behind me. A fresh start. Nothing to remind me of Amy or the life we never had together.

An hour later, the service wound-up and an endless line of strangers wanted to hug me and offer their condolences. I did my duty, nodding, smiling and thanking them for coming but all I could think of was how badly I wanted to be anywhere but there. But 'be careful what you wish for', as they say. We'd almost said our goodbyes when a big, black limousine emerged from the carpark and pulled up to the curb just in front of where we were all standing. I knew immediately who it was. The conversation paused as the remaining crowd watched to see who the expensive ride belonged to.

The back door opened and a black Louboutined shoe landed

purposefully on the footpath. Sandrine rose on her svelte leg and, as her huge brimmed black hat appeared above door level, the crowd gasped simultaneously.

"Well, I guess we know who paid for the funeral," muttered Nathan quietly.

"Why would Sandrine pay for Amy's funeral?" Ash asked sceptically, "she didn't even know Amy."

"No, but she was shagging Ritchie," Kat said with a shrug, as I kept my eyes glued to the French woman. She stood against the limo with her arm draped over the open door, staring in my direction. At least I assumed she was staring in my direction, it was hard to tell through her big, black sunglasses. I turned to my friends and shrugged my explanation, feeling Sandrine's dark eyes boring into my back.

"Ritchie, I have a weird feeling about this," Ash said, grasping my arm. I patted her hand reassuringly.

"I know how to deal with Sandrine," I assured them all. "I'll see you guys at the wake," I added, sensing their collective hesitance. I smiled confidently and sauntered over to where the Black Widow was waiting for me. I had no idea why she was there, or how she'd heard about the funeral, but I did agree with Ash that something didn't feel quite right.

"Richard," Sandrine cooed apologetically, "I'm so sorry for your loss." It was hard to judge her expression underneath the big glasses and over-sized hat, but she didn't appear to be particularly sorry at all.

"Thanks Sandrine."

"Ride with me?" she asked nodding stoically towards the limo.

"Sure," I agreed with another shrug. Shrugging was easier than talking. I climbed into the car and slid down the long seat as she joined me. She closed the door behind her, and the car pulled away. I peered around the black leather interior, which looked identical to the interior of her limo in Paris.

"How are you, Richard?" she asked, resting her well-manicured hand on my thigh.

"As well as can be expected," I said flatly.

"I can't even imagine," she breathed, attempting to sound sympathetic while the slight smirk on her lips suggested otherwise.

"What are you doing here Sandrine?" I asked, bluntly, "how did you even know about this?"

She cocked her head innocently. "The team have been talking Richard and I wanted to come and make sure you were alright."

I snorted with grim amusement. "Right," I said, for lack of a better response. Given her demeanor I found it very hard to believe that her motives were selfless.

"Don't be like that," she said, taking my chin in her hands so that I'd look her in the eyes. "You know how I feel about you Richard, I only want what's best for you."

"As long as it aligns with what you want," I said flicking my head to shake off her grasp.

"I know you're grieving, so I won't take that personally," she said with her school-teacher tone, "but I want to assure you Richard, that my offer still stands. Come to Paris with me and leave this tragedy behind."

"Sandrine, I can't go to Paris with you," I said with a mixture of anger and disbelief. "I'm moving back to Australia."

"Whatever for?" she asked with surprise.

"It's my home Sandrine. Plus I'd already booked my ticket before Amy…" I let my words trail off and cleared my throat. "As I said in Paris, I really appreciate the offer but it's time for me to settle down and home is the only place I can see myself doing that. Especially now that Amy's gone." I knocked on the divider window to signal the driver. He wound down the tinted divider and I leaned towards the gap. "Can you please pull over here?" I asked. He nodded his agreement and I turned back to Sandrine. "We had a lot of fun Sandrine, but this is over now. I'm going home and I don't plan on coming back any time soon."

"Is there nothing I can say to change your mind?" she asked desperately.

"I'm sorry," I said, patting her hand apologetically, "but my mind is made up. I'm done with Europe." Sandrine nodded solemnly, a spark of anger flaring behind her eyes.

"I understand," she said with a tone that indicated the exact opposite. I gave her a kiss on the cheek as the car came to a halt.

"Bye Sandrine," I said, opening the car door.

"Au revoir Richard."

I climbed out of the limo and shut the door behind me. The long black limo pulled away as I waved at the dark tinted windows. I couldn't see Sandrine; all I could see was the reflection of a bald, broken man.

The Broken Man

Yeah. So there's that death I warned you about.

Things do get better, I promise. Once the grief wears off, life will go on, but right now we're stuck in the thick of an emotional shitstorm.

Ash and Nath will be back with me in Book three: Stories from the Sea, as we depart London for our respective coast lines.

Tails and Ryza are taking a break, but they'll be back with their own book soon enough. As I said... life goes on.

RITCHIE

Stories from the Sea

With one of their best friends gone forever, the Artemis crew are no more. As they scatter to different corners of the globe, they must learn how to move forward without each other. For the couples, it's time to settle down into family life, but for Ritchie, life must begin again. It's time for him to leave behind the bad memories and carve out a new life in the Land Down Under.

RITCHIE CARLTON has just lost the love of his life. He's moved back home to Perth to start a new life, but struggles to leave the past behind him. That is, until a chance meeting at his brother's wedding, with local entrepreneur Kane Thompson, changes everything. Ritchie doesn't realise it, but Kane is about to make all his dreams a reality.

NATHAN STONE has everything he never knew he always wanted. With his bachelor days a thing of the past, and his previous dramas behind him, Nathan is on top of the world. He and Ashley have a baby on the way, nuptials upcoming and a move to the coast imminent. The only thing that would make it better would be to have his mum around. Would she ever be well enough to leave the hospital and join his new family?

ASHLEY GRANGER finally has her happily-ever-after. After ten years of hell, followed by six months of chaos, Ashley has found true love with Nathan Stone and, for the first time in her adult life, feels safe and free. Letting go of her new job however, is proving to be difficult. How will she balance motherhood, her career and a life by the sea? Can Ashley figure out a way to have it all?

KANE THOMPSON is known as the Golden Child. He's always done everything 'right' and spent his entire life living up to everyone's expectations. He was the dux of his primary school; Head Boy of his high school; President of the University Student Guild; and now he's the CEO of Perth City's largest technology company. But Kane's outstanding life isn't all it's cracked up to be. On the outside, things look perfect, but on the inside, he's cripplingly unhappy. Will Kane's new friendship with Ritchie pull him out of his funk?

Sneak Peek...

- ASHLEY GRANGER -

"Can I have everyone's attention please?" Nathan called loudly, as he tapped a spoon against his Champaign glass. Our jovial crowd of family and friends slowly fell quiet and I squeezed Nathan's hand as we waited for the silence to descend. "I just wanted to thank you all for coming today. I know it seems weird for us to have a party, given everything that's happened, but this is the last time we'll all be together in one place for a while, so we wanted to mark the occasion, and celebrate a few major events in one go."

The crowd muttered in agreement, with head nods all-round. Nathan quickly glanced at Ritchie to get his attention, and then gave me a wink to indicate that it was my turn to speak.

"As you all know," I said loudly, to get over the murmur, "our lovable Aussie Larrikin is moving back home to Oz. Ritchie can you come up here please?"

The attendees all turned to look at a very bashful Ritchie, who bowed his head and humbly joined us on the little stage.

"You promised no speeches," Ritchie argued with a smile as I threaded my arm around his waist

"I promised that you wouldn't have to do any speeches," I teased, before continuing my speech. "Ritch, you're one of the most caring, down-to-earth, fiercely loyal and loud-mouthed people," I said with a cheeky grin, eliciting quiet laughter from the crowd, "that I've ever had the honour of calling a friend. You really have been the heart and soul of our little crew and I know for a fact that Artemis won't be the same without you." I felt my throat tightening with emotion, so I quickly pushed on. "We're going to miss you fiercely, but England's loss will be Australia's gain."

"Aww Granger...," Ritchie said with a sad smile, "I was only on loan anyway," he joked, and then wrapped me up in a bear hug. I tucked myself inside his huge frame and rested my head against his solid chest as he squeezed me tight. In six months, this giant of a man had become my family, and I couldn't believe that we'd have to move into the next phase of our lives without him.

It wasn't just Artemis that wouldn't be the same without him. Our lives were going to have a Ritchie sized-hole that could never be filled.

Want to learn more about N.J. Ewing? Visit: brandartisans.com.au/njewing

331

About N.J. Ewing

Born and raised on the West Coast of Australia, N.J. completed a Bachelor of Arts with a double major in Communications and Media Studies at Murdoch University in 2002.

Although writing was part of her degree, she never expected to write a book (let alone three!) when she left Uni and embarked upon a marketing career. Her professional ambition led her to London for a large part of her twenties, which was where the idea for Stories from the City was born.

With the first two books in the series complete, and the third in progress, N.J. is excited to get the story out into the world a decade after its inception.

brandartisans.com.au/njewing

Another Feature Title from Brand Artisans Australia:

This debut novel from Australian Author, Monica Ritz is just the first in a series that's set to take the romance genre by storm.

Combining romance with mystery, and some corporate espionage thrown in for good measure, this story will captivate readers of both genres.

Two jobs, two men, two lives all waiting to collide.

This world is tough, but exciting as Cari learns to live with the fact that she has become a passenger in her own life.

This is an epic roller-coaster ride of relationships and emotions, trust and betrayals, never knowing who really knows what, but Cari has to survive as there is no way out!

Genre: Fiction - Romance; Mystery; Corporate Crime

brandartisans.com.au